BEYOND THE ICE LIMIT

BEYOND THE ICE LIMIT

A GIDEON CREW NOVEL

DOUGLAS PRESTON & LINCOLN CHILD

GRAND CENTRAL
PUBLISHING

NEW YORK   BOSTON

Copyright © 2016 by Splendide Mendax, Inc. & Lincoln Child
Cover design by Flag
Cover art by Stanislaw Fernandes
Cover copyright © 2016 by Hachette Book Group, Inc.

Grand Central Publishing
Hachette Book Group
1290 Avenue of the Americas
New York, NY 10104
grandcentralpublishing.com
twitter.com/grandcentralpub

First Edition: May 2016

Grand Central Publishing is a division of Hachette Book Group, Inc.
The Grand Central Publishing name and logo is a trademark of Hachette Book Group, Inc.

The publisher is not responsible for websites (or their content) that are not owned by the publisher.

The Hachette Speakers Bureau provides a wide range of authors for speaking events. To find out more, go to www.hachettespeakersbureau.com or call (866) 376-6591.

Library of Congress Cataloging-in-Publication Data
Names: Preston, Douglas J., author. | Child, Lincoln, author.
Title: Beyond the ice limit : a Gideon Crew novel / Douglas Preston & Lincoln Child.
Description: First edition. | New York : Grand Central Publishing, 2016. | Series: Gideon crew series ; 4
Identifiers: LCCN 2015050544 | ISBN 9781455525867 (hardcover) | ISBN 9781455566136 (large print) | ISBN 9781455588978 (int'l) | ISBN 9781478909118 (audio CD) | ISBN 9781478909125 (audio download) | ISBN 9781455525881 (ebook)
Subjects: LCSH: Human-alien encounters—Fiction. | Antarctic Ocean | BISAC: FICTION / Thrillers. | GSAFD: Adventure fiction. | Science fiction.
Classification: LCC PS3566.R3982 B49 2016 | DDC 813/.54—dc23
LC record available at http://lccn.loc.gov/2015050544

ISBNs: 978-1-4555-2586-7 (hardcover), 978-1-4555-2588-1 (ebook), 978-1-4555-8897-8 (int'l), 978-1-4555-6613-6 (large print)

Printed in the United States of America

RRD-C

10 9 8 7 6 5 4 3 2 1

To Jamie Raab

BEYOND THE ICE LIMIT

1

GIDEON CREW STARED at Eli Glinn. The man was standing—standing!—in the kitchen of Gideon's cabin high in the Jemez Mountains, gazing at him with placid gray eyes. His all-terrain wheelchair—the wheelchair in which Glinn had always sat, virtually helpless, since Gideon had first met him several months before—sat unused ever since he had, to Gideon's great astonishment, risen out of it minutes before.

Glinn gestured toward the wheelchair. "Forgive this tiny bit of drama. I staged it, however, for an important reason: to show you that our mission to the Lost Island, despite certain regrettable aspects, was not in vain. Quite the opposite: I'm living proof of its success."

A silence ensued. It stretched into a minute, two minutes. Finally Gideon went to the stove, picked up the sauté pan containing the wild goose breast in a ginger and black truffle emulsion that he had just finished preparing with exquisite care, and dumped it into the garbage.

Without a word, Glinn turned and walked, a little unsteadily, toward the cabin door, using a hiking pole as a brace. Manuel

Garza—chief of operations at Glinn's firm, Effective Engineering Solutions—offered to help Glinn into the wheelchair, but Glinn waved this away.

Gideon watched the two men leave the cabin, Garza guiding the empty wheelchair, the words Glinn had spoken a few minutes earlier reverberating in his mind. *That thing is growing again. We must destroy it. The time to act is now.*

Gideon grabbed his coat and followed. The helicopter that had brought the EES men to this remote site was still powered up, its rotors whistling, sending ripples of waves through the meadow grass.

He followed Glinn inside the chopper and took a seat, buckling in and donning a headset. The chopper rose into the blue New Mexico sky and headed southeast. Gideon watched his cabin get smaller and smaller, until it was a nothing more than a dot in a meadow in a great bowl of mountains. Suddenly he had a strange feeling he would never see it again.

He turned to Glinn and spoke at last. "So you can walk again. And your bad eye...can you see with it now?"

"Yes." Glinn raised his left hand, formerly a twisted claw, and flexed his fingers slowly. "Every day they get better. As does my ability to walk without aid. Thanks to the healing power of the plant we discovered on the island, I can now complete my life's work."

Gideon didn't need to ask about the plant. Nor did he need to ask about Glinn's "life's work." He already knew the answers to both questions.

"There is no time to waste. We have the money, we have the ship, and we have the equipment."

Gideon nodded.

"But before we take you back to EES headquarters, we have to make a little detour. There's something you must see. I regret to say it will not be pleasant."

"What is it?"

"I'd rather not say more."

Gideon sat back, mildly irritated: typical inscrutable, enigmatic Glinn. He glanced at Garza and found the man to be as unreadable as his boss.

"Can you at least tell me where we're going?"

"Certainly. We're going to pick up the EES jet in Santa Fe and fly to San Jose. From there we'll take a private car into the hills above Santa Cruz, and pay a call on a gentleman who resides there."

"Sounds mysterious."

"I don't intend to be enigmatic."

"Of course you do."

A small smile—very small. "You know me too well. But since you do, you also know everything I do is with a purpose."

The chopper left the mountains behind. Gideon could see the shining ribbon of the Rio Grande crawling through White Rock Canyon below them, and beyond that the hills of the Caja del Rio. The town of Santa Fe spread out to his left. As they proceeded over the southern end of town, the airport came into view.

"This talk about your final project," said Gideon. "You mentioned an alien. A seed. You say it's threatening the earth. That's all pretty vague. How about giving me details—starting with why, exactly, you need my help?"

"All in good time," said Glinn. "After our little excursion to Santa Cruz."

2

A LINCOLN NAVIGATOR, driven by an elfin man in a green cap, met them at the San Jose airport. From there, they had driven south along Route 17 into redwood-clad hills. It was a beautiful drive through towering, haunted forests. Both Glinn and Garza stayed resolutely silent; Gideon sensed they were ill at ease.

Deep in the redwoods, the car turned off the highway and began winding its way along a series of valleys, past small farms and ranches, isolated villages, shabby trailers and run-down cabins, through deep pockets of redwoods, meadows, and burbling creeks. The narrow, cracked asphalt road gave way to gravel. The evening was advancing and dark clouds tumbled in, casting a pall over the landscape.

"I think we just passed the Bates Motel," said Gideon, with a nervous laugh. No one else seemed amused. He sensed a gathering atmosphere of tension in the car.

The gravel road entered another redwood forest and almost immediately they came to a large wrought-iron gate, set into a high stone wall. A wooden sign, once elegantly painted and gilded but now somewhat faded, read:

DEARBORNE PARK

Below that, an ugly, utilitarian placard had been bolted:

NO TRESPASSING

VIOLATORS WILL BE PROSECUTED

WITH THE UTMOST RIGOR OF THE LAW

As they approached, the gate opened automatically. They passed through and halted at a small gatehouse. The driver in the green cap rolled down his window and spoke to a man who came out. He quickly waved them along. The road, winding through gloomy redwoods, rose ahead. It began to rain, fat drops spattering on the car windshield.

Now the feeling in the car was one of oppression. The driver turned on the wipers, which slapped back and forth, back and forth, in a monotonous cadence.

The SUV climbed to the ridgeline and suddenly the redwoods gave way to a high meadow, many acres in extent. Through the sweeping rain, Gideon thought he glimpsed a distant view of the Pacific Ocean. At the far end, the meadow rose to a high lawn, at the apex of which stood a mansion of gray limestone, in Neo-Gothic style, streaked with damp. Four towers rose to crenellated turrets and battlements framing a grand central hall, its Gothic arched windows glowing dull yellow in the stormy twilight.

They approached the mansion along a curving drive, wheels crunching the gravel. The wind picked up, lashing rain against the windshield. There was a distant flicker of lightning, and a few moments later Gideon heard the delayed rumble of thunder.

Gideon swallowed a crack about the Addams Family as the driver halted under a pillared porte cochere. A red-haired orderly in a white jacket waited on the steps, brawny arms crossed, as they emerged from the vehicle. No one came forward to greet them. The orderly made a brusque gesture for them to follow and turned, walking back up the stone steps. They followed him into the great hall that served as the entryway. It was spare, almost empty, and their footfalls echoed in the large space as the door boomed shut behind them, slammed by an unseen hand.

The orderly pivoted to the right, passed beneath an arched portal, then continued down a long hallway and into a parlor. At the far end stood a carved oaken door, on which the orderly knocked. A voice summoned them in.

It was a small, comfortable office. A gray-haired man with a broad, kindly face, wearing a tweed jacket with leather elbow patches, rose from behind a desk. The walls were covered with bookshelves. A fireplace stood against the far wall, logs ablaze.

"Welcome, Mr. Glinn," he said, coming from around the desk, hand extended. "Mr. Garza." They shook hands.

"And you must be Dr. Crew. Welcome. I am Dr. Hassenpflug. Please, sit down." He accompanied this with a gesture indicating the chairs in which they were to sit, arrayed comfortably around the fire. His easy warmth contrasted strongly with the unease that surrounded Garza and Glinn.

A brief silence ensued. Dr. Hassenpflug finally broke the ice. "I imagine you wish to hear how the patient is doing? I'm afraid the news is not encouraging."

Glinn clasped his hands and leaned forward. "Thank you, but we're not here to learn about the patient's condition. As we discussed, our only purpose today is to see the patient. His prognosis is not our concern."

Hassenpflug sat back. "I understand, but a word of caution might be in order—"

"I'm afraid any such word would be out of order."

The doctor fell silent, a frown gathering on his face. Much of his amiable air was dissipating under Glinn's curt and unfriendly tone. "Very well, then." He turned to the orderly, who had been standing behind them, his hands clasped in front of his white jacket. "Ronald, is the patient ready to receive visitors?"

"As ready as he'll ever be, Doctor."

"Please show the visitors into his quarters. You and Morris remain close by." Hassenpflug turned back to Glinn. "If the patient becomes excited, the visit may have to be terminated. Ronald and Morris will be the judges of that."

"Understood."

They crossed the parlor and great hall, passing beneath another arch into what had once apparently been a large reception room. At the far end was a door, not of wood, but of riveted steel, and toward this door they headed. The orderly named Ronald paused before it, pressing a small intercom button.

"Yes?" came a tinny voice.

"Mr. Lloyd's visitors are here."

The buzzer sounded and the door opened with a *click*, to reveal a long, elegant marble corridor, lined with ancestral portraits. There was nothing of the air of an institution about this place, although it was now clear to Gideon that it was, in fact, just that. The corridor gave onto an elegant room, ablaze with light. The room was furnished with dark Victorian sofas and armchairs, the walls covered with Hudson River School paintings of mountains, rivers, and other wilderness scenes. But what attracted Gideon's attention most strongly was the robust man, about seventy years old, with a shock of white hair, seated on one of the sofas. He was wearing a straitjacket. An orderly—Gideon assumed this was Morris—sat next to him with a tray, on which sat an array of dishes, each holding a mound of pureed food. The orderly was spooning dark brown goop into the man's mouth. Gideon noticed that a bottle of red wine sat on the tray—a Château Pétrus, no less. A plastic sippy cup filled with the wine stood adjacent to the bottle.

"Your visitors are here, Mr. Lloyd," Ronald announced.

The man named Lloyd raised his massive, shaggy head, and two piercingly blue eyes widened—at Glinn. Despite the strait-jacket and the man's age, he still radiated strength and physical power. Slowly, slowly, the man stood up, staring at them and seeming to swell with a singular intensity, and now Gideon could see that his legs were cuffed and hobbled, rendering him unable to walk except in the tiniest of steps.

He leaned over and spat out the brown stuff that the orderly had just put in his mouth.

"*Glinn.*" He ejaculated the name the same way he had the puree. "And Manuel Garza. What a pleasure." His tone indicated it was no pleasure at all. His voice was strange, quavering and deep, shot through with gravel. It was the voice of a madman.

And now those concentrated blue eyes settled on Gideon. "And you've brought a friend?"

"This is Dr. Gideon Crew, my associate," said Glinn.

The air of tension had gone off the charts.

Lloyd turned to the orderly. "A friend? How surprising."

He turned back to Glinn. "I want to look at you—*up close.*"

"I'm sorry, Mr. Lloyd," said Glinn, "but you have to remain where you are."

"Then you come to me. If you have the guts."

"I don't think that's advisable..." Ronald began.

Glinn approached Lloyd. The orderlies stiffened but did not intervene. He halted about five feet away.

"Closer," Lloyd growled.

Glinn took another step, then another.

"*Closer,*" he repeated. "I want to look into your eyes."

Glinn walked forward until his face was only inches from Lloyd. The white-haired man stared at him for a long time. The orderlies shifted nervously and remained close, tensing, it seemed, for whatever might happen.

"Good. Now you can step back, please."

Glinn complied.

"Why are you here?"

"We're mounting an expedition. To the South Atlantic. The Ice Limit. We're going to take care of the problem down there once and for all."

"Do you have money?"

"Yes."

"So you're not only criminally reckless. You're an idiot, as well."

A silence.

Lloyd continued. "It was five years and two months ago when I said to you, when I begged you, when I *ordered* you, to pull the dead man's switch. And you, you crazy obsessed son of a bitch, you refused. How many died? One hundred and eight. Not counting the poor bastards on the *Almirante Ramirez*. Blood on your hands, Glinn."

Glinn spoke in a calm, neutral tone. "There's nothing you can accuse me of that I haven't done the same a hundred times myself."

"Cry me a river. You want agony? Look at me. For the love of God Almighty, I wish I'd gone down with the ship."

"Is that why the straitjacket?" Glinn asked.

"Ha! Ha! I'm as gentle as a kitten. They've got me in this to keep me alive, against my will. Free one hand and give me just ten seconds and I'm a dead man. A *free* man. But no: they're keeping me alive and burning through my own money to do it. Look at my dinner. Filet mignon, potatoes au gratin with Gruyère, lightly grilled cavolini di Bruxelles—pureed, of course, so I won't attempt suicide by choking. And all washed down with a '00 Pétrus. Care to join me?"

Glinn said nothing.

"And now, here you are."

"Yes, here I am. Not to apologize—because I know no apology would be adequate or accepted."

"You should have killed it when you had the chance. Now it's too late. You've done nothing while the alien has grown, swollen, and engorged itself—"

"Mr. Lloyd," said Morris, "remember your promise not to talk any more about aliens."

"Glinn, did you hear that? I'm forbidden to talk about aliens! They've spent years trying to rid me of my psychotic talk of aliens. Ha, ha, ha!"

Glinn said nothing.

"So what's your plan?" said Lloyd, recovering himself.

"We're going to destroy it."

"Excuse me," said Morris, "but we're not to encourage the patient in his delusions—"

Glinn silenced him with an impatient gesture.

"Destroy it? Brave talk! You can't. You'll fail just like you failed five years ago." A pause. "Is McFarlane going?"

Now it was Glinn's turn to pause. "Dr. McFarlane has not done well in recent years, and it seemed imprudent—"

"Not done well? Not done *well*? Have you *done well* in recent years? Have I?" Lloyd cackled mirthlessly. "So. Instead of Sam, you'll take others with you, including this poor sap, what's his name? Gideon. You'll send them to a hell of your own making. Because you've no sense of your own bloody weakness. You figure everyone else out, but you're blind to your own arrogance and stupidity."

He fell silent, breathing hard, the sweat coursing down his face.

"Mr. Glinn," warned Ronald, "the patient is not allowed to become excited."

Lloyd turned to him, suddenly calm, the voice of reason. "As you can see, Ronald, I'm not the least bit excited."

The orderly shifted uncertainly.

"I'm not here to justify myself to you," said Glinn, quietly. "I deserve all of this and more. And I'm not here to ask you to excuse my actions."

"Then why are you here, you son of a bitch?" Lloyd suddenly roared, spraying spittle and brown flecks of pureed filet mignon into Glinn's face.

"That's enough," said Ronald. "Visit's over. You have to leave now."

Glinn removed his handkerchief, carefully wiped his face clean, and spoke quietly. "I'm here to seek your approval."

"You might as well ask if the lamppost approves of the dog pissing on it. I *disapprove*. You're an idiot if you think you can still destroy what has grown down there. But you always were an arrogant shit-eating grifter. You want my advice?"

"That's enough!" said Ronald, moving in and taking Glinn by the arm, directing him toward the door.

"Yes, I want your advice," Glinn said over his shoulder.

As Gideon followed the orderly who was gently, but firmly, escorting Glinn from the room, he heard Lloyd hiss out: "*Let sleeping aliens lie.*"

3

BACK AT EES headquarters on Little West 12th Street, in the boardroom high above the old Meatpacking District of New York City, Gideon took his place at the conference room table. There were only three of them, Garza, Glinn, and himself, and it was three o'clock in the morning. Glinn, having apparently dispensed with the need for sleep, seemed to expect his employees to do so as well.

Gideon had begun to wonder if Glinn really had changed. He had never seen the man quite so driven, in his own quietly intense way. The meeting with Lloyd in the gigantic, one-man mental hospital had evidently shaken him badly.

The man serving them all coffee silently retreated, shutting the door behind him. The room was dim, the lights low. Glinn, seated at the head of the table, his hands clasped in front of him, allowed the silence to gather before speaking. He turned his two gray eyes on Gideon.

"Well, what did you think of our visit to Palmer Lloyd?"

"He freaked me out," said Gideon.

"Do you know now why I wanted you to meet him?"

"As you said. To seek his approval, get his blessing. After all, that thing down there cost him a lot of money—not to mention his sanity."

"That's part of it. I also wanted to—as you put it—freak you out. To impress on you the gravity of our undertaking. You need to walk into this with your eyes open: because without you, we cannot succeed."

"You really caused the deaths of a hundred and eight people?"

"Yes."

"Wasn't there an investigation? No charges were filed?"

"There were certain, ah, unusual circumstances touching on the relationship between Chile and the United States that encouraged both state departments to make sure the investigation was not overly thorough."

"I don't like the sound of that."

Glinn turned to Garza. "Manuel, will you please give Gideon the necessary background?"

Garza nodded, taking a large folder from his briefcase and laying it on the table. "You already know some of this. I'm going to start from the beginning anyway. If you have any questions, feel free to interrupt. Six years ago, EES was approached by Palmer Lloyd for a peculiar assignment."

"The same Palmer Lloyd I just saw in Dearborne Park."

"Yes. The billionaire was planning to build a natural history museum in the Hudson River Valley. He was collecting the rarest, finest, and biggest of everything—money was no object. He had already snagged the biggest diamond, the largest *T. rex*, a real Egyptian pyramid. Then he got a report that the largest meteorite in the world had been found. It lay on Isla Desolación, an uninhabited island in the Cape Horn Islands at the very tip of South America. The islands belong to Chile. Lloyd knew that

Chile would never allow the meteorite to leave. He therefore hired EES, and a meteorite hunter named Sam McFarlane, to steal it."

"Excuse me," said Glinn, "*steal* isn't quite the right word. We did nothing illegal. We leased mineral rights to Isla Desolación, which allowed us to remove iron in any form."

"*Steal* may not be the most apt description," said Garza, "but it *was* a deception."

At this rebuke, Glinn fell silent. Garza continued. "The meteorite was extremely heavy—twenty-five thousand tons. It was a deep-red color, very dense, and it had other, ah, peculiar properties. So under the cover of this iron-ore-mining operation, we outfitted a ship, the *Rolvaag*; sailed to the island; excavated the rock; and loaded it on board. Suffice to say, this was a challenging engineering project. But we succeeded—quite brilliantly, in fact. And then we were caught. A rogue Chilean destroyer captain figured out what we were up to. He commanded the *Almirante Ramirez*, the ship Lloyd mentioned. Instead of informing his superiors, he decided to play the hero and chased us southward to the Ice Limit."

"Ice Limit. You've used that term before. What is it, exactly?"

"It's the frontier where the southern oceans meet the Antarctic pack ice. We played hide-and-seek among the bergs. The *Rolvaag* was shot up in the confrontation, but ultimately we managed to sink the destroyer."

"You sank a destroyer? How?"

"It's a complicated story, best left to your briefing book. In any case, the *Rolvaag*, carrying the twenty-five-thousand-ton meteorite in its hold, had been badly damaged by the destroyer. The weather worsened. A point came where we had a choice: either jettison the rock—or sink."

"How do you jettison a twenty-five-thousand-ton rock?"

"We'd installed a dead man's switch for that purpose, just in case. Throw the switch, and the meteorite would be dropped through a door in the hull."

"Wouldn't that founder the ship?"

"No. A large amount of water would come in before the door could slide shut, but the ship was fitted with pumps and self-sealing bulkheads that would have handled it. The crew and captain wanted to dump the rock…" Garza seemed to hesitate, glancing at Glinn.

"Tell the full story, Manuel. Spare nothing."

"In the end, everyone wanted to dump the rock. Even Lloyd came around. But Eli alone had the code to the dead man's switch. He insisted the ship could ride it out. They begged, pleaded, threatened—and he refused. But Eli was wrong. The *Rolvaag* sank."

Garza glanced at Glinn again.

"Let me tell the rest," said Glinn quietly. "Yes, I refused to pull the switch. I was wrong. The captain ordered an evacuation. Some got off, but many did not. The captain…" He hesitated, temporarily losing his voice. "The captain, a woman of great courage, went down with the ship. Many others died in the lifeboats or froze to death on a nearby ice island before help arrived."

"And Lloyd? What happened to him?"

"He was evacuated in the first lifeboat—against his will, I might add."

"How did you survive?"

"I was in the hold, trying to secure the meteorite. But it finally broke out of its cradle and split the ship in half. There was an explosion. It seemed as if the meteorite, when it came into contact with salt water, reacted in an unusual way, generating a shock wave. I was thrown clear of the ship. I remember coming to on a raft of floating debris. I was badly injured. They found me a day later, close to death."

Glinn lapsed into silence, toying with his cup of coffee.

"So now the thing's just lying on the seabed. Why all the worry, the talk of danger? And...of aliens?"

Glinn pushed the coffee cup away. "It was McFarlane, the meteorite hunter, who figured out what it really was."

This was followed by a long silence.

"There's a respected theory in astronomy called Panspermia," Glinn finally continued. "It holds that life may have spread through the galaxy in bacteria or spores carried on meteorites or in clouds of dust. But that theory assumed microscopic life. Everyone missed the obvious idea that life might be spread by *seeds*. A gigantic seed would better survive the cold and intense radiation of outer space by its sheer size and resistance. It's the same reason why coconuts are so large: to survive long ocean voyages. The galaxy has many water-covered planets and moons in which such a seed might fall and then sprout."

"You're saying this meteorite was actually just such a seed? And when the *Rolvaag* sank, it went to the bottom and was...*planted*?"

"Yes. Two miles beneath the surface. And then it sprouted."

Gideon shook his head. "Incredible. If true."

"Oh, it's true. It sank roots and grew upward like a giant tree—rapidly. Seismic stations around the world noted a number of shallow quakes on the seafloor at the site. Several small tsunamis raked the coasts of South Georgia and the Falkland Islands. But it was all happening two miles deep, and the seismic signature

of the quakes looked like the product of undersea volcanic erup-
tions. So did the mini tsunamis. Since it was in an area far outside
of any shipping lanes and posed no risk to anyone, the 'undersea
volcano' was generally disregarded. Even volcanologists ignored
it, as it was simply too deep and too dangerous to study. And
then it went quiescent. All of which explains why nobody figured
out what was really going on—except me, of course. And Sam
McFarlane. And Palmer Lloyd." He shifted in his chair. "But over
the past five years, we've developed a plan to deal with this problem. Manuel will summarize it for you."

Garza looked at Gideon. "We're going to kill it."

"But you said it had gone quiescent. Why go to the trouble and
the expense—not to mention the danger?"

"Because it's alien. It's huge. It's dangerous. Just because it's
quiescent doesn't mean it will remain so—in fact, our models
predict exactly the opposite. Think about it for a moment. What
will happen if it blooms, or produces more seeds? What if these
plants spread to cover the bottom of the oceans? What if they
can also grow on land? No matter which way you look at it, this
thing's a threat. It could destroy the earth."

"So how are you going to kill it?"

"We have in our possession a plutonium core of about
thirty kilograms, a neutron trigger device, fast and slow shaped
HE, high-speed transistors—everything needed to assemble a
nuke."

"Where in hell did you get that stuff?"

"Everything's for sale in certain former satellite states these
days."

Gideon shook his head. "Jesus."

"We also have a nuclear weapons expert on staff."

"Who?"

"You, of course."

Gideon stared.

"That's right," said Glinn quietly. "Now you know the *real* reason I hired you in the first place. Because we always knew this day was coming."

4

THE ROOM FELL silent. Gideon slowly rose from his chair, making a successful effort to hide his anger. "So you hired me to oversee the building of a nuke," he said calmly.

"Yes."

"In other words, four months ago, back when Garza first walked up to my fishing spot on Chihuahueños Creek and offered me a hundred thousand dollars for a week's work, stealing the plans for some new kind of weapon off a defecting Chinese scientist—it was really this moment, *this* job, that you had in mind."

Glinn nodded.

"And you want to use the nuke to kill a gigantic alien plant that is supposedly growing on the bottom of the ocean."

"In a nutshell."

"Forget it."

"Gideon," said Glinn, "we've been through this tiresome dance several times before: your heated refusals, your storming out, and then your eventual return once you've thought it through. Can we please skip all that?"

Gideon swallowed, stung by the comment. "Let me try to explain to you why this is a crazy idea."

"Please."

"First, you can't do this on your own. You need to take this problem to the UN and get the whole world behind the effort to kill this thing."

Glinn shook his head sadly. "Sometimes you amaze me, Gideon. You seem so smart—and then you say something so remarkably stupid. Did you just suggest that we ask the *United Nations* to solve this problem?"

Gideon paused. He had to admit, on reflection, that it didn't sound like a very intelligent idea. "Okay, maybe not the UN, but at least take it to the US government. Let them deal with it."

"You mean, let our most excellent Congress deal with this situation in the same way it has handled our other pressing national problems, such as global warming, terrorism, education, and our crumbling infrastructure?"

Gideon fished around for a snappy rejoinder to this but could not find one.

"This is no time for waffling," said Glinn. "We're the only ones who can do this. It's got to be done now, while the life-form is quiescent. I hope you'll help us."

"If not?"

"Then sooner or later, the world as we know it will end. Because without you, we *will* fail. And you'll reproach yourself for the rest of your life."

"The rest of my *short* life, you mean. Thanks to what's growing in my own brain, I've got maybe eight, nine months left to live. You and I both know that."

"We don't know that anymore."

Gideon looked at Glinn. His face looked years younger; as he spoke he gestured with both hands, and his dead eye had healed up and was now clear and deep. His wheelchair was nowhere to be seen. On their last mission together, he had partaken of the restorative, health-giving lotus—just as Gideon himself had. It had worked for Glinn; but not, apparently, for Gideon.

"You really believe you'll fail without me?" Gideon asked.

"I never say anything I don't believe."

"I'll need to be convinced this thing is as dangerous as you say before I help you with anything nuclear."

"You'll be convinced."

Gideon hesitated. "And you have to make me a co-director of the project."

"That's quite absurd," said Glinn.

"Why? You said we work well as a team. But we've never worked as a team. It's always been you telling me what to do, me doing it my own way, you protesting, and then, in the end, I turn out to be right and you're wrong."

"That is an oversimplification," Glinn said.

"I don't want you second-guessing and overruling me. Especially if we're dealing with something as dangerous as nuclear weapons—and this seed of yours."

"I don't like governing by committee," Glinn said. "At the least, I'll have to run this through our QBA programs to see if it's feasible."

"You yourself said there's no time," said Gideon. "Make your decision now or I walk. For once, do something without your damn QBA programs."

For a moment Glinn's face flashed with anger, but then it smoothed out, the neutral mask reasserting itself, until he once again looked like the Glinn of resolute mystery.

"Gideon," he said, "think for a minute about the qualities that a leader—even a co-leader—is required to have. He's a team player. He's good at inspiring others. He's able to hide his true feelings, put up a false front when necessary. He projects confidence at all times—even if he doesn't feel confident. He can't be a freelancer. And he's certainly not a loner. Now, tell me: do any of these qualities describe you?"

There was a pause.

"No," Gideon finally admitted.

"Very well." Glinn rose. "Our first stop is the Woods Hole Oceanographic Institution. And then it's off to the South Atlantic—and beyond the Ice Limit."

5

As the helicopter banked, the afternoon sun shimmered off the waters of Great Harbor, Massachusetts, and the R/V *Batavia* came into view. Gideon was surprised at how big it looked from above; just how much, with its massive prow and tall central superstructure, it dwarfed all the other research vessels and boats in the mooring field.

"A *Walter N. Harper*–class oceanographic research vessel," Glinn said from the adjoining seat, noticing Gideon's interest. "Three hundred twenty feet in length, beam of fifty-eight feet, twenty-one-foot draft. It has two thirty-five-hundred-horsepower Z-drives, a fourteen-hundred-horsepower azimuthing jet, full dynamic positioning, two-hundred-fifty-thousand-gallon fuel capacity, eighteen-thousand-nautical-mile range at a cruising speed of twelve knots—"

"You lost me with the part about the 'azimuthing jet.'"

"All it means is that the jet drive can be rotated in any horizontal direction, so the ship doesn't need a rudder. It allows for very exact dynamic positioning, even in rough seas with winds and currents."

"Dynamic positioning?"

"Keeping the ship in one place. Gideon, surely you know all about boats after your recent adventure down in the Caribbean."

"I know I don't like them, I don't like being on the sea, and I'm quite content to remain ignorant of all things nautical."

The helicopter finished its turn and began to descend toward the midships helipad. A deckhand with wands motioned them into place, and a moment later the door was opened and they hopped out. It was a brilliant fall afternoon, the sky a cold blue dome, the sun slanting across the deck.

Gideon followed Manuel Garza and Glinn across the helipad, the EES director crouching a little stiffly against the backwash of the rotors. They went through a door into a waiting and staging room, sparely furnished. Three people immediately stood up, two in uniform and one civilian. Outside, the chopper lifted off.

"Gideon," said Glinn, "I'd like you to meet Captain Tulley, master of the R/V *Batavia*, and Chief Officer Lennart."

The captain, a man of no more than five feet, stepped forward and shook Gideon's hand with gravity, his tight and humorless face breaking into a poor semblance of a smile. One brisk up-and-down motion, and then he stepped back.

Chief Officer Lennart was worlds apart from Tulley: a blond, Nordic woman in her early fifties who towered over the diminutive captain, full of warmth and fluid motion, with a hand as warm and as enveloping as an oven mitt.

"And this is Alexandra Lispenard, who is in charge of our fleet of four DSVs. She'll be your driving instructor."

Lispenard tossed her long, teak-colored hair and took his hand with a smile, giving it a slow shake. "Nice to meet you, Gideon," she said, her contralto voice in contrast to the formal silence of the others.

"DSVs?" Gideon asked her, trying not to stare as he did so. She was about thirty-five and stunningly attractive, with a heart-shaped face and exotic, agate-colored eyes.

"Deep Submergence Vehicles. A motorized bathyscaphe, really. A marvel of engineering."

Gideon felt the pressure of Glinn's hand on his shoulder. "Ah, here's the doctor. Gideon, I'd like you to meet Dr. Brambell, the expedition's physician."

A wiry old man with a glossy pate, wearing a white lab coat, had appeared in the doorway. "Pleased, very pleased!" he said in a wry Irish accent. He did not offer to shake hands.

"Dr. Brambell," said Glinn, "was on the *Rolvaag* when it went down. I'm sure when he has a chance, he'll tell you all about it."

This unexpected statement was greeted by a short silence. The two ship's officers looked surprised—and displeased. Gideon wondered if Brambell might be considered a kind of unlucky Jonah.

"That isn't a fact I care to have bandied about," said Brambell shortly.

"My apologies. In any case, Gideon, you've now met several of the most important people on board. Alex will take you down to the hangar deck. I'm afraid I have another engagement."

With no further talk, Lispenard turned away, and Gideon followed her through an open bulkhead door, down a circular metal staircase, and along a maze of cramped passageways, stairs, and hatches until—quite suddenly—they came out into a vast, gleaming space. Along the sides stood several bays, some covered with drop cloths, but four of which were open. Inside three of these were small, identical rounded vessels, painted bright yellow with turquoise trim. They sported a variety of thick portholes, along with various extruding bulges and projections and a kind of robotic arm set into the bows. The stern wall of the hangar contained a large door, which had been rolled open, exposing the ship's fantail deck. A fourth vessel was visible there, under an A-frame crane.

Lispenard began humming "Yellow Submarine."

"My sentiments exactly," said Gideon. "Very cute."

"Twenty million dollars' worth of cute. That one under the crane is *George*. The other three are *Ringo*, *John*, and *Paul*."

"Oh, no."

She walked through the hangar, stepped up to *George*, and placed her hand on it, giving it a little pat of affection. It was surprisingly small, no more than nine feet long and about seven feet high. She turned to Gideon. "Inside, there's a titanium personnel sphere, almost a sub within a sub, with a hatch at the top and three viewports. There's a panel of electronics, a seat, controls, videoscreens—and that's about it. Oh, and there's a receiving basket in front for the robot arm to place items in. If something should go wrong, there's an emergency release that jettisons the sphere and sends it to the surface. The rest of the DSV is taken up with ballast tanks, a mercury trim tank, cameras, strobes and lights, sonar, a bank of batteries, a stern propulsion motor, propellers, and a rudder. Simple." She shrugged. "Shakedown dive tomorrow."

Gideon turned from *George* to her. "Great. Who's going?"

She smiled. "You and me. Oh seven hundred."

"Wait. You and me? You think I'm going to drive one of those? I'm no Captain Nemo."

"They're designed to be driven by anyone. They're idiotproof."

"Thank you very much."

"What I mean is, they have self-driving software. Like a Google car, but controllable with a joystick. You just move the joystick indicating where you want to go, and the mini sub's AI does the rest—making all the dozens of little adjustments necessary, avoiding obstacles, maneuvering through tight spaces, doing all the fine control without you even being aware of it. You can't crash it even if you try."

"Surely there are other people along for this joyride who have more experience with DSVs."

"There are. Antonella Sax, for example, our exobiology chief. But she won't be joining the ship for some time yet. Besides, Glinn said there was a reason you should get comfortable with operating a DSV. Something to do with your role in the overall mission."

"He never mentioned I'd be driving a submarine. I don't like being *on* the water, let alone *in* it—and two miles down, for Chrissakes."

She peered at him with a half smile. "That's strange. I didn't take you for a wimp."

"I *am* a wimp. I am most definitely, without doubt, a lily-livered, spineless, cowardly, gutless poltroon."

"Poltroon? Nice word. But you're going down with me tomorrow. End of discussion."

Gideon gave her a stare. God, he was sick of bossy women. But there was no point in arguing with her for the moment; he would take it up with Glinn. "So what else is there to see around here?"

"There's the various labs—they're fantastic, you'll see them soon enough—along with the mission-control room, a library, galley, dining room, lounge and game room, and crew quarters. Not to mention the engine room, machine shop, commissary, sick bay, and all the other shipboard necessities." She checked her watch. "But now it's time for dinner."

"At five o'clock?"

"When breakfast is at oh five thirty, all the mealtimes are shifted."

"Breakfast at five thirty?" This was another thing he'd take up with Glinn, this totally unnecessary nod to military discipline. "I hope to God this isn't a dry ship."

"Not now. It will be once we arrive on target. We've quite a long journey ahead of us."

"How long?"

"Nine thousand nautical miles to the target site."

It hadn't occurred to Gideon there would be a long preliminary voyage before they even reached their goal. Of course, if he'd given it even a moment's thought, he would have realized. What had Glinn said about the cruising speed of the ship? Twelve knots. Twelve nautical miles per hour, divided by nine thousand nautical miles—

"Thirty-two days," said Alex.

Gideon groaned.

6

Lᴇᴛ's ᴛᴀᴋᴇ ᴏᴜʀ drinks out on deck," Gideon said to Alex Lispenard.

"Good idea."

Gideon rose from the bar, trying to keep his second martini from slopping over the rim. The bar on the R/V *Batavia*, an alcove off the dining room, was small and spare but pleasing in a kind of nautical way. It sported a row of windows, presently looking over Great Harbor to the low-lying shores of Ram Island. After negotiating the low door, they emerged on deck. It was a faultless October evening, cool and deep, the golden light falling aslant the ship, the cries of seagulls in the distance.

Gideon took a good slug of the drink and leaned on the rail, Alex joining him. He was feeling good—very good, in fact: a total reversal from how he'd felt just two hours before. It was amazing what an excellent meal and a martini could do to one's outlook on life.

"Think we're going to get fed like that throughout the voyage?" Gideon asked.

"Oh, yeah. I've been on a lot of research vessels and the food is always good. When you're months at sea, bad food means bad morale. On a trip like this, food is the least of any expense, so you might as well stock the best. And in Vince Brancacci, we have one of the finest chefs afloat."

"You mean that guy I saw in the white smock, with the laugh of a hyena and the build of a sumo wrestler?"

"That's the one."

Gideon took another slug and glanced at Alex, leaning on the rail, the breeze stirring her glossy brown hair, her upturned nose and agate eyes aimed at the blue sea horizon, her breasts just pressing into the rail.

He averted his eyes. As attractive as she was, there was no way—none—that he was going to get involved in a romance on a long voyage to the antipodes of the world.

She turned toward him. "So, what's your history?"

"You haven't been briefed?"

"The opposite of 'briefed.' Beyond asking me to familiarize you with the DSVs, Glinn was totally mysterious. I got the sense he wanted me to find everything out for myself."

Gideon was relieved. This meant she knew nothing about his medical situation. "Where to begin? I started my professional career stealing art, then I got a job designing nuclear bombs."

She laughed. "Naturally."

"It's true. I work at Los Alamos designing the high-explosive lenses used to implode the cores. I was part of the Stockpile Stewardship program, running computer simulations and tweaking those lenses to make sure the bombs would still go off after years of rotting in some nuclear vault somewhere. I'm, ah, on extended leave at present."

"Wait . . . you're *not* kidding?"

Gideon shook his head. His drink was disappointingly empty.

He thought of going back for a third, but a little voice in his head told him that would not be a good idea.

"So you actually design nukes?"

"More or less. That's why I'm on this voyage, in fact."

"What do nuclear bombs have to do with this voyage?"

Gideon stared at her. She really hadn't been briefed. He quickly backtracked. "It's just that I'm an engineer with a knowledge of explosives—that's all."

"And you weren't kidding about the art thief business, either?"

"No."

"One question. Why?"

"I was poor, I needed money. And more important, I loved the pieces I stole, and I only stole from historical societies and museums that weren't taking care of their collections, stuff that nobody saw anyway."

"And I suppose that made it morally okay."

This irritated Gideon. "No, it didn't, and I'm not excusing myself. Just don't expect me to grovel in guilt and self-reproach."

A silence. He really might need that third drink now. Or maybe it was time to change the subject. "I also worked as a magician. Prestidigitator, to be precise."

"You were a magician? So was I!"

Gideon stood up from the rail. He had heard this many times before: somebody who learned a few card tricks and then bestowed on themselves the hallowed title of magician. "So you can pull a coin from behind someone's ear?"

Alex frowned and said nothing.

Gideon leaned back on the railing, realizing he'd offended her. "I was a professional," he explained. "I went on stage, got paid well. I even developed some original tricks. Worked with live animals—rabbits and the like. I had a great trick with a six-foot python that would clear out half the audience." He fiddled with his empty glass. "And I still keep my hand in—picking pockets for fun, that sort of thing. It's like playing the violin: you have to keep practicing or your skills go to hell."

"I see."

"Turns out magical tricks and art thievery are, in fact, related fields."

"I imagine they would be."

Gideon had an idea. A really good idea. This would be amusing. He leaned toward her. "I'm going back in for another—can I bring you one?"

"Two's my limit, but you go ahead. Bring me a glass of water, if you don't mind."

As he departed he brushed against her, casually, using the distracting touch to lift the wallet out of her open purse. Tucking it into his pocket with his own wallet, he went back inside and returned to the bar. "Another Hendrick's on the rocks with a twist, and a glass of water, please."

He watched as the bartender mixed the martini. Alex suddenly appeared next to him. "Getting a little chilly out there." To his surprise, and more, she leaned against him. "Warm me up?"

He put his arm around her, feeling his heart accelerate. "How's that?"

"Good. That's fine, I'm warm now, thanks." She shrugged off his light embrace.

Vaguely disappointed, he picked up his drink while she took her water, clumsily, spilling a little on herself.

"Drat." She took a napkin and brushed the water off her blouse.

He sipped. "So what's your history?"

"I grew up on the coast of Maine. My dad had an oyster farm

and I helped him out. I basically grew up on the water. We grew 'diver' oysters, so I got my PADI open-water cert when I was ten, PADI wreck diving at fifteen, nitrox cert at sixteen, and then I got my certs in cavern, deep diver, ice diver, and the rest. I love the sea and everything under it. Majored in marine biology at USC, went on to get my PhD."

"In what?"

"The benthic life of the Calypso Deep. That's the deepest part of the Hellenic Trench, seventeen thousand feet."

"Where is that, exactly?"

"The Mediterranean, west of the Peloponnesian Peninsula. I spent a lot of time on the R/V *Atlantis* over there, dove down on the *Alvin*—that was the first real DSV, actually."

"Cruising off Greece—nice way to get a PhD."

"I never feel more at home than when I'm on a ship."

"Funny, because I never feel less at home. The sea makes me sick. Give me the high mountains of the West and a stream full of cutthroat trout any day."

"You get seasick, I get altitude sickness."

"Too bad," said Gideon. "There goes my marriage proposal."

The joke fell flat, and Alex sipped her water in the awkward silence that followed.

"And the magic thing? Do you still do that?" Gideon quickly asked.

She waved her hand. "I could never compete with you! It was just a little thing I did to amuse myself and my friends."

"I'd be happy to teach you a few basics."

She raised her eyes to him. "That would be wonderful."

"Maybe we should go back to my quarters—if I can locate them, that is. I actually packed a few magic tricks. I'm sure with a little help you'd pick them up quickly."

"Let's go. I'll show you the way to crew quarters."

He finished his drink, pretended to slap his jeans. "Oops, forgot my wallet. Would you mind picking up the tab? I'll get the next one." He watched with a smile of anticipation as she delved into her purse for her wallet, knowing that she'd find it missing. To his vast surprise, she pulled it out and placed it on the bar.

"Wait...that's your wallet?"

"Of course." She took out a twenty and paid the tab.

Gideon reached for his pocket, and found her wallet was gone. His wallet was gone, as well.

"Oh, shit," he said automatically, "I think I may have dropped something out on deck." He rose from his stool and immediately fell flat on his face. Stupefied, he looked at his feet—only to find that his shoelaces had been tied together. He glanced up to see Alex laughing hilariously, holding his wallet in her hand—along with his wristwatch.

"So, Gideon," she said between gusts of laughter. "About those basics?"

7

GIDEON FLUSHED FROM embarrassment. God, he felt like an idiot. He untied his shoes while Alex stood over him, not bothering to conceal her triumph. He stood up and dusted himself off. His embarrassment began to turn to something else as she handed him the wallet and wristwatch.

"You're not angry?" she asked, recovering her composure.

He looked at her standing there, face aglow, agate eyes twinkling, long glossy hair in unruly coils over her tanned shoulders, breasts still heaving from the recent hilarity. Here she'd humiliated him—and what was his reaction? Overwhelming desire.

He averted his eyes and swallowed. "I guess I deserved it." He glanced at the bartender but he was inscrutable, as if he'd seen nothing.

"You still want me to show you the crew quarters?" she asked.

"Sure."

She turned and strode out of the bar and through the dining room while he followed. They navigated another maze of corridors and stairs—through a bulkhead hatch, and into a long narrow corridor with rooms on one side.

She stopped at a door and opened it. "The scientists have private rooms. This is mine."

He followed her in. It was surprisingly spacious, with a queen-size bed, two portholes, built-in dresser, writing table with a laptop computer, mirror, walls painted cream-white.

"Here's the bath." She threw open another door to reveal a small bathroom with a third porthole.

"Very nice," he said. "Quite the room for a...well, a scientist."

She turned. "I'm not just a mini sub driver. I'm the mission's head oceanographer, as I'm sure you know. I've been with EES for five years now."

"Actually, I didn't know. I haven't really been briefed, either. How come I've never met you before?"

"You must know Glinn's mania for compartmentalization."

"And your position vis-à-vis Garza?"

"He's an engineer; I'm a scientist. EES doesn't have a normal corporate structure, as I'm sure you've realized. Things change from mission to mission."

He nodded, watching her move around the room, smoothly and gracefully. She had a swimmer's body, lithe and athletic. He had sworn, absolutely sworn, that he would not get into another romantic entanglement. Given the medical death sentence hanging over his head, it wasn't fair, either to him or to the woman. But that was theoretical; she was real.

"What's your room number?" she asked.

"Two fourteen."

"That's at the end of the hall. Let's check it out." She headed out the door and he followed.

They went down the hall to the door marked 214. He took out the magnetic key card he'd been given when being processed earlier in the day, waved it at the lock, and the door clicked. He pushed it open and switched on the light—to be greeted by a luxurious, spacious cabin, with a row of portholes, a king-size bed, a sitting area with a sofa and two chairs, The floor was covered in thick cream-colored pile, the lighting soft and indirect. His luggage had already been placed in one corner, neatly arranged.

"Wow," said Alex, stepping inside. "And what's *your* position at EES to merit all this?"

"I don't know. Slacker in chief?"

He followed her in and watched as she took a turn around the room, her hand stroking the quilted bedcovers, adjusting the lights. She opened the door to the bathroom. "A tub, no less!" Making herself quite at home, she next explored the sitting area, where there was a kitchen nook with a microwave oven, coffee machine, and small fridge. She opened the fridge. "And look— Veuve Clicquot!" She took out a split of champagne and waved it at him.

"Great, let's open it and celebrate."

She put it back, shut the fridge door firmly. "Two's my limit, remember? And you're already over yours. I need you clearheaded for tomorrow's dive. And besides, I don't drink champagne in strange men's rooms."

"Me? A strange man?"

"Art thief, nuke designer, magician—very strange."

"We'll enjoy it tomorrow evening, then. You and me."

"We'll be wiped out after our shakedown dive." She glanced at her watch. "In fact, I'd better be getting back to my quarters. I've got a lot of work to do before bedtime."

He walked up to her and put his hand on her shoulder as she turned to go. What was he doing? He knew that third drink was a mistake, but he wasn't going to stop now. He felt his whole body aching with longing. She paused at his touch and he leaned toward her. But then she deftly ducked out from under his hand and stepped aside. "None of that, mister. Not on a ship. You know better."

"I wish I did know better."

"Breakfast at oh five thirty, remember; then we go to the DSV hangar and prep. See you then."

And she was gone.

He sat down on the bed with a sigh. He also had a ton of work to do: files and documents to review, a computer to set up and get networked into the ship's system. And he couldn't go to Glinn and argue himself out of the dive—not after three martinis, smelling like a drunk.

He stretched out on the bed, hands behind his head. Alex's faint perfume remained in the air and he inhaled it, feeling another surge of longing. What was wrong with him? He should be pissed off at the way she'd humiliated him, but instead it seemed to be having an altogether different effect.

Alex, he decided, was right about one thing: he had better get himself under control or this was going to be a very long voyage indeed.

8

A BIG AUTUMN sun rose over the distant Nobska Lighthouse and Vineyard Sound, casting gold across the water as they came out on deck early the next morning. A stiff breeze blew in from the east, kicking up whitecaps across the harbor and the sound beyond.

The A-frame crane had moved two DSVs out of the hangar deck and onto the fantail. To Gideon they looked stubby, even cartoonish; almost too small to fit a human inside, let alone everything else. Alex had told him to wear tight-fitting but warm clothing. She was dressed in a sleek tracksuit of dark blue with white racing stripes, which hugged her muscled legs, rear, and torso in a way Gideon found most distracting. He, on the other hand, was dressed like a slob in jeans and a long-sleeved undershirt.

Glinn and Garza were standing together when they arrived. Glinn was dressed in a black turtleneck and pants, a thin, even spectral figure on the windswept deck. Garza wore a suede jacket with the collar turned up, his salt-and-pepper hair stirred by the wind.

"Right on time," said Glinn, approvingly, coming over with an outstretched hand and giving Gideon a shake. "Are you ready to go deep, Gideon?"

"I wish you'd told me I was going to be piloting a Yellow Submarine."

"To what end? It would only have worried you. These DSVs are idiotproof."

"So Alex tells me."

"She's an excellent instructor. You'll do fine."

"But I thought my job was to be your expert on nuclear explosives. Surely you could have hired an extra sub driver."

Instead of answering, Glinn patted him on the shoulder in a way that Gideon found patronizing. Gideon glanced at Garza for an explanation, but the engineer was, as usual, silent and unreadable.

"You'll be driving *George*, and I'll be in *Ringo*," Alex told him. While Glinn and Garza watched, Alex gave him an external tour of *George*, pointing out and naming the various parts—cameras, strobes, viewing ports, CTFM sonar, sail lights, current meter sensor, emergency identification strobe, emergency homing radio, lift propellers, rudder and ram propeller, underwater telephone transducer, collecting basket, and robot arm. "The ladder goes up to the sail hatch," she explained. "It's pretty simple—just climb up and lower yourself inside, using the two grab bars. The personnel sphere is five feet in diameter. I'll get into *Ringo* and we'll communicate through radio, do a dry run on deck—and then get lowered into the water."

"Should I climb up now?"

She nodded. "Just lower yourself into the chair. On a hook just above your head you'll find the communications helmet; put that on and toggle the switch on the lower right. Wait for me to talk.

You don't have to press a transmit button—it's full duplex above water. Underwater, the range of actual conversation is limited to five hundred meters. Beyond that, there's only communication using digital sonar—text and synthetic voice only."

He nodded, trying to follow it all.

"Okay, up you go."

Gideon climbed the ladder, grabbed the bars, and lowered himself into the sphere. Someone shut the hatch and dogged it down as he settled into the lone chair and put on the headset.

The interior of the sphere was almost completely covered with electronics, screens, panels, buttons, and dials. The forward viewport was directly in front of his face, and there were left and right viewports as well as a downward-looking port. A small console to his right contained a keypad, a joystick, and a few emergency buttons in little cages that could be flipped up. Everything was illuminated dimly in reddish light.

A moment later Alex's voice came in. "Gideon, you read?"

"Loud and clear."

"I'm going to go through every console and screen, from left to right."

For the next sixty minutes, she proceeded to describe everything in the sphere in excruciating detail, until Gideon despaired of remembering it all. At last she concluded with the joystick panel.

"This is really all you need to know," she said. "The joystick works like any normal joystick: forward, back, port, and starboard. The more you push it in any one direction, the faster the sub will go. But it's always on fine autopilot control, which means it will correct any mistakes you make. If you push the stick forward to enter, say, a hole in the side of a ship, it will automatically steer you through the hole, touching nothing. It will navigate you down tight passageways without touching any walls. It will keep you from grazing the bottom or striking underwater obstacles. The autopilot takes its cues from you, but then handles the details itself. It won't enter a space too small for it, and it won't obey if you direct it into the seafloor or a cliff."

"Is there any way to shut it off?"

"Not directly—that's the whole point. If necessary, control of your DSV can be transferred to the surface, however. Now: do you see those two red buttons under the flip-up cages? The one that says EMERGENCY EJECT will jettison your titanium sphere, which will rise fast to the surface. This has never been tested and the rapid rise might kill you, so don't do it. And the EMERGENCY BEACON activates your beacon if you get into trouble."

"What's the point of an emergency eject if it might be lethal?"

"It's a last resort. Okay, ready for the wet run?"

"No."

"The crane'll pick up your DSV, put it in the water, and release it. You'll begin to sink automatically, controlled by the autopilot software. Normally, there would be two hundred pounds of iron ballast aboard to rapidly take you the two miles down to the wreck. But the water here is only a hundred feet deep or so, so that won't be necessary. The autopilot will bring you to a halt ten feet off the bottom. You wait and do nothing until I tell you what to do."

"Yes, Captain."

He felt the sub being hoisted, then swung out over the water. Then he was lowered, ever so gently, until blue water appeared in the viewports. And then, with a *clank*, the sub was released and began to drift downward. Running lights came on automatically, front, astern, and below. He could see bubbles ascending around him. The water was murky, but in a few minutes the bottom began to take shape. As promised, the sub slowed and came to a hover about ten feet above a bed of waving kelp, in dark-green water. There was a soft hiss of warm air. Gideon didn't like the feeling of claustrophobia. He almost could feel the press of water above him, the thickness of it in the air he was breathing.

And then, twenty feet in front of him, he saw the other yellow sub drift down and come to a halt, its running lights winking at him.

"Gideon, do you read?"

"I read."

"Why don't you start by getting a feel for the joystick. Move it forward, sideways, and back, and see how the DSV responds."

"How do I go up and down?"

"Good question. You see the thumb toggle on top of the joystick? Forward moves you up, backward goes down. Go ahead and play with it while I watch and comment."

Ever so gingerly, he pushed the joystick forward. A faint humming noise sounded and the sub moved, very slowly.

"You can be a little more aggressive. The autopilot smooths out any sharp motions you might make."

He gave it a bigger push and the sub moved forward faster.

"You're coming right at me, Gideon. Try a turn."

Instead of turning, Gideon toggled the sub up and it went up and over her sub, then he toggled back down and the sub settled just above the layer of kelp. He pushed it sideways and the sub went into a smooth turn. In a moment Alex's mini sub reappeared in the viewport.

"Gideon? How about learning to walk before you fly?"

Her instructional tone was beginning to irritate him. He accelerated toward her, then toggled up again; but this time his coordination was off and the sub went almost vertical, climbing sharply toward the surface.

"Toggle down."

He pushed the toggle down, but accidentally pushed the joystick forward as well. The problem, he began to realize, was that the sub's response wasn't as instantaneous as a car's; water gave everything a sluggish, delayed effect. And now he was heading straight for the bottom—fast.

"Oh, shit." He pulled the toggle and joystick back, but in his panic overcompensated once again and gave it an inadvertent twist. The sub slewed around like a corkscrew before coming to an abrupt halt—unbidden—just above the kelp. A small red light was blinking and a genteel alarm was sounding; on the main control screen a message appeared:

FULL AUTOPILOT TAKEOVER
RELEASE OF CONTROL TO OPERATOR IN
15
SECONDS

He watched as the numbers counted down.

"Son of a *bitch*," he muttered.

Alex's cool voice sounded in his ear. "Well, Gideon, congratulations. That was the most remarkable display of ineptitude I have ever seen in a DSV. Now that you've gotten your teenage ya-yas out, want to try again? This time as an adult."

"If you weren't yammering in my ear all the time," he said angrily, "I might have pulled it off. Bloody backseat driver."

Alex's cool voice came through. "Keep in mind that our conversation, and everything we do, is being closely monitored in mission control."

Gideon swallowed his next comment. He could just picture Glinn, Garza, and the rest assembled in the control room, listening and frowning with deep disapproval. Or perhaps laughing. Either way he felt annoyed.

"Right." The seconds had now ticked off and the screen read:

CONTROL RELEASED TO OPERATOR

He eased the joystick forward and the sub moved slowly in a straight line; then he executed a gentle turn, came back, and halted.

"There's a good boy," said Alex. "Nice and easy."

Gideon almost thought he could hear a faint snigger sounding in his headset.

9

THE R/V *BATAVIA* had "crossed the line" with all the silliness and concomitant ceremony that passing the equator entailed, which Gideon had retreated from with alacrity. For the past fifteen days, since leaving Woods Hole, life on board the *Batavia* had been dull: seasickness alternating with bored overeating, reading, watching *Game of Thrones* in the ship's theater, playing backgammon with Alex (where he was now about a hundred games behind), and trying not to drink too many cocktails in the evening.

Although by now he had met numerous scientists and many of the ship's other major players—nattily dressed Ship's Chief Engineer Frederick Moncton; Eduardo Bettances, dour and formidable chief of security; and Warrant Officer George Lund, who seemed intimidated by everything and everybody—he had made few friends on board. Most of the crew were ex-navy, with crew cuts and pressed uniforms—not Gideon's type at all. And the various scientific and technical teams were too busy preparing for their upcoming duties to do much socializing. Glinn was as remote as ever. Gideon and Garza, despite the recent thaw in their relations, remained wary of each other. The only one he really liked—liked far too much—was Alex, but she had made it clear that while she, too, enjoyed his company, shipboard romance was out of the question.

But there was one character aboard ship who, over time, began to intrigue him: the ship's doctor, Patrick Brambell. He was like a gnome, a devious old fellow with a head as shiny as a cue ball, a small face, sharp crafty blue eyes, and a stooped way of slinking about the ship, like a ghost. He always had a book tucked under one arm and never appeared in the mess hall, apparently taking his meals in his room. The rare times Gideon had heard him speak, he'd detected a soft Irish accent.

What intrigued Gideon most of all was that, aside from Glinn and Garza, Brambell was the only member of the expedition who had been on the *Rolvaag* when it sank. Gideon had the nagging sense that Glinn and Garza were withholding information about the shipwreck, perhaps even lying about the fate of the *Rolvaag* in order to secure his nuclear expertise. For this reason, Gideon decided to pay Brambell a surprise visit.

So one muggy tropical afternoon, he made his way to the crew quarters and, making sure Brambell was in his room, knocked on the door. At first there was no answer, but he knocked again, loud and persistent, knowing the devious old coot was holed up inside. After the third knock, an irritated voice finally responded. "Yes?"

"Can I come in? It's Gideon Crew."

A pause. "Is this a medical issue?" the voice filtered through the door. "I'll be glad to meet you in the sick bay."

Gideon didn't want this. He wanted to beard Brambell in his element.

"Um, no." He said no more; the less explanation, the less Brambell would be able to find a reason to say no.

A soft rustle and the door unlocked. Without waiting for an invitation, Gideon pushed in and Brambell, taken by surprise, automatically stepped back. He was holding a Trollope novel in one veined hand, his finger marking where he'd been reading.

Gideon took a seat, uninvited.

Brambell, his wizened face wrinkling with annoyance, remained standing. "As I said, if it's a medical issue, the clinic is the proper place—"

"It's not a medical issue."

A silence.

"Well, then," said Brambell, not exactly defeated but resigned, "what can I do for you?"

Gideon took in the large room. It astonished him. Every single inch of wall space, even the portholes, had been covered with custom-built shelves, and those shelves were completely lined with books, all kinds of books, the most eclectic range imaginable, from leather-bound classics to trashy thrillers to nonfiction books, biographies, histories, as well as titles in French and Latin. As his eye roamed the collection, the only type of book he did not see in evidence was medical.

"This is quite the library," said Gideon.

"I am a reader," came the dry voice. "That is what I do. Medicine is a sideline."

Gideon was impressed by this frank announcement. "I guess, being on a ship, you get a lot of time to read."

"That is the very point," said Brambell in his high, whistling accent.

Gideon clasped his hands and looked at the doctor, who was eyeing him curiously, no longer irritated—or at least, so it seemed. The doctor put down the book. "I see you are a man who has come to me with a purpose."

Gideon already sensed that Brambell would respond well to directness. He knew when a person could not be socially engineered, and the ship's doctor was just that person.

"Glinn says he's given me the full story on the sinking of the *Rolvaag*," said Gideon flatly. "But something tells me he left part of it out."

"That would be like him."

"So I'm here. To hear the story from you."

Brambell gave a small smile, grasped the arms of what was evidently his reading chair, and eased himself down. "It's a long story."

"We have all the time in the world."

"Indeed." He made a tent of his fingers and pursed his lips. "Do you know about Palmer Lloyd?"

"I met him."

Brambell's eyebrows shot up. "Where?"

"At a private mental institution in California."

"Is he insane?"

"No. But I'm not sure he's sane, either."

Brambell paused, considering this a moment. "Lloyd was a curious man. When he learned that the world's largest meteorite had been found on a frozen island off Cape Horn, he became determined to have it for the museum he was building. And he hired Glinn to retrieve it. EES bought their ship, the *Rolvaag*, from a Norwegian shipbuilding company. It was a state-of-the-art oil tanker, but they disguised it to look like a shabby old tub."

"Why an oil tanker? Why not an ore carrier?"

"Oil tankers have sophisticated ballast tanks and pumps, which would be necessary to stabilize the ship. Not only was the meteorite the largest ever, but it was incredibly dense—twenty-five thousand tons. So Glinn and Manuel Garza had to develop elaborate engineering plans to dig it up, transport it across the island, load it on the ship, and bring it back and up the Hudson River." He paused again, reflecting. "When we arrived at the island, it was surely one of the most godforsaken places on earth. Isla Desolación: Desolation Island. And that was when things started to go wrong. To begin with, the meteorite was not a normal iron meteorite."

"Manuel told me it had 'peculiar qualities.' I'd say being an alien seed is peculiar enough."

Brambell smiled mirthlessly. "It was a deep red in color, made of a material so hard and dense that the best diamond drills wouldn't even scratch it. Indeed, it seemed to be composed of a new element with a very high atomic number. Perhaps one of the hypothesized elements in the so-called island of stability. This of course made it far more interesting. It was gotten aboard ship with great difficulty—but successfully. But as we started for home, we came under fire from a rogue Chilean destroyer. Glinn, through a typically brilliant stratagem, managed to sink the destroyer. But the *Rolvaag* was badly damaged herself and a storm came up, with a heavy sea. The meteorite started to shift in the hold, the cradle becoming more and more damaged with each roll of the ship." He glanced at Gideon. "You know about the dead man's switch?"

"I know that Glinn refused to use it."

"That was the damnedest thing. Even when Lloyd himself was begging Glinn to throw that bloody switch, he wouldn't do it. He's one of those men who *cannot fail*. For all his talk of logic and reason, underneath Glinn's as obsessive as they come."

Gideon nodded. "I understand the captain went down with the ship."

"Yes. What a tragic loss." Brambell shook his head. "She was an

extraordinary woman. Sally Britton. When Glinn refused to acti-
vate the dead man's switch, she ordered an abandon-ship, which
saved dozens of lives. She insisted on remaining aboard. Then the
meteorite broke free, tore a gash in the hull, and there was a huge
explosion. Britton died, but Glinn was somehow blown free and
survived. A true miracle. He's a cat with nine lives."

Gideon did not go into the story of Glinn's previous crippled
condition, or how he had been cured. "And you? How did you
survive?"

Brambell went on in the same dry, jaunty voice, as if he were
describing something that had happened long ago to someone
else. "After the explosion, most who survived found themselves
in the water, but there was a lot of floating debris and a couple of
drifting lifeboats. Some of us were able to get aboard the lifeboats
and make our way to an ice island. We spent the night there, rescued the next morning. But a number of people froze to death on
the island in the darkness. As a doctor, I tried my best—but I was
helpless against the overwhelming cold."

"So Glinn really was responsible for all those deaths."

"Yes. Glinn—and the meteorite itself, of course." Brambell
glanced around at the walls of books. "It was only later that
McFarlane figured out what the thing really was."

"Glinn mentioned McFarlane to me, but there wasn't anything
about him in the briefing files. What was he like?"

Brambell gave another of his half smiles. He spread his hands.
"Ah yes. Sam. He was a good soul, a bit rough around the edges,
sarcastic, blunt. But a fellow with a good heart. Brilliant, too, one
of the world's experts on meteorites."

"I understand he survived."

"Survived, yes—but scarred. Bitter, angry, haunted—or so I've
heard."

"And you? You're not scarred by what happened?"

"I have my books. I don't live in the actual world. I am imperturbable."

Gideon looked at Brambell. "I have to ask: given all you know about Glinn and his limitations—and all the horror you went through—why did you agree to return for this expedition?"

Brambell laid a veined hand on the book. "Plain old curiosity. This is our first encounter with an alien life-form, even if it's just a big mindless plant. I couldn't say no to the chance to be part of that discovery. And—" he patted the book—"in the meantime, I can read to my heart's content."

And with that he smiled, rose, and offered his hand.

10

As they approached the Ice Limit, drifting icebergs began appearing in the southern ocean, and Gideon found their deep-blue color and sculptural beauty to create one of the most amazing sights he had ever witnessed. He stood at the rail, watching the ship glide between two gorgeous bergs, one with a hole in it, a kind of ice-arch through which the morning sun shone brightly. It was November 20, which Gideon reminded himself was spring—the weather equivalent to April 20 back home—but the air was surprisingly warm and gentle, the ocean utterly calm. It looked nothing like the "Screaming Sixties" he had heard about, so named because at sixty degrees of latitude, the earth was fully girdled by ocean; the winds blew incessantly around the globe, raising enormous seas that circled the planet and—with no land to arrest their course—growing ever bigger and bigger.

But this was anything but screaming. The ocean was a mirror that reflected the stately forms of the icebergs drifting northward from the glaciers of Antarctica, shed during the spring calving season.

In an effort to orient himself, Gideon had spent some time examining the charts in his briefing book. They truly were in the middle of nowhere. The tip of South America was six hundred and fifty miles northwest, the Antarctic Peninsula two hundred and fifty miles to the southwest, and the closest land—Elephant Island—a hundred and forty miles west. No, that wasn't quite right: the chart in his briefing book did show a speck of rock, a glacier-covered peak thrusting from the sea less than a hundred miles from their position, called Clarence Island.

He breathed deeply of the fresh, clean, salty air—and then felt a presence approach from behind.

"Calm as a millpond," Alex Lispenard said, leaning on the rail beside him and gazing across the iceberg-dotted sea, the breeze stirring her long brown hair, her profile etched in the golden sun.

Gideon took a deep breath. "They told me it would be rough."

"There'll be plenty of that, don't worry."

The ship had now slowed to almost a stop, and Gideon could feel the faint vibration of the deck as the engines began to work first one way, then another.

"Feel that?" Alex asked. "That's the dynamic positioning system being activated. We've arrived. The ship will hold a steady position from now on, right here, no matter what the currents or winds do. You'll feel the azimuthing jet stopping and starting from time to time."

Gideon nodded. Staring down at the cold, blue-black water he felt a shiver, thinking of what lay beneath his feet, thinking that he'd be going down there—almost two miles. It filled him with dread.

"Yeah," said Alex, "it's right below us now, I guess."

"Not exactly below," said Gideon. "We're about half a mile offset—for safety's sake." He knew this from all the cramming he'd been doing in his briefing book. He had also dined a few times at the captain's table, where Glinn and Garza also frequently sat, and he had picked up a lot of information about the project that way as well. But he still felt uninformed, and it annoyed him.

He checked his watch. "Walk you down to the briefing?" he asked.

"Sure." He felt her body moving next to his as they descended the companionway to mission control, the electronic nerve-center of the ship.

They were early, but Glinn was already waiting on the briefing platform, flipping through a sheaf of papers. During the voyage south, the man had continued to heal, almost miraculously, before Gideon's very eyes. Far from the once-crippled figure in a wheelchair, now he no longer needed even a cane to support himself.

Glinn motioned for Gideon to join him on the platform. Reluctantly disengaging himself from Alex's warm grasp, he stepped up.

"What is it?" he murmured.

"I might need some assistance in this briefing from the EES slacker in chief," Glinn replied.

"How do you know about that?" Gideon demanded. But Glinn's only reply was a wintry smile.

The seating area in the center of the room began to fill with the more senior members of the ship's crew and scientific personnel. It was an impressive space, oval in shape, crammed with high technology. The walls were covered with giant LCD screens, most of which were now dark. These screens could supposedly display feeds from a host of underwater cameras, Deep Submersible Vehicles, ROVs, satellite downlinks, shipboard radar and sonar, GPS and chartplotters. There were rows of computer workstations and large, sweeping consoles festooned with dials, buttons, keypads, and small LCDs, along with so much else that Gideon could hardly keep it straight. Mission control looked like it came straight out of a science-fiction movie.

The meeting hour arrived and a hush fell over the murmuring group. Looking out, Gideon recognized many faces: Captain Tulley, as colorless, respectable, and duty-bound as they came, sitting in the front wearing an impeccably pressed uniform; and next to him Chief Officer Lennart. Gideon had come to like her quite a bit: she reminded him of a Nordic goddess, a giant blonde, but with a down-to-earth personality, someone who, when off duty, appreciated dirty jokes and seemed to have an endless store of them. She had a low, resonant laugh that was truly infectious and a subversive, bad-girl attitude. At the same time, she had a distinct Jekyll-and-Hyde personality, becoming scarily professional when on duty and projecting an almost supernatural level of competence. Directly behind the captain and chief officer sat the ship's chief engineer, Moncton, and the security chief, Eduardo Bettances.

And then, sitting in the back behind a scattering of scientists and technicians, was Prothero. He had forgotten Prothero's first name, because nobody used it, especially Prothero himself. The man slouched in his chair in his usual faded T-shirt and jeans, Keds propped up on the chair in front, face partially hidden under an unruly mop of black curly hair. A tall, pretty Asian woman sat next to him. Prothero's pale, moon-like face and receding chin with a silly tuft of hair seemed to float in the dim light of the instrumentation, his large eyes and lips glistening with excessive moisture. In every way, Gideon found Prothero to be an off-putting dude. Normally Gideon was attracted to nonconformists, but Prothero had met his friendly overtures with complaints about his berth, the ship's lack of computing power, the lousy speed of the satellite Internet connection, and a host of other grievances, almost as if Gideon were the responsible party. Prothero was the expedition's sonar specialist, said to have the largest collection of recorded cetacean communications and "songs" in existence. He was rumored to be deciphering their language. He never, however, spoke of this to anyone—at least, not so far as Gideon knew.

Glinn cleared his throat. "Greetings," he said in a cool voice. "Ladies and gentlemen, we have arrived on the target area. Let me welcome all of you to the Ice Limit."

He paused for a smattering of applause.

"To be precise, we are at the shifting boundary of floating ice that surrounds the Antarctic Continent, at the edge of the Scotia Sea, about two hundred and fifty miles northeast of the Antarctic Peninsula. The wreck of the *Rolvaag* and the target object both lie in about thirty-five hundred meters of water more or less below us, in an area of the seafloor called the Hesperides Deep. Our position is 61°32'14" South, 59°30'10" West."

Nobody was taking notes; it was all in their briefing books.

"As the Antarctic spring progresses, we will begin to see more and more icebergs start to calve in the warming waters. They offer much spectacle and little or no danger. The true danger here is the weather. We are in the Screaming Sixties, and even though it is spring, we will probably experience high winds and heavy seas from time to time."

He walked slowly across the platform, then turned. "Our mission objectives are simple. We will study this alien life-form with the single goal of identifying how it is vulnerable *in order to destroy it*." He paused, the emphasis on the last phrase hanging in the air. "We are not here to satisfy our own curiosity, to benefit science, or to enlarge our knowledge. We're here to kill it."

Another dramatic pause.

"Our first objective in the coming days will be to recover the two black boxes from the *Rolvaag*, which will contain vital information about the sinking of the ship, as well as video feeds of the meteorite in the hold and the actions of personnel on the bridge and other spaces in the last minutes of the ship's existence. We will also map and survey the wreck—and the entity itself."

Out of the corner of his eye, Gideon saw Prothero shift in his chair, flinging one leg over the other, his face propped up by one hand.

"The fact is, since arriving, we have already come face-to-face with a confounding mystery." Glinn turned to one side and an LCD panel behind him popped into life, displaying a false-color image. "Here is a sonar image of the wreck of the *Rolvaag*, which we have just scanned in twenty-five-meter resolution. It's rough, but you can see the ship is in two pieces on the seafloor, about fifty yards from each other. Tomorrow we will undertake an initial survey dive in a DSV."

He turned.

"Now here is another sonar image of the area, two hundred yards to the south."

Another image appeared on the LCD panel. This one was odd—blurry, a vague, almost fog-like swirl of colors.

"This is a sonar image of the life-form that we believe has grown from the so-called meteorite seed dropped on the seafloor."

A silence.

"But there's nothing there," said a technician.

"That," said Glinn, "is the problem. There's nothing there. Not even the seafloor is visible. The sonar signal is simply vanishing as if into a black hole, and what small return we're getting is stochastic and constantly shifting."

"Is something wrong with the sonar system?" said the technician.

Prothero sat up, his abrasive voice loud in the room. "No, there isn't, as I've said repeatedly. I've checked and triple-checked it."

"Well," Alex joined in, "it seems to me the likeliest explanation is equipment malfunction—"

"Hey, hey, hey, there's *no* equipment malfunction," came the querulous reply. "It's all working perfectly. I'm tired of being blamed for this."

"Any idea, then, what's happening?" Alex asked politely.

Listening, Gideon's dislike of Prothero went through the roof.

"How would I know? Maybe there's a vent spewing clouds of suspended particulate matter, like clay, into the water. Maybe there's a small erupting undersea volcano. I'm sick of these questions."

Gideon spoke up. "No need to get your knickers in a twist, Prothero. Alex is asking legitimate questions."

Prothero laughed loudly. "Oooh, the white knight comes to rescue the damsel in distress."

Gideon, feeling the blood rush to his face, was about to respond when Manuel Garza interjected: "No one is blaming anyone. We've got an enigma on our hands, which tomorrow's recon mission will solve. So let's focus on that and keep the discussion civil."

Prothero gave an audible snort and went back into his slouch.

"Regarding the recon," Glinn went on, "we're going to keep it simple. One DSV will go down to photograph the target object, along with doing a quick photographic and sonar survey of the wreck so we can get a better idea of its position on the seafloor. Extracting those black boxes will be critical."

He paused.

"We'll be doing this recon tomorrow. It took us a month to get down here, and there's no point in wasting any time. Alex Lispenard, as DSV chief, will assign the mission. Any questions?"

There were none.

"That's all—thank you very much."

As the room was emptying, Glinn laid a restraining hand on Gideon's arm, indicating he should stay. When everyone had left, including Garza, he leaned over. "Give Prothero a wide berth."

Gideon felt a swell of irritation. "He had no business attacking Alex like that. He's a jerk and I called him out on it."

"And you were humiliated. You'll never win a nasty exchange with him. His IQ is forty percent higher than yours."

Gideon laughed. "Really? You've got all our IQs memorized?"

"Of course. Now, about the recon. As I said, Alex will be assigning the mission. And she'll want to do it herself. Your job is to convince her to let you do it. If necessary, I'll order her to let you."

"Me? What the hell do I know about driving those DSVs? This is a bit too important for a honeymoon dive, don't you think?"

"A baby could drive those DSVs. But here's why I want you: I sense this recon is more dangerous than people realize, precisely because we *don't* know what's down there. Why can't we see it on sonar? That's very disturbing."

"So you're saying I'm expendable? I thought my nuclear knowledge was priceless to you."

"You're not, and it is. I never thought I'd say this, but you're . . . *lucky*. You get yourself out of the most amazing scrapes."

"Despite my low IQ?"

"Perhaps because of it," Glinn said drily.

"How reassuring."

"Listen to me carefully, Gideon. I want you down there, seeing things firsthand with your own eyes. You said you needed to be convinced this thing is dangerous before you'd lend your expertise—this is your chance. Besides, the more you know about what we're dealing with, the more you understand, the more useful it will be when the time comes to build—and position—the bomb that will destroy it."

And with that, he nodded his dismissal.

11

THEY TOLD HIM the descent would take forty minutes—if all went well. Gideon, strapped into the DSV known as *Ringo*, fought back a growing sense of unease and claustrophobia as the submersible was lowered into the water.

He'd had a right good argument with Alex when he'd asked her to assign the recon to him instead of herself. Nothing had worked—wheedling, cajoling, demanding: even telling her to fuck off. In the end, though, he hadn't needed to go to Glinn—she'd taken the matter to him herself, and Glinn had endorsed Gideon's request. The whole incident had left her furiously angry, and that pained Gideon—especially since he wasn't exactly thrilled to be the volunteer guinea pig.

The surface of the ocean was visible through the forward viewport, rippled by the breeze but otherwise calm. He could feel the faint swing of the DSV as it entered the water. In a moment the submersible was under, with glistening bubbles swirling around the viewport, and then he was staring into the infinite, sunspeared depths.

He took a deep breath. He tried to take his mind off the fact that he was going down into the blackness beyond—almost two miles deep.

"Ringo, do you read?"

"Loud and clear."

Gideon's mission-control contact was Garza, who, although he wasn't exactly the warmest human being, was one of the most competent. For that, Gideon was grateful.

"We're going to hold you at a depth of twenty feet while we go through the in-sea checklist. You ready?"

"So far, so good."

While the DSV hung in the water, still on its cables, Garza ran through a checklist, telling Gideon to flick one switch, read a second dial, turn on this pump and turn off that one, while he confirmed that all systems were go. Finally, Garza said: *"Ringo,* ready to release in one minute."

The procedure, Gideon knew from the topside briefing, was to release the DSV into the water, where it would sink straight to the bottom, drawn down by its iron ballast. At the bottom, the weights would be jettisoned, giving the DSV neutral buoyancy. Because acoustic or electromagnetic communications between the DSV and ship at a depth of two miles were impossible, for this first dive *Ringo* would remain in contact with mission control by a wire cable, which would unspool as the DSV descended. If the cable broke—apparently, this was a common occurrence—the autopilot would automatically take over and bring *Ringo* back to the surface. The cable would carry all of the DSV's operations, video, and sonar data to mission control, so that if anything started to go wrong they would know it in real time.

"Release in ten seconds."

Gideon listened as Garza's voice counted down in his headphones. Then he heard a muffled *thunk* and felt himself begin to sink. He could see small particles in the water drifting upward past the viewports at a steadily increasing rate. The surrounding sea began to darken: from light blue, to blue, to a deep indigo.

"All systems green," came Garza's neutral, reassuring voice, every two minutes.

Now the viewports had faded into black. Occasionally something—a bit of particulate matter—would flash through the DSV's running lights, moving upward as the vehicle sank.

"Take a deep breath, Gideon. Your vitals are starting to rise."

He realized he was breathing fast and shallow, and he could feel his heart racing. They were monitoring his vital signs, of course, and he knew this incipient panic would not look good. He made a supreme effort to regulate his breathing, calm himself down, telling himself this was far less dangerous than crossing Seventh Avenue at rush hour.

"Better," said Garza.

Gideon checked the clock—Jesus, it had only been seven minutes. Thirty-three more to go. One screen showed a continuous sonar image of the seafloor below, and he focused on it to distract himself. The image gradually grew clearer. Two brighter images began to resolve themselves, representing the two pieces of the *Rolvaag* on the seafloor. To the west of the wreck he could see the strange, ever-shifting, pixelated cloud of sonar return that cloaked the place where the meteorite had landed.

Twenty minutes. He glanced around, refamiliarizing himself with the controls, then checked the depth gauge, continuously reeling off his depth. Two thousand meters, two thousand ten, two thousand twenty...

The sonar image of the wreck continued to sharpen. But the sonar cloud to its west was, if anything, getting bigger and blurrier.

Thirty minutes. He was almost there.

"Slowing descent to fifty meters per minute," said Garza.

Gideon felt the change. Or perhaps it was his imagination? Now he could see the *Rolvaag* in detail on the sonar screen. It lay on the seafloor, torn in half, with a debris field scattered around it. Both pieces of the ship—each one impossibly huge—were lying on their sides, at an angle of perhaps one hundred and twenty degrees. Other than that, the seafloor extended flat in all directions—except for an area about a hundred meters in diameter at the spot where the meteorite was estimated to have landed, which was still just a blurry, shifting cloud of pixels—random sonar return.

The wreck grew until it filled the sonar screen, and still kept growing. He could see the DSV was aiming for a spot on the seafloor perhaps fifty meters from the ship's stern.

"Slowing descent to twenty meters per minute," said Garza. "Gideon, *Ringo*'s lights have a reach of about a hundred meters. You'll be able to see the *Rolvaag* in visible light through the downward viewport at any moment now."

"Roger." Gideon kept his eye fixed on the viewport.

"The autopilot will bring you to rest on the seafloor," said Garza. "Then the DSV will automatically blow the ballast tanks to achieve neutral buoyancy, and the autopilot will bring you up ten meters. Hopefully the action won't throw up too much silt, but if it does, you're downcurrent from the ship and you will remain stationary until the silt clears away."

"Understood."

So far Gideon had done nothing but monitor the screens.

Gazing through the viewport, he could now see the details of the bottom approaching, faint in the DSV's lights. It was smooth mud with a few scattered depressions and some unrecognizable pieces of debris. The wreck itself was still out of view.

The DSV settled down ever so slowly, the bottom coming up to meet him. The muck of the bottom obscured the view out the lower port, and he shifted his gaze to the left and right viewports. To his right, with a start, he realized he could see the dim form of the *Rolvaag*'s stern, with two gigantic, mangled screws affixed to what looked like pods. The crumpled hull, split along riveted seams, extended on into the blackness.

"Ready to blow tanks," came Garza's voice through the communications wire.

"Roger."

Now he felt a series of jolts, and a cloud of silt rose up to obscure his view. The DSV ascended briefly, then became stationary again. The viewports remained completely obscured by silt, which was reflecting the headlights back into the DSV, making it bright inside.

"We're waiting for the silt to drift downcurrent," said Garza.

Within two minutes, the silt had cleared away. He was, as Garza promised, about thirty feet off the bottom. Now he could see the *Rolvaag* in more detail, still faint and at the edge of the spotlights' penetration. Strangely, there was no sign of any deep-sea life, no fish or sea creatures around, and nothing on the ocean floor save scattered bits and pieces of debris.

"*Ringo*, the DSV is yours. Begin recon."

"Roger that." Gideon's briefing had been very specific: to pass over the length of the wreck at a height of twenty meters, from stern to bow, then make a second, sideways pass. The

DSV was pre-programmed to do a complete photographic, sonar, and magnetic survey. All he had to do was pilot it, making sure to steer clear of any snags—not that it mattered, since *Ringo*'s autopilot would avoid them anyway. Then, in phase two of the recon, he was to make his way toward the site of the meteorite and see what the sonar cloud was all about— whether it was a cloud of silt, seafloor venting, or something else.

Gingerly moving the joystick, Gideon turned the DSV to face the ship's stern, then pushed it forward. With a smooth motion, the DSV hummed along at a slow pace. He maneuvered the mini sub to a higher altitude above the seafloor. Gradually the stern came into sharper view, each of its two giant screws larger than his entire vessel. He increased altitude, the DSV responding with the brief delay he was now used to. He made continuous adjustments to keep the path steady and even.

"Proceed to the predetermined waypoint," said Garza.

A chartplotter on the main screen showed the waypoint in x-, y-, and z-axes, and it took only the merest nudging for the submersible to reach it, at which point he came to a halt.

"Commence survey."

Again the DSV needed almost no help from Gideon, who only had to push the joystick slightly for the craft to follow the predetermined survey line, smoothly and expertly. The whole thing was pre-programmed and Gideon began to feel that his presence was more or less optional.

As he cruised about fifty feet above the wreck, Gideon became even more impressed by its enormous size. They had told him it was bigger than the Empire State Building, and now he was experiencing just how true that was. It went on and on, the warped hull sliding past. He passed the superstructure, then the bridge, lying on its side, crushed and scattered about the seafloor in great wrinkled heaps, with all kinds of cables draped about. One bridge wing stuck up from the hull, its windows shattered.

Odd, thought Gideon, that there were no signs of life around the wreck—no fish moving in and out, no plant growth. The entire place seemed dead. But that would be explained, perhaps, by the great depth and lack of light.

He reached the spot where the hull had split, the great riveted plates of the ship ripped apart, the petaled pieces of metal warped outward. Clearly, an explosion inside the hold had torn the ship in half. And in the space between the two halves of the ship lay a huge, rotten pile of debris, a gigantic tangle of split timbers and metal struts, which he assumed must be the remains of the "cradle" for the meteorite.

Suddenly he had a jolt: he could see, lying on the seafloor just outside one section of the hull, an oblong shape that—as he peered more closely—was all too obviously a human corpse. It was missing its head and both of its arms. And as he continued scanning the slowly passing view, he saw another folded shape nearby that, too, was a body. This one was not only headless and armless but missing one leg as well. Apparently, the limbs had been torn away by the force of the explosion that sank the *Rolvaag*.

Jesus.

"I see human remains down here," he said.

Garza's calm voice came back. "We see them, too. This is not unexpected. Carry on."

"Roger."

He swallowed. Why hadn't he thought of that before? And why hadn't they mentioned this in the briefing? Other than the violence done to them by the explosion, both corpses seemed remarkably well preserved, which, he figured, must be due to the great depth.

Now he could see the blunt bow approaching.

"Nearing waypoint two," said Garza.

As he passed the bow, the water suddenly became dark again, the seafloor almost too far away for the headlights to reach.

"Reaching waypoint two."

Once again the DSV came to a smooth hover.

"We're going to make a second pass," Garza said, "to the north and offset from the ship along its deck side. Proceed to waypoint three."

For this scan, the DSV would be close to the seafloor, scanning the wreck sideways. Gideon maneuvered to the waypoint and began the scan.

This was more dramatic, driving only thirty feet above the seafloor, looking at the wreck sideways. Because the two pieces of the ship were lying on their sides, Gideon was now looking down on the decks, which had been slightly accordioned by the impact with the seafloor.

"What's that?" Gideon suddenly asked. He could now barely make out a thin, thread-like line, lying on the seabed and twisting off into the darkness.

"We see it," said Garza. "All right, slow down. Divert from the pre-programmed path and get closer to it."

Gideon eased the DSV over until it was positioned about ten feet above the thing. He peered at it through the viewport. "Is it a wire from the ship?" he asked.

"No," said Garza. "It's too long. Get a little closer, please."

Gideon worked the joystick and the DSV lowered to within five feet of the cable. It was smooth, featureless, pencil-thin, and the same gray color as the seafloor it was lying on. Now that he was closer to the bottom, he could see other, similar cables lying on the seafloor, some partially buried, some appearing and disappearing in the muck, all snaking off in one vague direction into darkness.

"Did you notice they're all heading in the direction of the meteorite?" said Gideon. "I'd like to follow these."

A brief silence. "We don't advise that," said Garza. "Finish up the survey; we can examine it later."

"My survey of the *Rolvaag* is complete. Since I have to go that way anyway, I'd really like to follow these."

More silence. No doubt they were conferring topside, out of his hearing. "Very well," said Garza. "Go slow and do not—I repeat—do *not* enter any cloud of silt, if there is one, or approach any venting structures. Stay well away from anything that looks unusual or unnatural."

"Roger."

Gideon turned *Ringo* and began following the narrow snake-like cables lying on the seafloor. For some reason they gave him the creeps.

And then, through the forward viewport, Gideon could see a large, indistinct, looming form start to take shape.

"Do you see that . . . ?"

"Yes," said Garza in a clipped tone. "And we're losing you in the sonar cloud."

"But the water is totally clear."

"We see what you see."

Gideon instinctually slowed the DSV to a crawl. His sonar screen dissolved into a wash of noise. However, the submersible's headlights now picked up the form ahead, outlining it with clarity.

"Oh, my *God*," he murmured.

Looming ahead out of the darkness was a gigantic, tree-like thing: a grotesque, ribbed growth rising from the seabed, with a fissured, bark-like surface. It towered so far above him that the top of it disappeared into blackness, out of the range of his lights. It went on and on and on.

"Go no farther," said Garza, but Gideon had already stopped the DSV.

There was silence topside. Gideon stared. The loose bundles of cable he'd followed ran along the seabed until they reached the vast growth, combining together and running into its base like a root. Gideon could see a vast number of other, similar appendages converging in from other directions as well, going into the base of the structure.

"Holy shit," Gideon said.

Garza spoke again, his voice uncharacteristically tense. "Time to return to the surface."

"I'm going closer." Gideon eased the joystick forward.

"No, you're not." A message popped up on the DSV control screen:

CONTROL TRANSFERRED TO SURFACE

The craft stopped responding to the joystick. He heard a clang as the iron ballast was released and the sub began to rise.

"Hey—!"

"Sorry," said Garza. "We're bringing you up."

But now Gideon was rendered speechless as the submersible rose and the enormous size of the thing became fully revealed. He was rising at an angle, away from the tree, and just when its central trunk started to divide into what appeared to be clusters of branches, the thing disappeared into the murk, out of range of his lights.

"Thirty-nine minutes to surface," came Garza's tight voice.

As blackness reasserted itself around the viewports of the DSV, Gideon could only imagine the consternation now taking place in mission control.

12

GLINN CALLED A meeting for one o'clock, barely giving Gideon enough time to change out of his sweaty clothes and shower. When he arrived in mission control it was already packed; it seemed that everyone who was anyone on board ship was there, every chair was taken, and in the back it was standing room only.

Garza was seated on stage with Glinn; as Gideon entered, Glinn beckoned to him and he joined them.

To his surprise, a scattering of applause greeted his arrival on stage, which became general. He quickly sat down, embarrassed.

Wasting no time, Glinn gestured for a wireless mike and spoke into it. "This debriefing is called to order."

At the sound of his cool, neutral voice, an instant silence fell.

"Most of you have already heard about this morning's recon dive by Dr. Crew. I'm sure I speak for everyone in saying that he is to be congratulated for a successful mission."

Another round of applause. Gideon noticed Lispenard, sitting in the front row. He expected to see anger and disapproval on her face. Instead, he saw an expression he didn't quite understand.

"The purpose of this meeting," Glinn went on, "is to briefly review footage and data from that recon, and then open the floor to ideas, analysis, and discussion. Finally, we will address the next steps to be taken."

He gestured to the tech in the A/V booth and the main screen came to life. The assembled company watched in silence as an edited version of Gideon's reconnaissance played on the screen, with the communications dialogue included. At the end of the reel came a series of magnified stills of the huge' thing he'd discovered and the tendrils that snaked away from it.

"And now," said Glinn as the footage ended, "I'll share with you a few additional images. The first are sonar readings *of* the organism, collected on the recon."

This was followed by a series of images similar to the cloud observed previously—ever-shifting pixels of sonar noise.

"And here are some sonar readings *from* the creature. It generates sonar—in other words, it makes a low, continuous noise—in the two-hertz range, far below that of human hearing. Here is a computer-generated image of its sonar fields."

The images showed an eerie, glowing, blurred outline of the thing, with streamers coming off it.

He continued with some additional images in various modes, and then paused, looking around the room. "Very well. I'm going to open the floor to anyone who has anything to say, or any questions to ask. This free-flowing discussion will last thirty minutes, so be succinct."

A bunch of hands went up. Glinn pointed to the back. "Prothero?"

Why, Gideon thought, *call on him first?* He was likely to hijack the discussion.

Prothero rose. "Okay, it's pretty obvious to me what's going on with the sonar." He looked around. "Nothing wrong with the equipment, by the way. That Baobab's got a surface that looks like bark. You saw that? So I took a close look at it, under magnification, and right away I noticed that it has a remarkable mathematical quality: it scatters sonar almost perfectly. In other words, the Baobab's invisible to sonar. And I can also tell you why."

He paused, looking around again, aggressively, as if waiting for someone to challenge him.

"Please do explain," said Glinn, encouragingly.

"The Baobab grows in deep salt water, in the complete absence of light. That's evidently its natural environment. Sonar is about the only way to 'see' in that environment, and so, to avoid predators, it evolved to be invisible to sonar. Obviously, its home planet was a deep watery world, perhaps an ocean covered in miles of ice, like Europa or Callisto. That also explains the two-hertz sound it produces—it's pinging its surroundings, so to speak."

He sat down abruptly. Gideon found himself startled, indeed astonished, at the clear logic of the analysis.

Prothero's observations were greeted with a burst of murmuring that filled the room. "Thank you," said Glinn after a moment. As the room died again into silence, Alex Lispenard raised her hand.

"Alex?"

"Two things struck me. First, the complete absence of sea life in the vicinity. In the benthic zone you don't typically see a lot of life, but this area is *dead*."

"What sea life would you normally expect to find?" asked Glinn.

"A few scavengers—hagfish, crabs, and such, which feed on carcasses that sink from the upper regions. You'd also see detritivores, which feed on decomposing animals and plants and also gobble up feces sinking from above. And epifauna and infauna would live on and in the seafloor itself. But I saw no evidence of any of these at the site."

"Any speculation why not?"

"On land, there's a phenomenon called allelopathy. Some trees and plants reduce competition around themselves by releasing chemicals into the soil that harm other plants or stop the germination of seeds. We may be seeing that here."

"And the other thing that struck you?"

"The human corpses. Beyond what I assume to be damage caused by the initial explosion, they show almost no signs of decomposition that I could see."

"Any theory as to why?" Glinn asked.

"At that depth and pressure, organic remains begin to dissolve even if they're not attacked by microorganisms. I have no idea why they're so well preserved."

This generated a long discussion. Glinn managed it, giving everyone a chance to speculate and ask questions. When the half hour was over, he gently closed the conversation. "I'd like to conclude by pointing out something that has undoubtedly occurred to many of you already." He stood and began to pace the stage, slowly.

"Dr. Prothero, it seems, has put a name to this organism—the Baobab—and I endorse it. The Baobab is currently quiescent. It went silent, so to speak, after an initial burst of activity and hyperactive growth following its 'sprouting.' I privately hoped we might have found it dead. But these images suggest it is very much alive...and healthy. It seems certain that at some point it will 'fruit' and produce seeds. We already know what these seeds look like, because the so-called meteorite was one of them—and we planted it. The seed weighed twenty-five thousand tons, was virtually indestructible, and was composed of a material many times denser than any known element on earth. Obviously, it evolved for the rigors of interstellar travel. It is a seed designed for Panspermia, but not the normal Panspermia of spores envisioned by exobiologists: drifting in space or hidden in meteorites. This is Panspermia with a vengeance. Terminator Panspermia."

There was a nervous titter from the audience.

"Which brings me to my point: once the Baobab produces seeds, *how will they be dispersed into outer space?*"

He let that hang in the air.

"Think about it a moment. Each seed weighs twenty-five thousand tons. There seems to be no way for them to escape the gravitational field of any planet they land on. And yet they *do* escape. So I ask again: what is the dispersal mechanism for these seeds?"

Another silence.

"I suggest that there can be only *one* mode of dispersal, only one way for these incredibly heavy seeds to be released back into outer space and go adrift—to find fertile new oceans in which to sprout and grow. No doubt you can guess what that mode is, as well."

He took another turn, almost like a television evangelist, and faced the audience again. "Once you understand that, you understand what it means for the fate of the earth—and *why we cannot fail.*"

After the meeting had adjourned, and as Gideon was getting ready to go, Alex Lispenard approached him. "Gideon?"

He turned.

"Look. I want to apologize for arguing with you earlier, escalating the discussion, taking it to Glinn."

"Forget it," he said. "It was my fault. You're the DSV chief. I just felt—"

She touched his arm. "No need to explain. I understand now. What you did, going down there alone—on your second dive, no less—took real guts. And you kept your cool amid a nasty shock."

"Well, as you said, anyone can drive a DSV. And Garza yanked me up before I did anything stupid."

"When I was in mission control and that gigantic thing appeared on the screen, I was really taken aback. For a moment, I was damned glad it was you down there, and not me."

"It's just a tree."

She shook her head. "I wouldn't make any assumptions about what it is. None at all."

13

GIDEON HAD NEVER seen so many stars in his life.

After dinner, he'd retired to his cabin to unwind in solitude. But the events of the day, the unsettling descent and even more traumatic ascent in the DSV, and the revelations and speculations of the briefing session that followed, had affected him deeply. He couldn't seem to shake the feeling of the cramped submersible, or the sight of the monolithic, cliff-like flank of the Baobab as he had ascended beside it. Even his big stateroom felt claustrophobic. And so he'd come up on deck. He wanted to feel the infinite space of the heavens above him as he brooded.

Standing at the railing, a gentle spring breeze ruffling his hair, he stared southward. The lights from the ship provided just enough illumination to outline the nearest icebergs, which towered out of the black water like ruined castles, broken spires reaching toward the sky. The sea was a black sheet, reflecting the stars and the bergs, creating a surreal mirror of the dark world above.

"Hello, there."

He turned. "You like to sneak up on me."

"It's almost as much fun as tying your shoelaces together." Alex joined him at the rail, leaning her elbows on it, gazing out. "This is what I love most," she said. "Being right here, out in the great ocean like this, far from land. Have you ever seen anything so beautiful?"

"I admit it's magical. But I still prefer the mountains."

He could just catch the scent of her freshly washed hair, and he felt the same hopeless attraction wash over him. Part of him wished there were no Alex Lispenard on board to torment his dreams and disturb his peace of mind, but mostly he was glad of her presence and friendship—even if she did beat him relentlessly in backgammon. "That observation you made—about the bodies not decomposing—was really disturbing."

"At that depth and pressure, salt water is like a mild acid. It goes to work on organic remains right away. You may recall that no human remains were found with the *Titanic*—not even bones. While most of that was done by scavengers and tubeworms, the seawater and pressure sure helped it along."

"I can see why the Baobab-thing might excrete chemicals that kill off the surrounding microbial life—but how would it stop the action of pressure and salt?"

"That's the mystery."

Silence fell. They remained at the railing. Alex was so close to him her arm was brushing his. She had turned her head toward him, and he in turn swiveled to look at her. Their faces were very close. He resisted the impulse to lean in and kiss her.

Instead, she kissed him. Her lips were soft and warm. The kiss lingered for a long, slow moment, and then her lips parted and their tongues touched. He reached up and stroked her hair, pulling her toward him in a deep, long embrace.

She withdrew, smiling. Gideon was so out of breath he couldn't speak.

He leaned in to kiss her again but she stopped him with her finger. "Not where we might be seen."

"Right." He wondered where this was going; why she'd changed her mind about shipboard romances. He knew this was probably not a good idea for either of them, but at the moment he really, truly didn't care.

"We haven't done any magic tricks together," she said in a low voice.

"I'm not sure I can teach you anything."

"Oh, I don't know. There are always new tricks." She paused. "Do you still have that bottle of Veuve Clicquot?"

"I've been saving it."

She took his arm. "Let's go enjoy it."

He looked at her a long time. He couldn't believe this was happening. "All right."

They walked back into the *Batavia*'s interior, arm in arm. It was almost midnight and most of the ship, except for the bridge and the night watch, had gone to bed. Down through the corridors and passageways they walked, and into his stateroom. To his relief they met nobody along the way.

He closed the door behind them with his foot. Silently they came together and kissed again. She began unbuttoning his shirt, slowly, and he did the same with her blouse. He resisted the impulse to tear off all her clothes.

She pulled the shirt over his head and ran her fingernails lightly along his chest. "Mmm, I like this."

He tossed her blouse aside, unhooked her bra, and released

her breasts, cupping them in his hands. He lightly ran his fingers around her nipples, feeling them stiffen at his touch. He could hear her breath quicken.

Her hand crept down his stomach and slid under his belt buckle. "Want to teach me some magic?"

"Yes," was all he could manage to say.

They made love slow, deep, and hard.

Afterward, he lay collapsed on top of her, kissing her lazily. Then he propped himself up, looking down at her lips, her nose, her hair disheveled over the pillow, her eyes looking into his.

"We forgot the champagne," she said.

"It's still there, waiting for us."

They looked at each other for a long time. "What about your...you know, rule about no romance on board ship?" Gideon asked at last.

"Oh, well." She shrugged. "I just couldn't stop myself."

"You mean, this isn't just a moment of weakness, never to be repeated?"

"I've been thinking about doing this for thirty-two days," she said. "I'm afraid I'm hooked. There's no going back now."

"For thirty-two days? I had no idea."

"Come *on*! All those backgammon games? All the time we spent together? You men just don't have a clue, do you?"

"But why now?"

"It was when you went down alone this morning—insisted on it, said there was no point in arguing, told me to fuck off. It sure made me mad, but oddly enough it also made you irresistible. I didn't expect you to be so...forceful. Knowing how afraid you are of the deep."

He shook his head. "It was Eli's idea, to be honest."

"Well, he admitted that when I escalated the issue, complained to him. But you *did* it."

A silence. "So...is this...for real?"

"I hope so."

"Are we going to hide it?"

She laughed. "On board ship? Impossible. But as long as we're discreet, I doubt anyone will object."

"Eli might."

"Are you kidding? With all his psychological profiling, I imagine he *expected* this. Maybe he even engineered it to happen, which is why he suggested you lead the recon. He's the world's most skillful manipulator. But in this case it was a good manipulation."

"Speaking of manipulation..." He looked down at her naked body, still unable to believe what had just happened; how suddenly his fortunes had changed.

"Uh-oh," she said. "Is something happening down there again—so soon?"

14

T HREE DSVs HAD been removed from the hangar deck and now rested on the fantail, casting long shadows in the golden light of morning. Gideon arrived a few minutes before the scheduled briefing, cup of coffee in hand, pleasantly exhausted by the long night of lovemaking. Alex was already there, dressed in a sleek black leotard-like outfit, as if channeling *The Avengers'* Emma Peel. She looked well rested—intimidatingly so, he thought, all things considered. Manuel Garza had arrived as well and was chatting with Alex. To Gideon's surprise, he appeared to be dressed for a dive.

"Hello, Gideon," said Garza, offering his hand.

Gideon took it. He thought Garza looked a little nervous, but maybe that was wishful thinking. "So you're piloting a DSV, too?"

"Assigned to *George*. You're going down in *John*."

"And I'm in *Paul*," said Alex, sauntering over.

Gideon tried to maintain a nonchalant look and avoid staring. He glanced around at the others in view: a few DSV techs and the ship's second engineer, Greg Masterson, a powerfully built man who was on hand to look over the DSVs' engines and give the dive a green light. Did they know? But there weren't any knowing glances; just an air of professional gravity.

"Coffee before a dive?" Alex asked, arching her eyebrows. "That's brave."

"How so?"

"Coffee's a diuretic."

Gideon hadn't thought of that—although he had already been down twice. "Um, what happens if you have to pee?"

"In your pants."

Gideon set his coffee cup aside.

A deck door opened and Glinn emerged, limping ever so slightly, carrying an iPad and blinking in the bright sunlight. He clasped his hands behind his back and bestowed on them a cool smile of welcome.

"Nice day for a dive," he said. "We've been lucky in the weather."

Nods of agreement.

"You've all studied the mission plan, but I'm going to run through the main points briefly and see if there are any questions."

He paused. Gideon glanced surreptitiously at Alex. Her eyes were on Glinn. With an effort, he turned back to the briefing.

"First, a word about communications. Unlike yesterday, all of you will be in communication with mission control via your UQC underwater phones. The UQC is an acoustical modem that operates at a speed of twelve hundred baud maximum—very slow. It can carry voice communications and minimal data, but almost all the heavy data has to be archived for downloading once you surface. We'll deploy special sonobuoys above where you're working to pick up the signals and relay them to mission control.

But because of the minuscule throughput, there will be a time delay before we'll actually be able to view them on the surface. Also, because these are acoustical signals, they're easily blocked. Gideon, when you're inside the *Rolvaag*, your communications will be temporarily cut off—not just from mission control, but from the other DSVs."

Gideon nodded.

"The two black boxes are vital. One contains all data and communications to and from the ship's bridge. The second stored the CCTV video from security cameras set up throughout the ship. If we can recover both, we'll have a detailed picture of the ship's last moments. We know exactly where they're located: in the electronics hub on the forecastle deck. With the *Rolvaag* lying on its side, you'll have to enter the hull, make your way through the wreckage of the hold and beyond to a point underneath the forecastle deck, then cut through the deck to reach the electronics hub. The route has been fully programmed into your DSV, but we don't know the condition or layout of the interior, so once you enter the hull you'll have to use your own judgment. The *John* has a cutting torch on its mech arm. It's AI-assisted, so there's no fear of making a mistake. Questions?"

"Not at the moment."

Glinn shifted, turning toward Alex.

"Since we can't map the, ah, Baobab with sonar, we'll scan it using visual light and LiDAR. That's your job. The LiDAR is a green-wavelength laser capable of penetrating sixty feet of water. We need to know the extent of this thing—not only the trunk, but its branches as well. Also, what are those tendrils Gideon saw on the ocean floor, and how far out do they go? And do they go to anything in particular?"

Gideon, looking at Alex again as Glinn spoke, found his mind wandering back to the previous night. He quickly squashed the vivid images that rose in his mind. Given his own precarious medical condition, he thought, what was he doing, getting into a relationship like this? Following the awful events that had transpired during their time on the Lost Island in the Caribbean, Glinn had healed amazingly well—and Gideon still held out some hope he might also be cured of his condition. Or was that just wishful thinking? As of yet, there was no evidence that anything had medically changed—no evidence that he might have any longer than nine months left to live. Was he becoming an old softie, or did this really feel, already, like more than a shipboard romance? What the hell should he do? Once again, he made a mighty effort to tune back in to Glinn, who was now talking to Garza.

"Manuel, you will undertake a high-resolution sonar and LiDAR scan of the *Rolvaag* and the surrounding seafloor, extending out a radius of half a mile. I also want you to do a five-mile transect, starting at the Baobab and going out, to see how far the dead zone extends."

Glinn looked at the three in turn. "Finally, all three DSVs today are equipped with science baskets. If you see something interesting, notify mission control. We will use the UQC to look at it and decide whether it can be picked up and brought to the surface. If so, you'll use your mechanical arms to place it in the science basket. The operation of the arm is simple and it, too, is AI-assisted, so previous experience is not required."

He ran through a few more details, then finished with a simple: "Let's mount up."

Gideon climbed his submersible's ladder up to the sail hatch. He stood there a moment, looking at the other two, watching as Alex gave him a smile and a wave, then lowered herself gracefully through the hatch. A moment later he grasped the bar and stepped into his own hatch, climbing down the miniature ladder into the personnel sphere. Unlike the previous day, he felt calm and confident.

Ten minutes later, Gideon once again found himself staring through the forward viewport at a swirl of silver bubbles as *John* was lowered into the water. He heard the *clank* as the DSV was released and watched through the viewports as he drifted down into the infinite, darkening blue.

15

Oᴜᴛ ʜɪꜱ ʀɪɢʜᴛ and left viewports, Gideon could see the yellow gleam of lights from his two companion DSVs, drifting down at approximately the same rate. He could hear the faint hiss of the air tanks and CO_2 scrubbers. During the forty-minute trip to the bottom, he eventually lost them in the blackness. After a long, boring ride he picked up their lights again as they slowed, nearing the bottom.

His first waypoint was a spot fifty meters from the split hull of the *Rolvaag*, at an altitude of thirty feet off the ocean floor. The autopilot gently brought him to the waypoint, the sub coming to rest. Gideon looked about, rotating the sub and peering into the gloom. He could see, a few hundred yards to his left, the blurry cluster of lights from Alex's DSV, *Paul*, also hovering thirty feet above the seabed. Through the forward viewport he saw a similar cluster of lights from *George*.

Following protocol, he made contact using the UQC. "*John*, at waypoint one, calling *Paul*."

"*Paul* here, I read you. At waypoint two."

"*John*, calling *George*."

"*George* here, I read you. At waypoint three."

These names, Gideon thought, were starting to feel a little silly.

Glinn's voice came in, from control, inflected with digital distortion. They were all on the same channel, and they now made their way through a set of safety checklists and review of the search protocols.

"Commence the mission," said Glinn at last.

Gideon moved the central joystick, aiming the autopilot toward the *Rolvaag*. The engines hummed and the craft moved forward, approaching the wreck, headlights illuminating the gaping, petaled hull. Inside, he could see what looked like a forest of twisted metal beams.

He felt not a little twinge of claustrophobia at the thought of going in there.

On a flat-panel to his right, there was a schematic of the wrecked ship. This was overlaid by a blinking red dot, indicating his location. The black boxes appeared on the panel as a small orange target. The ship was huge; judging from the schematic, he would have to travel almost two hundred yards from the point of entry.

As he moved toward the gaping hull, the little red dot moved on the screen. In the background, he could hear Alex on the common frequency, speaking to mission control while she maneuvered *Paul* toward the Baobab. Manuel's voice came through as well as he circled the area, surveying the ship and surrounding debris field.

Gideon, Glinn had told him, *when you're inside the* Rolvaag, *you'll be temporarily cut off—not just from mission control, but from the other DSVs.*

During the briefing, Gideon had learned that the normally open hull of the former supertanker, the *Rolvaag*, had been modified: it was webbed with struts and beams that braced the so-called cradle intended to hold the twenty-five-thousand-ton meteorite. Some of the beams, and the cradle itself, had been made of wood, because wood was a more flexible and giving material than steel, and the EES engineers had determined it would hold up better to the rolling of the ship in a storm, should they encounter one. They had indeed encountered a storm, a terrible one, made worse by the lack of engine power and damage to the ship inflicted by the pursuing Chilean destroyer. The rocking of the meteorite had eventually weakened the cradle and caused it to break loose, followed by an explosion that split the ship in two just as it was starting to sink. The source of this explosion had never been determined, but the theory was that the meteorite had reacted with the seawater.

As he moved toward the vast, wrecked area of the gigantic hold, the voices of *George* and *Paul* began to dissolve into digital static.

Gideon paused at the hull opening and used his controls to shine the spotlight around, probing the recesses ahead. It was a mess. He saw what he believed must be a portion of the former cradle, a huge, sled-like object, mangled and splintered, jammed up against a broken bulkhead. The forward part of the hull offered a relatively clear pathway for his DSV, but deeper in he saw a tangle of cables and struts that would have to be dealt with.

"Control, this is *John*. Entering the hull."

The briefest of pauses over the low-baud UQC. Then, full of static: "*John*, we read you. Report back as soon as you can."

He eased the stick forward; the DSV hummed as it entered the wrecked space. Skirting a massive, torn edge of slab steel, he moved deeper into the hold. Without any effort on his part, the sub smoothly avoided some hanging cables and a strut. The hiss of UQC now ceased entirely and a message appeared on the screen, indicating he had lost communications. Bubbles rose in front of the main viewport. A layer of silt lay over everything, softening the contours. He would have to take great care not to stir it up.

He was moving at the pace of a walk. Orange blobs of rust grew from the iron struts and particles drifted in the water, dancing sluggishly through his light. Below, the side of the hull was littered with splintered beams and struts, torn to pieces by the violence of the explosion. The splintered wood, while waterlogged and sunken, looked fresh. Clearly, this had been a massive explosion, strong enough to bulge out the iron hull plates, pop the rivets.

There was another body here: wearing a mechanic's uniform, head torn away, crushed torso held in place by two broken beams.

Averting his eyes, Gideon checked the schematic; the red dot that represented his sub was now a third of the way to the access point inside the hull space.

A tangle of I-beams loomed ahead. The autopilot slowed and he moved the joystick, looking for a way around. There was a space between two girders that looked big enough, and he aimed for it, the autopilot easing through with finesse. But it was beginning to feel as if he were in a shattered forest after a battle, the girders like warped, broken trees. He probed this way and that through the maze-like jungle, each time finding a hole just wide enough to get through.

As he penetrated deeper into the wreck, it grew increasingly difficult to shake off the feeling of claustrophobia. The radio silence didn't help; Gideon began to feel very much alone.

...Or was he? Because, strange as it seemed, he was also aware of a sense of being watched. *Followed.* He dismissed this as best he could: it was the sort of anxiety that occurred when walking in a dark forest at night, he told himself, and it dated back to the early days when humans were, in fact, hunted. And hadn't he compared this environment to a forest—albeit a wrecked one?

And now, quite suddenly, he reached a point through which there seemed no way to pass. He maneuvered forward, slowly, until he was blocked. He turned one way, then another, and then another. There seemed no passage forward. Hovering in place like this, his engines stirred up the silt; he could no longer tell from which direction he'd come.

Jesus, what was I thinking—agreeing to pilot my way through hundreds of yards of wreckage, miles below the surface? No way do I have the experience to do this. And now I've gotten myself trapped—and can't call for help. He started to panic, then quickly forced himself to calm down; the autopilot would, of course, know the way out. But to go farther, he'd have to do some cutting.

Doing his best to breathe slowly and deeply, he centered his attention on the beam blocking his way and raised the robotic arm, activating the underwater acetylene torch. It had its own set of controls and, to his relief, was surprisingly easy to use; the arm seeming to know exactly what he wanted it to do. Another example of a quasi-AI automatic control.

The torch popped to life, sending up a stream of bubbles and a white pinpoint flare. He maneuvered it toward the beam and began cutting, careful to make the cut slanted so the beam would fall away from him. But the AI software of the arm already knew that. In a few minutes, with a muffled *snap*, the beam toppled away and he was able to proceed.

He continued maneuvering, this time to the left, and paused to cut through another beam. Now his spotlight shone on the bulkhead of the forecastle deck. Because the ship was lying on its side, the deck was a vertical wall of steel, which made it much easier to deal with. His screen schematic showed him exactly where he was supposed to cut in order to reach the electronics hub, where the two black boxes—actually orange in color—were stored. A second flat-panel contained a diagram of the hub's interior, indicating the exact location of the boxes. They should be easy to get at, as they were supposedly designed for ready access in a wrecked ship at depth.

He maneuvered the DSV to align it with the pre-programmed cutting lines, and then, with a mere touch of the controls, the arm flared once again into life. The protocol called for cutting the access opening in five stages: removing five smaller plates of steel, each cut designed so that the plates would drop away and not present a further obstacle.

Practically by rote, the mech arm cut the plates with unerring precision, and one by one they fell away. In ten minutes, the hole was big enough for the DSV to pass through. But still impeding the opening was a forest of pipes between the decking, and he had to cut through each pipe in turn. They, too, fell away cleanly.

Gideon positioned the sub and probed the space ahead with the spotlight before entering. It was an utter mess. The cabinets that once held computers and electronics had burst open, spewing their guts everywhere; the space was a tangle of wires, bundles, cables, and fiber optic.

As if that weren't enough, beyond the tangle of wires was a body, arms and legs splayed, slowly drifting about, neutrally buoyant. Long blond hair floated in the silty cloud—it was the body of a woman. It was clothed in a uniform. Four bars: a captain. What was the name of the *Rolvaag*'s captain? Britton. Sally Britton.

So this was her. Gideon felt a strange mixture of regret and horror.

The corpse had its back to him and floated in the middle of the room, turning ever so slowly in what seemed a slow-motion ballet.

Behind the corpse, on the far wall, were two bright orange cubes, each about eighteen inches square, affixed to the wall with easily removable bolts, and with nothing nearby to impede access.

Except the floating body.

Gideon eased forward, extending the robotic arm. He lit the torch and cut his way through the cables. In a few minutes he had cleared a path and eased into it, approaching the corpse. With the arm extended he gently touched its torso, attempting to nudge it to a far corner; the push was uneven and caused the body to rotate more, turning to face him as it drifted away, arms outstretched as if yearning to be rescued.

Gideon stared in fascinated horror. The face was perfectly preserved, the blue eyes flashing in the intensity of the headlights, the mouth partly open, just a bit of pink tongue visible, the blond hair swirling into a coil of gold: a woman of about forty, attractive even in death.

Perhaps harder than he intended, he pushed the joystick forward and the DSV surged past the body. Reaching the orange boxes, he used the arm to pull the emergency bolts and put each box into the science basket in turn, securing them with tie-downs designed for the purpose.

Now to get the hell out.

Twisting the joystick, the sub made a one-eighty—and once again the body came into view, drifting toward him as if to block his way.

"Son of a bitch," Gideon muttered, maneuvering around it and heading for the hole he'd cut in the bulkhead. A few keystrokes on the control board and the sub's autopilot was retracing its route, with no input from him—and doing it perfectly.

In ten minutes he could see the ragged edges of the hull, and in another two he was outside the ship. He found himself taking deep gulps of air, as if emerging from a cave. The vise-like feeling of claustrophobia ebbed, and he mopped his brow, trying to get his heart rate back to normal. The UQC crackled back into life, the voices of mission control and the other two subs resuming. *Thank God.*

He radioed up. "Control, this is *John*. Mission accomplished. Black boxes retrieved."

"Very good," came Glinn's voice. "Proceed to waypoint one and commence transmitting your data and the video feeds. You're the first to complete your mission, so hold tight at the waypoint until all three of you are ready to ascend together."

"Roger that." He entered the pre-programmed waypoint into his control stack and the mini sub glided back to the location, about a hundred yards from the wreck, then came to a hovering stop. Gazing through the forward viewport, he saw a single tentacle from the anomalous life-form wandering across the mud. It looked like a thin snake or a worm of endless length. He thought of the huge Baobab-like thing towering above them all, and felt a shiver of both disgust and dread.

Then, shaking these feelings away, he settled in, preparing to transmit his datastream while waiting for the others to complete their assignments.

16

Eli Glinn preferred to stand, even to the point of exhaustion. He could never get enough of standing. He had been in a wheelchair for so long he felt he had done enough sitting for a lifetime.

As a result, in anticipation of being liberated from his wheelchair, he had designed the central command console of mission control in a U-shaped form, the keyboards and screens positioned for the height for a standing man, with no chair or option to sit. If others had to stand when in control, so be it. But now he was in control, the others in the room at their own distant posts. He was surrounded by screens, and he carefully shifted his attention among them, from one to the next to the next, so as not to miss any development.

So far things had gone well. While he knew it was pure superstition, Glinn did not feel comfortable when everything went as planned. Perfection seemed a mockery to him; in his view, perfection was not only impossible, but the enemy of success. The real key was flexibility in the face of the unexpected, or, as someone once said, the "known unknowns." But he was willing to accept

each accomplishment as it came, realizing that much more difficult decisions, and greater unknowns, lay ahead.

John, under Gideon's control, had been inside the wreck for
thirty minutes, unable to transmit due to interference from the
hull. The baud rate on the UQC was abysmally low even in the best
of circumstances, acceptable for voice but a mere soda-straw for
data. He wanted to see what the interior of the ship looked like.

Suddenly he heard Gideon's voice pop back on the frequency.
"Control, this is *John.* Mission accomplished. Black boxes retrieved."

"Very good," Glinn said. "Proceed to waypoint one and commence transmitting your data and the video feeds."

A few minutes of silence. Then: "This is *John,* back at waypoint
one. Transmitting."

"Understood," said Glinn. "Any issues?"

Another, briefer silence. "No. Except I encountered another
two corpses."

Glinn did not inquire further. He would see it soon enough on
video.

He shifted his attention to the other two DSVs. Garza was fully
engaged in mapping and he, too, was ahead of schedule, with
just the five-mile transect remaining. Lispenard was cautiously
circling the Baobab, moving higher in a spiraling fashion, using
LiDAR to scan the entity at millimeter-level resolution, as well as
videoing it in visible light. So far there had been no sign of life
from the Baobab; no sign, in fact, of anything. It was inert.

That concerned Glinn.

A faint beep from the console indicated the compressed video
upload from Gideon was complete. Glinn hesitated, and then
tapped a few keys, directing the upload to play on a spare screen
at four times normal speed.

He watched in silence as the sub passed through the open hull and made its way deeper into the ship. The explosion had blown away most of the bracing around the cradle and reduced it to a splintered hulk; the force of the compression could be clearly seen radiating from the cradle.

No question: the meteorite—the seed—had reacted violently on coming in contact with salt water. Perhaps this was the beginning of its sprouting process. If indeed the word *sprout* could be applied: so far they had gathered no evidence this was a plant, nor the meteorite an actual seed. It could be anything—spore, rhizome, egg, gametophyte. Or it could be something utterly alien. Even though he had been there in that hold during those final critical moments, Glinn reminded himself once again to stay detached; not to make assumptions.

He cut the playback speed to normal time.

On the screen, Gideon cut through the blocking struts. Glinn watched as the sub's mech arm then cut a hole in the decking below the electronics hub and moved into the space, slicing away the deck piping as it did so.

And then Glinn froze. There was one of the corpses Gideon had mentioned. In uniform. Four bars on the sleeves.

The captain.

He felt a sudden, strange buzzing in his head. The body, its back turned, blond hair floating, was slowly rotating, turning its face toward him.

Glinn experienced a momentary cessation of thought. And then, despite all his carefully constructed defenses, his deliberate blocking out of certain memories for so long, the pain came rushing in, along with the sick horror of her death—a death for which he was responsible. Here it was, his guilt, in the very flesh, come back to haunt him.

A single decision had done this: the most inexplicable decision of his life, a decision he believed at the time was founded on logic, but which in retrospect was the product of emotion, fear, and panic; a decision that had forever stripped him of certitude and self-confidence. And it was a decision that led to the death of the only woman he had ever loved.

He could not breathe as he watched the body turn toward him, the hair forming a golden halo. He did not want to see the face, which he knew even now would be a sight to haunt him forever. But he was paralyzed; he could not turn away.

The face came slowly into view, profile first, then full-on, like a moon rotating on its axis; lips pink, skin as pure as marble, the small nose dusted with freckles—but worst of all were the eyes, those staring blue eyes, coming around to drill into him: accusatory.

His legs began to shake; but before he could seek a chair he felt all muscle tension slacken and he folded to the floor.

After that there was only a confused jumble, muffled shouts, people bending over, Brambell's bald and shining head, the sting of a needle, the sensation of being lifted, the murmured commands, and a welcoming absence of thought.

17

Aᴌᴇx Lɪsᴘᴇɴᴀʀᴅ ᴡᴏʀᴋᴇᴅ her DSV controls, circling the trunk of the Baobab from a distance of about forty feet. The trunk was massive, far larger than even the largest sequoia: around sixty feet in diameter, and covered with a rough, bark-like surface of crude, parallel vertical grooves.

As her spotlight probed the trunk, she could see it was vaguely translucent, almost like a cloudy jellyfish, of a pale-greenish color like sea glass. Within, she could see the blurry outlines of what appeared to be internal organs, folded tubes and sacs that made no sense, looking like no terrestrial organism she knew of. There were also some round globules with a yellowish tinge, along with spidery networks of darker, reddish strands. The entity's flesh was scattered with shining flecks and spots that drifted around in slow motion, like snow in a snow globe. It was simultaneously beautiful and grotesque. From this vantage point, seeing the complexity inside, it appeared to her more animal than plant, or perhaps something in between. And yet so far she had seen nothing that looked like sensory or feeding organs. Nor did it seem to have a mouth or anus.

At any rate, she was getting everything on video and LiDAR. They would have plenty of time to examine the images and scans topside and try to determine how the creature lived, how it fed, what it needed to stay alive—assuming, of course, it *was* alive.

She continued her slow circuit, maintaining a spiral pattern in order to create a three-dimensional digitized model of the thing. In another loop she would have reached the point where the branches forked out—not like a tree, but all at once, to form a kind of starburst pattern like a sea anemone.

Sea anemone... once you got past the scale of the thing, she thought, it did vaguely resemble a sea anemone—although the branches looked rigid, not like the flexible tentacles of an anemone, and Alex saw no signs of stinging cnidocytes on them.

At the very base of the fork, she noted something unusual: a dark, oval shape deep inside. It was the size of a large watermelon, and it looked out of place to her somehow, as if it didn't belong with the rest of the creature.

"Control, this is *Paul*," she said. "I see something unusual at the fork in the trunk. Something dark."

A brief pause. "Okay, we see it," came the voice of Chief Officer Lennart.

Alex wondered briefly what had happened to Glinn. "It doesn't look like the surrounding tissue. Request permission to take a closer look."

"Permission denied."

Alex swallowed her momentary irritation. She wondered how Gideon would react to such an order.

At the thought of Gideon, a small smile formed on her face. Then her lips set once again in a straight, determined line.

The sub came around, the autopilot accomplishing its complex spiraling maneuver without effort. She had reached the forking section of the trunk.

As the DSV rose above the fork, she looked down and, at last, saw what could only be a mouth: a round opening, three feet in diameter, surrounded by what appeared to be three sets of clear, rubbery lips. It was flexing rhythmically, as if pumping water in and out.

"I think we just found its mouth," she said. "And from what I can see, it's very much alive."

"Stay well away," warned Lennart.

"It looks like it's sucking in water—filter feeding."

The pulsing, rubbery, huge, translucent lips were truly disgusting. Alex shuddered.

Now the sub commenced another autopiloted loop above the mouth, taking in the sudden coruscation of branches. She could see, deep below the mouth, the dark melon-shaped object she had noticed earlier.

"Hey, I think that dark shape I mentioned earlier is something it swallowed."

More scanning.

"Wait . . . the mouth stopped flexing."

"Noted."

"It's gone still."

"Back off to two hundred feet," said Lennart sharply.

"Roger." Lispenard touched the joystick and sent the sub on a radial away from the mouth.

Suddenly she felt a lurch. An alarm went off in the sub and a flashing message appeared on the main screen.

WARNING: STRONG CURRENT DETECTED

She instinctively knew what it was, and a quick glance at the hideous mouth confirmed it. The orifice had expanded grotesquely, the lips protruding, the whole thing sucking in water at an abruptly increased pace. She grabbed the joystick and gave it full reverse, the engine thrumming up fast, arresting the forward movement of the sub.

"Get out *now!*" she heard Lennart say in her headset. "Back away, full power!"

This was what she was already doing—but now the mouth ballooned further, the lips stretching, and the current increased. The sub shook and rocked in its effort to pull free. Lispenard pushed the joystick sideways and rotated the sub, trying to exit the current diagonally. For a moment it seemed to work; the sub jerked violently sideways and almost broke free, but then the mouth gulped more water, swelling like an enormous toad, snagging her once again in its suction.

"Not free yet!" She struggled to keep the sub stable in the vortex created by the flow of water, the mouth seeming to loom ever bigger. Such a huge current had been generated by the suction that now a curtain of silt was rising in plumes from the ocean floor—or was it caused by the *motion of the roots?*

As the sub began to spin, she slammed the joystick sideways, trying to break free of the maelstrom—to no avail.

"Emergency eject!" Lennart said. "Trigger the eject!"

Alex reached for the red eject lever, but was thrown back by an unexpected lurch. And then the mini sub was suddenly swallowed in a green, milky globe of light, the creature's translucent tissue flaring in the headlamps. She both heard and felt a wet, sucking sound, and she could see the tissue flecked with bright specks, flexing and contracting horribly, as the thing swallowed her whole.

"I'm inside," she said, doing her best to keep her voice even.

"Use the arm torch—cut your way out," was the last message she heard before the UQC ceased working, the acoustic connection crackling out into digital hiss.

She activated the arm and tried to extend it, but the pressure of the thing's internal tissue blocked any movement. She tried a second time, pushing the joystick all the way forward, but now multiple alarms were going off, warning messages flashing everywhere.

Screw this. She activated the acetylene torch, the flame flaring into life. The effect was instantaneous: a sudden, jerking reaction, along with a low booming groan, and then she managed to pull the emergency eject, designed to jettison the titanium personnel sphere from the sub housing, inflate the ballast tanks, and send it screaming to the surface.

18

Gideon throttled his DSV to its max as he sped toward the scene of the disaster. He had heard the exchange over the UQC and watched in horror as the lights of Alex's sub winked out as it was apparently swallowed. But they were not gone entirely—there was a ghastly, greenish glow now from inside the creature, and as he approached he could even see the dark, blurry outline of the sub within.

The titanium sphere, he knew, was incredibly strong, resistant to pressure down to a depth of three miles; she would be safe inside it. She could cut her way out of the Baobab with the torch or, perhaps, irritate the creature enough to regurgitate her...

"Gideon," came Lennart's voice. "What are you doing?"

He didn't bother to answer, keeping himself focused, cursing the slowness of the sub's propulsion.

"Your orders are to remain at the waypoint."

"The hell with orders."

As he closed in, he could now make out sounds: not digitally through the UQC, but through the water itself, picked up by his sub's exterior hydrophone and broadcast into the interior. He turned up the gain.

"There's nothing you can do. Stop now."

A sloppy, wet groaning sound filled his capsule, along with a rapid clicking, overlain by some kind of low rumble.

"Stay back, Gideon. *That's a direct order.*"

Ignoring this, he dropped down, coming in low, only ten feet above the seafloor. If he approached the creature from below, the mouth wouldn't be able to reach him; he'd cut into its trunk with his torch, chop the whole damn thing down if that's what was necessary. But even as he descended he saw, inside the monster, the sudden bright spark of Alex's own acetylene torch lighting up, and—in reaction—the upper trunk of the creature flexing abruptly. The lights of her sub winked out and there was a muffled popping sound; a huge, roiling belch of air bubbles was expelled from the creature's mouth.

She'd hit the eject.

The creature writhed horribly. But the sub didn't emerge; didn't break free. More air erupted.

"No!" Gideon cried.

Now the trunk was warping toward him, bulging grotesquely like a puff adder.

"Gideon!" came Lennart's voice. "What you're doing is suicide. Get the hell away from it!"

He lit his torch, waving it at the creature as he motored forward. A tiny voice in his head told him that this was crazy, David coming at Goliath, but he pushed it aside. Through the forward viewport he saw one of the strangely thin tentacles of the creature whipping sinuously across the ocean floor. He had to do something *now*. He pushed the joystick down, reached the root, halted, and extended his torch, slashing at it, the heat making it pop and sizzle like seared meat. The tentacle coiled frantically, causing silt to cloud the water. He slashed again, each movement riling up more silt and engulfing him in hazy darkness.

An all-too-familiar message popped on the screen:

CONTROL TRANSFERRED TO SURFACE

He felt the joystick stop responding.

"No!" he cried.

"We're getting you out of there."

And now the sub started to rise. The silt cleared and Gideon— in a last, spontaneous move—grabbed a long, floating section of root that he'd chopped free with the mechanical arm and stuffed it into the science basket, next to the black boxes.

And then a voice came through the hydrophone. It was Alex's voice: calm, pleasant, remote as the stars.

"... Let me touch your face."

19

THE SEEDILY DRESSED man wheeled his cheap roller bag down Santa Fe's West San Francisco Street. He passed a Starbucks and hesitated, craving a venti macchiato—or even a single shot of espresso—but realized he didn't have the money. Turning down Galisteo Street, he stopped at a shopfront with a sign identifying it as PROFESSOR EXOTICA. It sported a window stuffed with bizarre and fantastical rocks, minerals, gems, and fossils. There was a cave bear skull, mounted; a dinosaur egg; a mummified crocodile; a spectacular azurite geode; a four-inch tourmaline; and a large, sectioned meteorite with its etched face displaying a riot of Widmanstätten lines.

The man paused at the window. He hadn't called ahead to make an appointment, but the proprietor, a guy named Joe Culp, was almost always there. Besides, an appointment hadn't seemed like a good idea—the last one hadn't gone all that well, and he'd been afraid of being turned away before he even got in the door.

He collapsed the handle of the roller bag, then picked it up. Jesus, it was heavy—maybe eighty, ninety pounds—but that weight was what was going to buy his dinner and a place to spend the night. He pushed through the door, bells tinkling, and lugged the bag down the staircase into the basement shop, crammed floor-to-ceiling with natural wonders.

"Hey, hey, Sam McFarlane!" Joe Culp came around from behind the counter, arms spread wide, and gave the man a big embrace. McFarlane didn't like to be hugged, but it seemed prudent not to object. "What you got for me? Where you been? Teaching?"

"I *was* teaching. Didn't work out. So I headed to Russia."

"Whereabouts?"

"Primorye."

At this, he saw Culp's face take on a faint look of disappointment. He glanced at the suitcase. "These are Sikhote-Alin specimens?"

"Yeah."

"All of them?"

"Trust me, these are good ones. The best. Shrapnel, thumbprints, oriented—all unique. One with a hole in it."

"Let's take a look," said Culp with what McFarlane sensed was slightly forced, artificial cheer.

McFarlane unzipped the roller bag to reveal a row of shoe boxes of sorted specimens, each labeled with a Sharpie.

"Let's take a look at the ones with regmagylpts," said Culp.

McFarlane pulled out a box and laid it on the counter. He opened it up. Inside he had wrapped the specimens in paper towels. He sorted through them and picked out a few of the biggest, then unwrapped them. Culp brought out a velvet-covered board and placed it on the counter to keep the meteorites from scratching the glass.

"How about that?" said McFarlane, laying his best specimen

on the velvet. "Thumbprints on one side, fusion crust. Totally unique."

Culp grunted and picked it up, examining it. "How'd you get these?"

"There's a lot of guys in Primorye with metal detectors that go out there, sweep the area. There's still tons of shit out there."

Culp turned the piece around in his hand and finally put it down. "What else?"

"You don't like it?"

"It's not that I don't *like* it. It's just that we specialize in unique stuff. This... well, there are pieces like it selling on eBay. Let's see the one with the hole in it."

McFarlane searched through the box until he found it, unwrapped it, and laid it on the velvet.

Again he saw disappointment in Culp's face, which annoyed him. When Culp didn't pick it up right away, McFarlane took it in hand. "See?" He peered through the hole. "This is pretty unique."

"It's also pretty small. I might be able to sell it, though. How much you want for it?"

"Twelve hundred."

"Whoa! No way can I get twelve hundred. Or even six. Sam, you know I'd be lucky to get two."

McFarlane felt his irritation grow. "Bullshit. It cost me three thousand bucks to get to Primorye. Who's going to pay for that? And I had to pay the guy who *found* it two hundred!"

"Then I would say you overpaid."

"Come on, Joe. How many Sikhote-Alin specimens have thumbprints and a hole?"

"The market's awash with Sikhote-Alin. Just go on eBay and look."

"The hell with eBay. This is way better than eBay." McFarlane reached into the box and pulled out another. "Look at this—wicked good piece of shrapnel, two hundred grams. All twisted up. And this—" He unwrapped another, then another, with increasing rapidity. "And how about this? Beautifully oriented with flow lines and fusion crust."

Culp spread his hands. "Sam, I just don't need them. I've got meteorites, *unique* meteorites, selling for ninety, a hundred grand. This is not the kind of stuff I handle. Now, if you had a really good pallasite, say, I would definitely be interested. Like that incredible Acomita pallasite you brought me five years ago—if you could get me another slice like that, I could sell it tomorrow."

"I told you, I just got back from Russia. I spent my last nickel on these meteorites. Surely you need some less expensive stuff in this shop—I mean, who can afford hundred-grand meteorites?"

"That's my clientele."

McFarlane hesitated. "I'll sell you the whole collection for six grand. Take them all. Forty kilos of iron—that's only fifteen cents a gram!"

"Honestly, Sam, your best option is eBay. There's no shame in that. And then you wouldn't have to absorb the dealer's cut."

"So after all the great stuff I've brought you, all the money you've made off me—you want to shuffle me off to eBay?"

"I didn't mean it that way. I'm just offering advice—you do what you want."

McFarlane felt the disappointment and rage building. "eBay," he said, shaking his head.

"Sam, you haven't brought me anything I could use in years. Not since that...that expedition to wherever it was. Bring me something good and I'll pay you well, *really* well—"

"I told you never to mention that expedition!" McFarlane said, rage finally breaking through the dam. He swept the box off the counter to the floor, the meteorites flying and rattling everywhere.

Culp rose. "I'm sorry, Sam, but I think you should leave now."

"With pleasure. And you can go ahead and keep that shit on the floor, I don't want it. Give it away to your rich fucking clients or use it for fucking paperweights. Jesus, what a ripoff artist!"

McFarlane seized his suitcase and climbed the stairs in a fury, emerging onto the street. But the sudden bright light dazed him, and already he felt his fury subsiding. Son of a bitch, he needed those meteorites he'd left scattered on the floor—those were his best. He didn't even have enough money to buy a cup of coffee. He felt a sudden overwhelming shame for his outburst. The guy wasn't in the charity business. And McFarlane knew, underneath it all, that Joe was right: the meteorites he had were run-of-the-mill specimens. The trip to Russia had been a bust—other meteorite hunters had already cleaned out the good stuff, and he was left buying the shit everyone else had rejected. Joe had helped him before, advanced him money, financed his trips...He owed the guy five thousand dollars and Joe hadn't even brought it up.

After a long, burning hesitation, McFarlane turned and headed back down into the shop. Joe was just putting the last of the meteorites back into the shoe box. He silently handed it to McFarlane.

"Joe, I'm really sorry, I don't know what got into me—"

"Sam, I'm your friend. I think you need to get some help."

"I know. I'm a mess."

"You need a place to stay tonight?"

"No, I'm good, don't worry about it." McFarlane put the shoe box back into his roller bag, zipped it up, and manhandled it back up the stairs, mumbling a good-bye. Back in the street he wondered where he was going to get the money for a meal and a place to spend the night. Maybe he could get away with sleeping in Cathedral Park again.

He felt a vibration and realized his cell phone was ringing. He pulled it out, wondering who was calling him. He hadn't had a call in days.

The caller ID said DEARBORNE PARK. Where the hell was that?

"Hello?"

"Is this Dr. Samuel McFarlane?" came the voice on the other end.

"Yes."

"Please hold the line a moment. There's someone here who'd like to speak with you."

20

Evening light raked the deck of the R/V *Batavia*, casting golden lines and shadows. An iceberg, drifting past the ship, was lit from behind by the setting sun, its edges glittering in fractures of turquoise and gold. The surface of the ocean was like a polished sheet, the air utterly still. The peacefulness of the scene, knowing how Alex would have appreciated it, struck Gideon as grotesque as he walked through the double doors into the fluorescent-lit darkness of the DSV hangar.

The entire ship's complement had gathered in the cavernous hangar, oddly empty with the two DSVs from the morning dive still on deck for maintenance—while of course the third was gone. The hangar was necessary, because there was no conference room big enough to accommodate everyone.

Wordlessly, Gideon took up a position next to Glinn and Garza, standing and facing the group. The silence was absolute, but the atmosphere was anything but calm: the air was electric with tension. Gideon himself was numb with shock, unable to process what had happened on an emotional level, although—intellectually—it was all too horribly clear. He scanned the sea of faces, looking angrily for Lennart, who had overridden his attempted rescue of Alex. The chief officer was standing with Captain Tulley, Chief of Security Bettances, and a clump of other senior officers, staring carefully at nothing. He knew she had done the right thing—his actions were impulsive, self-destructive—but he nevertheless felt impotent rage mingling with the grief.

Beside him, Glinn stood motionless, more of a cipher than ever. According to the scuttlebutt among the officers, he had apparently had a breakdown in mission control upon seeing the video of Captain Britton; he had been below in sick bay when the accident occurred. But he'd quickly recovered and now looked normal—or rather, normal for him, with his face having resumed its mask-like detachment. He was dressed in khaki pants and a beige short-sleeved shirt, his gray eyes looking out from underneath a smooth, seemingly untroubled brow.

Gideon glanced at his watch: five PM sharp. As usual, Glinn began the meeting on the very second, stepping forward.

"I want to apologize for my temporary incapacitation," he said, his voice cool.

This was met with an intense silence.

"More important: I am terribly, terribly sorry about what happened to Alex Lispenard. I know you all liked and respected her, and that you all share my grief. It is a tragedy for this ship and for this mission. But right now, the best way we can honor her memory is by pushing ahead with our work."

Another silence.

"Her death was not in vain. We successfully retrieved the black boxes from the *Rolvaag*. The boxes were hardened against many kinds of potential damage, including explosion and extreme water pressure. Unfortunately, it appears that at the moment of sinking, something caused a massive EMP—an electromagnetic pulse—to course through the ship. The boxes were electromagnetically shielded, but that EMP blew through the shielding and the storage media was compromised. The data is salvageable, at least most of it, but it will be a delicate, painstaking process. Hank Nishimura is handling data recovery."

Nishimura, a tall, thin, and alarmingly young-looking fellow, wearing a white lab coat over a loud Hawaiian shirt, gave a little nod.

"I'll now turn the floor over to Dr. Garza, who will provide a postmortem on the loss of *Paul*."

Garza stepped forward, his dark face furrowed with controlled emotion. "I won't sugarcoat things. This is tough for all of us. We're going to show you the footage we were able to recover from Alex Lispenard's DSV, which wasn't much: only the low-res video feed had been uploaded before the sub was lost. In addition, all the LiDAR data was lost. We have some footage of the last moments of *Paul* taken from the camera of *John*, which was nearby, piloted by Dr. Crew. My own DSV, *George*, was too far away to capture anything beyond the UQC audio feed. Dr. Nishimura is going to run this video and audio now, without comment. Discussion will follow."

He turned and a two-hundred-inch UHC flat-screen monitor, commandeered from mission control, flickered into life.

Gideon turned to watch reluctantly. The trunk of the Baobab appeared, in low resolution, translucent in the spectral light, giving off a greenish glow. The vantage point was from the *Paul* as it circled the upper part of the trunk, shining its headlights at the entity. The light disclosed a dark object enclosed in a jelly-like sac, perhaps a foot and a half long, but with a strange, convoluted surface, wrapped by what looked like engorged veins. But the resolution was low and the object blurry and pixelated, and he could make out no specific details.

Now Alex's voice broke in. *Control, this is* Paul. *I see something unusual at the fork of the trunk. Something dark.*

Okay, we see it, too, came the voice of Chief Officer Lennart.

Nishimura froze the video, showing the object encased near the fork of the trunk, digitally enhanced.

Son of a bitch, thought Gideon as he stared at the dark object. *It looks like a brain.*

The video restarted and now the DSV spiraled up above the level of the fork. Gideon could clearly see the mouth, with its translucent, rubbery lips gulping water, like some gigantic, revolting fish.

I think we just found its mouth, came Alex's distorted voice.

The scene unfolded in enhanced slow motion. Underneath the voice exchanges, there was that low rumble Gideon had heard earlier. He watched as the DSV was sucked in; he saw Alex struggling to move the mech arm and then the bright flash when she fired up the torch. The UQC was barely functioning and the final video stream was little more than a blur of light and shadow. But the flash of the acetylene was unmistakable, and that, it seemed, was what had triggered the creature to react, apparently crushing the DSV.

The screen went briefly black. Then Gideon's own video feed took over and he was viewing from a distance, once again, the eruption of bubbles from the creature—probably the outrush of air from the ruptured DSV—and then came the final, inexplicable message: *Let me touch your face.*

This finally broke the agonized silence. From the assembled group came a burst of murmuring, expostulation, even a few suppressed sobs. Glinn stepped forward as the lights came up. "Discussion?" he rapped out.

"What's going on with that last message?" It was Lennart.

"Our belief—myself and Dr. Brambell—is that it appears to have been some sort of hallucination, rapture of the deep, that Alex experienced as the pressure failed on the DSV."

"That doesn't explain the timing," said Lennart. "She spoke seconds after the sub was already crushed."

A restive murmur.

"That," said Glinn sharply, "is clearly a technological artifact of the UQC communications system. A delay. We're working it out."

"But it didn't come through the UQC. It was picked up on *John's* hydrophone."

Another burst of talk.

Glinn held up his hands. "The UQC and the hydrophone use the same acoustical system. There was a lot of sonar interference from the Baobab. It's an imperfect audio delivery system. We're working on an explanation."

Lennart retreated, an unsatisfied frown on her face.

Prothero raised his hand.

"Yes?"

"Okay, you heard that low background rumble at the very end of the tape?" He looked around. "Play it again."

Glinn ran it through again.

"I helped Nishimura enhance the video, and as soon as I heard that, I knew what it was." He walked up onto the stage with a certain triumph in his face. "Here it is, sped it up ten times." Prothero plugged his cell phone into one of the monitor's audio input jacks, activated it. An eerie, loon-like sound came from the speakers: half moaning, half singing.

Prothero let it play for about fifteen seconds, then switched it off. "Classic. That's the vocalization of a blue whale. Your acoustic network picked up a whale somewhere in the vicinity."

"Blue whales can't dive anywhere near that deep," said Antonella Sax, head of the exobiology lab.

"No. But their vocalizations can travel for up to a hundred miles. The loudest sound ever recorded from an animal came from a blue whale. There must've been a pod of them traveling somewhere above, which *John*'s hydrophone picked up by accident. Very cool. I'll do a triangulation and find out where those whales were when this was picked up. Great blues are not common this far south—this could be important."

He left the stage, looking around as if for approbation.

"Further discussion?" said Glinn.

Gideon raised his hand and spoke. "That dark, oblong thing inside the creature—anyone else think it looks like a brain?"

Many murmurings of agreement.

"If so," he went on, "then killing this son of a bitch might have just gotten a lot simpler."

This observation was greeted with general assent. The discussion went on until—as it began to veer into ever more speculative territory—Glinn stepped forward and cut it off. "All right," he told the assembled crew. "Thank you. Now I'm going to dole out some assignments. The exobiology team under Antonella Sax will examine the root-like piece Dr. Crew brought back. Dr. Sax, your team will also attempt an analysis of the organism's internal systems—in particular, I'm interested to learn whether the creature has a brain and nervous system, and especially if that dark thing is in fact its brain. Prothero, I want you to try synchronizing the hydrophone and UQC audio streams. As for the stray whale sound, I'm not sure it's worth spending time on."

Prothero shrugged.

"Dr. Nishimura should be able to provide us with data from the black boxes in a day or two, and that will give us a lot more to work with. And the team reporting to Manuel Garza—"

"Just a moment." A beefy man in coveralls stood up. It was the ship's second engineer, the man named Masterson. "What I'm not hearing is how we're going to protect ourselves. That thing just crushed a titanium sphere engineered to withstand fourteen thousand psi."

It was Garza who responded. "We believe we're safe here on the surface. The top of the Baobab is still almost two miles below us. That's a lot of water."

"Pure assumption."

There were murmurs of assent.

"Admit it, we're in over our heads," Masterson went on. "That thing down there is a lot more dangerous than you told us. I suggest we move the mother ship a safe distance away from here— like ten, fifteen miles—just in case."

"That would fatally impede our research," said Glinn.

"Yeah, but that son of a bitch has already 'fatally impeded' one of us."

Glinn let a moment pass before responding. "Alex Lispenard's death is a shock and a tragedy. We learned something about the creature and its capabilities in the hardest way possible. But—" He cast his eyes around—"we must take risks if we're going to terminate this thing."

"There are legitimate risks and then there's foolhardiness," said Masterson, to more murmurings. "I'd put that last mission in the foolhardy category. You sent three subs down there, one of them circling less than fifty feet from the creature. Not smart. I think we'd better back off, or maybe even rethink the whole expedition."

"We're in uncharted territory," Glinn said, with an edge to his voice now. "We don't have the luxury of playing it safe. We *must* have information." He paused, casting his gray eyes over the assembled group. "You were fully briefed on our situation. All of you understood that we would be completely isolated here. There can be no evacuation and no rescue. The one helicopter we have, an AStar, has a range of three hundred sixty nautical miles. The nearest heliport is Grytviken, on South Georgia Island—six hundred nautical miles distant. Our two launches are not rated for blue-water travel, especially in the Screaming Sixties of the South Atlantic. So for better or worse, we're here, and we're in this together. Now, Mr. Masterson, is it your intention to demand we back off the target site?"

Masterson looked chastened. "All I'm asking for is a little caution."

"And that is perfectly reasonable. Thank you, Mr. Masterson." Glinn glanced around with impassive eyes. "Meeting concluded."

As the group was breaking up, Glinn laid a restraining hand on Gideon's arm. "Meet me down in the exobiology lab," he said quietly. "Ten minutes."

21

By the time Gideon reached the exobiology lab, Glinn was already deep in conversation with Antonella Sax, the lab's director. They were bent over a stainless steel box with a glass top, in which the root-like tentacle he'd retrieved—remarkably thin and long—lay sealed inside. Four other technicians were busy in various corners of the spacious but crowded lab.

Glinn motioned him over. "Dr. Sax is explaining what she and her team plan to do with this specimen."

Gideon had not had much contact with Sax, who was a short, stocky, serious woman with brown hair pulled back tight, glasses, about forty—smart and all business. He shook her hand and she turned back to the coiled tentacle.

"What we have here," Sax said quietly, "is humanity's first real example of exobiology. That is beyond outstanding. But it presents all kinds of challenges. For example, under normal circumstances we'd be running the most painstaking and meticulous sterile procedures possible. But we don't have time for that. We need to know as much as we can about this thing, as fast as possible. Quick and dirty. The more we know, the better we'll be able to prepare."

"No quarantine procedures?" Gideon asked. "We don't want an Andromeda Strain event."

"The fact is, the ship itself is a kind of quarantine—the ultimate quarantine. Before we return to port, we'll incinerate this thing and any other parts of the creature we bring up, then sterilize the lab."

Gideon hesitated. He was still in shock, dazed from what happened to Alex, and he found it hard to focus. "Do you feel the ship is at risk from any sort of disease or microbes this thing might be carrying?"

Sax looked at him, brown eyes clear. "In a word: yes."

"This creature is already exposed and open to the ocean," Glinn said. "So whatever microbes it might be carrying are already present in the environment."

"What I find remarkable," said Sax, "is that this specimen reached the surface, where the pressure is about four hundred times less, intact, with no obvious alteration. Normally, when you bring a deep-sea specimen up to surface pressure, it completely falls apart."

"So this thing can live at all depths?" Gideon asked.

"A reasonable inference."

Sax went on to describe the plan of research, starting with sections of the specimen for various scans and examinations—frozen, microscope, SEM, TEM, histological. Also, she said, CAT scans, MRIs, electrical impulse tests, microbiological and biochemical analyses. "We don't know what this is," she told them. "Plant, animal, or something else entirely. We're not sure what it's made of. Does it have DNA? Is it even carbon-based? The most elementary questions still have to be answered. But by the time we're done, our tests will tell us about its anatomy, nervous system—if it has one—the flow of fluids and electrical impulses, its cellular energy cycles—assuming it even has cells—its biochemistry and molecular biology. But for the time being..." She shook her head. "It's like landing on an unknown planet."

"Then we'll let you proceed with all haste." Glinn turned, indicating for Gideon to follow him. Once out in the hall, and alone after turning a corner, Glinn halted. "There's something I want to talk to you about—in confidence."

"Of course."

"Back there in the meeting, I squelched speculation on Lispenard's last words."

Gideon took a deep breath. "I noticed."

"There's something profoundly disturbing about them, and I don't want a lot of speculation about it."

"You're...um, you're referring to the timing?"

Glinn looked at him steadily. "Prothero is working on that, and I do believe it has to be some kind of glitch. No: I'm referring to *what* she said. The meaning. *Let me touch your face.*"

Gideon said nothing. She had spoken those words to him, or something very similar, the night they had spent together. *My God. Was it just last night?*

"I said it was some sort of rapture of the deep. But I don't believe that's true. The sphere was crushed immediately. And at two miles down, there's no 'rapture'—death at that pressure is absolutely instantaneous. In listening to those words...I sense there's real meaning in there, not some random, crazy utterance of a failing brain. This is something..." He paused. "Something beyond our understanding."

He turned his piercing gray eyes on Gideon. "This is a line of inquiry that you and I will pursue, quietly—just the two of us. I know, Gideon, what Alex's death meant to you. I know this isn't easy. But I also know this anomaly is something you won't let drop until you get to the bottom of it. Prothero is working on the timing glitch. I want you to keep tabs on what he's doing—and make sure rumors about anything he might discover aren't disseminated haphazardly. We've lowered a camera to the seafloor and placed it about two hundred yards from the creature. We're going to be watching it twenty-four seven."

"All right," Gideon heard himself say.

Glinn looked at him thoughtfully for a moment. Then, with the briefest of nods, he turned and headed back in the direction of mission control.

22

Eli Glinn dimmed the lights in his stateroom and began undressing for bed. He slipped off his shirt and paused to examine his left arm. It was the one most injured during the sinking of the *Rolvaag*; the limb had taken the brunt of the explosion. Despite the low light he could still see smooth, shiny areas that had once been knotted burn scars, along with rills and ridges of wounds and shrapnel cuts. He flexed his arm and the muscles rose under the skin, their power slowly returning, helped along by his daily workouts.

The bones in his arm had fractured into dozens of pieces, which the doctors had to reassemble, like jigsaw pieces, screwing everything back together with plates and rods. Most of the metal had now been removed—a few fresh scars attested to that.

He raised his hand and stared at it. It amazed him how that awful claw, which he'd thought he would never use again, was now almost normal. He held it up and moved his fingers. He'd never be a concert pianist, but at least he could now dine at table like a human being instead of an animal, spilling his food and barely able to dab his own lips with a napkin.

He flexed his fingers, then his arm again, rotating it this way and that, enjoying the freedom of movement, the lack of stiffness or pain. He turned with a sigh. This was unlike him; he was not the kind of person to admire his own body, to take pleasure in it. At least, he hadn't been. But now, with his injuries almost healed, he was far more aware of—and grateful for—his healthy limbs. Somehow, that gratitude made him recall those who hadn't survived—one in particular—and he felt the old guilt and sadness come creeping back in, like the tide.

Stripping down to his underwear, he went into the bathroom and brushed his teeth before the mirror. His face looked better, the bad eye healed up. Strangely enough, its color was a slightly different shade of gray: just a touch darker. Fresher. Younger.

The lotus root he'd ingested, on that strange distant island two months before, had performed nothing less than a miracle.

He washed his face, dried it, combed his thinning hair, and returned to his stateroom. From his closet he removed a silk dressing gown, slipped it on, then went to the nearest porthole. Undogging it, he pulled it wide and breathed in the fresh, incoming air—the scent of salt and ice. A nearby berg was a mere gray shape in the darkness, dimly illuminated by the lights of the ship. The sea was calm, the moonless night full of stars.

With a sigh he moved away from the porthole and lay on the bed, putting his hands behind his head, his thoughts, like water in a well-worn groove of rock, inevitably going back to the terrible events of the sinking of the *Rolvaag*.

He reached out and slid open the bedside drawer and removed a slim volume: *Selected Poems of W. H. Auden*. Turning the well-thumbed pages, he arrived at the poem titled "In Praise of Limestone." He did not need to read the poem; he knew it by heart; but still he took a measure of comfort from the printed words.

...But the really reckless were fetched
By an older colder voice, the oceanic whisper:
'I am the solitude that asks and promises nothing...'

After a long time of reading and re-reading the poem, he laid the book aside and rose from the bed. Once again he went to the window and breathed in the sea air, and then, tightening the belt of his dressing gown, he put on slippers. He went to his desk, took a spare flash drive out of a drawer, slipped it into his pocket, and quietly left the room.

It was one forty-five: almost two hours into the midnight watch. The ship was quiet, motionless, all but the watch sleeping. He made his way noiselessly down the corridor, up a set of stairs and down another, until he arrived at mission control. It was locked, but he had the key. The room was, as he'd hoped, empty. Going to the central station, he flicked on the main screen, pulled up a series of menus, hit some additional keys. Moments later a video started: the feed from Gideon's mini sub as it entered the *Rolvaag's* hold. He fast-forwarded to the point where the deck plates and pipes were cut away—and the DSV's headlights illuminated the corpse of the captain. Sally Britton.

He stopped the video, inserted his flash drive into a USB slot, typed in a few commands, then resumed the video as he copied it to the drive.

There it was again: that swirl of blond hair; the body's arms thrown out as if in surprise; the uniform, still neat and clean despite years in the water. Slowly the face turned to him once again, those sapphire eyes wide open, the lips parted, the neck and throat so real, so white, so life-like...

He abruptly stopped the video. The download was complete and he removed the flash drive and made his way back to his cabin. Lying down again on the bed, he pulled his laptop over, inserted the USB stick containing the video, and replayed it, slower this time, and then again, frame by frame, finally freezing the image as the face turned to the point where the eyes were looking straight into the camera. He stared at it for a very long time.

He was still staring at it when the blood-red light of the rising sun speared through the porthole into his stateroom, signaling the start of another day.

Now he closed the notebook, pulled out the flash drive, and went to the porthole window. He stood there a moment, watching the day rise out of the calm ocean, and then took the flash drive and flung it as far as he could into the deep-blue water, where it made a tiny splash. And then something incredible happened: one of the many seagulls hanging around the ship swooped down and grabbed it from the water before it could sink and flew away with it, growing smaller and smaller until it vanished into the brilliant orange sky.

23

At eight am, Gideon knocked on the door to Prothero's marine acoustics lab with a feeling of foreboding. He had managed little more than an hour or two of sleep the night before—if it could be called sleep.

His instinctual dislike of the sonar engineer had only deepened after the man's galling comment about the "knight in shining armor"—a comment made all the more offensive by Alex's death.

"Door's unlocked," came the muffled voice within.

Gideon eased it open and was greeted by a wave of electronic heat and a fantastical jumble of electronic gadgetry. There, in the corner, he could see Prothero in a torn T-shirt, hunched over a circuit board with a soldering iron. It was exactly as he imagined the lab would look, a god-awful mess, and Prothero himself was utterly predictable in his shabby T-shirt and disheveled contempt for civility. There was nobody else around; the tall Asian woman who had been at Prothero's side during the earlier briefing had not yet, apparently, reported in.

He waited while Prothero continued to work.

After a long silence Prothero said, without turning: "Be with you in a sec."

Gideon looked around, but there was no place to sit. Every chair and table was covered with electronic crap; the very walls were invisible, hidden by racks and shelves of exotic equipment. Even Gideon, who had advanced computer skills, did not recognize some of it, especially the stuff that looked jerry-built. But it was clear enough that much of it—the speakers, microphones, and oscilloscopes—involved acoustics.

Prothero finally gave a loud snort of annoyance, straightened up, put away the soldering iron, and swiveled around on the office chair. He came toward Gideon, still seated, pulling himself along with the heels of his feet, the casters of the old chair creaking.

He came to a halt a foot in front of Gideon. "What is it?" he asked.

"We had an appointment?"

A grunt. "Okay."

And now Gideon had the distinct feeling Prothero didn't even recall the appointment.

"I wanted to chat with you about the, ah, last transmission from Alex Lispenard."

Prothero ran a hand over his limp, longish black hair, combing the greasy strands back with his fingers. He rubbed his neck. He looked like he'd been up all night; but then, he always looked like that.

"Have you managed to figure out the glitch?" Gideon asked.

Prothero rotated his head on his scrawny neck, getting the kinks out. "There is no glitch."

"Of course there's a glitch, or some other sort of technical problem. I mean with the timing."

"Just what I said. No glitch."

"I saw the mini sub crushed," said Gideon. "I *witnessed* it. Then five seconds later, her voice came through the hydrophone. If there was no glitch, then obviously there was some sort of delay in the transmission, some kind of time lag."

"No delay."

"Come on. What are you saying?"

"What your hydrophone picked up was a direct acoustic sound coming through the water, at that moment."

"Impossible."

A shrug from Prothero; some scratching of his arm.

"So you're saying a dead person spoke," Gideon pressed on.

"All I'm saying is, there was no glitch."

"Jesus Christ, of *course* there was a glitch!"

"Ignorance combined with vehemence doesn't make it so."

Gideon tried to hold down his anger. He took a deep breath. "You're telling me that Alex spoke when, *a*, she was dead, and *b*, she was inside the creature?"

"I haven't gotten far enough to draw those conclusions. Maybe it wasn't her speaking at all."

"It *was* her. I know her voice. Who else could it have been?"

Another maddening shrug.

"Besides, a person can't speak underwater anyway. You're telling me someone was able to speak a sentence clearly through four hundred yards of water? Of course there's a technical issue here. Whatever she said somehow got stuck in an analog conversion algorithm, or whatever, and took a few seconds to come through to my sub."

"Hey, Gideon?" Another round of neck rotations. "Why don't you just get the fuck out of here?"

Trembling with rage, Gideon forced himself not to utter his

next, escalating comment. This was getting nowhere—and he realized it was partly his fault. He had come in here with a chip on his shoulder; he was way too emotionally invested in the outcome; and he was letting this jackass get under his skin.

"I'm just trying to understand," he said with barely maintained calm. "You see, a good friend died."

"Look, I get it. I get that you're freaked out. I'm sorry about what happened. But don't come in here telling me my job. I'm way ahead of you."

"Then how about filling me in on where you are? I would appreciate that very much." Someday he would kick this son of a bitch's ass all the way to the South Pole—but not just now.

"Thank you." Prothero scratched his arm again, like an ape. Gideon waited, letting the silence build.

"I've been working on the physics of how that message was actually transmitted through the water. And here's where I'm at."

He fell silent.

"Go on," Gideon said after a minute.

"It's weird as shit."

"How so?"

"It was digital."

"What do you mean?"

"You know the difference between analog and digital sound waves? One looks smooth, while the other is made up of individual samples. Time slices. Little steps, like a staircase. This one was digital. And the wave was constructed to pass through water so it would sound normal when it emerged from the speaker, back in the air, the way it did coming out of your hydrophone."

"But...how?"

Another shrug. "No biological system produces digital sound. Or digital *anything*. Only electronics do that. And that blue whale vocalization? Also digital. It came from the Baobab—not from above."

"The Baobab made a blue whale sound? Digitally?"

"Yup."

"So...this thing isn't alive? It's a machine? It's like—recording audio signals and playing them back at us?"

"Who knows what the hell it is, or what it's doing?"

Gideon stared at the engineer. "We don't have to know what it is," he said slowly, "to kill it."

24

Deep within the belly of the R/V *Batavia*, inside an unnamed and unlabeled storage area that was always kept carefully locked, Manuel Garza stood, examining the massive steel racks that held the partially assembled pieces of the bomb. It was all here, everything but the plutonium core, which was in a secret, shielded vault in another location. As he looked over the tidy racks with their components, carefully sealed and vacuum-packed in silvered plastic, and sitting in custom-made Styrofoam cradles, he felt concerned. He did not like the way Gideon, after showing no interest for weeks, had suddenly, angrily, insisted on seeing the nuke. It struck him as primeval: the vengeful warrior seeking comfort in the presence of his weapons. Since the death of Lispenard, he knew, the atmosphere on the ship had changed. It had become grim and purposeful. Under ordinary circumstances, that would not necessarily be a bad thing—but Garza was concerned nevertheless. He was deeply suspicious of vengeance as a motive, and he did not believe that the life-form they were going to kill should be thought of as an enemy any more than, say, a grizzly bear or a virus should. The hungry bear did what it did; the virus did what it did. And this thing did what it did, too. There was no intelligence about it, he was sure; just instinct.

The turning of a key; the undogging of the hatch; and then Glinn was in the room, Gideon at his side.

"Here it is," said Garza. "It's all sealed up—nothing much to see."

He watched as Gideon silently moved past him, staring at the bomb. He reached out and touched the plastic. "This looks pretty small for a nuke," he said after a moment.

"It's an efficient one," said Glinn. "Originally the payload for an R7 Semyorka ICBM."

"Soviet-era."

"Of course."

"How did you get it?"

"We already told you all you need to know about that."

"The yield?"

"About one hundred kilotons."

"Weight?"

"One forty kilograms."

"How big is the plutonium pit?"

"Twenty kilograms. Oval."

He watched Gideon run his hand along the plastic. "What type of trigger?"

"It's got a polonium-210 initiator."

"Jesus. I can't believe you were able to get all this. Makes me worried about where the rest of those old Soviet bombs are ending up."

"There is much to worry about. But that's a problem for another day and someone else."

Gideon withdrew his hand. "Was it expensive?"

"Extremely."

"And how has it been modified for underwater use?"

"The obvious engineering challenge," said Glinn, "was dealing with water pressure. We plan to put it inside a small titanium sphere and send it down in an ROV, operated remotely. We have an ROV specifically designed for that task, in fact, standing by in the hangar."

"I see. And how will the weapon be deployed?"

"That, Gideon, is your department. You're the expert on modeling nuclear explosions. No one's ever detonated a bomb two miles deep, in water pressure four hundred times that of the surface. We want to make sure it's maximally destructive."

Gideon looked from Glinn to Garza and back again. "You're talking about a massive computational problem."

"Yes. And we have the computing power on board to do it. A Q machine."

Gideon said, "The explosion has to wipe that thing out completely, leaving nothing that could take root and grow again. So we need to know where it's most vulnerable, where its vital organs are, how its tissue might respond to the bomb's effects. It wouldn't do any good to blow it apart if all the pieces just drifted to the seafloor and re-rooted themselves."

"You clearly understand the problem," said Glinn. "It might be as simple as killing the brain. On the other hand, it might be as complex as atomizing the entire Baobab."

Gideon turned to Garza. "I want to start assembling this as soon as possible."

"Hold on," said Garza. "We've got a long way to go before we're ready to nuke this thing."

"We need to put the son of a bitch together and have it ready to go at a moment's notice. We've no idea what that thing's going to do."

"As soon as we start opening these packages," Garza replied, "we'll be dealing with high explosives, fragile computer components, and a hunk of deadly plutonium. And having an armable nuclear weapon on board the ship for an extended period is dangerous as hell."

"What's dangerous as hell is sitting here with a useless nuke, unable to defend ourselves if that thing figures out what we're up to and decides to take us out."

"That thing isn't going to 'figure out' anything," said Garza. "It's not an intelligent life-form. Probably a plant or some kind of giant anemone." Garza felt exasperated; this was Gideon letting his emotions take over, letting his thirst for vengeance drive his thinking.

"We've no idea what kind of intelligence this thing has," said Gideon. "If that dark thing I saw is its brain, it's pretty damned big—bigger than yours," he added drily.

"Having a live nuke on board the ship," said Garza, "is insane. What if a storm comes up? What if a component fails? What if the device is jarred or struck by lightning?" He turned to Glinn.

"Gideon wants to assemble it," Glinn said. "Not arm it. And don't forget the fail-safe. That should allay your concerns."

"What fail-safe?" asked Gideon.

"The three of us—and only the three of us—will have the code to arm the nuke and start the detonation sequence. But as a precaution, we also have a code to abort it, should we jointly or singly determine that using the device is an unsound idea."

"That's neither here nor there," Garza said. "We're not on a military base. We're on a ship full of civilians. The security here is porous. As engineer in chief, I strongly recommend against assembling the nuke until just before we need to use it."

A long silence, and then Glinn told him quietly: "Arrange for delivery of the plutonium core."

Garza was startled; this was so very unlike Glinn. As he was about to object, Glinn's radio crackled. Glinn listened for a moment, then turned to them. "Lispenard's DSV seems to have reappeared—it's in the clear, on the seabed outside the creature."

Gideon quickly swiveled away from the weapon. "What condition is it in?"

"Sonar seems to indicate...smaller. Denser."

"Crushed," said Garza. "Just as we thought."

"I'm going down to get it," said Gideon immediately.

Garza expected a protest from Glinn, but instead he saw the man nod. "Manuel?" he said. "Let's prep *John* for another dive."

What is it between these two? Garza asked himself, shaking his head, as he left for the hangar deck.

25

Once again, Gideon found himself trying to control his breathing and stave off feelings of claustrophobia as he sank into infinite black nothingness. Forty minutes later, the bottom came into sight in his lower viewport: a gray expanse of abyssal mud, scattered here and there with twisted pieces of debris, looking like a surreal landscape by Yves Tanguy. His target landing waypoint was south of the shipwreck, a thousand yards from the Baobab.

John settled into a hover fifty feet above the seafloor. This time, the sub was wired to the surface; mission control was packed, he knew, and at least a dozen eyes were monitoring his every move. A slender steel cable for lifting the crushed DSV was attached to his mech arm, unspooling from the crane on the *Batavia*, and he had to be careful to move in such a way as to prevent the wire and the cable from tangling.

"At waypoint zero," he said.

"Roger," came the voice of Garza, who was manning the control hub. "Proceed to waypoint one."

Gideon moved forward, the low hum of the propellers reverberating through the sub. The crushed remains of *Paul*, at the position of waypoint three, were sitting on the seafloor about fifty feet from the trunk of the creature.

Fifty feet. Given yesterday's tragic, catastrophic events, that seemed way, way too close for comfort.

Gideon headed for waypoint one. Reaching it, he moved the joystick and the autopilot made a sharp course change, heading immediately for waypoint two, where it would make another sharp change. The idea was that making a zigzag approach to the creature might confuse it. Gideon thought the plan was counterproductive and did nothing but increase the time he would be on the bottom, but he had been overruled by Glinn.

Halfway to waypoint two, his beams began to illuminate the Baobab—and at the same moment he heard a rapid buzzing noise, rising and falling in cadence, come through the hydrophone—and the hull of the sub.

"What the hell is that?" he spoke into the mike.

"It appears you're being painted with sonar," said Garza. "Higher frequency than the usual two hertz."

"Son of a bitch."

Gideon could hear consternation over the channel. "Hold on," said Garza. "Do not approach further. We need to take stock."

"No more delays," said Gideon. "I can see *Paul* now. I'm going in."

More rapid discussion in the background.

"Okay," said Garza. "Move as fast as possible and then get out of there."

"My sentiments exactly."

The buzzing of the sonar sped up, slowed down, rose and fell in register. It sounded like a swarm of angry hornets and it gave Gideon the creeps.

As he approached, his headlights fully illuminated the ruined

DSV. It sat on the ooze of the bottom as if it had been placed there: a compact, neatly crumpled ball of metal with things embedded in it. It lay atop a veritable maze of the thin, tendril-like roots that extended away from the Baobab in every direction. The jagged and mashed pieces of the honeycombed titanium hull had been folded over themselves as easily as a sheet of tinfoil. It was almost beyond belief that the creature could have accomplished so easily what the weight of two miles of water could not. A faint, cloudy trail drifted downcurrent from the crumpled mass, forming a comet's tail. In the beam of his light, reddish water could be seen seeping from a small rent in the structure.

Gideon looked past the wreck to the trunk that loomed above: a solid, rugose wall that resembled some kind of horrible, organic skyscraper. The bloated thing was stationary, no movement or sign of life visible...save for the hideous buzz of the sonar.

He felt apprehension mingling with fury and hatred.

He slowed at the wreck and extended the mechanical arm, which was carrying a steel cable with an explosive anchor bolt at its end. The pre-programmed arm, acting as usual with very little operator input, held the bolt out and placed it against a solid part of the crushed mini sub; with a *thud* and a burst of bubbles, the bolt was anchored.

The sound seemed to irritate the creature; the sound of its sonar rose in both pitch and volume.

"Bolt secured," said Gideon.

"Ready to raise," said Garza.

The mission protocol was for him to wait until the surface team had begun raising the wreck, to ascertain visually that it was holding together during the lifting process. Gideon backed away, watching the slack being taken out of the cable, seeing it gradually go taut. Another moment, and then, with a puff of silt, the wreck rose like some ghastly oversize Christmas ornament into the blackness.

"Looks good," he said. *"Paul* secure."

"We concur," said Garza. "Drop ballast and surface."

Only too happily, Gideon hit the release lever, dropping his iron ballast, and *John* began to rise—fast.

At the same moment, the huge creature began to flex in the most grotesque way: the mouth emerging from the center of the stalk, swelling with water, rubbery lips quivering. Gideon felt a shudder as his sub was caught in the sudden current, and it lurched and began to spiral. There was a snapping sound that he knew instantly was the communications wire breaking free. Half of his screens went dead, the voice of Garza in his headphones went silent, and a bunch of alarms went off, warning screens popping into life.

He jammed the joystick sideways to counteract the spinning, and the sub abruptly slowed, the nose tilting sharply up, the tail being pulled back toward the sucking, grasping mouth. Fighting against this, Gideon goosed the forward thrust and cleared the emergency ballast tanks of water, filling them with an explosive burst of air, increasing the sub's buoyancy to maximum.

He could feel the sub's need to rise fighting against the down-sucking current. A vibration started, a rattling, with the thrumming sound of fast water—and then, with a sudden lurch, the sub broke free and tumbled upward, rotating head over heels like a crazy bubble toward the surface. Fighting the controls, Gideon could feel the autopilot trying to correct the chaotic motion. Sensing a rhythm to the ship's gyrations, he rotated the joystick in the opposite direction, and, with a lurch, *John* stabilized.

By the time his heart rate had returned to a semblance of normality, blue light was appearing in the viewports and, a moment later, the sub broke the surface. Through the left viewport, Gideon could see the clean, white profile of the *Batavia*. As soon as he was above water, Garza's voice came from his headset radio.

"Gideon? Gideon? Do you read?"

"Loud and clear."

"Are you all right?"

"Shaken up, but fine."

"We're getting you out of the water."

Without his input, the mini sub headed across the smooth water toward the mother ship, half a mile away.

26

MANUEL GARZA ENTERED the forensic lab filled with a sense of foreboding. Half a dozen metal chairs had been set up before a large flat-panel: a movie theater in miniature, all ready for a most macabre showing.

Garza had lived through the sinking of the *Rolvaag*. They say that with time, memory of even the worst experiences begins to fade, and this, in fact, was what had happened with him. He wasn't sure if this was an unhealthy form of repression or merely a self-protective psychological reaction. All he knew was he had spent years avoiding thinking about that terrible night, pushing away any and all thoughts of it, to the point where—he told himself—he hardly remembered what had happened. He had no interest in remembering. Maybe some people dealt with PTSD by going over the events in their mind again and again. Not him: his way of dealing with it was to repress the shit out of those memories, squash them, pretend they never happened.

And now here he was, about to be spoon-fed all those carefully banished memories, one at a time.

"Dr. Garza, welcome!" said Hank Nishimura a little too brightly.

Garza silently took the proffered seat. He knew full well his reputation aboard ship was of someone rude, aloof, and taciturn. He had the same reputation at the EES home office. It had bothered him at first, but when he realized he wasn't able—or willing—to change, he'd decided the better route was not to care. The mission at hand was all that mattered; screw the rest.

He was early, and as he waited First Officer Lennart came in, followed by Antonella Sax, the exobiologist. Nobody spoke. Finally Glinn arrived. Nobody else had been invited: not Gideon, not Brambell.

Garza looked at Glinn curiously. What they were about to see was, without doubt, going to put the EES director in a very bad light. *Bad* wasn't even the word: it would pretty much draw back the curtain on Glinn at his most obsessed and homicidally negligent moment. If these tapes ever made it out into the world, it was quite possible Glinn would spend the rest of his life in prison.

And yet Glinn was wearing his usual mask—his face neutral, ambiguously pleasant, vaguely intelligent, the face of an accountant, perhaps, or a mid-level manager at a consumer goods company.

Glinn sat down.

And now Garza could see just how nervous Nishimura was. He was the only one who had seen the tapes so far, and what he had seen must not have been very nice.

"Dr. Glinn, would you care to say a few words by, ah, way of introduction?" asked Nishimura, hopefully.

Glinn waved his hand. "Play the tapes."

"Um, yes. Okay." Nishimura's eyes darted around, the rictus of an inappropriate smile on his face. "What I did—what Dr. Glinn asked me to do—was to create a composite video of the *Rolvaag's* last moments, in strict chronology, highlighting the defining events. The video starts about an hour before the sinking, and continues to the point where the ship broke up and the recording systems went dead."

He clasped his hands, took a breath.

"We were able to recover most of the data. There were two cams on the bridge, two in the hold, and several others scattered about the ship. Sometimes the quality of the image is degraded, and often the audio is hard to understand, unless it was an electronic communication. There are some...difficult moments in here...Obviously, all this is confidential to this room. That's why, at Dr. Glinn's orders, the audience has been kept small. No discussion of this is to take place beyond our circle—correct, Dr. Glinn?"

"Correct."

An uncomfortable pause. "Dr. Glinn, are you sure you don't want to say any words about what we are to view?"

Another dismissive wave of the hand.

Nishimura swallowed. "All right, then. I'm going to roll it with no further comment. You'll note I've inserted a running time stamp in the lower right corner of the frame."

The lights in the room went down. The screen came up black and the time stamp began running:

19:03.44

Then the video began. A scene materialized. It was the bridge of a ship—the *Rolvaag*. The point of view was from above and to the side, showing the helm, the master's position, the officer of the watch. The light was gray, a stormy twilight. The bridge was dark, as was normal, with only the red glow of the electronics and several low-lit screens displaying radar and chartplotters.

Garza recognized Captain Britton at the master's station, the figure next to her Eli Glinn. The first officer, a man named Howell, stood beside the helmsman, whose back was at present turned to the camera. In the rear of the bridge, out of the way, was the rest of the voyage's main cast: Palmer Lloyd, the billionaire financier of the expedition; Sam McFarlane, the rogue meteorite hunter; and Rachel Amira, the chief scientist. All silent. All watching.

Through the bridge windows was the prow of the ship and, staring at it, Garza's heart almost stopped as the repressed memories came flooding back.

It was the height of the storm. Enormous seas were erupting over the bow and sweeping the forward deck. Most of the containers and several davits had already been torn from their moorings and swept overboard. Beyond was the sea, a chaos of towering waves with boiling crests—waves the height of ten-story buildings. Only the sheer size of the *Rolvaag* was saving the vessel. If there was any talk on the bridge, it was completely drowned out by the roaring thunder of the sea. Each person was focused on his or her task, fixated on trying to keep the great tanker under control. As the ship rose on each wave, the winds climbed to a gibbering wail. At the peak of the waves the entire superstructure shook, the camera image trembling, as if the winds were attempting to rip the top off the ship. Then, as the ship sank into the trough, there would be a shudder, the howling of the wind dying off as it fell into the canyon of water—and then it would begin to roll, slowly, achingly. The view through the bridge windows would go down, down, into the looming wall of dark water, webbed by foam, and then, with agonizing slowness, it would heave up again, the view raising past the dirty water to a dirtier sky with no terminus.

Staring, remembering, Garza tried to control a sense of unexpected, overwhelming panic. It was all he could do to maintain his composure.

Now Captain Britton was speaking with Glinn, gesticulating. Glinn was on a handheld radio. "It's Garza," he was saying. "I can't hear him over the storm."

Britton turned to First Officer Howell. "Patch him through."

Suddenly Garza heard his own electronic voice, calling from the hold.

"Eli! We're losing the primary crosspieces!"

Glinn responded with eerie calm. "Stick with it."

"The whole thing's unraveling faster than we can keep up with—" A screech of tearing metal drowned out the rest. The ship was slanting crazily, the sea boiling over the rails, the bow buried in water: it looked as if the ship were going to drive itself straight into the ocean.

"Eli, the rock—*it's moving!* I can't—" The audio dissolved in static.

Abruptly, the video cut to the hold of the ship—a place Garza knew well, as he'd been principal engineer of the massive web of struts and braces that held the twenty-five-thousand-ton meteorite in place. There it was: the meteorite, shrouded in canvas, nestled in its cradle, wrapped in giant rubber-coated chains and hawsers and surrounded by a forest of wooden timbers and, beyond those, steel struts for rigidity and strength. Designing that cradle had been one of the great engineering achievements of Garza's life. And it had worked. It had *worked*, damn it, and it would have saved the ship, if Glinn, the bastard, hadn't . . .

Then he went stiff. There he was: his younger self, on the lower catwalk surrounding the meteorite, madly working the levers of the power-control console, which adjusted the tension on the chains and hawsers and kept the rock snug and tight in the cradle.

Only it wasn't snug anymore. As the ship rolled—an angle-meter in the power-control console showed the degree of pitch—the rock was moving, the chains slipping a little, the wood flexing, the iron groaning. He felt a wave of shock and nausea roll over him as he watched. And then he saw a shadow on a catwalk above, a furtive scurrying, and he suddenly remembered the Cape Horn native they'd brought on board for his local knowledge. What was his weird name? Puppup. John Puppup. There he was, staring down with a maniacal grin on his face: a grin of satisfaction, even triumph. The figure faded back into the forest of struts. And then there was so much sound in the hold, such a roaring and screeching, that nothing else could be heard. It was a mere five-second image—then the video cut back to the bridge.

Now Captain Britton turned and gestured, and Palmer Lloyd approached. The audio had been obviously enhanced, but it remained distorted, full of echoes and digital artifacts—the words, however, were chillingly clear.

"Mr. Lloyd," she said, "the meteorite *must* go."

"Absolutely not," Lloyd replied.

"I am the captain of this ship," Britton said. "The lives of my crew depend on it. Mr. Glinn, I order you to trigger the dead man's switch. I *order* it."

"No!" screamed Lloyd, seizing Glinn's arm. "You touch that computer and I'll kill you with my bare hands."

"The captain gave an order," shouted the first officer.

"Only Glinn has the key, and he won't do it!" screamed Lloyd. "He can't, not without my permission! Eli, do you hear me? I order you not to initiate the dead man's switch."

The argument about whether to initiate the "dead man's

switch," which would jettison the meteorite into the sea, became increasingly heated. Garza had not been present at the argument—he had been down in the hold—and he strained to hear over the increasing roar of the sea. As the argument reached its height, McFarlane, the meteorite hunter, spoke clearly, and his sudden interjection seemed to take everyone by surprise. "Let it go."

Even as Lloyd was protesting, the ship began yet another roll—but this one was different. The wave lifting the ship was truly staggering in size. All talk ceased. One of the bridge windows blew out, the high-impact plastic flying away in shards as the wind shrieked through. Then a terrible sound began. The bridge slanted, slanted some more, the ship now thirty degrees on its side, while everyone clung desperately to whatever handholds were available, the vessel wallowing broadside-to. Nothing but black water could be seen through the windows. A moment of stasis—and then, with an immense shudder, the ship began to right itself.

This was the moment that changed everyone's mind.

As soon as the deck leveled, Lloyd released his grip. "All right," he said. "Let it go."

There was more discussion, lost in the roar of the wind as the ship came up to the summit of the following wave. Glinn was at the keyboard, ready to enter the command, the code that only he knew, which would open the dead man's doors and drop the meteorite. But he wasn't typing—as Garza knew he wouldn't. His long white hands fell away from the keys, and he turned slowly to face the others. "The ship will survive."

Cut back to the hold. There he, Garza, was again. The meteorite had shifted, several wooden beams had splintered, and the cradle looked bent. "Eli!" he was calling into the radio. "The web is failing!"

He heard Britton's voice on the ship's radio, ordering him to throw the dead man's switch. His voice answered, "Only Eli has the codes."

Britton's furious answer: "Mr. Garza, order your men to abandon stations."

Cut back to the bridge: Glinn refusing steadfastly to jettison the meteorite, despite now universal entreaties.

And then came the key command, from Captain Britton to the first officer: "All hands, abandon stations. We will abandon ship. Initiate 406 MHz beacon, all hands to the lifeboats."

As First Officer Howell broadcast the order over the ship's intercom, Britton left the bridge.

27

Aт тне request of Ronald—a request it had seemed wise to comply with—Sam McFarlane left his battered roller bag in Dr. Hassenpflug's office and followed the burly, red-haired orderly down echoing corridors and beneath the ornately carved archways of the Neo-Gothic mansion named Dearborne Park. At last, a door of heavy steel sprang open with the clicking of locks, revealing an elegant reception room. Yet as McFarlane looked around he realized this was an orchestrated illusion. The expensive landscapes in oil that hung on the walls were encased in clear Plexiglas. The plush armchairs and sofas had their legs discreetly bolted to the floor. There were no sharp objects anywhere in sight. This, he realized, was not only a reception room, but also an asylum—a lavish, expensive asylum.

At the far end of the room, an elderly man sat in a high-backed chair. The stiffness and rigidity of the man's posture radiated a pride that was at odds with the straitjacket snugged tightly around his arms and torso. The man looked at him, his blue eyes glittering with recognition. An orderly had been feeding him some kind of crimson liquid through a plastic cup fitted with a straw. "Take that away," Palmer Lloyd said in a sharp aside. Then he turned his focus back on McFarlane.

"Sam. Come closer."

But McFarlane did not move. He'd recognized Lloyd's distinctive voice immediately, of course, when he'd received that call on his cell phone in Santa Fe. Ever since, he'd been mentally preparing himself for this meeting. But now, actually seeing the man in person, he was unprepared for the storm of emotions—anger, hatred, guilt, remorse, grief—that washed over him.

"What the fuck do you want?" he asked, his voice sounding strange and husky in his own ears.

Lloyd's seamed but still vigorous-looking face broke into a smile. "Ha ha!" he laughed. "That's the Sam I remember." He pierced McFarlane with his eyes. "That's the Sam I need. Come closer."

This time, McFarlane complied.

"Guess who came to see me a few weeks ago, Sam?" Lloyd asked.

McFarlane did not reply. He was shocked by the look in the man's eyes. The failure of the expedition, the sinking of the *Rolvaag*, had, he knew, touched all its survivors in one way or another. He'd heard Lloyd had taken it particularly badly. But to see this powerful, confident billionaire reduced to such a state was difficult to take in.

"Eli Glinn came to see me," Lloyd said.

"*Glinn?*"

"Ah! Ah, ha! I can see just by looking at your face that you hate him as much as I do."

McFarlane grasped the arms of a nearby chair, lowered himself into it. "What did he want?"

"What do you suppose the son of a bitch wanted? What we

all want." Lloyd glanced at the two orderlies, then leaned in and lowered his voice. *"To kill that thing."*

McFarlane went rigid. For the past five years, as he'd drifted from one place to another—unable to hold a job, disdainful of attachments, restless, aimless, yet never for one minute at peace—he'd been haunted by their shared past. He knew that "thing" Lloyd was referring to. It had never been far from his mind.

Looking intently at McFarlane's expression, Lloyd nodded. "We both hate the man. Don't we, Sam? It was his fault—all his fault."

"Not just his," McFarlane said. "Yours, too."

Lloyd sat back up in his chair. "Mine!" He gave a harsh laugh. "Oh—I suppose you're blaming me for roping you into the expedition in the first place? For ruining your life?" His voice rose tremulously. "As I recall, your life was ruined already. Have you forgotten the Tornarssuk meteorite? *I* gave you a chance for redemption. It was Glinn, not I, who took that chance away—and you know it."

The orderly named Ronald, standing near the door, stirred. "Don't excite the patient," he warned.

Immediately Lloyd became calm again. He gestured for the other orderly to give him a sip from the plastic cup. "What have you been doing with yourself, Sam?" he asked in a quieter voice. "Other than peddling worthless meteorites, I mean."

"This and that."

"Such as?"

McFarlane shrugged. "Taught geology at a community college for a while. Worked at a steel mill in Braddock, Pennsylvania."

"But you couldn't stay still, could you? The demons kept driving you on, right? Ha! Well, it turns out you're not the only one. Glinn, too. He came to see me with that right-hand man of his,

Garza, and some younger fellow, can't recall his name. Seems he's been haunted by that thing we planted in the South Atlantic all this time, too." Lloyd leaned in again. "Except his demons are worse than ours. He didn't throw the dead man's switch. He sank the *Rolvaag*. He killed a hundred and eight people. Worst of all: he left that thing there, all these five years. He let it grow. Grow, grow, until now it's—"

"Mr. Lloyd," Ronald said, mildly but firmly.

"What?" Lloyd said, craning his neck around to look at the orderly. "I'm just talking to an old friend." He turned back to McFarlane. Now his tone became hurried, almost anxious, as if he knew his time was short. "I've thought about Glinn's visit, ever since he left. I've thought about nothing else. He's going back there, Sam—after all these years. I thought his inaction was cowardice. But it wasn't that. It was a question of money. Now he's got it. And he's down there by now. God only knows what's going on there, this very minute."

He made a gesture from beneath the straitjacket, as if desirous of grasping McFarlane's hand. The chains on his legs clinked as he shifted in his chair. "But I know what's going to happen. If you have any brains, you know, too. He's going to *fail*—again. He's born to failure; he seeks it out. The patterns of thought that doomed the *Rolvaag* are going to doom this expedition, too. He's acting egotistically, judgment clouded. He's got no humility, no sense of the uncontrollable randomness of events. He's made a living out of solving engineering problems, *terrestrial* engineering problems—and this isn't like that at all. Oh, no, not at all."

"Why are you telling me this?" McFarlane asked.

"Why do you think, man? *You have to go down there.* He needs your expertise. Your familiarity with those bad old days. Your ability to stand up to him, tell him he's wrong to his face. Damn it, he needs somebody who was as—as close—to that thing as he was. He needs an interfering angel—someone as *wrecked* as he is!"

"Go yourself," McFarlane said.

For a moment, Lloyd stared at him in surprise. Then he dissolved into laughter once again. "Go myself? These gentlemen would protest. Besides, even if they let me out of these restraints, I'd never make it past the front door. I've thought of a hundred, a thousand, ways to kill myself. I'd be dead within sixty seconds of being free." Lloyd stopped laughing. "Look, it's not a question of money, you have to go, and go *now*, I'll bankroll you—"

"So you're as big a coward as you thought Glinn was," McFarlane interrupted. "You know what's going to happen—what that seed will do to the world—and you can't stand the thought of it. So you want out before it happens."

"Sir—" Ronald said in another warning tone.

"Well, you know what? You're right. We're all dead—or will be, soon. And a good thing. I've wandered the world for five years now, and in all that time I haven't seen a whole hell of a lot worth saving. I hope that thing *does* destroy humanity—before we go out and ruin the galaxy. Good riddance to us. And you especially."

For a moment, Lloyd stared in mute surprise. Then his face colored with rage. "You...How dare you come here and patronize me with your insectile world-weariness, your faux ennui! You're worse than he is. You disgust me! You're dogshit! You're...no, wait! Don't go. Come back, Sam—don't go! *Don't go!*"

But McFarlane had risen and was heading quickly for the door—even as the orderlies were hurrying to escort him bodily from Dearborne Park.

28

In the video room, Garza glanced at Glinn to see how he was taking it. Once again, he could only marvel at the man's coolness.

The video now cut to several quick shots of the ship's corridors; the running of personnel to the lifeboats; and then to the lifeboats themselves, enclosed orange boats that were not on davits but of the free-fall type, in which the lifeboat sits on a downward-facing track and is launched by sliding off the main vessel.

Back to the bridge. Everyone had abandoned their stations save for First Officer Howell and the helmsman. The helmsman would die, Garza knew, but Howell would survive. But where had the captain gone? Garza recalled that he himself had ordered his men to abandon their stations and then had followed the captain's orders, leaving the hold and proceeding to his own assigned abandon station: one of the free-fall lifeboats.

Another cut to the hold. Glinn could now be seen arriving at the upper catwalk, greeted by the Tierra del Fuegan, Puppup. The hold elevator was broken, and so Glinn began climbing down to the lower catwalk around the cradle, clinging to the ladder as the ship heeled and the ladder departed from the vertical. The hold was filled with the sound of groaning steel and cracking wood. The tarp around the meteorite had torn, exposing its massive crimson surface.

Garza peered more closely at the screen. Fascination was now replacing his initial shock and horror. These were images he had never seen; events he had never known. Glinn, of course, had never spoken of them.

Glinn began working the rubber-coated chains that had shaken loose, using the motor-assist to tighten them back around the meteorite. Puppup was helping him, their conversation partially drowned out by noise.

Then another figure suddenly appeared on the upper catwalk: Captain Britton. "Eli!" she called in a loud voice. "The ship's about to break up!"

Glinn said nothing. He continued to work with Puppup, trying to retighten the chains, which had ratcheted loose in the previous roll. Garza himself had tried again and again to tighten the chains in the same way, only to have them slide back out under the immense weight of the meteorite with each roll of the ship, as the ratcheting gears were becoming stripped.

"Come back to the bridge with me," she called out. "There may still be time to trigger the switch. Both of us can still live."

Now Glinn shouted back, "Sally, the only people who are going to die are the foolish ones in the lifeboats. If you stay here, you'll survive."

The ship heeled once again; the meteorite shuddered; and still the captain pleaded with Glinn to abandon ship. But Glinn refused to stop work on the chains, even as the ship rolled again, more dreadfully, the hold a riot of screeching, tearing metal, the great meteorite shifting with a sound like thunder.

"I could love you, Eli..." came Britton's last call to him, but he ignored her—and then she disappeared.

Her body had been found in the electronics hub of the ship; Garza guessed she must have been trying to bypass the codes and trigger the dead man's switch from there.

I could love you, Eli. My God. Garza had had no idea. He hadn't known just how much Glinn held back from him—just how much he'd been keeping bottled up all these years. No wonder the man had fallen apart on the bridge at the sight of Britton's body.

As he watched, the ship continued its long roll. And there was Glinn, climbing on top of the rock itself, holding a wrench, attempting to tighten the chain bolts by hand—a completely insane undertaking. He straddled the massive rock, crisscrossed with ropes and chains, like Captain Ahab astride Moby Dick, wrench in hand, desperately flailing and struggling with a massive chain shackle.

There was a tearing sound as the meteorite shifted and the tarps rent, the meteorite now almost completely naked, its strange, crimson surface practically glowing. Hull rivets began popping. And still the ship yawed on its side, more and more steeply. There was an almost bestial sound of rending metal, a shower of sparks, a ratcheting of chains...and the web unraveled. The meteorite rolled out of its cradle, almost leisurely, Glinn atop it; the rock impacted the web of struts and beams, splintering wood and pushing steel aside like butter, descending slowly but inevitably in the inexorable pull of gravity. The ship was now canted almost on its side. The hull began to unzip and the sea came roaring in, white with fury. As Garza watched, the meteorite came in contact with the seawater.

At this point, Nishimura had slowed the video. It now progressed frame by single frame. As the water hit the surface of the meteorite, it seemed to froth or boil, and the meteorite's skin appeared to split apart and contract, exposing a glassy interior. It reminded Garza of a chrysalis splitting to release a butterfly.

Now the video slowed even more, one frame every second. The boiling of the water around the meteorite intensified, and the red skin of the rock peeled away explosively as the translucent insides appeared to swell; the water rushing into the hold frothed around it; a rippling flash of white light erupted from the interior of the meteorite; Glinn disappeared—and then the video froze.

"That," said Nishimura, "is the last frame before the feed went dark. I've enhanced it as much as possible."

The image showed the interior of the meteorite, filled with light; and there, suspended in the middle, was the brown, ropy, engorged, melon-shaped thing resembling a brain that they had seen encased in the trunk of the Baobab.

After lingering on this final image, the monitor went dark and the lights came up. After a moment, Glinn rose and, at last, faced the others. Garza was bathed in sweat, profoundly shaken by what he had seen. Reliving the nightmare had been bad enough, but witnessing the unexpected profession of love on the part of Britton, and the callous rejection by Glinn...It was too much.

Glinn was standing before them, silently. A strange expression was on his face. For a moment, Garza worried he would collapse again. A single shudder passed through his frame. And then the moment, whatever it was, passed. His look became as cool, as detached, as unreadable, as always.

He cleared his throat. "Dr. Nishimura and Dr. Sax are analyzing that final image, but it appears that on contact with salt water, the object, which as we now know was not a meteorite, underwent an explosive sprouting or hatching event." He glanced around. "We hope these last few seconds of footage will provide some insight into the creature's life cycle and vulnerabilities. In particular, whether that object inside the creature, visible in the final frame, is in fact its brain."

Glinn looked around. "Are there any questions?"

Total silence. People were too shaken up to ask questions now, although they would surely have some later. Having seen what happened, Garza marveled that Glinn had survived at all; the explosion, evidently tamped by water, had blown him free with just enough force to propel him beyond the sinking ship but not enough to kill him. Many others hadn't been so lucky; and some, like Britton, had refused to abandon ship.

"If anyone has any insights or theories," said Glinn, "please bring them privately to me. Recall that the details of what you have just seen should be kept confidential—for obvious reasons. And now, good morning."

And with that he turned and left the forensic lab without another word.

29

Rosemarie Wong was used to working in labs full of male jerks, but Prothero really took the cake. He was a jackass—a brilliant jackass. And not just brilliant, but a truly creative scientist, something as rare in science as it was in music or literature. He was someone who habitually thought outside the box, whose mind made startling connections across entire categories, who cleaved mundane reality to find the gem within, and whose acidic skepticism ate away at even the most universally accepted truths. Many of his intellectual leaps were crazy, but once in a while they were not. When she had started working with him two years ago, he had just gone through a string of lab assistants, one after the other, nobody lasting more than a few months. Wong had decided that, come hell or high water, she was going to get along with this prize ass because she believed he was a great scientist who, someday, was bound to go somewhere unusual. Somewhere important. And when that day came, she would be there with him.

In this, she had been spectacularly correct. This secret mission to the South Atlantic was giving Wong a chance to do science beyond her wildest dreams. Just to be part of humanity's first encounter with an alien life-form was mind blowing. If it meant she had to put up with world-class asininity, juvenile crudeness, and preteen temper tantrums on a daily basis, that was the price to pay. As a protective carapace, she had developed a sort of sarcastic, bantering relationship with him that seemed to earn at least a modicum of his respect—and kept his nasty temper at bay. She also had come to realize the vulgar nastiness was a form of respect: it was Prothero demonstrating to her that he wasn't going to treat her nicely or gently, because he considered her his equal.

"Wong, where the fuck is my hat?"

Prothero came around the corner of her work bay, holding a screwdriver in one hand and a motherboard in the other.

"It's on your head."

Prothero clapped his hand to his head—his bare head—and then grimaced. "Ha, ha. Where is it?"

"Probably in the bathroom, where you always leave it."

Prothero went out the door and came back a moment later, wearing his hipster hat. "Here's what I've been thinking: we're going to translate that whale signal."

"Translate it? As in, decipher whale-speak?"

"Exactly." He pulled up a chair backward and sat down. "And I know just how to do it. I've got the world's biggest collection of blue whale vocalizations, here in this lab. We're going to reverse-engineer it."

"So you think the Baobab is trying to *talk* to us?"

"That thing's been sitting there on the seafloor for, what, five years? Listening. And what does it hear? Well, two miles down there isn't much sound. The only sounds that carry that deep are whale vocalizations. Whale-talk is damned loud. It carries a hundred miles. You following me?"

"Yes."

"All right. So the Baobab is listening, listening, listening...and maybe it starts to figure out what the whales are saying. And now it's trying to communicate with us in the only language it knows."

This was one of those crazy Prothero leaps. "So what's it saying?" she asked.

"*I'll gladly pay you Tuesday for a hamburger today,*" said Prothero, and laughed hilariously at his own lame joke.

"Here's what I think," she said, when Prothero had stopped wheezing.

"You know I don't give a shit what you think. But tell me anyway."

"It's randomly playing back sounds it recorded. They mean nothing."

Prothero shook his head. "This thing's intelligent—I'll bet anything on that. And it's sending us a message."

"So how exactly are you going to translate it?"

"You mean, how are *you* going to translate it. *You*, Wong, are going to find the closest digital match between that Baobab sound and the blue whale vocalizations in my database. And then we're going to find out what the blue whale was doing when it was recorded making that sound—and that'll give us an idea of the meaning. Like, was the whale chasing prey? Was it a mother calling her calf? Was it fucking?" Prothero laughed again.

Wong shook her head. "If it's trying to communicate, why not by some other means than whale calls?"

"No doubt it's highly attuned to sound. Sound is the best way to communicate underwater. Electromagnetic fields dissipate, and light can't penetrate more than four or five hundred feet. This thing evolved to live in the dark depths of a watery world. It developed a sonar-resistant skin; it used sonar to "look" at Gideon Crew when he was down there collecting the wreck of *Paul*. Naturally it uses sound to communicate. And whale calls are all it has heard."

"*Digital* sound. Which means it's a machine. There's no way for a biological system to evolve so as to produce digital sound."

"Wong, Wong, Wong..." Prothero shook his head. "Maybe it's a machine, maybe it's a biological system, maybe it's a combination of the two. Whatever it is, *it's talking to us*. Now get your ass to work and find out what it's talking *about*."

30

Dr. Patrick Brambell chewed on a Mars bar as he stared pensively at the crushed ball that had formerly been the DSV *Paul*, sitting on a tarp in the hangar deck. The immediate area had been cordoned off with yellow curtains. Two engineers and as many roustabouts were wheeling in a bizarre device they had jerry-rigged in order to dismantle the submersible so they could extract the remains of Lispenard's body from the wreckage. It looked like nothing so much as a large, villainous Jaws of Life. Glinn stood silently in the background, taking in everything.

The workers began positioning the jaws of the contraption at two sides of the wreckage, in order to draw apart the wrinkled, shattered mass of the titanium sphere; huge eyebolts had been affixed at the two places and the machine was now set to draw them apart, unfolding the metal the way someone might unfold a balled-up piece of paper.

Brambell turned to his medical assistant, Rogelio, who was standing next to a polished stainless-steel gurney. This gurney was where they would reassemble the body. The idea did not overly disturb Brambell—he had seen far worse—but he was worried about his assistant, who looked a bit green around the gills.

"We must recover every, ah, piece, no matter how small," Brambell told the workers. Glinn's silent presence in the back made him nervous. He felt like a student teacher being monitored by the principal. He had never liked Glinn—the man was cold, remote, a cipher. Never mind the fact he was largely responsible for what had happened to the *Rolvaag*.

The assistant nodded weakly.

The "jaws" were affixed to each eyebolt and a deep hum started up as the machine began to spread them apart. With a creaking, cracking noise, the crumpled ball began to separate along its fracture zones, and water began draining from within it.

"Halt!" Brambell called. Immediately, the machine stopped. Rogelio rolled the gurney in close and, with large, rubber-tipped tweezers Brambell and his assistant began picking out mashed pieces of flesh and pulverized bone, mingled with bits of clothing, and laid them all out on the gurney in turn.

After a few moments he turned to the assistant. "Rogelio, how are you doing?"

"Hanging in there," Rogelio said in a strangled voice.

"Good man."

It took at least ten minutes to remove every little bit from the fissure in the wrinkled titanium, and then they backed off and signaled the engineers to continue.

The procedure went on for hours, prying first one piece of metal apart, then another, and another, in between stopping to pick out the remains, sometimes with the help of a portable magnifier on wheels with built-in illumination. At least it was a cool day, the good weather holding; the temperature inside the hangar was about sixty degrees—not bad, Brambell mused, for the preservation and handling of human remains. And a large proportion of the remains were of workable size, which was also a good thing: he'd feared the corpse might have been little more than tomato paste.

Slowly the body began to take shape on the gurney—in a grotesquely altered state. Brambell and his assistant had been able to identify virtually all of the pieces by a combination of their position in the wreck, the bone fragments, and the clothing present. By chance, they had started working from the feet upward. Brambell knew that recovering the head and skull would be the last, and most difficult, part.

As he worked, Brambell was mightily impressed by the immense forces that must have been applied to the submersible—especially the titanium sphere—to crush it so violently. In some areas, the pressure had been so intense and so sudden that it appeared to have softened or even melted the metal.

It was disagreeable work, and Rogelio bore up relatively well under it, not losing his lunch as Brambell had feared. The two roustabouts operating the machinery, and the two engineers, were another story: turning their backs, looking away whenever possible, averting their eyes assiduously to avoid seeing the remains to the point where Brambell had to speak to them sharply to keep their eyes on the job. Glinn, on the other hand, was just the opposite: watching the entire procedure in silence, face expressionless. He could have been observing a golf match. Nobody spoke except the fellows operating the jaws, and then only to communicate tersely about the equipment.

Now they separated the personnel sphere, laying the pieces out in jigsaw position on a large tarp spread precisely for that purpose. As they pried apart the last two large pieces, the upper torso, neck, and crushed head became visible.

Brambell glanced at Rogelio and was dismayed to see the man had gone pale. The two roustabouts were not even bothering to cover up their horror and disgust. An engineer turned away, retching. Only Glinn seemed unmoved.

"All right, let's keep going," said Brambell, moving in with a pair of rubber-tipped forceps and picking up the jaw, teeth and skin still adhering. He laid it all on the gurney. Another piece followed, then another. The face itself had survived almost entirely whole, flattened without being mashed to a pulp. Rogelio worked on the opposite side of the gurney while a great silence collected in the hangar. As they continued, Brambell found himself becoming disturbed by something. It wasn't the gruesomeness—it was an odd feeling that something was not quite right. But he said nothing. He didn't want to seem like a crank—or, worse, cause a panic.

As they neared the end of the dismantling process, the titanium sphere lay in neatly arranged and numbered pieces on the spread tarp, along with mashed equipment from inside the sphere. Everything had been thoroughly picked over by Brambell and Rogelio, and all the remains were laid out on the gurney. Brambell, bending over them, putting body pieces into place like a puzzle, felt a presence behind him. It was Glinn.

"Have you recovered all of the remains?" he murmured.

Brambell did not answer right away. He wondered just how to phrase it. Finally he said: "We'll know when we weigh the remains if a substantial portion is missing. Of course, we'll have to factor in the loss of blood and the infusion into the tissues of a certain amount of salt water..." He swallowed.

"Of course."

One of the roustabouts, having recovered somewhat, asked, "Why the hell did the creature crush up the DSV like this? Was it defense?"

"It happened right after Lispenard switched on her acetylene torch," said Glinn. "So I would say yes—it felt pain and reacted."

Brambell said nothing.

"I think it was fear," said the roustabout. "The thing was afraid."

Another silence, then Glinn turned to Brambell. "Doctor, you don't agree?"

Blast Glinn, he thought. "If it was a purely defensive action, why would the thing swallow it in the first place?"

"Part of that very defensive reaction."

"But Lispenard was trying to escape, not attack. It sucked her in. It wasn't afraid."

"What are you suggesting?" said Glinn.

You asked for it. "Think about what the DSV looked like when the thing expelled it," said Brambell. "All crushed up in a ball like that."

"Meaning?"

Brambell drew in an irritated breath. "As a child, I used to roam the Killarney National Forest with my brother Simon—may he rest in peace. Two would-be naturalists, collecting wee skeletons of mice and shrews. And we knew the best place to get them. Near owl nests."

"May I ask where this recollection is going?"

"It's a pellet," Brambell said flatly.

"A what?"

"A pellet. Like an owl pellet. Good God, man, need I be more plain?" He waved a hand at the remains—metal and organic both. "*It's a shite.*"

31

THE NUCLEAR WEAPON had been broken down in a most ingenious way, Gideon thought, so as to form six easily assembled pieces. Five of them were on racks, sealed and ready to go; the sixth, the gold-plated plutonium "pit," had been housed elsewhere and would have to be loaded last, using special equipment.

The room was deep in the bowels of the ship, the close air smelling faintly of diesel fuel. Gideon gazed at the deadly pieces and considered the situation. The main body of the nuke was like two halves of a giant beach ball, already sporting slow and fast high-explosive lenses. The initiator was in a separate package, smaller than a golf ball and sealed in heavy lead foil. The detonators were in the fourth package, attached to wires, ready to be inserted into the brass chimney sleeves. The fifth package contained the small computer into which the detonator wires would be plugged and would—ultimately—send out the detonation signal.

Garza would soon be delivering, at Glinn's orders, the final package containing the plutonium. Once he'd done that, the assembly sequence was simple. And then the bomb would be ready for arming.

The racks had been specially engineered to allow a single person, using computer-controlled mechanical assists and a ceiling winch, to assemble the bomb in about an hour. Testing would take another hour. Gideon was amazed at the elegant, beautifully simple engineering work Garza had done. As long as you knew what you were doing, it was almost as simple as putting together a set of shelves from Ikea.

Stuff like this didn't exactly grow on trees. He wondered once again just how much EES had spent in order to procure it.

The actual arming of the bomb wouldn't happen until just before it was to be used. It would be armed with a code, nicknamed ARM, to be entered into the computer by keypad. Only Glinn, Gideon, and Garza knew the code. The countdown to detonation could then be started with a simple keypress on that same keypad—or by a remote-located computer in mission control.

But the nuke—as Glinn had previously explained—had a fail-safe mechanism built into it. This was a second code, ABORT, that would immediately stop the countdown.

Again, only the three of them knew the abort code.

Gideon frowned. The more he thought about this arrangement, the less he liked it. His dislike was due in part to Lispenard's horrible death. But it was also a result of the rumors swirling about the ship: that the sonic signals emitted by the creature were a form of communication; that, in its years sitting on the bottom of the sea, it had learned the only language it heard—whale-speak—and was now trying to communicate with them. If that were the case, it meant the Baobab was intelligent. It wasn't some unthinking life-form operating on instinct, like a shark. It *knew* what it was doing.

It was evil. And yet it was—or might be—sentient. Even intelligent.

He did not like the idea that Garza or Glinn had the opportunity to stop the countdown and abort the bomb at the mere stroke of a key. Glinn did not particularly worry him: even though he was the one who'd refused to use the dead man's switch on the *Rolvaag*, Gideon understood this time around the man's deep animus toward the creature, his obsessive, Ahab-like desire to kill it. But he didn't trust Garza. While he knew they all shared the same goal, the death of Lispenard and the creature's attempt at communication had transformed Gideon's view of the life-form growing underneath them. He was a different man from the one who had begun this mission, deeply concerned at the idea of setting off a nuclear explosion. He understood now the threat the entire planet faced if this malevolent thing was allowed to reproduce and spread. There could be no hesitation or pusillanimity in killing it.

And that was the problem. He had yet to complete the complex computer simulations modeling what would happen when a hundred-kiloton nuke was detonated two miles deep, either directly under or within triggering distance from the ship. Would the water diminish the effects of the blast—or magnify them? Air was a forgiving and flexible medium that allowed the force of such a blast to expand and disperse. But what would happen in an incompressible medium such as water under the pressure of four hundred atmospheres? And how would that affect the *Batavia*? It seemed to him that, at the very least, a gigantic eruption of steam would break the surface. The P-wave, traveling through water perhaps dozens of miles, could easily rupture the hull. And he was pretty sure it would generate a tsunami-type disturbance on the surface that might swamp or overturn the ship. When all the effects became known—and he would soon have to provide them with the results of his simulations—Gideon didn't want Garza chickening out. He wanted to make sure that, once he assembled the bomb, he could arm and detonate it—and that no one could stop it.

No: he wasn't worried about Glinn. The man had nerves of steel. But Garza...he was the cautious one. Even after the device was armed and the countdown started, the man might change his mind about the whole plan, decide it was too dicey, and code in ABORT before Gideon could stop him.

That could not be allowed to happen.

Gideon reached out and picked up the computer controller, peeling off its metallicized plastic wrap. He hefted it. It was a stainless-steel box about three by three by six inches, with a key-pad, plus input and output ports. Inside was a single-function computer. Nothing overly complex. Nothing that couldn't be re-programmed.

Gideon had to smile.

32

Despite herself, Wong was mightily impressed by Prothero's library of whale sounds, which he claimed was the largest in the world. At his request, she had devised a small program that scanned that database of audio files, looking for any matches with the sounds emitted by the Baobab. She had come up with two solid hits and several partials. As she finished the final run, she heard a stomping in the hall outside the lab and knew it was Prothero returning. His ridiculous Doc Marten boots made an unmistakable sound on the steel plating of the ship.

"So," he said, removing his hipster hat and flinging it down on a table piled with junk. "What's taking you so long?"

"I just finished."

Prothero pulled up a chair, swept some printouts onto the floor, and sat down. "What you got?"

"Two pretty close matches."

"Let's hear them."

She played the Baobab sound first, as a control, and then the two similar sounds from Prothero's whale database, all sped up ten times to put the pitch into the best range for human listening.

Prothero grunted. "Play those hits again, first the whale, then the Baobab."

She ran through them again in reverse order.

"That's close! So—did you look up the circumstances when the two whale calls were recorded?"

"I did. The first recording was made by a Greenpeace vessel a few years ago, about five hundred miles south of Tasmania. It had been shadowing a Japanese whaler. This was the sound the whale made as it was dying, after being hit by two penthrite grenade-armed harpoons by the Japanese."

"Fucking barbarians. And the other one?"

"That was recorded by a Woods Hole oceanographic vessel from a blue whale stranded and dying on a sandbar on Sable Island, off the coast of Nova Scotia. Some kind of virus had interfered with its internal navigation, apparently, and it beached itself. It died not long after."

"Both dying sounds..." Prothero was silent for a long time, his brow furrowed. Finally he stirred, picked his nose. "What do you think?"

"I still think the creature was merely repeating, parrot-like, a whale sound it had heard."

Prothero made a face. "Just tell me what you think it *means*. I mean, to the whales that made the sound. We'll deal with the Baobab later."

"My first thoughts were that it might have been a cry for help, or maybe a growl of warning or fear. Or the equivalent of a whale death-scream."

"Did you find any other matches?"

"Only partials. Some matched the first part of the Baobab's sound, some matched the second."

"Play those."

She played a few of them.

"Hmmm. Notice how all these whale utterances tend to fall into one of two categories. Two *words*. Some sound like one word; some like the other." Prothero scratched himself. "So tell me under what circumstances those partials were made, starting with the first. What was going on when it was recorded?"

"That sound was made by a pod of three blue whales, all together, when one was attacked by a gang of orcas. The blue whales managed to drive off the killer whales through ramming and blows of their tail flukes. They made those sounds as they were doing it."

Another grunt from Prothero.

Wong reached toward her equipment. "Let me replay the other, similar sounds."

Prothero waved his hand. "You don't have to. I already know what they mean."

"You do?"

"Yeah," said Prothero. "You hear it all the time in pods of whales as they're traveling together. Lone whales never make the sound. It's one of the first 'words' I was able to translate."

Wong was surprised. "You've already *translated* some blue whale speech?"

"Yeah. Don't tell anyone." Prothero made a face. "I intend to publish someday."

"So what does it mean?"

"That sound is the whale referring to itself. It means 'me' or 'I.'"

"Wow. So what do you think the initial sound means?"

"It's a verb. That much I'm sure of."

"Whales have verbs?"

"Sure they do. All they do is move. Everything to a whale is movement or activity. I think the entire blue whale language is made up of verb-like sounds."

"Okay." This did not sound very scientific to Wong, but she was in no mood to argue with Prothero.

"It's a verb, and it's used by whales that are dying, or whales that are trying to drive off attacking orcas. I think it's pretty obvious what it means." He gave her a superior smirk. "You don't get it?"

"No."

"It means *kill*."

"Kill?"

"Exactly. Think about it. What's a whale's going to say that's dying in agony from a Japanese harpoon? *Kill me.* What are whales saying as they chase a gang of orcas? *Kill, kill!* That's what the Baobab was saying over and over to us, that's the Baobab's message to us. *Kill* is the first word and *me* is the second."

"That's crazy," said Wong.

Prothero shrugged. "It may be crazy, but that's the message it's sending. It's telling us something, urgently. And that something is: *Kill me.*"

33

Barry Frayne was tired. It was ten o'clock at night and the exo lab had been going almost nonstop since noon, when the long, string-like tentacle had arrived and Glinn had ordered Dr. Sax to prepare it for study. Frayne reported directly to Sax, and his lab contained the front-line workers, the prep guys, the bio grunts. Each guy—and as it happened they were all guys—was a specialist in a particular area of biological lab preparation. Under Sax's scrutiny, they had done sections for microscope, TEM, and SEM studies; they had set up biochemical assays; they had done pre-dissections and dissected out unusual inclusions and organelles for analysis. All of this had then gone out to specialized labs elsewhere on the ship. They were, you might say, the heavy lifters, the prep cooks who got everything ready for the PhDs to work on.

Frayne at least had an MA, but the other three guys just had college degrees. Didn't matter: they were all good at what they did.

The gross and fine anatomy of the tentacle, or root, or spaghetti, or worm—a lot of crazy nicknames had been proposed—was stunningly different from any biological organism Frayne had seen before. It was hard to tell whether it was even a plant or animal, or perhaps it was neither. It had cells, or membrane-enclosed packages with interior cytoplasm—that, at least, looked normal. Beyond that, nothing was recognizable. Inside the "cells" there were no normal-looking organelles, no nuclei, endoplasmic reticulum, mitochondria, or Golgi bodies. Nor did the thing have the types of organelles you'd expect to see in plant cells: chloroplasts, dermata, vacuoles, or rigid cell walls. There were things inside the cells, of course, but they looked like complex inorganic crystals. They glittered like diamonds in the light of the microscope, and seemed to come in different colors, although that appeared to be iridescence or light refraction. Frayne had isolated a bunch and sent them off to be analyzed. He was curious to know what they were.

The narrow tentacle had no blood vessels that he could see, nor phloem or xylem channels for the movement of fluid. Instead, it had an incredibly dense and complex tangle of fine microfibrils like nerves or wires, wrapped in bundles. They were very hard to cut and seemed to be stiffened with something equivalent to plant cellulose, though of a different material, more like inorganic mineral than woody fiber. But what was strangest of all was that, when you really got down to it, there was nothing in the tentacle that actually looked like living tissue. It looked instead like an incredibly finely built machine.

Sax had been in and out, supervising the work. He knew she'd seen the same things he had—she *must* have. But she'd kept her thoughts to herself.

Now he finished up on the microtome, placed it on a slide, sealed it, labeled it, and slotted it into the holder. It was the last one, and they were almost through—as long as Sax didn't come back with yet another last-minute request.

"Hey, Barry, take a look at this."

Frayne looked up and walked over to where one of his co-workers, Waingro, was standing over the main length of tentacle, getting ready to slide it back into cold storage. The thing lay coiled like a thin rope in its shallow tray.

"What's up?"

"Look at it. It's shorter."

"Of course it's shorter. We've been cutting off sections."

"No," said Waingro. "I mean, before the last break we took, I could swear it was longer."

While they were talking, Reece, another lab assistant, came over and stared down.

Frayne turned to him. "What do you think? Is it shorter?"

Reece nodded. "Yup."

"You...you think someone swiped a piece?" Frayne asked. He was alarmed. They had locked the lab when they left for their last break, but they hadn't locked up the tentacle. They weren't working in sterile conditions—that would have been an unacceptable impediment to the speed being demanded of them. They were taking their chances that the thing didn't infect them with some exotic disease or pathogen. But that seemed highly unlikely, given how far from human biology the thing clearly was. Still, when they left the lab, they always locked it as a precaution.

"I wouldn't be surprised," said Reece. "Make somebody a hell of a souvenir."

Frayne felt a swell of irritation. "Let's take it out and measure it. We'd better be sure."

Still gowned up and wearing latex, the four unlocked the specimen tray and removed the thing. It was hard and stiff, like a piece of cable. They kept it under refrigeration, but it sure didn't look like it would deteriorate or rot if kept at room temperature. It wasn't edible to any earth-origin microbes. And coming up from four hundred atmospheres to one didn't seem to have altered it at all. The thing was, essentially, weird as shit.

Working with care, they laid it out on the long, stainless work-table, which had built-in measuring marks.

"Six hundred eighty centimeters," said Frayne. He pulled a clipboard down from the wall and scanned it. "It was originally eight hundred and nine." He started adding up in his head the pieces they had removed; thirty centimeters for sectioning; forty for dissection; ten for biochemical assays; five for miscellaneous.

"We're forty-four centimeters short," he said. He looked around. "Did anyone forget to log a removal?"

No one had. And Frayne believed them: they were all careful workers. You didn't get to be on a project like this if your lab work was sloppy.

"Looks like someone couldn't be bothered to make a request through ordinary channels. Liberated a piece for themselves."

"You think they just came in and cut off a piece?" asked Stahlweather, the fourth assistant.

"What else am I to think?"

"But the lab was locked during break."

"So? Lot of people have keys. Especially the ones who think themselves important enough not to have to follow the rules."

Heads nodded all around.

"I'll have to put in a report about this to Sax and Glinn," said Frayne. "They're not going to be happy about it. And this happened on our watch."

"Maybe Glinn did it."

"Or that asshole Garza."

More nods. This was a likely explanation. And it would deflect blame from them.

Frayne looked around. "Time to close up shop. The top brass won't like the fact that somebody liberated a piece of that thing. But you know what? We followed procedure. And you guys put in a good day—well done."

"Speaking of liberation..." Reece climbed onto a stool and reached up to the top of a cabinet, slipped his hand deep out of sight. Waingro was smiling knowingly.

Reece produced a gallon jug of red wine. "I think we owe it to ourselves to have a little party."

Frayne stared. "What, with that rotgut?"

"And what if Sax comes back?" Stahlweather asked. "Now that we're at the work site, it's ix-nay on any drinking."

"Come come, the speakeasy is open for business. Sax isn't coming back—not tonight." Reece's smile grew broader. He reached up again to the hidden store and brought down a bottle of brandy, another of triple sec, and a bag of oranges and lemons. "Sangria, anyone?"

34

It was by now after dawn and Patrick Brambell was mightily relieved to be alone in his medical quarters, without Glinn or his assistant, Rogelio, breathing down his neck. He wanted to be alone, to think, to contemplate, to figure this thing out. He never could think clearly when there were other people around, and he was particularly relieved that he'd gotten rid of the shadowy presence of Glinn, lurking in the background like a specter. That, and the four workers in the adjoining exobiology lab, who—hours before—had grown as boisterous as a bloody frat party and he'd almost had to go tell them to pipe down.

In the silence, he got back to work.

In front of him, arranged with precision on the gurney, were the remains of Alexandra Lispenard. It was a singularly gruesome sight, much of it looking like coarse-ground hamburger mingled with mashed bits of flesh, shot through with shreds of clothing, strands of hair, and fragments of bone. Having arranged and re-arranged just about every piece over the course of the last several hours, he had become thoroughly numbed and now gazed upon the scene not with horror but with scientific detachment.

The problem, he mused, was simple. If the crushed DSV was indeed a pellet—a shite—then the creature had to have absorbed some nourishment from it, the same way an owl ate a rodent whole, digested its flesh, and expelled the bones and fur. Nothing else made sense. The DSV seemed intact, nothing missing or dissolved, and besides it was hard to imagine the creature eating metal, glass, or plastic. It seemed much more likely it had digested or absorbed some of Lispenard.

He wondered exactly what that might be. It could have been her blood: naturally, the body was completely drained of blood, all five liters of it. But he remembered from the video of the recovery of *Paul* that there had been a faint cloud of blood trailing away from the crushed DSV when it was first discovered.

So the creature probably hadn't absorbed the blood. It had washed away.

What he needed to do was weigh the body and see how much, if any, was missing. That could help him determine what had been absorbed.

He called up Lispenard's chart on his computer and noted that her weight had been fifty-eight point eight kilograms. With the blood gone, that would lighten the remains by five kilograms, for a total weight of fifty-three point eight kilograms. The amount of wet clothing embedded in the remains, he calculated, was about one kilogram.

The gurney came with a built-in scale. He unlocked its weighing latch, activated the keypad, and waited while the digital screen ran through the kilograms.

It stopped at fifty-three point three kilograms.

So the body was missing about one and a half kilograms of weight. Some of that might be pieces they'd missed, or other liquids, such as lymph or bile, that had dispersed into the ocean.

But some, if not most, of that liquid would have been replaced by salt water. Brambell was pretty sure he'd gotten every last piece of her. They'd been fanatical about it, and the pieces had sort of clung together in a stringy way, one leading to the next.

What part of the human body weighed one point five kilograms?

The answer came to him immediately. The brain.

Brambell exhaled loudly in chagrin at his stupidity. Here he had carefully assembled the face and skull on the gurney: ears, nose, lips, hair, the works. But he'd forgotten about the brain. Where was it? He bent over the gurney, but there was no trace of it. Could they have overlooked it when extracting the body from *Paul?*

No. Impossible.

Could the brain, which was also watery, have dissolved and drifted away in the extreme water pressure?

The feeling he'd had when they'd taken apart *Paul*, back on the hangar deck—the feeling that something wasn't quite right—came back again now, full force.

He picked up a pair of rubber tweezers and leaned over the assembled cranium, turning over the largest pieces of skull. The inside of the cranium was totally clean—licked clean, one might even say. Even the dura membranes normally found inside the cranium were gone—gone completely. And those were tough.

He pulled the tray of surgical tools close and carefully dissected the first two cervical vertebrae, C1 and C2. They had survived the crushing fairly intact. He quickly located the main anatomical points, the dens of axis and the transverse ligament of axis. With the utmost care he rotated C1 and teased apart the partially crushed mess to expose the vertebral foramen. There, inside, he found the spinal cord enclosed in the thecal sac. The top of it, right where the cord emerged from C1 and connected to the medulla oblongata, looked precisely as if it had been cut with a scalpel. Indeed, it had a seared aspect that suggested heat had been involved.

"Bloody hell," Brambell muttered to himself. He was utterly discomposed. Had the creature eaten the brain? But no: that didn't seem likely, given such a clean-cut removal. Rather, the bastard had—with almost surgical precision—*taken* the brain.

Brambell backed away from the gurney, a feeling in the pit of his stomach that was not good. He took a few deep, shuddering breaths. And then, recovering himself, he did a quick bioassay of the brain stem. Then he pulled off his gloves, hung up his apron, washed his hands, straightened his lab coat—and went off to look for Glinn.

35

GIDEON CREW STOOD with Glinn and Manuel Garza at the foredeck rail. They were speaking in low tones. Their conversation was about the nature of the Baobab, but as usual it seemed to wander into wild speculations and crazy theories. It frustrated Gideon that, even now, they had so little hard evidence on the thing. They didn't know even the basics: was it a machine or a life-form, or some bizarre combination of the two? Was it intelligent—or just a dumb plant? This lack of information was becoming a serious problem on board ship, because the resulting vacuum was being filled with rumor and speculation.

At least the remarkable weather was still holding, the ocean as calm as a millpond. Every day brought them closer to summer, and the calving of the icebergs seemed to be accelerating in the advancing spring weather. As Gideon looked out, he counted six stately bergs dotting the sea. The rising sun hung low, casting a golden pathway over the water. The calmness of the scene belied the turbulent atmosphere on the ship.

"Excuse me, gentlemen?"

Gideon turned to see Dr. Patrick Brambell approaching, looking neat as a pin, but with such a concerned expression on his normally placid face that Gideon grew instantly alarmed.

"Dr. Brambell?" said Glinn.

Brambell came up with tentative steps, hands clasped together. "I've completed the autopsy," he said. "Of Lispenard," he added, unnecessarily.

Gideon felt a tightness in his chest. He had viciously suppressed all thoughts of Alex, which otherwise seemed to erupt regularly out of nowhere and stagger his peace of mind. But this he had to hear. He waited.

"Well?" Glinn asked when Brambell didn't go on.

"The brain is missing," said Brambell.

"What do you mean, missing?"

"Absolutely missing. Not a trace of it, not a trace." The words came tumbling out, his Irish brogue heavier than usual. "It appears to have been removed at the brain stem, severed as if with a scalpel, and with evidence of the application of searing heat. I did a quick section and bioassay, and found that the proteins at the site of the removal had denatured—proof of heat."

Gideon stared at him. "Removed? Not crushed?"

Brambell ran a hand across his bald head. "It appears the brain was removed *before* the skull was crushed—otherwise there would have been traces of it on the inside of the skull, neural matter forced into the fractures. But no—there's no trace of gray or white matter anywhere in the remains. Not even microscopic traces. The Baobab seems to have...well..."

His face collapsed into confusion.

"Eaten it?" Garza completed the sentence.

Listening, Gideon heard himself tense up.

"That's what I thought at first. But if it was going to be absorbed as nourishment, why remove it intact? And I have no doubt it *was* removed. What happened to it after that, I don't have a clue—eaten, absorbed, whatever."

"Scanned?" Gideon heard himself ask.

Garza turned sharply. "What do you mean by that?"

"Her brain was removed intact," Gideon said. "Why? Maybe the creature wanted to interrogate it, download its contents— that would be a good reason to take the brain out undamaged."

"Improbable," said Garza. "To say the least."

"Think about Alex's final message. *Let me touch your face.* She was in contact with something. She spoke—or, at least, her brain did."

"If your theory is true," said Garza, "how did she speak? She had no mouth—her body was crushed."

Gideon winced inwardly. *Don't remind me.* He tried to stay focused, to think through the problem logically. "Her brain, removed intact, spoke through the creature. *Let me touch your face.* Her brain was in contact with something, but her brain was confused, disoriented. I mean, it had just been removed from her body."

Garza's face displayed broad irritation. He shook his head. "Good God, if this isn't pure science fiction."

There was a long silence. Glinn, as usual, took everything in while displaying an impassive face. *Maybe Garza's right*, Gideon thought: *maybe it is science fiction.* It sounded pretty ridiculous in retrospect. But he wasn't going to give Garza the satisfaction of admitting it.

"And there's another little thing," Brambell said after a moment.

Glinn raised his eyebrows.

"It seems someone swiped part of the specimen from exo lab. The four lab assistants kept a log of all sections removed, but there's a large piece missing—and no one seems to know where it went. Did any of you by any chance take a piece without logging it?"

Garza turned an accusatory stare on Gideon.

"Not me," said Gideon. Garza was proving to be a bigger pain in the ass than usual this morning.

"None of us would have done anything that irresponsible," said Glinn crisply.

"Well," said Brambell, "the lab might have made a mistake in its initial measurement of the tentacle. Or maybe they forgot to log a removal." He cleared his throat. "Or perhaps the whole thing is a smokescreen to conceal unprofessional behavior. I say this because those four gentlemen had a party last night in the lab—when I passed the lab just now on the way here I found the remains of a bash, the four of them fluthered and washing the barroom floor, so to speak."

"You mean, passed out?" Garza asked.

"That is precisely what I mean. The only one conscious was Frayne—if you can call it conscious—and it was he who told me of the missing piece of tentacle."

"Where are they now?"

"Speak of the devil." And Brambell turned as Frayne himself approached. His lab coat was stained with purple, and he stank of wine. He looked like hell. Frayne didn't strike Gideon as the partying type—but there he was, obviously hung over.

Glinn stepped aside as Garza turned on the man. "What the hell's this?" he demanded.

Frayne began explaining, in a bumbling sort of way, that they'd had a bit of a sangria party, but nothing outrageous—

Garza cut him off with a gesture. "What about the missing specimen?"

At this, Frayne launched into a complex, rambling explanation, claiming it had happened long before the party, wasn't their fault, they kept impeccable records, someone had probably stolen it for a souvenir, and anyway they really hadn't drunk all that much...

"You know the rules," said Garza. "No drinking once the ship came on station. I'm docking you a week's pay. And because you're the chief assistant, I want you to report to the brig for twelve hours—and to get some sleep."

"Brig?" The man looked devastated. "You mean, jail?"

"Yes. Brig. Jail. I'll have a security detail meet you there."

"But—"

Garza stared hard at him until the man wilted and slunk off. Then he turned to Glinn. "This sort of lapse in discipline is like poison on board ship. I hope you agree with me."

A faint incline of the head indicated Glinn's agreement. And then, after consulting his watch, he turned to Gideon. "We'd best wrap this up," he said. "You and I are needed in Prothero's lab."

36

GIDEON CROWDED WITH several others into the small, messy lab. It was like an electronic cave. An acrid smell of solder and burnt electronics hung in the stuffy air. Prothero was sitting at a rack of computer and audio components, cables dangling everywhere, wearing a dirty Hawaiian shirt, half unbuttoned. His concave, white chest, covered with a scattering of wiry black hairs, was hideous.

Standing to one side was Prothero's assistant, the tall, thin, elegant woman named Rosemarie Wong. She looked exactly like Prothero's antithesis. Gideon wondered how she could stand working with him.

"Sorry there's no place to sit," said Prothero, gesturing at two chairs, both stacked high with stuff. "I keep telling you I need a bigger lab. This one sucks."

Glinn ignored the comment. "Dr. Prothero, tell us what you've found."

Prothero began hammering away on a keyboard. "In a word: we did it. We translated the message from the Baobab. Hey, Wong? Play the tape."

She keyed up a tape and moments later the song of a blue whale came through, followed by the sound that had been generated by the Baobab. Prothero talked at length about the nature of blue whale language.

Gideon felt himself getting increasingly vexed. "So what does it mean?" he finally interrupted.

"I want to warn you: the message is kind of strange." Prothero rolled his eyes dramatically. "The thing said—" He hesitated— "*Kill me. Kill me.*"

"How sure are you of this hypothesis?" asked Glinn.

"I'm pretty damn sure. If you'd let me explain..." And explain Prothero did, again at length, playing the tape one more time, and then playing other recorded blue whale sounds, elucidating in self-congratulatory tones how they'd broken down the sounds, deduced the meanings, verified their findings.

Gideon, despite his skepticism, found himself impressed—but not convinced. When Prothero was finished, he asked: "So why would the creature be begging us to kill it? Especially after destroying one of our DSVs?"

Prothero shrugged. "That's for you guys to figure out."

"How do you know it's not just mimicking blue whale sounds it heard?"

"Blue whale speech travels a hundred miles or more in water. So this thing's been hearing all sorts of blue whale vocalizations. Why would it repeat just this one? No, my friend, it's *communicating* with us."

The "my friend" part especially grated on Gideon. "If this is communication, it makes no sense."

"Maybe it's confused," said Prothero, shrugging. "Maybe it's like the guy who goes to France and makes an ass of himself trying to speak the language." He brayed loudly.

"We're dealing with an alien life-form," said Glinn. "Possibly an alien intelligence. It doesn't surprise me we wouldn't understand its first attempt to communicate."

Gideon shook his head, then glanced at Wong. She was keeping her cards close. "What do you think, Rosemarie?"

Wong gave a little cough. "I think Gideon may be right. It may just be playing back sounds, like a parrot."

Gideon felt gratified. His opinion of Wong and her intelligence rose still further.

"Well, if science were a democracy, I guess I'd be wrong then," said Prothero, adding: "But it ain't—and I'm right." And he laughed again, raucously.

At that moment the warrant officer, Mr. Lund, appeared at the door. "Dr. Glinn?"

"I was not to be disturbed."

"We've got an emergency. The Baobab—it's starting to become active."

37

By the time Glinn and Gideon arrived in the control center, it was a hive of activity. Glinn took his position at the central command console and Gideon stood to his right, at the secondary console. Chief Officer Lennart came up smartly, carrying an iPad.

"Brief me," Glinn asked quietly.

"Very well. About twenty minutes ago, the surface sonobuoys began to register some unusual sounds coming from below. They were very similar to the types of P-waves that come from small temblors on the ocean floor, around one point five to two on the Richter scale. When we mapped the sources, we found they were clustered around the Baobab, but not coming from it."

"Is it on the ship's net? Bring it up."

Lennart hit some keys on the console keyboard and a seismic map appeared.

Glinn frowned, staring at it, Gideon looking on. "Seems to form a roughly circular pattern around the creature."

"Yes."

"Can you tell how deep the temblors originate?"

"Shallow. At least, by seismic standards: a few hundred feet below the seafloor. But as we monitored, we noticed the temblors appear to be going deeper, and occurring farther away from the creature—basically, in a spreading and deepening ring."

"As if the thing was extending its root system?"

"Perhaps. And that's not all. As you know, we dropped a camera and anchored it to the seafloor, trained on the Baobab, monitoring it in green light. We've seen no unusual activity—until now. We've just begun to see some movement of the creature itself."

"What kind of movement?"

"A swaying motion in the branches. Very slow. And the mouth, or suction hole, has extended itself several times while inspiring and expelling large amounts of seawater. The amplitude of the two-hertz sound it emits has gone up."

"I want a detailed analysis of the temblors," Glinn said. "With three-D mapping in real time."

"Very good."

There was a sudden commotion to the right, and a technician came running up. "A DSV, *George*, has just gone missing."

Glinn frowned. "Missing? Aren't they under lock and key—and alarmed?"

"The thief evaded electronic security."

"Who was it?"

The technician spoke into his headphones, then listened. "They're not sure, but it might have been a lab assistant named Frayne."

"Frayne?" Gideon asked. "Isn't he in the brig?"

The man listened for another moment. "He never arrived at the brig. They've had a detail looking for him, but it seems he managed to sneak down to the DSV hangar. They're reviewing security video now . . . yeah, it's definitely him."

"Was he still drunk?"

"They don't seem to have information on that. Wait... They're saying he smelled of liquor."

"How did Frayne get the DSV in the water?" Gideon asked. "It takes a crew to launch."

"He seems to have had help. We're still figuring that one out. Again, they're reviewing the tapes, trying to determine exactly what happened."

"Where's he taking the DSV?"

"Straight down, it seems. Fast. No response on any frequencies."

"Prepare *John* right away," Glinn said. Then he turned to Gideon. "Get over to the hangar deck. You're going down after him."

38

Twenty minutes later, Gideon was in the water, watching once again through the forward viewport as the DSV sank into blue darkness. They hadn't gone through the usual safety checklist, but *John* had been used so recently that they assumed—correctly, Gideon hoped—that one was unnecessary.

It was unbelievable—Frayne, drunk and joyriding a ten-million-dollar mini sub. If it was indeed joyriding. But what else it might be, Gideon couldn't even hazard a guess. Revenge? Some crazy suicide mission to kill the creature?

Gideon was descending at the maximum allowable rate, with the control room monitoring his DSV through the wired connection to the surface. He might have to drop the wire if extensive maneuvering were involved on the seafloor, but for now he had a good connection to the ship. Which, at least, was a comfort: they were seeing everything he was, in real time, as well as monitoring his mini sub and its life-support systems.

The viewport had now turned black. A few bubbles flared white as they passed upward through the light of the DSV's headlamps. He had a sonar lock on *George*: it was about three thousand feet below him, but he was catching up quickly. Frayne, he knew, was a rank novice in DSV handling, and he was no doubt having difficulty maneuvering. At the rate he was descending, he calculated he'd catch up with Frayne a few thousand feet above the seafloor.

Looking through the viewport, he strained to get a visual on *George*'s lights. But he knew it was fruitless; he wouldn't see them until they were about five hundred feet apart.

What the hell he was going to do when he caught up with Frayne was still being discussed in mission control. If he wasn't able to persuade him to turn around and return to the *Batavia*, there were various options—but all of them were difficult and dangerous. The technicians above were trying to prioritize and work them out, step by step.

There was no manual on this one.

The interior of the sub felt particularly claustrophobic. He hadn't had time to psychologically prepare himself for the descent—hadn't even had time to change his clothes. He had dressed for the cool morning air of the south, and he was now hot and sweaty, his shirt itching around his collar. He watched as the meters ticked off on the depth gauge. He was six hundred meters from the bottom; any moment, and *George* should come into sight.

And there it was: a blurry blob of light directly below him.

"Got a visual fix," he reported.

"Keep descending," Glinn's voice crackled through his headset. "Try to match his rate and come up beside him."

"Copy."

The blob began to resolve itself into a wavering cluster of lights. Gideon increased his descent rate slightly into the red, impatient to catch up before they reached the bottom. God only knew what Frayne was planning to do, and he wanted to stop him well before they came within the purview of the creature.

Now the outlines of *George* began to materialize.

"Hail him," said Glinn.

Gideon turned up the gain on the UQC. "*George*, this is *John*. Acknowledge."

Nothing.

He repeated the call. Still no response. He was catching up fast, and now he paused to slow his own descent, to position his sub to ensure it was not directly above *George* but safely to one side.

"Frayne? Do you read?"

No answer.

"Hey, Barry! It's Gideon Crew. Can you hear me?"

Silence.

"Look, Barry, can we please talk? What's going on?"

Now he was only about thirty meters above *George*. He could see the clear outline of the DSV, see the dull red glow from the viewports, see the mech arm folded up in descent position. He slowed still further as the two mini subs closed in until he was almost matching its speed. In a moment he'd be able to look directly into *George*. God, maybe Frayne was unconscious, passed out.

He finally drifted level with *George* and peered through the side viewport. He was surprised to see Frayne, not passed out, but looking perfectly normal, working the controls with focus and calm.

And the man didn't look in his direction. Not even a glance.

Gideon waved. "Hey, Barry. Look at me, will you please?"

No recognition that the man had heard.

Gideon glanced at the depth monitor. They were closing in on the bottom. If he didn't stop soon, the AI would kick in and slow him down; so would the AI of *George*. Neither submersible would be allowed to slam into the seafloor.

"Frayne? Can you hear me?"

No response.

Gideon switched to a private frequency to speak with mission control. "Can he hear me?" he asked.

"He certainly can. And he can hear us, too. We know his UQC is on and at full gain."

"It's as if he's a robot."

"We can see that."

"Can't you transfer control to the surface and just bring his DSV back up, like you did to me?"

"He's got the override sequence," Glinn told him. "We don't know how. Nobody is supposed to have it but me, Garza, and the maintenance technicians."

"Jesus, what a balls-up." Gideon shook his head. They hadn't even given the sequence to him. He'd take that up with Glinn later.

"Okay," said Glinn. "Listen closely. If he won't respond, the technicians here say there's a way for you to disable *George*."

A schematic image of *George* flashed on his screen. Glinn's voice went on, cool and even. "We want you to use your science arm for a simple procedure. His DSV has six thrusters. Insert the end of the arm into each thruster, wrecking the blades. They say you'll only need to disable three to leave *George* DIW. Then we can attach a tow cable and haul it up."

"There's no other way besides wrecking the thrusters?"

"Everything else that's vulnerable is protected by the outer hull. What we're suggesting is simple and foolproof. We're temporarily modifying the AI on your DSV so that it can be done— otherwise, it would be prevented."

"Roger. Will do." Now he saw, out the lower viewport, the faint outlines of the seafloor, just coming into illumination. At the same time he felt the autopilot begin to slow the sub.

"I can see bottom," he said.

"AI modifications complete. Move in and perform the disabling maneuver as quickly as possible."

"*George* is slowing, too—and veering off."

"Pursue."

Gideon maneuvered his joystick and accelerated to the max. But *George* was also moving at full speed, parallel to the seafloor. It seemed that Frayne was growing more accustomed to the mini sub's controls.

"He's heading for the Baobab," said Glinn. "The creature's active. Very active. Stay well away from it."

"I've got it floored—I just can't catch up."

And now Gideon could see the faint outline of the creature, resolving itself in the glow of their headlight bars. It was moving—rippling—and the trunk was swelling frightfully, as if filling with water.

"It's extruding its mouthparts," said Glinn. "The Doppler sonar is picking up a current."

Suddenly *George* angled upward, straight toward the extruding mouth. The funnel-like orifice was swelling with water and swinging toward the sub, pulsing and gaping.

"Break off!" Glinn ordered Frayne over the public channel. "Retreat!"

The *George* accelerated, caught in the current. Even as the order came in, Gideon could feel his own DSV being drawn upward and inward. Gideon jammed the joystick sideways, trying to get out of the current. He felt *John* being tugged toward the creature, heard the all-too-familiar thrumming of water along the hull...but then his vessel broke free, wobbling in the sudden turbulence. He immediately reversed course, pulling away from the monstrous creature and retreating at full speed. Reaching a safe distance, he stopped and turned back...

...And then he watched, horrified, as *George*—drawn closer and closer—began to tumble in the violent current. Moments later it was sucked bodily into the creature's maw. In a horrible moment of déjà vu, he saw its shadow pass inside the semi-translucent gullet...and then there was a violent flexing of the trunk; a popping sound; and a sudden expulsion of air in a cascade of bubbles.

And over the hydrophone, he heard Frayne's voice: calm, strange, distant.

Who are you...?

39

GIDEON PUSHED OPEN the personnel hatch and pulled himself up and out of *John*, gulping down fresh air. God, he was glad to be back on the ship. He felt badly shaken at what he'd just seen. At least Alex had struggled to the last. Frayne, on the other hand, had driven straight into the creature's maw. Was he drunk? But he sure hadn't looked drunk through the viewport. On the other hand, his actions had hardly been normal, either. Like a robot—or zombie.

He felt steadying hands grasping him as he came down the ladder. When he reached the deck, his legs almost collapsed from underneath him; Garza helped hold him up. The man looked flushed and tense; even Glinn was not his usual inscrutable self.

"What the hell did Frayne think he was doing?" Gideon said, gasping.

"Fuck if any of us know," said Garza. Gideon was grateful for the man's iron grip as he pulled himself together.

"I'm okay now," he said after a moment. Garza eased his arm off.

"You figure out who helped him?" Gideon asked, smoothing down his clothes.

"One of his lab partners, Reece. We questioned the guy, and he insists he didn't do anything—even though we have him on tape, clear as day, working the A-frame to lower *George* into the water. Claims he must have amnesia." Garza scoffed. "Obviously bullshit. He's in the brig now."

Gideon turned to Glinn. "And you? What do you think?"

"The only rational explanation I can put forward at this point is that Frayne was on drugs. Maybe he himself didn't know what he was doing."

The focused, fixated expression he'd seen on Frayne's face did not look like that of a drugged-out man. And how had he convinced his lab partner to help him? "Are you sure Frayne and his lab partner aren't involved in some sort of sabotage?" Gideon asked.

"For whom?"

"Perhaps Chile is still pissed off about the *Rolvaag*'s sinking of the *Almirante Ramirez*. Inserted a saboteur on board."

"That's a possibility," said Glinn.

Striding across the deck came the tall, impressive form of Chief Officer Lennart. "Mr. Glinn? We've got an incoming aircraft. Helicopter."

Glinn turned sharply. "Identity?"

"It's an EC155, originating in Ushuaia, Argentina, but registered in the US. The pilot says they're transporting a passenger to us."

"A passenger? Who the devil is it?"

"They won't say. They've asked permission to land."

"Deny—unless they identify their passenger."

"I'm sorry, maritime regulations require we allow a landing. They have to refuel—they don't have enough for a return."

Glinn shook his head. "I want armed security at the helipad. I don't want that chopper leaving until we have a chance to learn who it is and what they want."

"Our bird's on the pad," said Lennart. "We're going to have to take off and hover to let them land. That means we can't hold them too long."

Glinn turned. "We'll hold them long enough to find out what their game is. Gideon, Manuel, arm yourselves at the arms locker and meet me by the helipad."

The helipad was amidships, on a raised platform forward of the DSV hangar. As they collected weapons from the locker and then worked their way up stairways and corridors to the metal steps leading to the helipad, they could hear their own AStar chopper taking off. Standing in the hatchway, Gideon watched as it cleared the pad and moved off into a holding pattern to the south. Soon a new sound could be heard: the faint throbbing of another chopper, coming from the opposite direction. Emerging from the hatch, Gideon glanced toward the sound and saw a large helicopter emerging out of the clear blue sky, moving fast. The .45 he had been given was heavy and cold on his hip.

Gideon, Glinn, Garza, and a security team remained crouching to one side of the helipad, at the bottom of the stairs, to keep out of the backwash and also to provide cover if shooting began. As the chopper thundered in and began to descend above them, Gideon raised his head, squinting through the powerful rotorwash to watch the landing.

The roar subsided. Glinn was already shouting orders into his headset. "Security, move in and cover the chopper. I want answers before we refuel and allow them to depart."

Three security men, guns drawn, scrambled toward the cockpit. Glinn rose. "Come with me," he said.

They mounted the stairs and crouched on either side of the

chopper. Meanwhile, the rear cabin door opened; a scuffed and worn leather bag was thrown out; and then a single man emerged. He was lean to the point of gauntness, face lined and weathered to the texture of brown leather, his blue eyes glittering with suspicion and antagonism. He paused, skewering one person after another with his gaze. When Glinn saw him, he rose, then shoved the gun back into his belt. The man's gaze paused at Glinn, then passed him by and came to rest on Garza, who was also holstering his weapon, a sour expression on his face.

"McFarlane," Garza finally said. "Sam McFarlane. You son of a bitch."

"Yeah," McFarlane said after a moment, with a cold smile that held no trace of mirth. "I'm here. And now things are really going to get fucked up."

40

GLINN QUICKLY DISBANDED security and authorized the EC155 to refuel and take off. "My cabin," was all he said, pointing at Gideon, Garza, and the new arrival.

A few minutes later they were in Glinn's large stateroom. Before they could even sit down, Garza turned on McFarlane. "What are you doing here?"

McFarlane returned the question with a bitter smile. "Once part of the team, always part of the team."

"How did you find out about us? And how did you afford that chopper? The last I heard, you were broke and peddling a sack of second-rate meteorites."

McFarlane did not answer this. Instead, he calmly took a seat, crossed his legs, and bestowed a cool look on Glinn. "Glad to see you looking so well, Eli."

"Thank you."

Garza refused to sit. "I want to know how you found out."

"I've had a long journey," McFarlane replied. "It took me forty-eight hours of travel to get here. Do you think a cup of coffee might be managed? Two creams, two sugars. A buttered scone would also be lovely." This request he directed, in a supercilious tone pitched for maximum offensiveness, at Garza.

Gideon stared at the man. Was this really Sam McFarlane, the meteorite hunter he'd heard so much about? But of course, it had to be: he recognized the face from the video footage they'd rescued from the *Rolvaag*. And yet the man looked different now—very different.

Glinn picked up his radio, murmured into it, and set it down again. "All taken care of. Now, Sam, please tell us how you heard about our effort and what you're doing here."

"Palmer Lloyd hired me."

This was greeted with shocked silence.

"Oh, this is classic," said Garza. "A defective, hired by a madman."

Glinn held up a staying hand. "Go on."

"A few days ago, I got a call from Lloyd. He invited me to visit him in that posh asylum of his, gave me plane fare." He shook his head. "What an experience that was. But I'll tell you one thing: the man isn't mad. He's as sane as anyone. He asked, *begged* me to come down here."

"For what purpose?" Garza demanded.

"To save you all from yourselves."

"And how do you intend to do that?" Glinn asked mildly.

"He said that you, Eli, were once again acting the egotist; that your judgment was clouded—and that you thought you had everything in hand, when in fact just the opposite was true. He said you were setting yourself up to fail again, and that you were going to take down a bunch of innocents with you. Just like last time."

"Did he say anything else?"

"He said you were a man born to failure. That you instinctively seek it out."

"I see," said Glinn. Throughout this recitation, his expression had not changed. "And how are you going to bring about our salvation?"

"My job is to stop the stupid. To warn you when you're about to fuck up. Lloyd tasked me with being your 'interfering angel.'"

"How long are we going to listen to this horseshit?" said Garza. "You can interfere all you want—from the brig."

Gideon listened, with no intention of opening his mouth and getting drawn into the argument. To him, this seemed like the last thing they needed—yet another variable in the equation. This McFarlane might be an entertaining son of a bitch, but he promised to be a disruptive presence.

A knock came at the door and a steward entered with a tray of coffee cups, a pot, cream and sugar—and buttered scones. He placed the tray on a table. Glinn thanked him and he left. As Glinn began preparing McFarlane's coffee, he asked: "And how do you propose to become this 'interfering angel'?"

McFarlane took the cup, drank deep. Glinn began pouring coffee for the rest.

"Put me on the team," said McFarlane. "Give me total access. Allow me free run of the ship. And *listen* to what I say, for a change."

Garza shook his head in wonder at the man's effrontery.

"Agreed," said Glinn.

Garza looked over sharply. "What?"

"Gideon, I'm going to put you in charge of briefing Dr. McFarlane." Glinn turned. "Manuel, let's put aside history and look to the future. And Sam, you would do well to change your tone, which is immature and unbecoming."

Garza stared. "You're really going to let this joker join the team? After all that's happened? What's his role?"

"Dr. McFarlane," Glinn said, "is going to be our very own Cassandra."

41

LATER THAT AFTERNOON, with the utmost care, wearing a radiation suit with an air supply, Gideon manipulated a small, overhead crane to maneuver the two assembled hemispheres of the nuclear device closer together. The plutonium pit was now in place, plated in twenty-four-karat gold, shining like a golden apple in the center of the layered implosion device. The two hemispheres looked like an exotic fruit, sliced down the middle. The device had been cleverly designed to slot together, with male and female plugs that fit with machined precision. The high-explosive lenses surrounding the core were also precisely machined. The shaped charges were in different colors—red for fast and white for slow—designed to focus the detonation wave into a contracting sphere so that it evenly compressed the core into a supercritical state.

The HMX explosive material gave off a faint chemical smell, a funky, plastic-like scent, that brought back memories of his years working on the Stockpile Stewardship program at the Los Alamos National Lab. Nuclear weapons aged in complex ways, and keeping the nation's arsenal of nuclear weapons fresh and ready for use often meant disassembling bombs and replacing aging parts with new ones—a process not unlike what he was doing here.

Using two joysticks, he carefully worked the crane, making tiny adjustments, and finally was able to fit one hemisphere perfectly into the other, the cables and plugs slotting together, the machined HE parts sliding into place. He ran a quick electrical check and confirmed that all the electrical contacts had been made and were operating properly.

A double flange ran all the way around the stainless-steel outer shell, the holes lined up. He began inserting bolts through the holes cut into the flange and tightening them down.

He became aware of a presence behind him, and he straightened and turned. It was the new arrival, Sam McFarlane. Gideon felt a swell of annoyance at the interruption—and about how the man had crept up behind him. He had already spent an hour briefing him: what more did he want?

"This is a restricted area," said Gideon.

McFarlane shrugged.

"You should be wearing a monkey suit."

"Not necessary."

Gideon stared. This was a really unwelcome visit. He should have locked the door. And then he remembered that he had; McFarlane must have procured a key.

"The HE is mildly toxic, and plutonium and polonium, in case you didn't know, are poisonous in addition to being radioactive."

"That concerns me not at all."

"Well, then, is there something I can help you with?" he said, not trying to keep the annoyance out of his voice.

"I'm making the rounds. Trying to figure out how you plan to kill the thing. And you're in charge of briefing me—remember?"

He looked around. "So here it is—the heart of the matter. The nuke."

Gideon nodded.

"What are the specs?"

"It's an implosion device. Plutonium, of course." He wondered how much McFarlane knew about nuclear device engineering.

"What's the yield?"

"About a hundred kilotons."

"Nobody's ever detonated a nuclear device two miles underwater. Have you calculated just how that depth will affect the explosion?"

Gideon was a bit startled that the man had put his finger on the trickiest and most uncertain part of the whole operation. "It's a complex computer simulation. The water pressure appears to enhance the shock wave effects, but damp down the blast effects. It will completely kill the radiation, however—water stops neutrons."

"And how will you deliver it?"

Gideon hesitated. Some things were confidential, even on board the ship.

"Glinn gave me complete access to everything," said McFarlane.

"We've got a special ROV under wraps in the hangar. It'll deliver the weapon."

"And your calculations show the nuke will destroy the thing?"

"The blast effects will destroy the trunk and branches. The shock wave emanating from the detonation is essentially a P-wave so strong it will destroy even the creature's cellular structures—turn them, in effect, to mush. That's where the four-hundred-atmosphere water pressure really comes in handy."

"And what lies below the seafloor? Will it kill that, too?"

"The pressure wave will propagate into the ground and destroy the root structure."

"How far will it propagate, exactly?"

This was where the simulation began to break down, even pushing the limits of the onboard supercomputer. But he wasn't going to tell McFarlane that. "Well, it seems likely it'll sterilize the ground within a mile radius, to a depth of at least six hundred feet."

"Six hundred feet." McFarlane's eyebrows rose. "And just how extensive *is* the root system of the creature?"

"We're not sure. There's always been an assumption that if we kill the structure above the seabed, we'll kill the whole creature."

"Isn't that a risky assumption?"

"We think not. We can clearly see what we believe is the creature's brain inside the top of the trunk."

"What if it has other brains underground?"

Gideon took a deep breath. "Listen, Sam—may I call you Sam?"

"Of course."

"We can speculate all day. I've got a lot of work to do here. Maybe you should take these questions up with Glinn."

He found McFarlane looking at him rather intensely. "I'm taking them up with *you*."

"Why?"

"Because I have no respect for either Glinn or Garza. I saw how both of them operated during the last hours of the *Rolvaag's* existence. Glinn is a neurotic obsessive. Manuel is a superb engineer with no imagination whatsoever, which makes him doubly dangerous—talent married to convention."

"I see."

"If you want my opinion..." He paused, looking at Gideon. "Do you?"

Gideon was tempted to say he didn't, but decided the better course was to hear him out. "Sure."

"Your nuke's not going to work. It's going to kill the structure above the seafloor, sure, but I'll bet the main body of the creature is underground. It's too well engineered to be that vulnerable. You won't get it all—the nuke's not powerful enough."

"So if not a nuke, what?" Gideon asked with no little exasperation.

"Before you make that decision, you need more information."

"Such as?"

"Many years ago, when I was just getting started as a freelance meteorite hunter, I got a temporary job as a roughneck. Near Odessa, Texas. I was part of a team prospecting for oil. You know how they look for oil? They set an array of small explosive devices on the surface of the ground, along with seismic sensors. They detonate the explosives, which sends a pulse of seismic waves through the ground, which are then picked up by the sensors. A computer can process the information and draw a picture of what's underground—the layers of rock, the fault lines, the discontinuities—and, of course, the hidden pools of petroleum."

"Are you suggesting we do that here?"

"Absolutely. You need to map what's underground. You need to be sure you're going to get it *all*."

Gideon looked at McFarlane. The man was leaning toward him, his pale-blue eyes glittering in a way that made Gideon uneasy, breathing a little too hard. He was rail-thin and dressed in such a slovenly fashion he might have been a homeless person. And yet, despite everything, despite what he knew about the man and his history, Gideon recognized the suggestion was a good one. A very good one.

"We could do that."

"I sensed you were a person who would listen." He extended his hand, took Gideon's, and shook it. "I'll design the array. You set up the explosives and seismic sensors. We'll work together—partners."

"Not partners. Collaborators."

42

Two decks higher, in the marine acoustics lab, Wong and Prothero were monitoring an acoustic device that techs in the control center had lowered to within half a mile of the creature. Wong had on a pair of earphones and a headset in which she could hear Prothero's nasal voice.

"I'm ready to start broadcasting the *who are you?* blue whale vocalization," he said. "It's the sound two blue whales make when approaching each other from a distance—the whale hello, you could say. Let's see how the Baobab responds. Are you set?"

"Set."

"It's going to sound different from what we've been hearing so far. Those sounds were sped up ten times for clarity. The real vocalizations are in the ten-to-thirty-nine-hertz range. A human can't hear below twenty hertz, so it'll sound really low, almost like a stutter, and you probably won't catch it all."

"I understand."

"I'm going to broadcast for a minute, then give it a five-minute rest." Prothero fiddled with some dials. "Broadcasting."

It sounded to Wong like a series of extremely low groans and stutters. It went on for a minute, then fell into silence. Wong listened for a response. Five minutes went by. Nothing.

"I'm going to try it again," said Prothero. "Upping the amplitude."

He broadcast the whale greeting again. When it ended, there was a silence of about a minute—and then Wong heard another deep sound, very different: a long, drawn-out groan, followed by a stutter that faded over time into silence. A second sound followed, also long and low. She felt her heart accelerate. This was as unexpected as it was incredible: the thing had responded. They were communicating with an alien intelligence. Furthermore, she could hear that the Baobab was not simply repeating back what they had just played: rather, this was a new communication.

"You hear that?" said Prothero, his voice so excited it was squeaking like a teenager's. "Motherfucker! It's talking to us! There goes your theory that it's just mindlessly playing back shit."

"I concede the point," Wong said. She wondered briefly what would happen if she told Prothero what she really thought of him. No...that could wait until later. When they were back in home port, maybe.

"Okay. I'm going to repeat who are you."

The blue whale vocalization sounded. And the response came back, more rapidly this time.

"Did you get it on tape?" Prothero asked eagerly.

"Of course."

"I don't know what it means, but we'll sure as hell find out. Let's do it again."

They repeated the same message, getting the same response.

"Wong, put that sound into the acoustic database and see what matches we get."

"Already done."

It didn't take long for the computer to find a dozen matches in Prothero's vast database of blue whale sounds. Once again, she looked up the circumstances under which the sounds had been recorded and forwarded the results to Prothero's workstation. He labored for a while in silence.

"Okay," he said. "I've sort of got a translation. The Baobab's response was three distinct sounds. The first one seems to have something to do with time. It's really drawn out, though; I figure that means 'long time.'"

More typing. Prothero was muttering to himself, a number of *Jesum Crows* and *Fuckin' A*'s that she heard, unwillingly, broadcast through the headset.

"Okay," he said again. "The second vocalization involves distance. It, too, is abnormally drawn out. So it probably means something like 'long distance.' Or more like 'far away.' That's it! We asked it: Who are you?" and it answered: "Long time. Far away."

Wong felt a strange sensation, like ice, creeping down her neck. This was, without any doubt, a stunning moment.

"Then, there's this third one. It sounds like the warning sound whales make upon encountering a fishing net or a trawl line." He paused. "'Net.' I'm not a hundred percent sure about that one. And it doesn't seem to fit the other two, but..." Prothero grew animated. "You realize what we've done?" he crowed, as if the magnitude of it had just burst over him. "We're the first human beings to actually communicate with an alien intelligence! Holy fuck! It's telling us it came a long distance over an extended period of time. Just like the *Star Wars* opening crawl, *A long time ago in a galaxy far, far away...*"

The cold feeling spread. Wong had no idea why she suddenly

felt this way, but it seemed to her that buried in the message was something unutterably lost and lonely. *Long ago, far away*... That didn't feel like a message: it was more like a cry for help. And then how did that other word fit in, *net*?

Her thoughts were interrupted by Prothero. "Let's keep going. Let's see what else we can ask it—and get answers to."

But there was nothing. They broadcast sounds for another hour, but there was no reply. It was as if the entity—for whatever reason—had gone abruptly silent.

43

Gideon was damned glad he was in mission control this time, instead of down in the DSV. He stood at his usual console, watching the main screen along with everyone else in the room. McFarlane stood beside him, a silent, focused presence. McFarlane had rapidly integrated himself into the project, seemingly managing to be everywhere on the ship at the same time, intruding into every lab and machine shop and work space, making plenty of enemies in the process. Gideon had noticed that many on board ship not only disliked McFarlane but were, apparently, afraid of him. He was like a man who had gone through fire, been burned to the bone, and survived, leaving behind a scorched, skeletonized intensity; a being who followed none of the usual pleasantries and mannerisms that normally governed human interaction; a man who stated the truth as he saw it, in a way so stripped of social niceties that it was raw and offensive. Only Prothero seemed amused, even charmed, by his off-putting manner.

They watched as the remotely controlled *Ringo* hovered along the seafloor, a quarter mile from the Baobab, laying a line of charges and seismic sensors. The Baobab itself seemed to have gone somewhat quiescent as soon as the DSV arrived.

"The thing's like a cat," said McFarlane, who had taken on the task of overseeing the operation without being challenged. "Gone still. Waiting for the bird to hop a little closer."

Again, Gideon was surprised at the insight, which was not so far away from the lines along which he'd been thinking. But the plan was for the DSV not to get any closer; it would remain—or so they hoped—beyond reach of the grotesque, sucking mouth. Fortunately, the charges didn't need to be placed that close. The idea was to map the outer edges of the creature's underground presence.

It was a long process. There were few people in mission control; the operation had been last-minute. Glinn had decreed that, going forward, information was to be more compartmentalized, in an effort to put a lid on the crazy speculation and wildfire rumors. The ship was like the worst kind of a small town. It amazed Gideon how otherwise normal, educated people could be transformed into poisonous, vicious gossips, repeating and exaggerating every little thing, getting into petty disputes and absurd controversies. It was a measure of the toxic levels of anxiety and stress currently on board ship.

"You say you learned this roughnecking?" Gideon asked McFarlane.

"Yes. And then I tried the technique meteorite hunting. I figured it would be ideal for finding a large, heavy object underground."

"Did it work?"

"No. I tried it on the Boxhole Crater near Alice Springs in Australia. There *was* no main mass to find. The impactor must have vaporized on impact. Threw away forty grand. Left me bankrupt."

"So how did you get involved in the *Rolvaag* project in the first place?"

"You wouldn't know it to look at me, but I was once the world's most successful meteorite hunter. My former partner, Nestor Masangkay, found a gigantic meteorite in the Cape Horn Islands. He died before he could recover it. Palmer Lloyd got wind of it and hired me, along with Eli and his engineering company, to dig it up. I went down there on the *Rolvaag* with Eli's big team to recover it. I'm sure you know the story. Through criminal hubris, the entire ship went to the bottom—planting that son of a bitch right where it wanted to be."

"So why did Lloyd hire you to ride shotgun on *this* expedition? Since it's not a meteorite, where do you come in?"

"You heard what I said, back in Glinn's cabin. Lloyd observed my comportment during the last hours of the *Rolvaag*. He decided, with good reason, that I was better qualified to handle a challenging situation than the two G's."

"That would be Glinn and Garza."

"Yes." McFarlane turned his blue eyes on Gideon. "And now I've got a question for you."

"Shoot."

"How did Glinn heal up? The last I heard, he was a cripple, all hunched over in a wheelchair. Blind in one eye and barely able to move a finger."

The unexpected question threw Gideon for a moment. "He's had some...good medical treatment."

"Good? More like a miracle. If he weren't a hard-core atheist, I'd say he must have been praying awfully hard to Saint Jude."

Gideon changed the subject. "I didn't know Glinn was an atheist."

"Are you surprised? He doesn't believe in any power greater

than himself. And we all know he's God-like anyway—in his own mind, at least."

The DSV *Ringo* had finished laying the charges and seismometers, and now it was starting to ascend. As soon as it had reached a thousand meters, the plan was to detonate the charges, then measure the results: Glinn hadn't wanted to take chances that the creature would grow active again, or that the cables connecting the seismometers to the surface might become disconnected.

Now the chatter in mission control increased as the countdown toward the seismic test started. Detonation time approached, and the level of tension rose accordingly.

Gideon turned to his control screen. "We're ten minutes from detonation."

"The reaction of the creature should give us valuable information," McFarlane said. "If we survive its reaction, I mean."

That very thought had been going through Gideon's head.

"Five minutes," came the announcement.

"Understood," said McFarlane.

Suddenly Gideon heard a commotion at the main entrance to mission control. A man was shouting hysterically. Gideon looked over and saw another one of Sax's lab assistants, Craig Waingro, arguing loudly with security. He was gesturing wildly, screaming with almost inhuman intensity.

"Stop the explosions!" he shouted. "Stop them—*now!*" His voice sounded hoarse and muffled, as if he had swallowed sand.

The two security officers tried to restrain him, but Waingro started swinging at them. They both drew their guns. One tried to tackle the man; there was a brief struggle, and then suddenly Waingro wrenched free, the guard's gun in his own hand. He waved it about and it suddenly went off, the report deafening in the room. There were screams and shouts as people took cover.

"You won't do this!" Waingro cried, waving the gun and firing randomly again. "Don't even try! I'm warning you!"

The other guard rushed the man; he fired, but missed, and the guard tackled him. The first guard joined in and a massive struggle ensued. It was punctuated by the loud sound of another gunshot—and then silence.

The two guards, lying on top of the man, got up to reveal Waingro on the ground, arms splayed, gun still gripped in his right hand, the top half of his head shot away, brains sliding out into a widening pool of blood. In the struggle, he had evidently fired the gun inadvertently into his own head.

Gideon looked on in horror. There was something wrong—even more wrong than this awful sight would account for. Just as he felt McFarlane pull him roughly back, he saw what it was; there were gasps and expostulations of horror and disgust as others saw it, too. People backed away, shouting and shrieking.

Wriggling free of the man's ruptured brain, covered with blood and gray matter and membrane, was a dark-gray worm-like thing. As it thrashed free, it opened a tiny mouth, exposing a single sharp tooth; cut itself free; and then began to slither away.

44

Dr. Patrick Brambell looked down at the dead body of Wain-gro, Sax's lab assistant, lying on a gurney, still dressed and bloody from the tragedy that had occurred just a few minutes earlier in mission control. Dr. Sax stood beside him. Neither had been present at the disturbance. But the word was out, and the entire ship was in an uproar. Garza had demanded an immediate autopsy and a report on the worm, or tentacle, or whatever the abomination was that had slithered out of the man's brain.

"Dear me," muttered Sax, gazing at the body. "What a mess."

But Brambell's attention wasn't on the body itself; it had been arrested by the worm-like thing. Security had brought it down sealed in a stainless-steel tray with a glass top. Brambell felt a shudder pass through him as he looked at it. Following the melee in the control room, it had almost escaped, but at the last minute someone had recovered sufficiently from shock to slam a trash can over it, trapping it.

And here it was: a gray worm-like creature, about the diameter of a pencil and six inches long. It was wriggling about in the container, methodically exploring every nook and corner, clearly looking for escape routes. The head of the organism appeared to have two glittering black eyes, and between them a round mouth with a single razor-sharp black tooth protruding, made, it appeared, of a substance that resembled obsidian or glass.

"Dr. Brambell?" Sax asked. "Shall we begin?" Her hair was tucked under a cap and she was in full scrubs, as was he. They had established a formal relationship, which Brambell liked. Sax was both a PhD and an MD, and Brambell felt a little undereducated around her. One thing was certain—she was a lot better suited for this task, academically and emotionally, than his own lily-livered medical assistant, Rogelio.

He glanced over the large tray standing between them, neatly arranged with autopsy tools: #22 scalpels, skull chisels, rib cutters, forceps, scissors, Hagedorn needles, a long knife, and the obligatory Stryker saw.

Brambell did a visual inspection of the body. The video camera was running. He spoke his observations aloud, describing the head wound, the ingress and egress of the round, the state of the brain, and various other factors.

"Cut away the clothing, if you please, Dr. Sax?"

Sax began slicing off the clothes, putting them aside. Except for the mess that had been made of the head, the body was clean and in good shape. Brambell adjusted the overhead operating light.

"There's something odd here," Sax said. "With the nose."

Brambell took an otoscope, switched it on, and looked inside the nasal cavity. "What's this? It's some kind of injury."

He handed the otoscope to Sax. She took a look. "I think this is where the, ah, worm must have entered. Look—the nasal septum is damaged and the cribriform plate of the ethmoid bone has been pierced. Drilled through, almost. The hole is the same diameter as the worm."

Brambell took the instrument back, examined the nose more closely, and then—quite unconsciously—glanced in the direction of the worm.

"Uh-oh," he said.

The creature had stopped exploring the container. It seemed to have settled down, its "head"—for want of a better term—in one corner of the stainless-steel box. He heard a faint scritching noise.

Pulling down his glasses, Brambell peered closer. The thing was using its tooth to scrape away at the stainless-steel wall of its container. It looked at first like a hopeless task—what tooth could cut steel?—but then he could see that it was, indeed, scraping tiny curls of metal from the wall. Slowly, but surely, it was making a hole.

"Dear God," said Sax, looking over his shoulder.

"Indeed."

Without another word, Brambell grabbed the ship's phone and called the prep lab that, for security purposes, was now housing all the other tentacle specimens—in stainless-steel cases.

He looked at Sax. "No answer."

"The lab's probably locked up. Call security."

Brambell called security, told them to check on the specimens immediately—and to be careful. He hung up. "What now?"

They exchanged glances for a moment before Sax answered. "Let's dissect this little bugger before it escapes. The cadaver can wait."

"A most excellent suggestion." Brambell tried not to think about what the silence in the prep lab might mean.

He picked up the container and carried it across the room to the dissection chamber, mightily glad as he did so that the retrofitting designers of the ship had thought to include this unusual hooded and sterile dissection stage. He raised the hood and placed the latched container inside. The thing was disturbed by being moved; it reared up and displayed its black tooth, its head swaying back and forth menacingly.

"It's like a damn viper," Sax said.

Brambell shut and locked the hood. The dissection chamber had two sleeves, which manipulated remote dissection tools. Having inserted his forearms into the sleeves, Brambell used the manipulators to unlatch the box. The thing lashed out immediately, striking at the manipulator but bouncing off. It struck again and then wriggled out of the box, slithering fast across the space until it hit the wall, and then began exploring it, pushing and probing once again with its tooth.

Despite his best efforts, Brambell felt his hands begin to tremble. He had to fix the thing to the dissection surface—and the sooner the better. It was slithering all over the place, constantly in motion. Using the manipulator, he picked up a heavy dissection pin, hovered over the worm; and then—when it came into target range—he brought it down with a sudden movement, stabbing the worm and pinning it to the soft plastic surface.

With a faint but hideous squeal, the thing began lashing about, striking the pin with its tooth again and again.

Breathing hard, Brambell stuck in another needle, and then another, and another, until the thing was pinned almost as if sewn to the plastic board, yet still wriggling frantically, its mouth opening and closing, the tooth sweeping toward the gleaming pins that held it in place.

"Bring over the stereozoom," he said.

Sax wheeled over the microscope, used for fine dissection, and began to position it. She turned it on and an attached videoscreen popped to life, showing a blurry, magnified image of the worm.

She adjusted both the focus and the zoom until the image was sharp and at the desired magnification.

"Amazing that it refuses to die," murmured Brambell, fitting the eyepieces of the microscope to his face and inserting his hands again into the manipulators. He picked up a scalpel and positioned it at the posterior end of the pinned, but still frantically flexing, worm. He inserted the edge of the scalpel into the tip of the creature and began to make a lengthwise incision, opening it up from tail to head. The skin was hard, and it almost seemed to Brambell as if he were cutting through plastic. The creature made another squealing sound, louder this time. The cut exposed its insides, a grouping of bizarre internal organs— if they could even be called organs, given that they looked more like bundles of wires and translucent fiber optics, along with clusters of shiny black balls, like bunches of tiny grapes. The internal workings were, oddly, without color—a range of blacks, grays, and whites.

Still the creature struggled.

"Not dead yet," murmured Sax.

Brambell fixed the open incision in place with another set of pins, then removed the initial pins. Now it was splayed open on the dissection table, the skin held open, which caused the inner organs to pop upward, ready for dissection. They quivered and flexed, the black threads or wires contracting and relaxing as the thing, still alive, fought against the dissection. Brambell felt faintly sick. It just wouldn't die.

"May I look, Dr. Brambell?"

Brambell stepped away from the oculars with relief.

"It's too perfect, too well arranged, to be biological. It looks like a machine—don't you think?"

"I'm not sure I agree, Dr. Sax. It might just be a different mode of organization. The bioassays show the thing is carbon-silicon-oxygen instead of carbon-hydrogen-oxygen. This could very well be the product of carbon-silicon evolution."

Brambell could see the ugly little brute was now trying to saw away at one of the metal pins with its tooth. "I think all those threads are the creature's central nervous system," he said. "Let's follow them to the brain."

"Good idea."

With exquisite care, Brambell teased apart the sheaths and tissues covering the black and translucent threads, exposing them. Working his way forward, he saw they led to a cluster of black granules between the eyes, just behind the tooth—right where one might expect the brain to be.

"That must be it," said Sax.

"Agreed."

"Kill it, please."

"With pleasure."

Choosing a finer scalpel, Brambell inserted the gleaming tip into the cluster and made an incision. The reaction of the creature was sudden and dramatic: it made a sound like a high-pitched moan.

Brambell hesitated.

"Keep going, for God's sake."

He continued the incision, opening up the brain-like organ. Through the stereozoom, many complex structures could be seen. The creature gave one last piercing whistle, vibrated violently, then suddenly went still.

"Dead," said Sax. "Finally."

"Let's hope so."

He continued to dissect the tiny brain, removing slivers to be sectioned and examined with the scanning electron microscope;

another sliver for biochemical analysis; others for various additional tests. Slowly, he worked through the brain until it was completely exposed.

Through the stereozoom it was obviously complex, spheres within spheres, connected by countless bundles of tiny threadlike wires—neurons?—and translucent tubes.

Silently, he continued the dissection of the head. The tooth, black and exceedingly sharp, was shaped like a small shark's tooth; its root was attached to a massive bundle of wires that looked mechanical, and could contract or relax to control the motion of the tooth. The tooth obviously wasn't made of silicon dioxide; SiO_2 would not cut steel like that. He felt confident it was a carbon allotrope, probably related to diamond.

The creature's mouth led to nothing: no gullet, no digestive system, no stomach or anus. It just ended in another cluster of black and translucent threads. Maybe it *was* a machine—but if so, what a machine! Unlike anything created by humankind.

They worked rapidly but accurately, until they had dissected every visible organ and taken tissue samples for additional research. As with any dissection, the final product was a mess.

"Let us move on to the cadaver," Brambell asked.

"Before we do that," Sax said, "I would feel better if we put the remains of that thing in a blender and then incinerated it."

"Capital idea." Brambell chopped up the remains, put them in a small container, sealed it, removed it from the hood, dumped it in a bio blender, reduced it to gray mush, and then spatulated the mush into the small laboratory incinerator and turned it on. He heard the comforting sound of the flame popping to life, the gentle roar of the burner, the fan pumping the gaseous waste products out of the ship. It went on for a while, and then the unit indicated complete combustion had occurred.

"Shall we see what's left?" asked Sax.

"Why not?" Brambell opened the door to the incinerator and pulled open the drawer. A small bead of deep blue was present in the bottom of the container; no ash, no grit, just a gleaming ball of glass.

"How curious," said Sax, removing it with a pair of tweezers and holding it up to the light. "What a lovely color." She put it in a test tube and sealed it, labeling it for future analysis. She turned. "Dr. Brambell, I believe a cadaver awaits."

"Yes, indeed."

As they turned back to the body on the gurney, the ship's emergency public address system alarm went off, red lights flashing, a siren sounding. And then a voice sounded over the PA. Brambell was startled; this was the first time the emergency system had been employed.

"Attention: All personnel. Attention: All personnel. The specimens brought back on board from the organism appear to have escaped the prep lab. They may have calved into a number of smaller entities resembling small snakes, each with a single tooth. They are to be considered aggressive and extremely dangerous. All personnel are expected to remain on high alert. If you see such an organism, alert security and keep your distance. All personnel not engaged in essential business are instructed to meet on the hangar deck now—repeat, now—for further instructions."

Without a word, Brambell picked up the long knife and began to make the Y-incision from the xiphoid process to the pubic bone. "As far as I'm concerned, we're engaged in essential business."

As if in response, the ship's phone rang. Sax picked it up. "It's Garza. He wants us on the hangar deck. Glinn is requesting a brief."

Brambell laid down the long knife with regret. For now, at least, there would be no retreat into the comfort of the familiar.

45

GIDEON JOINED GLINN and a few other mission leaders at the far end of the DSV hangar. Glinn—who was in urgent conversation with Dr. Brambell and Antonella Sax—gave him a distracted nod. The golden orb of the sun had set into the ocean, leaving an orange glow across the horizon. The deck lights had just been turned on and were bathing the hangar in a ghastly yellow sodium-vapor light.

The hangar deck was a crowded and restless scene, some people talking in tense murmurs, others in loud expostulations. As Gideon looked over the crowd, he was shocked at the depth of anxiety, if not terror, he saw on many of the faces.

Glinn stepped forward. Gideon hoped he could work his calming magic, but given this crowd he was doubtful.

Glinn held up his hands and a hush fell. "As you all know, the specimen we brought on board—what we had assumed to be a long root or tendril—has vanished from the prep lab. We know that small, worm-like appendages, calved off from the main specimen, have managed to parasitize at least three people so far, and probably four, all assigned to the exobiology lab. Craig Waingro, the lab assistant who accidentally shot himself in a struggle in mission control, had a parasitic worm in his brain. CT scans have shown that the other two exo lab assistants, Reece and Stahlweather, are also infected, harboring worms in their brains. They are now anesthetized, restrained, and locked in the brig."

At this, the restless murmur of the crowd swelled in volume.

"Please. I have much more to tell you."

A half silence returned.

"It also seems likely Mr. Frayne, the lead lab assistant, was also infected, which, we believe, explains why he stole the DSV. Dr. Brambell and Dr. Sax have just completed a dissection of one of the worms, and we have more information and a tentative hypothesis to share with you."

Another swell of chatter; a few shouted challenges.

"Please!" said Garza stepping forward. "Keep quiet and let Dr. Glinn speak."

"The so-called worms have a single tooth. This consists of a diamond-like compound that can, it seems, work a hole in steel or pretty much any substance. We must assume that they are now dispersed throughout the ship. From what little we know, the worms appear to attack people when they sleep. They anesthetize the victim and enter the brain. This anesthetized period lasts perhaps two hours and, based again on the evidence, appears to take the form of an unwakable sleep."

"How do you know all this!" someone shouted.

"We don't know it. This is a working hypothesis, based on eyewitness testimony, inference, and deduction."

"We need to get the hell out of here!"

Gideon looked in the speaker's direction. It was Masterson—the second engineer who had riled up the postmortem meeting held in the wake of Alex Lispenard's death.

"That clearly won't solve the immediate problem," Glinn said calmly. "Now let me finish. The more you know about the situation, the better for everyone concerned. It *appears* that a person, once parasitized by the worm, becomes—for want of a better description—placed in the Baobab's thrall. Somehow enlisted to do its bidding, so to speak. This may be the reason Frayne stole the DSV, helped by Reece, and intentionally drove it straight into the creature's maw. And this is also why Waingro tried to interrupt the seismic charges we placed on the seabed—the Baobab must have believed them a threat and taken steps to stop us."

"That's bull!" someone said.

Glinn raised his hands. "The phenomenon is not unknown in earth biology—even in humans. *Toxoplasma gondii* is a parasite that lives in a cat's gut. It spreads to mice via cat droppings, invades their brains, and causes mice to lose their fear of cats—and thus get eaten. That is how the parasite spreads. People infected with toxo also become more reckless, get in more car accidents, seem to lose their sense of prudence. The worms seem to operate in a similar fashion. The parasitized person wakes up, goes about his business, unaware of what is in his brain or that he's been infected. But while he seems completely normal…he will go to any lengths to achieve his goal of trying to unite with the Baobab. As Frayne did. Or to protect it—as Waingro tried to do."

"Why?" someone shouted.

"We believe it may be for feeding purposes. It seems to have a specialized diet."

The *feeding purposes* phrase caused another tumult. Garza again shushed the crowd.

"Dr. Brambell is going to operate on the two remaining exo lab assistants tonight and try to remove their parasites. Meanwhile, we will be taking all possible precautions. Everyone on board ship is going to be CT scanned, on a twenty-four/seven schedule, which will be posted to the ship's net very soon. And I am sorry to say that all of us—everyone—are temporarily forbidden to sleep, because that is when it appears one is most vulnerable to attack. Sick bay will dispense phenethylamine to anyone who asks for it. Security, under the leadership of Manuel Garza, will be undertaking an intensive sweep of the ship, which we hope will find the missing worms."

At this the tumult became general. Garza stepped forward, crying out for people to simmer down, but the tide of anger rolled over him. The no-sleep order, in particular, seemed to spark both apprehension and anger. Suddenly Brambell, who had been waiting in the wings, stepped forward. The startling appearance of the man, and the universal respect in which he was held aboard ship, caused a temporary lull.

"My friends," he said in his Irish brogue, "it's quite simple. The worm enters through the nose, and works its way through the nasal bones into the brain. Remember that—until he is given instructions by the Baobab, or until he believes it to be threatened— a parasitized person will act completely normally. The only way to tell if someone is infected, short of a CT scan, is by witnessing a two-hour period of unwakable sleep—or by sudden and unexpected behavioral changes. We must all be vigilant."

This little speech was met with rapt silence. Glinn, taking tactical advantage, forcefully filled the silence. "We've told you all this for two reasons: First, to tamp down rumor and wild talk. Second, to alert you to the dangers and challenges currently facing us. Despite all this, indeed *because* of it, the program of killing the Baobab must go on full speed ahead. Everyone: back to business."

46

THE BLOOD ON the floor of mission control hadn't been cleaned up; many of the maintenance employees had been assigned to the teams sweeping the ship on worm detail. Gideon made a careful detour of it. Normally the lights were kept low in the room, because of the many monitors, but now they were turned up to dazzling brilliance. A two-woman security team, wearing gloves and face protection, was moving along a wall of equipment with pencil lights, a toolbox, and dental mirrors. They were unscrewing panels, searching the guts behind, then screwing each back and moving to the next one.

"At the rate they're going," said Sam McFarlane, appearing at his side, "it'll take months to sweep the ship."

Gideon shook his head. "Let's just get this done."

They joined Garza at the central command console. McFarlane, once again taking charge of the operation, ran a series of checks, first on the explosive array along the seafloor, then on the seismic sensors. The central screen showed a view of the creature itself, taken from the green-light video cameras that had earlier been placed on the seafloor. The thing appeared quiescent, like a giant, semi-translucent and sickly-green tree.

About fifty yards from the Baobab, sitting on the seafloor, lay the crushed and balled-up DSV that had been commandeered by Frayne. The creature had expelled it about an hour before. A faint cloudy trail drifted downcurrent from it.

"Everything's good to go," McFarlane said. "Let's restart the countdown at five minutes. Dr. Garza?"

"Initiating countdown," said Garza. "Five minutes."

A large digital timer popped up on the corner of the main screen. Gideon wondered if the creature would try to stop them again—if indeed it had initiated Waingro's psychotic break. How could it communicate with the worms through two miles of water? He wasn't as convinced of this as Glinn seemed to be. In his mind—and McFarlane's, he knew—the bigger question was how the thing might react to the explosions themselves. They were small charges, just enough to trigger seismic waves, nothing that would do damage...but the creature might well believe it was under attack.

"Four minutes," said Garza.

"Very well," replied McFarlane.

Garza and McFarlane had settled down into a kind of cold-war détente. They cooperated—in fact, they cooperated well—but on a professional level only.

Gideon felt his heart rate accelerate. It seemed unlikely the creature could do anything to them directly. Would the worms on board react? Was there really any potential communication between the parasitic worms and the mother creature? They had recorded no long-range sounds from the creature other than Prothero's whale song, nor any other potential mode of communication such as electromagnetic waves.

"Three minutes."

The tension in the control room, already high, was spiking. But at least it was controlled. The atmosphere throughout the rest of the ship was not. Already, Gideon had seen restless, angry knots of people talking among themselves, many calling for the mission to be aborted and the ship steered to Ushuaia, Argentina, the nearest port.

Glinn wasn't in mission control. Gideon wondered briefly what he could be up to that was more important than monitoring what they were about to do, but dismissed the thought. He was probably putting out fires all over the ship. The man had a unique ability to calm people down and project a feeling of unshakable competence and success. Gideon knew it was a mask, one of many Glinn put on.

"Two minutes."

Gideon transferred his attention to the screen of the Baobab. It sat there, swollen, ominous, the branches swaying almost imperceptibly. *George*, the crushed DSV, remained in place on the seabed, unmoving.

"One minute."

"Arming," McFarlane said. His thin hand unlatched and lifted the cage covering a red button on the console.

"All systems go."

Now Garza began to count down by voice: ten, nine, eight…

Gideon waited, staring at the screen.

"Fire in the hole," said McFarlane.

On the monitor, Gideon saw a dozen silt clouds erupt from the seafloor in a geometric array around the Baobab. A moment later the muffled sound was picked up by the sonobuoys on the surface—sound traveling faster in water than in air.

The Baobab reacted violently, the branches abruptly whipping and snapping about as if searching for an invader, the mouth extruding and opening, apparently sucking in vast amounts of seawater. The trunk swelled grotesquely, to the point that it became almost spherical, looking as though it might burst. At the same time, the creature's coloration underwent a swift, rippling change, turning from light green to an angry red, mottled with darker spots of purple.

And then an immense boom rocked the ship: a thunderous blast like a small earthquake that threw Gideon to the floor. The lights flickered and the ship shuddered strongly for a moment. There were some scattered screams. A shower of sparks spit out of a nearby console, and the sound of falling glass echoed from shattered monitors.

Gideon rose to his knees, but was thrown back to the deck again by another massive, booming noise. The lights flickered and this time went out, along with all the monitors, plunging mission control—which had no windows—into darkness. A second later the emergency lights came on, along with a series of alarms—including the fire-alarm siren.

A third thundering vibration struck the ship, weaker this time. Gideon rose to his feet, pulling himself up by a console. The monitors were still out, the dim emergency lighting barely adequate to illuminate the space.

McFarlane struggled up beside him, both of them bracing for the next attack. Nothing happened. Others were now getting up around them. Smoke was pouring out of a nearby console, and Gideon grabbed one of the ubiquitous fire extinguishers strapped to the walls and gave it a blast, extinguishing the embryonic fire.

Lennart's voice came over the intercom system. "General quarters. All crew to general quarters. Seal all bulkheads, security to bridge and engineering..."

As the emergency announcement went on, McFarlane said: "There's our reaction."

"It felt like an explosion. Must have been some kind of sonic attack."

"Yes. An ultra-low-frequency sonic attack with a remarkably high amplitude."

Gideon's radio buzzed and he pulled it out. It was Glinn. "I want you on the bridge," he said. While Glinn was speaking, Gideon could feel the engines coming to life, along with the incipient movement of the ship.

McFarlane overheard. "I'm coming, too."

Gideon did not argue.

47

I<small>T WAS NOT</small> a quick trip from the mission control room, deep inside the ship, to the bridge at the top of the superstructure. Gideon had only been on the bridge once before. It was a spacious area, far above the maindeck, with floor-to-ceiling windows giving sweeping views of the surrounding water and the ship itself, fore and aft. There was no internal illumination save a dull-red glow from the nighttime bridge lights and from a few hooded chartplotters and monitors. A gibbous moon hung in the sky, casting a remarkably bright light over the scattered icebergs, which looked like ghosts on the dark water. Bright stars bristled in the overhead dome of night.

As he stared at the moonlit view, Gideon saw something puzzling. The sea, as far as the eye could reach, was covered with shapes, big and small. It took him a moment to realize they were thousands upon thousands of dead fish, along with much larger shapes of what looked like sharks and porpoises. And, about a quarter mile away, he made out a cluster of huge white corpses, some fifty feet or longer each, just beginning to drift to the surface: dead whales.

The ship was gaining speed. The scene on the bridge was one of tight efficiency underlain with an intense urgency. First Officer Lennart was at the conn, relaying the captain's orders regarding heading, engine, and rudder. Captain Tulley stood next to her, a ramrod-straight fireplug of a man, murmuring his orders. Garza was nowhere in sight: he had gone off to oversee the security teams searching the ship for the missing worms.

Glinn was speaking to the officer of the watch, Warrant Officer Lund. Glinn turned and waved them over.

"Why are we under way?" asked McFarlane. "Are we running?"

Glinn looked at McFarlane. "No. We've been attacked, and we're moving out of range in order to effect repairs."

"The amplitude drops by the square of the distance," said Gideon. "Which means we probably don't have to go very far."

"Correct. The calculation was four miles. Mr. Lund, please brief them on the condition of the ship."

"Yes, sir." Lund, pale and blond, turned his narrow face to them. "We're taking on water. The bulkheads were sealed and the bilge pumps can handle it. The electricity generators are offline—fuel leaks—but should be fixed in an hour or so. The ship's navigational and engine equipment survived in pretty good shape. *Ringo*, which was at a depth of a thousand meters at the time of the sonic attacks, is a complete loss. The other major damage was to mission control, which is full of delicate and sensitive electronics. The damage appears to be severe but not catastrophic: monitors smashed, motherboards shaken loose, contacts broken. But the stand-alone computers, laptops and desktops mostly survived intact. They were shaken up but seem to be fine."

"Thank you, Mr. Lund," said Glinn. The warrant officer stepped back.

"And the nuke?" asked McFarlane.

"We haven't checked on it yet," said Glinn.

"Don't worry about the nuke," said Gideon. "Nuclear weapons are designed to be robust—built to be manhandled before being dropped."

"Please make an examination, just to be sure," said Glinn. "Now we have a decision to make: abort, or proceed?"

Gideon knew what he was going to say, but he waited. McFarlane looked at Glinn. "Let's hear your views first."

At this, a bitter smile gathered on Glinn's face. "Ah, Sam. For once, you want to hear my views. My apologies, but I'm not giving you the opportunity to disagree with me just for the sake of it. You two make the decision. If it's a tie, I'll break it."

"I say, go ahead," said McFarlane after a moment.

"Agreed," said Gideon.

"In that case, we go ahead. We'll repair the ship and head back to the target area, with the goal of deploying the nuke as soon as possible."

"Is there anything that can be done to protect the ship from a future attack like that?" asked the captain, who had overheard the conversation.

"I have an engineer working on it," Glinn told him. "He thinks we can lower a set of metal sheets into the water, to act as baffles. It won't block the sonic attack, but it may mitigate it. We have only a day, though."

The captain nodded. "The weather."

"Exactly. A serious storm is approaching that will preclude any progress for at least a week. Whatever we do, it must be done in the next twenty-four hours. And in any case..." He paused a moment. "If we can't isolate and kill the missing worms, we're fighting a losing battle. Besides, the ship's complement can't go indefinitely without sleep."

He looked at Gideon and McFarlane. "In other words, we can't afford to waste any more time with analysis. Let's go full speed ahead and take that thing out with the nuke."

48

MY DRINKING DAYS are past," said McFarlane, in answer to Gideon's invitation. It was one AM and McFarlane, in his usual brusque way, had invited himself into Gideon's cabin to discuss the seismic results, which Gideon had recently downloaded into his laptop.

The results couldn't have been worse—and were a bad shock to Gideon. McFarlane, Cassandra that he was, had been correct in his pessimistic speculation. Like the icebergs that surrounded them, almost ninety percent of the creature was below the seabed.

He heard a brief commotion in the hall; voices raised in argument. The entire ship was awake, and a few were already becoming strung out on amphetamines. Gideon felt the bulge in his own shirt pocket: a bottle of the pills sick bay had been liberally passing out. He hadn't taken any, and didn't intend to unless it became absolutely necessary. The truth was, he had no desire to sleep—and probably couldn't have even if he wanted to.

The sweep of the ship, now being led personally by Garza, was still under way, although half the search parties had been pulled off to help with repairs. Not a single worm had been found. But in the interim, someone had sabotaged the CT scanner—destroyed it completely. The same had happened to the X-ray machine. Clearly, more people had been parasitized and were apparently doing the bidding of the mother creature.

But how was the thing giving instructions? There was no way for it to communicate to the worms in the brains of the infected—was there? The very low-frequency sound it emitted was fully damped down before reaching the ship. How did it even know what to do? Sabotaging the CT and X-ray machines required not only intelligence but a sophisticated understanding of human technology. How was it possible?

And this thought was what led to a sudden revelation. It was a crazy, perhaps even insane idea. But it was the only thing that fit all the facts and explained everything—even the mysterious *kill me* plea.

Gideon would have to think hard about voicing his idea, because it seemed so outlandish. He glanced at the lean, weathered figure of McFarlane, bent over the laptop. He had rapidly come to respect, and in some ways depend on, the man's judgment, even if the way he expressed himself was frequently offensive. He would test his idea on McFarlane first.

"Look at this," McFarlane said. "That cluster, there." He turned the laptop screen toward Gideon, which displayed a picture of the area underground, surrounding the creature. "I've been using software to enhance it."

Gideon saw what looked like a grouping of ovoid objects, connected by thick cables.

"It's deep—over a thousand feet below the seafloor. You know what I think? I think those are developing seeds. Or eggs."

Gideon stared.

"Look closely at the structure. There's a hard shell around them, forming a covering. And then a liquid medium surrounds a round nucleus, a sort of yolk-like suspension."

"How large are these? What's the scale?"

McFarlane did some typing and a scale bar appeared. "Each one is about three feet in diameter along the long axis, two feet along the shorter axis. The nucleus inside is about nine inches by six."

"The size and shape of a human brain."

A long silence. He found McFarlane looking at him curiously.

"Note," said Gideon, "that there appear to be six of them."

"Noted. What are you getting at?" McFarlane asked.

"We've lost two people to the creature: Lispenard and Frayne. We also found three headless corpses in and around the wreck of the *Rolvaag*."

Gideon saw the light of dawning understanding in McFarlane's eyes. "Go on," the meteorite hunter said quietly.

"Note also that Lispenard videoed what appeared to be a brain-like organ in the trunk of the creature. But that brain is much larger: about fifteen inches in diameter."

A long silence. "And?"

"I have a theory."

"Let's hear it."

"The Baobab is a parasite, of course. But it's parasitism of a kind unknown on earth. It takes the brains of other organisms. Why? Two reasons. First, because it has none of its own. So it parasitizes the brain of another organism, *which provides it with the intelligence it requires.*"

McFarlane listened intently.

"Now for the second reason. Dr. Brambell said Alex Lispenard's brain was missing when the thing voided the remains of her DSV. Not just missing, but carefully removed. The same thing may well have happened to Frayne before his DSV was excreted. And as I said, we found three corpses from the *Rolvaag* that were all missing their heads. But the *Rolvaag* is a damned huge wreck. Who's to say there wasn't a fourth headless body somewhere inside that we haven't seen?"

"Two plus three plus one," said McFarlane.

"Precisely. That cluster of six objects, a thousand feet below the seabed, are developing into seeds. But I think that, at their core, they contain human brains. Six new creatures, each with its own intelligent brain. The fifteen-inch brain inside the trunk of the creature, on the other hand, is the one *it brought with it*—from outside the solar system."

"An alien brain."

"Exactly. *Kill me, kill me.* That was the alien brain speaking directly to us—that was not the Baobab speaking. The alien brain wants to die, desperately. Can you image what it would be like, to have your brain removed and incorporated into another life-form, used as a slaved processor or computer? And kept alive against its will—for millions of years? Kept nourished, functioning…and sane. Think about the four things Prothero has so far translated from blue whale speech: *Kill me. Long time. Far away.* And, perhaps most telling of all: *net.* It explains the final words of both Alex and Frayne—words that suggest a sudden, surprising meeting of some kind. A meeting between the human brain and…the alien brain. And it explains how the worms work. All they do is put a goal into their human's brain. A simple little goal. The parasitized human brain does all the complex thinking of how to *achieve* that goal—either to protect the mother plant, or to steal a DSV and drive down to unite with it. To make another egg. Just like the toxo infection in a mouse brain Glinn described. Makes the mouse go to the cat: to be eaten. The parasite in the mouse isn't giving it detailed instructions; it just causes the mouse to lose its fear of cats."

He paused, realizing how ridiculous it all sounded.

McFarlane didn't respond right away. He sat back in the chair, crossed his legs, and closed his eyes. For a long moment he made no movement. And then he said, without opening his eyes: "Think of the existential horror of it. A brain with no body, no life, no interactions, no sensory input. Just endless existence. No wonder it wants to die. And no wonder, as Prothero reported, the communication ended so abruptly, both times: the Baobab silenced the alien brain, kept it from continuing the conversation."

Gideon let that thought sink in. If McFarlane was right, that meant Alex, effectively, was still alive: her memories, her personality, everything she was. But trapped, disembodied, in the creature, to be used as a vehicle for its procreation. The horror of it was almost beyond imagining.

He opened his eyes.

"Are you all right?" McFarlane asked.

"No. Because you know the biggest irony of all? That thing had harvested four brains from the *Rolvaag*, probably when it first sank—yet it remained quiescent. Now it has two more—and it's suddenly growing active. I think by coming down here, we provided it with just enough additional brains for it to move to the next stage of development. Instead of killing it, we've helped it to propagate."

"Maybe so." McFarlane waved his hand. "But you know what? I think you've just figured out *how* to kill it. By destroying all seven of those brains."

49

Patrick Brambell had done six months of a general surgery residency, which was how he discovered that he was not cut out to be a surgeon. He was not a team player, which made for bad OR etiquette, and he did not enjoy working with his hands like a mechanic.

And now here he was, performing emergency brain surgery.

The patient, the exobiology lab assistant named Reece, lay anesthetized on the operating table, under bright lights. His head had been shaved and the surgery area cleaned and scrubbed with betadine. Reece's cranium had been placed in a three-pin Mayfield skull clamp, which held it rigidly in place. A testament to EES thoroughness that such a device happened to be in the surgical cabinets on board.

He had already gone through a stressful procedure—guided in real time by a neurosurgeon in Australia, via Skype—in which he had fixed a lumbar drain in the patient's lower back to remove some cerebrospinal fluid; this, the Australian neurosurgeon explained, was to "loosen" the brain and make it easier to operate on.

Standing at his side and assisting was Dr. Sax. This was little comfort; Sax was, indeed, an MD, but she had gone on to get a PhD and had never practiced medicine, let alone surgery. She was, if anything, more nervous than he was. As for his own assistant, Rogelio, after Glinn's crew-wide announcement about the parasitic worms, the man had locked himself in his stateroom, refusing to come out under any circumstances.

On a large monitor in front of him was Dr. Susanna Rios of Sydney, standing over a detailed plastic model of the head and shoulders of a human patient, lying facedown. Next to it was a real human cranium. These were the props she was going to use to guide him through the surgery.

This felt not unlike the nightmare that Brambell sometimes had: of finding himself in the cockpit of a plane, flying it after the pilot had suffered a heart attack, listening to the instructions of an air traffic controller on how to bring the plane in for a safe landing. The dream never ended well.

"The craniotomy will proceed like this," Rios was saying. "We're going to remove most of the suboccipital bone in what we call a skull-base surgical procedure. We're taking out an unusually large bone flap because, while we know the parasite is in the vicinity, we don't know exactly where it is. You're sure it's in between the dura mater and the brain itself?"

"Yes."

"And the parasite itself is of a rare variety, about which little is known?"

"Quite rare."

"Very well. I'm going to draw a line on this model, where you'll make the initial incision." She drew a line with a Magic Marker, just behind the hairline. "Now you copy it on the patient."

"Yes, Doctor." He drew the same line on his patient with a sterile pen.

"Dr. Brambell, your hand appears unsteady."

Brambell held it up. It was indeed trembling.

"Please close your eyes, take a deep breath, focus, and get that tremor under control." Rios spoke sternly yet calmly.

Brambell did as she instructed. The trembling steadied.

"Good. Make the incision, like this." She demonstrated with the scalpel on the plastic model.

He followed suit, the scalpel running lightly along the bone. Guided by the Australian surgeon, Sax followed the incision with an electrical cauterizing tweezers, zapping any bleeders. In between she used a sponge to keep the area wiped clear of blood.

"Now the skin and muscles are to be lifted off the bone and folded back, like this. Clip the edges of the incision with clamps and let the weight of the clamps hang down to keep the incision open."

She demonstrated with the plastic pieces of the model. Brambell followed suit.

"Very good. Now you're going to make four small burr holes in the skull with the perforator drill. Like this."

She drew four black dots on the real skull model and demonstrated. Brambell watched as, ever so gently and deftly, she cut a small hole in the cranium with the drill.

"Go slow. The perforator must be held perpendicular to the bone. Do not stop or pull back until the drill stops itself—which it will automatically just before it penetrates all the way through the bone. Ready?"

Brambell nodded. Sweat was running into his eyes, threatening to blind him. "Dr. Sax, please mop my brow," he murmured.

He drew four black dots on the cranium, as indicated. He

started the air-powered drill, which came up to speed with a soft whine. Then, taking another deep breath, he hovered over the bone with it.

"Do *not* use downward pressure," Rios said.

He lowered the drill until it bit into the skull with a high-pitched rasp. He immediately smelled the bone and blood atomized by the device even through his surgical mask.

"Slow...easy...that's it."

The drill stopped.

"Pull out and do the next hole. Your assistant needs to be ready with a little bit of saline in there to cool it."

Brambell eased off and raised the drill, following her directions. In a few minutes he was done with the four holes.

"The perforator," Rios said, "leaves a very thin layer of bone at the bottom of each burr hole. It has to be taken out, like this." She demonstrated with a funny-looking tool. Brambell did not have the tool.

"Use a small forceps instead," Rios said.

He used the small forceps to remove the wafer-thin pieces of bone. He could now see the whitish-bluish-gray membrane, the dura, peeping through the holes.

"Good. Now you're going to cut from hole to hole using the craniotome. You will cut along the lines, while your assistant uses the suction tube to draw up the saline solution and also gently push down the dura, keeping it away from the saw tip. She should be dribbling the saline into the cutting edge to keep it lubricated and cool."

Once again she demonstrated. "Ready? Both of you?"

Brambell nodded.

"Turn on the craniotome. Go slow. And steady: there's no hurrying anything in brain surgery."

He turned on the saw and it whispered up at a high pitch, like a mosquito. He began to cut along the line. Again that smell came.

As he eased it along the line, Dr. Rios talked him through the procedure, gently correcting him as he went. It took a long time, but was finally done. He expelled air. Sax mopped his brow again.

"Take a moment to rest."

Brambell closed his eyes, tried to think of something calming—and came up with *Hamlet*. He began quoting his favorite lines from *Hamlet* to himself. That worked well. He opened his eyes.

"Now you need to remove the bone piece with a pair of spurtles." Rios cleared her throat. "May I see your hands?"

Brambell held up his hands. They were steady.

"All right. Use the spurtles to remove the bone flap, but do it slowly and with the utmost care."

He took the spurtle set and, with infinite care, removed the oval piece of bone.

"Put it aside in the prepared sterile container, and—" Suddenly Rios stopped. "Oh, my God."

Brambell could see, under the translucent dura membrane, a section of the worm. It was about a quarter inch thick and was coiled, like a snake. It was moving slowly, with a continuous motion.

"What in the world is *that*?" Rios asked.

"It's the parasite."

"That's like no parasite I've ever seen—and I've been doing neurosurgery for twenty years."

"As I told you, it's rare."

"Right. Okay." Now Rios was the one trying to collect herself.

Brambell took a deep breath. He wanted to get this over with. "Dr. Rios, shall we continue?"

"Yes. Yes, of course. Ah, let's see. Next, wash the dura gently with saline and remove any bone tips." She demonstrated on her model with the suction tube and saline.

Sax did it.

"Now we're going to put in two traction sutures with 4-0 silk."

"What's a traction suture?"

"It's a suture that forms an open loop of silk you can stick your finger through and use to lift something up. In this case, you will elevate the dura off the brain, so you can cut it without nicking the organ itself. And...raise the membrane off that parasite."

Brambell nodded. As Sax gently washed down the dura and suctioned off bits of bone, the worm stopped its slow coiling, freezing in place. It seemed to have sensed something was going on. God, he hoped he hadn't disturbed the thing. If it slithered off into another part of the brain, they'd have to start all over again.

"This is new to me," said Rios. "How do you propose to get that thing out?"

"I was thinking I could grab it with forceps through the dura. Get a good grip before it...escapes. Then pull it out."

"The dura is a tough membrane. You can't pull it through— that would kill the patient. You've got to make an incision first."

"I understand. But I have to grab the thing by surprise." He paused. "I've got one shot at this."

"I'm beginning to see the problem. Might I suggest injecting it with an anesthetic first?"

"An anesthetic won't work." Brambell didn't bother explaining that the parasite came from beyond the solar system and had an alien biology; that, he knew, would not go down well with the good Dr. Rios. He cast his eye over the tray of tools, looking for one that would work. There were numerous sets of forceps, including several large ones with teeth.

"So tell me what you think I can do to get that thing out fast," he said.

"This is outside my area of competence," Rios said. "Shouldn't you consult with someone who's got experience removing these types of parasites?"

"There is no one. Just tell me how to do it, please."

"Well, the simplest way would be to start with those two traction sutures I mentioned, and use them to pull or lift the dura away from the parasite. Then you make an incision, grasp the parasite with forceps, and remove it."

Brambell looked at the worm. It had stopped moving, but it didn't seem alarmed; it looked almost as if it was waiting. "All right. Show me what to do on your model."

"Keep in mind that any movement that impinges on the brain, even a tiny bit, can cause damage."

"Noted. Let's go."

"First the traction sutures," Rios said. "These will be two loops of silk that your assistant can put her fingers through to lift or elevate the dura away from the, ah, parasite." She demonstrated on a second plastic model, using needles to form two loops of silk. She stuck her fingers through the loops and pulled upward, raising the membrane from the brain. "Got it?"

"Got it."

"The suturing needle should only go two-thirds of the way through the dura. Not all the way. Don't pierce it."

Brambell inserted the bent needle into the dura, worked it partway through and then out. He was concerned about disturbing the worm. And in fact, as he worked the bent needle through the membrane—which was very tough—the worm did seem to grow disturbed, and at one point gave a jerk, coiling up tightly. But it stayed put.

"Your assistant will now elevate the dura. Start the incision, and as she elevates it further, it will help you extend the incision to the desired opening. Keep in mind that working with forceps so close to the brain, even the smallest miscalculation—"

"I understand the risks," Brambell said with ill-disguised impatience. "Dr. Sax? Stick your fingers through those sutures and elevate the dura." Brambell took up the large, toothed forceps with his left hand and the scalpel in his right, ready to go.

Sax slipped her two forefingers through. The worm moved again, jerked a little. But it remained in place.

"Lift a little more."

She pulled up ever so lightly. Again the worm jerked, then coiled up tightly, as if to protect itself as the membrane was lifted from it. Brambell poked the tip of the scalpel through the dura, and with a quick, smooth movement cut an opening an inch long, exposing the worm. It remained quiescent.

"A little more."

The act of lifting helped him open the incision another inch. Now the worm finally seemed alarmed. It coiled itself still tighter. Then, suddenly, its head appeared, raising just like a snake into striking position, pointing at Brambell's hovering forceps. Its black tooth suddenly unsheathed, like a viper's fang.

"*Good Lord*," breathed Rios.

Brambell moved in with the forceps, slowly, like a cat.

The thing seemed to be watching his hand approach, its head weaving slightly.

Holding his breath, Brambell darted in and seized the creature across its body, the forceps's hooks sinking in. It slashed about, striking at him like a snake as he pulled it out, at the same time whipping around with its tooth, stabbing its head into the patient's brain, wriggling around and then pulling its head out with a sucking sound. Blood gushed out.

"Jesus!" cried Rios.

Now it went after Brambell, the head whipping back around again, the black tooth sinking into Brambell's hand. He gave a yell but didn't let go, the thing thrashing and stabbing, striking him again and again.

"Son of a bitch!" he cried, throwing it into a container previously prepared for it. Sax slammed the lid. A frantic skittering and high-pitched squealing filled the room. Ignoring his own slashed hand, Brambell turned back to the patient. Blood was welling out of the hole the worm had made, flowing down the sides of the head. The life-support alarms began to beep on the monitoring equipment; the EKG was going crazy—and then, even as he stared, it flatlined and the respiration fell to zero.

Reece died before his eyes, his blood running over the operating table and streaming to the floor.

"Doctor, you're bleeding," said Sax, grasping his forearm and pressing sterile pads on the cuts.

He turned on her. "Throw that devil in the blender!"

She obeyed. Brambell pressed the pads against his cut hand, hoping to the living God that the thing wasn't poisonous.

He turned back to the monitor. Dr. Susanna Rios was still there, staring at the scene with an expression of pure, speechless horror on her face. Her mouth was moving, but no sound came.

"So sorry, Doctor," Brambell said. "Please stand by—we have another patient." He heard the blender go on, the squealing of the worm cut short as it was reduced to a gray paste.

He experienced a wave of dizziness, felt Sax gripping his arm and leading him to a chair, sitting him down, giving him a glass of water, and then unwrapping his wounded hand. "Let's take a look at your injuries," she said. "Just sit back."

"We don't have time," said Brambell, rising. "We need to bring in Stahlweather."

50

AT FOUR IN the morning, Gideon was in his quarters, alone, working at his small desk. The simulation was almost finished. It was finally coming through after almost forty hours of CPU time on the ship's IBM "Vulcan" Q supercomputer.

He had a bad feeling. The fundamental question was how deep and wide the nuke's shock wave would penetrate into the seafloor. But the seafloor was composed of pelagic sediments—essentially loose, wet clay. It was like a soft blanket, the worst material imaginable for propagating a powerful shock wave. The six brains, which looked like they were being encapsulated into new seeds, were a thousand feet deep and off to one side of the creature.

McFarlane was surely right: if they could kill all the brains the creature had collected, they would certainly kill the creature itself as well. The thing was a parasite that needed a brain in order to survive—and additional brains to reproduce. Kill all of them and it would soon die—if it couldn't get any more.

He watched the window on his computer screen, meaningless numbers scrolling by. The Q machine was still thinking. Simulating a nuclear explosion two miles below the surface of the ocean was a massive computing job, but all indications were that it was almost done.

A soft knock came at the door. Gideon didn't answer. The door opened anyway and Glinn entered. "May I?"

"You're already in."

Glinn came in and eased himself onto the bed, iPad in hand. His face looked drawn, but otherwise he appeared fine—not tired, and certainly not half crazed, like so many others on board. But if you looked closely, there was a gleam in his eye that had not gone away: a gleam of deep and abiding obsession. Gideon knew that gleam, because he felt the obsession as well. It was a need, an overwhelming need, to destroy the thing, no matter what the cost.

"Where's Sam?" Glinn asked.

"He disappeared. Said he had some thinking to do."

Glinn nodded. "We now have a more complete report on the biology of the creature, which I want to share with you, because it may have a bearing on how readily it can be killed."

"Shoot."

"It's a carbon-hydrogen-silicon-oxygen form of life. Essentially, it's built of organic chemistry like us, but with the addition of silicon, mostly in the form of silicates and silicon dioxide. On our planet, marine diatoms seem the closest biochemical analogy. They extract silicon from water and build their bodies out of silicates. Some plant species also incorporate silicates."

"I don't really give a shit. I just want it dead."

Glinn went on, as if he hadn't heard. "And much of the carbon appears to be in pure form, in exotic allotropes—nanofibers, nanotubes, nanobuds, nanofoam, fullerenes, graphite, and diamond. It has silicon dioxide fiber-optic wires that transmit digital signals using light. The various exotic carbon fibers transmit electricity, some apparently with superconductance. Instead of muscle fibers, the entity has bundles of carbon fibers that can be contracted or relaxed. Many hundreds of times more powerful than any muscle fiber. That's how it could crush a titanium sphere."

"Where is all this going?"

"Patience, Gideon. The question is: Did this thing evolve? Or was it built? Is it a machine or a biological entity, or some kind of hybrid? We don't know. But here's what we *do* know."

He laid his iPad on the bed. "The temblors in the seafloor around it are almost constant. We've been analyzing them. The thing appears to be extending its roots or tentacles at an incredible rate—hundreds of feet an hour. The main body of those roots are heading for the South American continent."

"Good God."

Glinn paused, shifting on the bed. "We are out of time. The creature is growing too rapidly, the roots growing outward at a geometric pace. And now it looks like nodes are beginning to develop on those roots. In other words, it's getting ready to push up new Baobabs, like mushrooms after a rain. To collect more brains, more seeds. Which gives us an idea, an educated guess, about the creature's endgame."

"Tell me about it."

"In short order, a network of Baobabs will circle the globe, forming, in effect, a giant fist around it. Once that happens, the fist will flex—popping the surface off the earth like a giant tomato and breaking up the planet in the process—thus ejecting the seeds into space to find other worlds to parasitize. Each seed will contain its own parasitized brain."

"How did you figure this out?"

"Think about it. I've hinted at this before. Breaking up the planet is the *only* way for it to liberate those gigantic seeds."

Gideon glanced at the window on his monitor. The numbers were still flashing by.

"The situation on board this ship is becoming untenable," Glinn said. "We're losing control. The Q machine's Quantitative Behavioral Analysis indicates we have only about twelve hours left before discipline breaks down entirely and we have either a mutiny or chaos on board ship."

"So your QBA is what's been slowing down my simulation."

"My apologies. But understanding the human factor is crucial."

Gideon nodded.

"Despite all our precautions, other personnel have been parasitized by the worms. We know this because of the widespread sabotage—not just the CT scanner and the X-ray machine, but the ship's surveillance cams, as well. The whole system is down, and the vessel's intercom isn't working everywhere. All this is slowing down our efforts to find the worms—and identify the saboteurs."

"Again, I'm wondering where this is going."

"We must deploy the nuke now. And I mean *now*—within twelve hours."

Gideon glanced over at his workstation. "I need the numbers first. If the nuke won't kill those underground eggs, there's no point in setting it off."

"And when do you expect the numbers?"

"Any moment."

"Doesn't the computer tell you how long the calculation will take?"

"It's not a calculation. It's a *simulation*. A much vaster scale of complexity."

Glinn rose. "Forget the simulation. We've got the weapon. Let's use it." He looked at his watch. "I want the nuke armed and loaded in the ROV in a matter of hours." He turned. "Can you do it?"

As Glinn stared at him, Gideon became aware—once again—of the obsession they both shared.

"Fuck, yes," he said, almost surprising himself.

Glinn nodded. "Good." And then he left.

Just as the door shut, as if on cue, Gideon's monitor chimed. The window was blinking red. The simulation was complete.

Gideon rushed to the computer and, not even bothering to sit, began furiously calling up the numbers from the Q. The file came in slowly—it was fat—but in a minute it had loaded, numerical simulations made visual.

A schematic picture appeared and a slow-motion video began playing, simulating the detonation of the nuke, the expanding shock wave, the massive cavitation caused by the blast, the transitioning of seawater into steam, the effect of it on the Baobab, and the impact of the leading edge of the shock wave with the seafloor and its propagation beneath.

In a minute it was over. Still standing, Gideon now sought to sit down, placing an arm on the swivel desk chair. But something went awry; his legs were like jelly, and the chair slipped on its wheels sideways and he collapsed on the floor.

51

Brambell had never felt so shattered in his life. He was weary to the marrow. He sank into the chair in his clinic, eased his legs out one after the other, and leaned back. His limbs felt like lead.

He and Sax had lost both patients, one after the other. In the first case the parasite had killed Reece while it was being extracted; in the second, Brambell had followed Rios's recommendation and injected the parasite with hydrochloric acid, which did in fact kill it—but not quickly enough. As soon as he stuck the needle in the worm, it lashed out and killed the patient.

After Stahlweather had died on the operating table, he'd been forced to give the near-hysterical Dr. Sax a sedative, but to prevent her from sleeping he added to it a cocktail of mild stimulants, caffeine and methylphenidate Hcl, that had put her into a wakeful but dissociated state. He had installed her in a chair in the back room of the clinic, where she was resting but not sleeping. He had checked on her several times and found she was alert enough. Not that he really believed there were worms hiding in the clinic. They had killed both worms recovered from the patients, blending them into paste and incinerating them. The cuts on his arm were sore, but they were just cuts—so far there was no sign of any exposure to toxins. Which made sense: the worm's tooth did not have a channel to inject venom, as a viper's fang did, nor did there appear to be any venom-containing organs inside the creature.

His dispensary, down the hall and currently in the pharmacist's care, had been dispensing pills all night long. The steady stream of patients had ended, and it was close to dawn. He himself had not taken the speed. He had been a doctor too long to think it was a good idea, and he was surprised and even dismayed that Glinn had ordered it. But there it was: Glinn was not someone who consulted him on decisions like this. Brambell feared the wakeful atmosphere on board the ship more than he feared the unlikely possibility of being parasitized. The stress and fear, he believed, could easily deteriorate into stimulant-induced psychosis in many crew members.

In this ruminative state he found his eyes closing, and he jerked himself awake. Just two more hours to sunrise. What he should be doing was keeping busy, and the best way to do that was to start working on a blood test that would show if someone had been parasitized.

Brambell had drawn vials of blood from the two patients—and if he could find something unusual in that blood, something anomalous, something not present in the blood of an uninfected person, that could be used as a blood test.

He roused himself and shuffled over to the equipment cabinets. He would start with a standard CBC on the blood, measuring hemoglobin and red and white blood cell numbers. From there he would go on to a basic metabolic panel testing heart, liver, and kidney function, blood glucose, calcium, potassium and other electrolyte levels. Maybe a lipoprotein panel next, if nothing anomalous showed up. He hoped to God something *would* show up. And it very well might: surely the body would react in some way to having a six-inch parasite moving around in the brain.

God, he was tired. *Stay on your feet.* You couldn't accidentally fall asleep on your feet, he knew. Maybe he should take just half a pill...Once again, he put this thought out of his head. No amphetamines—he needed to keep his head as clear as possible.

Removing the rack of vials from the refrigerator—he had taken thirteen vials of blood from each patient—he began sorting and labeling them for the various tests. Then he went through the equipment lockers, taking out the necessary equipment and setting it up while going through the steps in his mind. As a doctor, he normally sent tests like this off to a lab. But back in medical school at RCSI, he had learned how to do them himself. On top of that he had the Internet, and surely somewhere there he would find the lab protocols. He jacked his laptop into the ship's network and went online. Yes: there it all was, in exacting detail.

He would start with a simple blood smear test. He took a drop of blood from one of the vials and spread it on a gridded slide, stained it, and covered it. He put the slide under the microscope and, pencil in hand, began counting the number, size, and shape of red blood cells, white blood cells, and platelets per grid, jotting down the figures. But he was so tired he was having trouble focusing. He blinked, blinked again, and adjusted the focus on the stage. God, his eyes were so shot from the failed operations he couldn't see through the eyepieces. And it had to be admitted he wasn't as young as he once was, less able to stand up to the grueling hours he had once endured as a resident.

He blinked again, then took some eyedrops out of the medicine cabinet and applied them to his eyes.

Once again he gazed through the eyepieces, but it was like trying to see underwater. Bloody hell. What he needed was a ten-minute break with his eyes shut. His judgment was growing affected; he needed to be sharp in order to continue the tests.

He glanced at the chair. Could he close his eyes without dropping off to sleep? But a quick ten-minute nap hardly seemed dangerous and, in fact, might work wonders. The idea that there were worms lurking somewhere in the room, waiting for him to go to sleep, was absurd. There would be no danger in just a ten-minute nap; and it would do him, and the work he had to do, a world of good. The ship was huge and the clinic was small and had watertight bulkhead doors all around, which could be dogged shut.

He went to the main door into the clinic, eased it shut, and dogged it. He shut the door to the inner lab as well. Then he took his cell phone out of his pocket, set the alarm to ring in ten minutes, and placed it on the counter, starting the timer as he did so.

God, he could hardly wait. He eased himself into the chair, leaned back, and closed his eyes. What a glorious feeling it was...

A dream woke him: a nightmare. With a muffled cry he jerked awake, feeling a sudden stinging pain, a horrible rasping vibration, inside his head. His mind, confused and frightened, took a moment to clamber up out of darkness into the real world; his hands flew to his face and he felt something and he fell out of the chair to the ground.

Good God in heaven, there was something on him. It was like a wriggling cable, hard and cold as steel; it was on his face and inside his nose. *Digging into his nose.* With a second muffled cry he managed to grasp the tail end of it and tried to pull it out; he could feel the thing's incredibly strong muscles rippling in his frantic grasp as he tugged, but it wouldn't come free. It had fixed itself inside and was working its way deeper, rasping and digging into his nasal cavity. He rolled about on the floor, hanging on to the thing's tail with maniacal intensity, trying to keep it from going deeper, but it was too well anchored, working its way in despite his every painful effort to pull it out.

Suddenly he felt, deep inside his head, a snapping of bone— like a finger poked through an eggshell—and then everything changed. The terror vanished and he felt a wonderful, spreading sensation of peace and contentment, and a blessed feeling of sleep stole over him: beautiful, serene sleep.

Dr. Antonella Sax stood in the doorway of the inner lab, rubbing her eyes and trying to focus. She had heard something, a cry perhaps, although she wasn't sure. But nothing was awry. Dr. Brambell lay on the floor, sleeping. His hands were folded on his chest and an expression of contentment lay across his face.

She leaned over to wake him up, gave him a little shake. "Dr. Brambell?"

No response. The poor man had been going thirty-six hours straight and was out like a light. He had locked the door and she noticed his cell phone on the lab table counting down the seconds. She picked it up. He had set it for a ten-minute nap and had two more minutes to go.

The poor tired man—ten minutes seemed like nothing. Seeing him asleep so peacefully made her feel the lure of sleep, herself. The shot Brambell had given her seemed to be wearing off, or at least it was no longer able to counteract the tidal wave of fatigue that pressed at her mind. She was aware that her rationality was still somewhat affected by the shot, that she wasn't thinking as clearly as she normally did—but who could be expected to, after the ordeal they had just gone through?

God knew the doctor needed a longer rest; and so did she. What risk would there be in a half-hour nap? That would be a lot more effective than ten minutes. The door to the clinic was securely dogged. And surely Glinn's no-sleep edict did not apply to herself and Brambell, who needed to be as sharp as possible if they were going to be effective.

She reset the phone alarm to go off in thirty minutes, and then eased herself into a lab chair and sat back, placing her feet up on the table, closing her eyes, and falling almost immediately into a delicious sleep.

52

Gɪᴅᴇᴏɴ ʟᴇꜰᴛ ʜɪꜱ cabin and headed for mission control, where he knew he would find Glinn. As he walked down the corridor, he heard, as he passed through crew quarters, voices raised in querulous complaint. A man came careening down the hall, smelling of alcohol, bumped into him, gave him an elaborate bow, and staggered on. As he passed the open door to the crew's mess, he saw that a crowd had gathered, talking urgently among themselves.

He hurried on. Glinn was right: they had very little time before things fell apart on the ship, if they weren't beginning to already. He wondered how the man would react to the news he was carrying.

The door to mission control was locked, but after identifying himself on the intercom he entered. Glinn was there, along with McFarlane. Both were hunched over a monitor. It was a view of the Baobab from the stationary camera. It was horribly active, the mouth extruding and swelling, then retracting, as if it were exercising some grotesque sex organ.

"The simulation is finished," said Gideon.

They both looked up.

Gideon had been debating in his mind the best way to say it, but when actually faced with the task his carefully crafted explanation vanished. "It won't work," he said simply.

"Won't work?" McFarlane repeated sharply.

"Not even close. The sediments act like a blanket. The shock wave won't reach that cluster of brains."

"I don't believe it," McFarlane said harshly. "Bury the nuke in the mud and set it off there. That'll excavate a crater down to them."

Gideon shook his head. "I already considered that. The simulation looked at various detonation altitudes above and within the seafloor. The best location is about two hundred meters above the bottom. The water pressure would propagate the shock wave to a larger area of seafloor, where it would penetrate the farthest. But not far enough."

"Let's see those simulations," said Glinn.

"They're on the ship's network." Gideon turned to the monitor, pulled up a keyboard, logged on, and ran the video simulation with all its various permutations, starting with the nuke exploding at the level of the seafloor, and then working up to a detonation half a mile above the Baobab. Each simulation showed the shock wave moving in slow motion through the water, hitting the ground, and continuing on—damping down and petering out in five to six hundred feet of depth. None of them reached the cluster of eggs, at a thousand feet deep.

"I can't believe it," McFarlane exploded. "This is a fucking nuclear weapon! You've set the parameters wrong."

"No," Gideon said. "The problem is, these deep-sea pelagic sediments are like a wet blanket. If it were solid rock it would be totally different. But it's not—it's like Jell-O."

"So what's the answer?" McFarlane asked furiously. "What have we got more powerful than a nuke? Can we go get an H-bomb? What else can we do? This is fucked up. Why wasn't this simulation done six months ago?"

He halted his tirade, breathing heavily. Gideon looked at him. He felt utterly defeated. And to think he'd seriously considered reprogramming the nuke's onboard computer so he could override an abort code, just in case the others got cold feet. What a joke. Now there was no question: everyone wanted to use the nuke. And every hour counted. But the damned thing wouldn't be enough to kill the entity.

Glinn spoke quietly. "Are there *any* options, Gideon?"

Gideon shook his head. "One nuke. One shot."

53

Rosemarie Wong had locked the door to the marine acoustics lab and was straightening up, trying to put the lab back into a semblance of order after Garza and his team had swept the place for worms. Prothero would have a fit if he came in and found it like this. Although it was just as messy when Prothero was there, he always claimed to know where every little thing was. And it was true: if she moved so much as a pencil in one of his staggering piles of crap, he would notice and berate her.

She was deeply concerned about what was happening on board the ship. Several times in the past hour she had heard groups of people passing by in the narrow corridor outside the lab, talking in loud, angry voices, their boots ringing on the metal floor. Some of them sounded like they had been drinking, while others appeared wired from the amphetamines that were being passed out like candy.

Where *was* Prothero? He had been working on his whale lexicon for much of the night, but then had excused himself and left, saying he'd be back in fifteen. But it had been almost an hour and he still wasn't back. Had he gone to sleep, defying regulations?

That would be just like him; the way to get Prothero to do some-thing was to ask him to do its opposite.

Wong told herself she shouldn't be worried. Prothero main-tained a completely unpredictable schedule, coming and going at all hours of the day and night, never eating in the mess but instead chowing down in the lab itself, at random times, on piz-zas and sodas brought in from the canteen. He would typically kick the trash into a corner, and it would then be up to her to retrieve it, put it in the garbage, and then empty the garbage at regular intervals to get rid of the oniony smell of pizza, which she loathed...

Once again through the door she heard a group pass by; once again she heard the muffled, angry voices. This was truly disturb-ing. Where was security? But she knew the answer to that: Garza had commandeered them all in the search for the worms. In the meantime, the ship's discipline was rapidly heading for a com-plete breakdown.

She heard the door rattle; a gasp. "Hey, Wong! Open up!"

Prothero. She got up, unlocked the door, opened it. He rushed in, slamming the door and locking it. He was gasping for breath, sweaty, his hair askew, sucking in air.

"What is it?" she asked. "What's happened?"

"Son of a *bitch*," he said. "The motherfuckers have gone crazy. It was only five minutes, maybe ten at most, I swear—"

There was a sudden thundering of footsteps outside the door; a rattling of the doorknob. "Prothero? *Prothero!*" a voice called, with an eruption of other voices behind.

Prothero backed away from the door. "Tell them I'm not here," he whispered to Wong.

Wong swallowed. "He's not here," she said through the door.

"Bullshit!" came the reply. "We know he's in there. Open up!"

A number of angry voices were raised on the other side of the door, and someone began pounding. "Who is that? Wong? *Open the fucking door, Wong!*"

Prothero, terror in his eyes, shook his head at her. He backed up, casting around the lab as if for a place to hide. There was none, of course.

"He's not here," she said again.

"Listen up, Wong! He's infected. We caught the son of a bitch sleeping. Couldn't wake him up. He's got a worm!"

Wong felt paralyzed. She glanced at Prothero. He didn't look right, but then he rarely looked normal.

"Are you listening? He's infected! Get your ass out of there and let us take care of it!"

Prothero shook his head, mouthing *no, no, no.*

Wong couldn't decide how to reply. She felt paralyzed.

Boom! Someone slammed into the door. *Boom!* The door was not a bulkhead and she could see it bow inward with each body blow.

"Open up, Wong! If you won't save yourself, we will!"

"*I don't have a worm!*" Prothero screamed. "I swear! I just took a snort nap, that's all!"

"He's in there!" There was a tumult of shouting and expostulation beyond the door. "Wong, for God's sake, he's dangerous! Let us in, *now!*"

"I'm not dangerous. I swear!"

Wong looked once again at Prothero. His eyes were bloodshot, he was soaked in sweat, and his body was twitching and jumping with panic and fear. He did look infected.

He read the meaning in her eyes. "No, no," he said, swallowing and trying to speak without screaming. "I'm not. Rosemarie, I swear it. They're crazy. I took a nap. Five minutes. I was out like a light. But I'm not infected! Remember, if you're infected they can't wake you for two hours, and—"

Boom! And now the metal door handle rattled and came loose. *Boom!*

Wong made a decision. "No!" she yelled at the men trying to break down the door. "You can't do this without evidence!"

Boom! The handle sprang off the door.

"You need proof!" she yelled.

Boom! The door flew open and a huge man forced his way through. She was shocked; it was Vince Brancacci, the ship's jovial chef. He did not look jovial now, with a meat cleaver in his hammy, hairy fist. A crowd surged in behind him, half a dozen men armed with tools, crowbars, wrenches, hammers.

"There he is!"

"No!" Prothero said. "Please God, no!"

The crowd, realizing they had Prothero trapped, suddenly seemed to hesitate.

"He's infected," Brancacci said, advancing with the cleaver. "He's finished. We need to get rid of the worm inside him."

"No, no, please!" Prothero whispered, shrinking back against a rack of computer equipment.

Wong stepped in between Brancacci and Prothero and drew herself up to her full height, towering above Brancacci. "You can't kill a man without evidence. You can't do it."

"We *have* evidence," said the chef.

"Which is?" Wong asked.

"He was sleeping. He couldn't be woken up. And look at him—just look at him! He's not acting normally."

"You wouldn't be acting normally if you were being chased by a mob."

"Get out of my way," said Brancacci threateningly.

She could smell the sour odor of Brancacci's sweat. "Don't do this," she said quietly. "Just turn around and go. You can't execute a man based on such weak evidence."

He reached out, grasped her shoulder with one powerful hand. "Please step aside."

"No."

With a wrenching motion he threw her aside. He was strong, and the action sent her tumbling into a rack of equipment, which fell with her to the floor with a crash. Momentarily stunned, Wong sat there as the mob moved in, stepping over and around her.

"God, God God please no *no noooo!*" she heard Prothero sobbing and pleading.

Brancacci swung the cleaver at his head, striking him above the eye with a sickening hollow sound. Prothero screamed, going down, blood splattering, his head already coming apart. Brancacci drew back and, taking careful aim, swung the cleaver again. The scream was cut short. Prothero lay on the floor, unmoving. The chef now stepped over Prothero, straddling him, and brought the blade of the cleaver down once again, driving it into his skull and opening it up like a melon.

Wong turned her head and closed her eyes. She heard a frantic struggle, shouts of *Find it! Get it! Get the worm!* But then the tumult rapidly fell into silence.

She opened her eyes. Brancacci was still standing spraddle-legged over Prothero's body, cleaver in hand. The rest had formed a silent circle around the fallen scientist, staring down at his remains, his skull and brains strewn across the floor in a pool of spreading blood.

"Stupid bastards!" Wong cried. "Are you satisfied now? Do you see? *There is no worm!*"

54

Manuel Garza paused at the bottom of the engine room stairs and wiped his face with a cloth. He was exhausted from the tedium of searching the ship and finding nothing. It was maddening: they knew the worms were on board. They had attacked several crew members, coming out of nowhere and then disappearing. But how do you find a six-inch, pencil-thin, gray worm on a research vessel packed with a million miles of wires and cables? And the engine room promised to be one of the worst places of all.

Frederick Moncton, the ship's chief engineer, a dapper French Canadian with a pencil mustache, was waiting for them, along with the first assistant engineer, two junior engineers, and a fireman. Garza had four guys in his immediate crew, Deputy Security Chief Eyven Vinter and three other security personnel. He had disarmed them; he didn't want pistols being fired in the confined spaces belowdecks, where rounds could ricochet all over and vulnerable equipment abounded. Instead, they carried heavy tools, hatchets and crowbars, as weapons.

Garza had not had occasion to visit the engine room before.

It was a large, hot, stuffy room smelling of diesel fuel and oil lubricants, but on the plus side it was at least a walk-around space, with steel floors kept spotlessly clean. The main diesel engine ran half the length of the room and was painted light gray, and it stood alongside three synchronized diesel generators, painted blue and yellow, that provided the ship with electric power, primary and backup. The rest of the room was a forest of pipes carrying fuel, seawater coolant, oil, and internal engine coolant. Running along the ceiling was a massive amount of ductwork.

It looked well maintained and organized. The personnel who had gathered, in uniform, to help his team go through the engine room appeared steady and professional. They had not succumbed to the hysteria that had been spreading topside. For this Garza was truly grateful.

He plucked the radio from his belt. "Eduardo, do you read?"

A moment later the clipped voice of Bettances, the chief of security, replied. "Roger."

"Your teams find anything?"

"Not a thing."

"Very well. Keep me informed. Garza out."

He replaced the radio. "Mr. Moncton," he said, bringing out several photographs of the worm, "we're looking for these. Any spaces where they might be hiding have to be opened and searched."

Moncton took the photos, flipped through them, and passed them around. "Yes, sir. We're at your service."

"You and your team know the ins and outs of this area. We'd like to start at the far end and sweep back to this point. It seems most efficient if your crew were to take the lead, opening every possible space where these things might be hiding."

"Yes, sir."

Moncton gestured to his men to follow him, and they filed to the back of the engine room via a narrow alleyway among pipes and the throbbing engines. "Most of what you see here," Moncton said, "the engines, the piping, those generators—those can't be opened. Or rather, opening them up would mean stopping the ship and shutting off power. But they're totally sealed environments, so I don't think the worms could get in, and they'd prove a very hostile environment anyway. Most of these pipes are carrying fuel and coolant under high pressure, the engines running at a hundred and sixty degrees."

"Understood," said Garza. "We won't deal with those now. Maybe later, if necessary."

They reached the rear wall, a riveted bulkhead of painted steel. "Chief, let's start with that row of control panels," Garza said. "We'll need to take off the covers and search each one."

"Very well, sir."

One of the junior engineers swiftly produced a large toolbox and they unscrewed the first panel and set it aside, exposing a close packing of wires and circuit boards. Moncton's engineers stepped aside as Garza's team came forward. They pulled on heavy leather gloves and face shields borrowed from the ship's metal shop. Garza watched closely as they poked around, sorting through various bundles of wires, pulling them aside, making sure all of them were real. They followed this up with dental mirrors and pencil lights to peer into the nooks and crannies.

"It's clean," Garza said. "Next."

There was an entire series of panels, switches, and control consoles. They went through them methodically. All were clean.

"Let's move on to the ductwork," Garza said, glancing up. This was going to be a bitch. "Where do those ducts go?"

"They're for engine air and ventilation. The engine air ducts go straight up to the deck. The ventilation ducts are supply and return from HVAC. You want to examine them?"

"You bet we do. Let's start up there, with that square ductwork on the ceiling."

The upper ductwork was accessible via a narrow ladder leading to a precarious catwalk. It consisted of a single large, square duct running the length of the engine room, spaced with oval, swinging gaskets that emitted air when ventilation was needed, but swung shut when off. It ended at a large T with an axial fan.

"Stick the video cam into each of those openings," said Garza. "Let's take a look."

Vinter and another security officer climbed the ladder, the second carrying a small camera and a light on a telescoping pole. Vinter pushed open the first gasket with a gloved hand while the other eased the camera in.

A video image appeared on the iPad Garza was carrying, transmitted via Bluetooth. The duct was empty—at least, as far as the light could reach.

"Next vent."

The men moved down the catwalk and repeated the procedure, looking into each vent in turn. Nothing.

They continued to the end of the duct, where it connected to a large horizontal T-fitting. An access opening was fixed into the underside of the duct, on hinges but screwed shut. The axial fan was humming at the vent's terminus. Below them, the ship's main engine throbbed, the heat rising from it in waves.

"Can we switch that fan off?" Garza asked.

"No problem." The fan was turned off.

"Okay. Swing the vent open and stick the camera in there."

The catwalk was tight, forcing Vinter, in the lead, to crouch underneath the ductwork in order to unscrew the vent door above his head. Two screws came out, which he tucked in his mouth, and then he reached up, grasped the vent flange, and wiggled it from side to side, loosening it from the grip of age. It opened with a screech of dirty hinges; a thin shower of soot came out, sprinkling his head and shoulders. Vinter wiped away the soot with his gloved hand.

The man behind him, carrying the camera on a stick, knelt and positioned himself underneath as well, easing the camera through the opening.

For a split second Garza was bewildered at what he saw pop into life on his screen: a tangled, gray, writhing mass. "Worms!" he cried. "Get back!"

It happened instantly: a sudden burst of scrabbling inside the galvanized ductwork, and then a mass of wriggling, squealing worms came spilling out of the open vent, falling onto the heads and shoulders of the two security officers. They screamed, flailing and twisting, frantically trying to slap and brush the things off them. In the process they fell against the thin railing of the catwalk and it gave way, sending them crashing to the engine room floor, the worms raining down along with them and skittering in every direction.

Garza leapt back, horrified. He could see several worms already squirming into the clothing and wriggling underneath the face protectors of the men on the floor, who were trying to beat them off in a panic. Vinter had torn off his face protector to pluck away the worms underneath, but even more worms converged and his face grew obscured by a solid, writhing mass trying to get at his nose.

"Son of a *bitch*!" Garza yanked a small hatchet out of its sheath on his belt and began chopping at the worms on the floor, trying to crawl toward the struggling men. The remaining two men of his team pulled out their weapons, a crowbar and a heavy wrench, and began beating at the worms. They came fast, making a keening, whining noise, like wounded rats.

"Fall back, there's too many!" Garza shouted, but nobody needed urging; every man was already retreating in the face of the onslaught.

Garza scrambled back himself, chopping at worms left and right as they wriggled toward him. This was clearly a fight they were not going to win.

"Get the hell out of here!" he cried. "Seal the engine room door!"

He retreated with the engineers, the fireman, and the two security officers single file, chopping and beating back the worms, which slashed and struck at them like maddened snakes. Moncton, the chief, grabbed a fire extinguisher and blasted the worms, to no visible effect. As they retreated, Garza could tell that Vinter and the other security officer were already in bad shape, apparently unconscious, twitching worms hanging out of their nostrils; a junior engineer lay on the floor as well, covered with worms, screaming and rolling around, trying to pull worms off his clothing. It was too late—several slipped into his nose despite all he could do, and in a moment he went still, as if suddenly asleep.

Even as they retreated, more worms were dropping out of the ductwork above their heads, falling down on them. They reached the door and Garza stood his ground, smashing at the worms as the others got out. Then he stepped back and the chief slammed the bulkhead door and dogged it down. Several worms, cut in half in the doorway, wriggled about in pieces before Garza beat them to a pulp.

"Christ!" Moncton said, as the others searched their clothing frantically.

"We're clean," said Garza after a moment. "God, those poor guys."

"We can't leave them in there," said Moncton.

"They're already done for."

A trembling silence fell on the group.

"What about the engine room fire-suppression system?" Garza asked. "Can we set that off—kill the worms that way?"

"The system uses FM-200," said the fireman. "Nontoxic."

"Okay, so how do we seal the engine room? Is there another door?"

Moncton shook his head. "These bulkhead doors are all watertight, but the air ducts go straight up to the deck. We can't seal them."

"Why the hell not?"

"Without engine air, the ship would be dead in the water. No propulsion, no electrical power. And the ventilation ducts go everywhere to and from HVAC—they reach into every corner of the vessel."

Garza shook his head. He wiped his face again. "Moncton, can you get me diagrams of all the ductwork on the ship?"

"The digital schematics are all loaded into the ship's network."

Garza nodded. "They're apparently breeding in that ductwork. There are many, *many* more worms just in that one space than we brought aboard with the specimen. This is our new priority. I'll be redeploying all sweep teams to clean out the ductwork, pinpoint their breeding source. And, Chief Moncton, you're going to mastermind the operation for me."

55

In the mission control room, Glinn replayed, yet again, the nuclear simulation as the others watched in silence. It was as if he was looking for something they had missed. But Gideon knew that nothing had been missed. The explosion would simply not reach the deeply buried seeds, no matter what parameters they changed.

Glinn shut down the monitor, pushed the keyboard away. There was a long silence. Gideon glanced at McFarlane, but his face was dark and inscrutable.

"All right," said Glinn. "We'll fire the nuke anyway and pray it works."

At this, McFarlane issued a low, dark laugh. "*Pray*," he said. "Is that where we're at?"

"What other choice do we have? We're out of time." He turned, "Gideon, arm the nuke."

"You can't do that," McFarlane said. "You're so eaten up with guilt about how you delayed acting on the *Rolvaag* that now you're making the opposite mistake—rushing headlong into a foolish, useless action."

Glinn ignored this. "Gideon? Arm the nuke. And load it on the ROV. I'll give you all the personnel you need to get this done as fast as possible."

Gideon once again saw the gleam in Glinn's normally unexpressive eyes. The man had a point. The nuke was their only option. It was only a matter of time until either they were all infected, or the chain of command aboard ship broke down completely. It *could* work. It would probably destroy the alien brain, at the very least—and they had no solid evidence that *all* the brains had to be destroyed in order to kill the entity...

"This is just what Lloyd warned about," McFarlane said. "You're too close to this. Your judgment is clouded. You're going to doom us all."

"What other options do we have? Unless we act—unless we detonate that bomb—the entire world is doomed." Glinn turned back to Gideon. "Arm the bomb."

Gideon took a ragged breath. "No," he said after a moment. "No. McFarlane's right. We only have one shot at this. We can't just detonate and hope for the best—not unless we're sure it's going to work. There *must* be another way."

"If you won't arm it, I will." Glinn got up to leave.

"Wait."

Gideon glanced over. McFarlane had grasped Glinn's arm. The meteorite hunter's face was hollow and dark and beaded in sweat.

"I have an idea," he said.

"I'm listening," Glinn said.

"Years ago, I explored Aklavik, an unusual meteorite crater in northern Canada. One in which a very small impactor resulted in a gigantic crater. I wondered: how did this small rock gouge such a large hole?"

"Go on."

"So I consulted several physicists. The meteorite hit a glacier. It appears the strike caused a phenomenon known as a liquid-liquid explosion."

"I've never heard of such a thing," said Glinn, dubiously.

"It's rare. What happens is two liquids, one cold and one super-hot, are violently mixed together. That in turn creates a huge surface area for immediate heat transfer, and one of the liquids undergoes instantaneous, explosive boiling. It's a big problem in steel mills, for example, if molten steel breaks out and flows over wet concrete. I ought to know—I worked in just such a mill for a while, three years back."

"So how did that work with the meteorite and ice?" asked Glinn. "Both are solids."

"The nickel-iron meteorite liquefied from the shock of impact. That's common. The ice also liquefied from the shock wave. The two mingled violently, and a vast quantity of water boiled in a millisecond, causing a massive explosion."

"You think that will happen with our nuke?" Gideon asked. "In the deep ocean?"

"No. The water won't do it. You need a second liquid—a very hot one—to mix with it."

"Such as?"

"Metal. Steel. You'd need a large amount of molten metal to mix with the water."

"So we put the bomb in a metal shell?"

"That's not nearly enough," said McFarlane. "You want as much metal as possible. Tons and tons of it."

"We can't wrap tons of metal around the bomb," said Gideon. "We wouldn't be able to deliver it."

"You don't have to wrap the bomb. You could lay sheets of

metal on the seafloor. Lay them flat. You do it above where those seeds are growing. That'll focus the explosion."

"Sheets of metal?"

"There must be huge amounts of steel plating on this ship. We could cut a bunch of bulkheads out, stack the sheets of steel on the bottom, then detonate the nuke above them. Close enough for the shock wave to liquefy the steel."

"How much steel are you talking about?" asked Glinn.

"I'd guess a couple hundred tons, at least. The more the better."

A silence. "How do you propose to stack hundreds of tons of steel two miles down?"

"Lower the plates on cables."

"We have two deepwater cables and one winch," said Glinn. "The cables are for emergency lifting of a DSV and are rated to no more than twenty-five hundred pounds displacement mass. It would take hours to lower each plate. Even if we could remove sufficient plating from the ship, we'd never get that much metal down there in time. And will the creature just sit still doing nothing while we stack iron around it?"

"We could dump the metal sheets overboard," said McFarlane.

"Those sheets would orient themselves as they sank," Glinn said. "They would end up being driven into the mud vertically. Would that work?"

"No," said McFarlane.

"Brilliant idea," Glinn said. "A shame it isn't feasible." Again he turned to leave.

Gideon stopped him. "Perhaps this is insane. But isn't there already a huge amount of metal lying down there?"

Glinn frowned impatiently. "Where?"

"The *Rolvaag*, of course."

56

GREG MASTERSON FELT like he was losing control of the mess hall. Someone had brought out a couple of bottles of scotch, from God knew where, and they were being passed around. Voices were raised, people were talking over each other, and nothing was being accomplished aside from useless venting.

This was really pissing him off. In frustration, he climbed up on one of the cafeteria tables. "Hey! Listen up!"

The roar of discontent went on.

"Goddamn it, *listen to me!*" He stomped loudly on the table. "Shut the hell up!"

That worked. The room quieted down.

"We need a plan. And I've got one." Masterson let the anticipation build. There were about twenty people there—crew, mostly, with a few members of the scientific staff. That should be enough. And they looked motivated—very motivated. "Are you ready to listen?" He deliberately pitched his voice low, soft, and this worked even better, as the room finally fell silent.

"Someone shut and lock the door."

It was done.

"Okay," Masterson said. "I think we all know the mission has failed."

A strong murmur of agreement.

"The ship is crawling with those damned alien worms. And they're multiplying. Rumor has it they're in the ductwork. They're in the engine room. They're everywhere."

He paused.

"We need to get the hell off this ship. As soon as possible."

A chorus of agreement. Masterson could feel the energy in the room. People were really listening and now they were coming together. He saw a whiskey bottle pass from hand to hand.

"Hey! Put the bottle down, for Chrissakes. We need to keep our wits about us. It's bad enough that we're all amped up on speed."

It was sheepishly put down.

"God knows how many of our crewmates have been infected. And remember: there's no way to tell. *No way to tell.* Not until it's too late."

Agreement all around.

"Okay. The closest mainland port is Ushuaia, in Argentina. It's seven hundred nautical miles northwest of here. If we start now, at full speed, we'll get there in fifty-eight hours."

A chorus of agreement.

"Up there in mission control, they're going on as if nothing had changed. They still think they can kill that monster. They're delusional."

"Or maybe they're infected!" someone cried.

"That's also a possibility," Masterson agreed. "As I said, there's no way to know. All I do know is, in fifty-eight hours, we could be off this ship and safe in Ushuaia."

This observation was greeted with a roar of approval.

"What do we do, then? Simple. We take over." He looked around fiercely. "In this room, we have the expertise needed—engineering, navigational, operational. And we have the manpower. We can do this."

Another dramatic pause. "We can do this!" echoed through the restive crowd. He also heard the word *mutiny* sprinkled here and there.

"Yes," he said quietly. "Mutiny. But a *necessary* mutiny. A mutiny to save not only our own lives—but the lives of every other uninfected person on board."

This suggestion silenced the room. You could hear a pin drop.

"Are you with me?" Masterson asked quietly.

A low murmur of agreement gathered steam.

"It's now or never. Stand up if you're with me."

One stood up, another, and then another, and within a moment they all rose with a loud scraping of chairs and a swell of voices.

"Is there anyone who disagrees?"

No one did. And this only served to reinforce Masterson's belief that they needed to carry off this mutiny as soon as possible.

Right now, in fact.

57

GARZA CRAWLED ALONG the horizontal supply-air duct that ran the length of the ship, with his two remaining men ahead of him, Moncton behind. They were all wearing construction helmets equipped with powerful headlamps. It was noisy and dirty, but there was, at least, a flow of fresh air. They were approaching the engine room, but so far had seen no sign of worms.

He had in hand an improvised weapon: an electric zapper. They all had them. Moncton had had the idea, and he'd assembled them quickly, using flashlight shells, a spark circuit and spark gap, and a capacitor, the whole thing powered by a pair of D batteries. Moncton was turning out to be some kind of genius: the chief engineer had taken a piece of worm, found it conducted electricity like mad, and decided they must be highly vulnerable to surges in voltage. In about fifteen minutes he assembled all the necessary zappers, and now they were on their way to the engine room, to see if they could find where the worms were breeding.

So far they'd found and zapped a couple of worms—and the zappers had worked beautifully. The zapped worms were *dead*—

or at least so they seemed, all withered and contracted into little gray knots.

Using his radio, he'd ordered Bettances, the chief of security, to deploy his own teams into the ductwork in the other areas of the ship. If they didn't locate the breeding source of the worms soon, they'd be overwhelmed—and fast.

Now they came to an X-junction. Garza consulted the HVAC diagram on his tablet and noted they were just a few bends away from the engine room duct. The two men in front of him used cameras on selfie sticks to peer around the corners, but saw nothing.

The crawling went on forever. They had to pause at every junction, every gasket, and inspect for worms. Garza believed that the worms might be like denning rattlesnakes, seeking each other out and gathering in one mass for mating. He believed that could very well be taking place in the ducts above the engine room—because of the heat. If he was right—if they were all assembled in a single nest—maybe they could take them all out at one go.

"Take the left duct," he said, and they crawled on. They were almost there.

Patrick Brambell awoke, feeling terrifically refreshed, although his body ached from lying on the floor. How had he gotten on the floor? He recalled going to sleep in the chair. As he sat up, he saw that Sax was sleeping in another chair, her feet propped up on the lab table, still set up for the blood tests. Her face was smooth and peaceful, her lips a little wet, her glossy hair spilling across her neck.

"Dr. Sax?"

She opened her eyes, then sat up. "Oops, sorry. I didn't mean to be sleeping." She glanced at her phone. "Not for that long, any-way. The cell phone alarm was supposed to go off."

Brambell picked his phone off the countertop. "Looks like we slept through the alarm. Well, we certainly needed it!" He chuckled, with a twinkle in his eye. "Haven't we been naughty—sleeping like this. Better not tell anyone."

"I feel so much better. I was just about dead. I feel like a new woman."

"Me, too. New man, I mean."

Sax laughed lightly. She stretched, stood up, and looked over the setup on the table. "Do you really think you can come up with a blood test for that thing?"

Brambell sighed. "I doubt it. It seemed worth a try, but you know, on further reflection it's pretty far-fetched." It was crazy, really, to think a simple blood test would somehow reveal an infection from an alien parasite.

"There must be better ways to spend our time," said Sax.

Brambell cast his mind back to the problem. What they desperately needed, he realized, was more information about the creature. That was *the* real problem: their ignorance of the Baobab, what it was, how it thought, why it was here. He felt extremely curious about it. It had come such a vast, lonely distance, and its life cycle was proving to be as complex as anything on earth—even more so.

"We're spinning our wheels in this lab," Sax said. "This isn't getting us anywhere."

"No, indeed."

"I wish there was a way for us to be more useful."

Brambell fell back into musing. "The problem," he said slowly, "is that the wrong people have been sent down to observe the Baobab. Gideon Crew: a nuclear engineer. Lispenard: a marine biologist. Garza: another engineer."

Sax nodded. "That's a good point."

"Technocrats all. None of them are humanists—not like you and me."

Sax nodded, running a hand over her glossy brown hair, smoothing it down. Brambell found himself admiring just how healthy it looked, and how delicate and white her hand was. He wondered why he hadn't paid more attention to her before.

"What they really should have done," Brambell said, "is to send someone like you or me down there—you, with an MD and PhD in medical science, or me, with an MD and decades of experience. We're the ones best suited for understanding an alien organism like that."

"I couldn't agree more."

Brambell fell into another musing silence, thinking. His mind seemed unusually clear; it was remarkable, really, what a good nap could do. As he went back over in his mind the progress of the expedition so far, it really did appear to him now to have been a dog's breakfast from the very beginning. Everything had been done the wrong way. The whole concept—of killing the creature—was flawed. It was clearly intelligent, and as such it could be communicated with. Reasoned with. *Understood.* Prothero had started down that path, but there had been no concerted effort; not really. If the Baobab could learn whale speech, surely it could learn human speech...

"You know?" said Brambell, turning to Sax. "I think one of us *should* go down there and try to communicate with that thing. That would solve all our problems in one fell swoop."

He found Sax looking back at him with admiration in her eyes. He hadn't noticed before how pretty she was. "Dr. Brambell, that is truly insightful." She hesitated. "But...how would we get down there?"

"We'll simply borrow a DSV. I believe *John* is right there in the hangar, ready to go. I truly feel that a simple conversation, a respectful meeting of the minds, would solve all our problems."

"We...just take it?"

"Yes," said Brambell. "We take it. Only one of us can go, of course, and that one will be me."

"I should be the one to go," she said. "After all, I've had some experience piloting DSVs."

"I'm not sure," Brambell said.

"Oh, please do let me go. You'll be with me every step of the way—in spirit."

Brambell thought about this. Then he nodded. "Very well. Since we'll be launching the DSV without any help, I suppose it might take my strength to manhandle the necessary equipment alone."

"Thank you, thank you!" Sax said, her eyes shining.

"Dr. Sax, I don't believe we should waste any more time—do you?"

"Dr. Brambell," she said, clasping her hands together, "I *so* admire your wisdom and courage."

58

As GARZA AND his team neared the engine room, he could feel and hear the vibration of the turbines coming through the ventilation duct. The focused beams of their headlamps cast a strong light down the duct to where it ended in a T. Beyond that T, and to the right, was the engine room duct. That was where they had initially encountered the nest of worms.

He felt fairly confident there were more.

He tapped the foot of the guy in front, and used hand signals to indicate they were to move up to the T and then pause. It was impossible to crawl through the ducts without generating a lot of noise and vibration, but Garza hoped that the worms would not be alerted, since plenty of noise and vibration was already traveling through the ductwork of the ship.

The ducts were of sturdy galvanized steel, and well attached, but even so they were not designed to carry the weight of four people, and as they moved the metal groaned in protest, swayed occasionally, even sagged a little. They had spread out to try to distribute the weight, but it still felt at times that the ductwork might just come loose and precipitate them to the floor of whatever room they were in.

As they neared the junction, Garza signaled another halt. He listened, straining to hear any scritching movements of shifting worms or the chalk-on-blackboard squealing sounds they made when excited. But there was nothing: just the humming of the engines and the whisper of moving air.

If there was a mass of them around the corner, there would be no running away. All four of them knew that. On their hands and knees in a confined space, with no possibility of turning around, they would have to stand their ground—stay and fight, like the defenders of Thermopylae.

The point man edged up to the T and, holding his camera out on its stick, eased it past the corner.

The image appeared on Garza's tablet. It took a moment to wrap his mind around it: the duct was free and clear for perhaps twenty feet, but then it became totally blocked by a large, bubbling mass that looked like thick, gluey porridge, or perhaps a giant glistening fungus. The surface of the mass was covered with what appeared to be giant pustules, but as he watched, a pustule burst and from it dropped a worm, which crawled off. And then another pustule burst; another worm dropped out.

So the worms *were* breeding, but not at all in the way he'd assumed. It was a single entity, pumping out eggs. Fine—that made it all the more vulnerable.

In silence he passed the tablet around so everyone could see what lay ahead, and then gestured for them to move back a little. When they had done so, he whispered: "That mass is right above the main engine. Probably attracted to the heat."

Nods.

"We can't get into the engine room. So we have to attack it from here—inside the duct."

"How?" asked one of his men.

Moncton, who was behind Garza, whispered, "We Tase it." He held up his electrical prod. "I can set these to shock on contact, like a Taser. We throw them at the breeding mass."

"The current from a couple of D batteries isn't going to kill it," one of Garza's men said.

"The circuitry in here produces low current but high voltage," Moncton said in a low voice. "Nine thousand volts, to be exact. So yes, it might kill it. It *will* kill it. That life-form conducts electricity better than copper."

"We're dead meat crammed into this ductwork. We can't even turn around!"

"Pass me your zappers," Garza said. "I'll do it. I'll toss two, keep one in reserve. Moncton, you take charge of the fourth zapper. Meanwhile, the three of you get back. And be ready to haul ass."

There was just enough room at the T-junction for Garza to squeeze past the two forward men. Moncton quickly unscrewed each device, tinkered with it, screwed it back together. "Just turn the flashlight switch on," he said, handing three of them up to Garza. "Then the current will flow between the prongs as soon as there's a connection—which there will be, the moment these prongs make contact with that thing. Okay?"

"Okay."

Garza began to crawl forward, past the T-junction and to the right.

His headlamp illuminated the pulsing mass. The worms were very responsive to light, and the bloated mass also reacted. The pulsing suddenly stopped. The worms crawling around it froze, coiled up, and took a protective, striking position.

Garza braced himself, switched on the first zapper, and tossed it as easily as a horseshoe. It was a good throw and its two prongs struck the mass squarely; there was a flash of electricity and the thing contracted violently, with a flabby rush of air, most of its pustules bursting and releasing worms in various stages of development.

There was a moment of stasis. And then worms surrounding the thing came whipping down the duct toward him, keening and scrabbling, their black teeth poking out.

He tossed the second zapper and made another direct hit, with its attendant flash of electricity. At this the thing ruptured open, expelling a foul, jelly-like mass of half-formed worms.

Garza crawled backward as fast as he could go, but the worms coming at him were faster. As they caught up to him he zapped them with a third prod; as he did so, the worms would make a little screech, then contract into grotesque, pretzel-like shapes.

"Get going!" he shouted. "Retreat to the nearest opening!"

A worm reached him, slashed at him; Garza zapped it, then zapped another. One after the other after the other. But his zapper's recovery time was slowing. The battery would soon be dead.

"Give me the other one!"

Moncton handed Garza the last prod.

"There's a big vent here!" a voice called from behind.

"*Exit!*"

The men dropped out of the vent, Garza last, followed by a river of worms.

"Forget the worms!" he shouted. "Run!"

They had come out in the corridor beyond the engine room, and they all immediately took off, ducking beneath a bulkhead door. Garza slammed and dogged it behind them.

"Jesus H. Christ," he said, leaning against the door and gasping for breath. He had cuts all over his hands from the slashing worms.

"You think there are more of those breeders?" Moncton asked.

"The way our luck is going, I sure as hell do," Garza replied, pulling out his radio to call Bettances. "And at the rate those worms are being pumped out, I'll lay you ten to one we're all zombies by lunchtime."

59

Patrick Brambell and Antonella Sax emerged onto the hangar deck shortly after the sun rose over the rim of the ocean.

"What remarkable weather we've been having," said Brambell cheerfully as they strolled across the hangar. "Nice of that approaching storm to hold off long enough for us to accomplish our goal."

"Really remarkable."

The DSV *John* sat in its rolling cradle, strapped down and draped in canvas. No one was around; the ship was in an uproar and all security personnel had been pulled off to assist in the hunt for worms.

"Are you sure you know how to operate this thing?" asked Brambell.

"Part of Glinn's habit of 'double overage,' you know: safety in redundancy. Really, it's rather like playing a video game. Joystick-controlled. Pretty simple. Although in this instance I'll have to disable the autopilot AI and turn off the surface override. Otherwise, the do-gooders might try to pull me back up and stop our mission."

"You can do that?"

"I was in mission control when they forced Gideon Crew's DSV back to the surface. Back when Alex Lispenard went to her new home. I saw them open the procedures manual on how to override the AI and the DSV operator's control. I saw the codes." She shook her head. "If they hadn't meddled so unnecessarily like that, maybe Dr. Crew could have come home then, too."

Once again, Brambell considered how profoundly misconceived the entire mission was. An intelligent, alien life-form had come to earth. And what was mankind's first response? Kill it.

How sad. And yet how predictable.

"All right, let's take a look at this," he said.

They each gripped an edge of the tarp and slid it off, exposing the mini sub. It looked fresh and new, gleaming in the sodium lights of the hangar, ready for its next dive, iron ballast already attached. Sax walked around, unclipping the tie-downs that held it in place on the cradle. She climbed into the motorized cart used to haul the DSVs to and fro, backed it up, and attached it to the towing pin.

"Open the hangar doors," she said.

Brambell rolled back the double doors, the sunlight pouring in. What a beautiful day it was, he thought, as he looked out to the distant sea horizon. A beautiful day in which to open a channel of communication—*real* communication—with the life-form. It had tried to speak to them in blue whale speech. If it could learn that, it could surely learn English. Indeed, with all the chatter it must have been picking up, chances were it *already* knew some English. He breathed deeply, thinking about the momentous step they were about to take—not for themselves, but for all humankind.

He stood in the warm spring sun and watched Sax expertly

tow *John* into position under the A-frame crane, get out, unhook it. She waved him over.

"What are you doing?" she asked.

"Daydreaming. About being part of a day that will go down in history."

She laughed and gave him a playful punch on the arm. "Come on, we've got work to do. Help me roll that ladder into position."

They took the rolling ladder and together wheeled it over to the DSV. Brambell held the ladder in place, then watched her derriere as she climbed up and attached the crane's two cables to hooks on the DSV. Then she came back down. "What are you grinning about?"

"You."

She smirked. "I'm getting inside. Do you see that console over there? Those are the controls for the crane. Once again, joystick-operated. You know how to use a joystick?"

"Oh, dear," said Brambell. "Never in my life."

She took his hand. "I'll show you. It's easy. Just try not to bump me around too much before putting me in the water."

At the console she demonstrated up, down, sideways for the boom, plus the control to raise and lower the cables. And finally, the button that unhooked the DSV. "Don't hit that button until I'm in the water, floating, with the cables slack."

"Understood. Ready?"

"I'm ready."

Brambell helped her onto the ladder and watched her climb up to the hatch at the top. The DSV really did look like the Yellow Submarine. Brambell had always felt a special affiliation with the Beatles, on account of his grandfather, the actor Wilfrid Brambell, having played Paul McCartney's fictional grandfather in the film *A Hard Day's Night*.

"Okay, Patrick!" She waved to him and gave him a thumbs-up. He smiled and waved back, and then she descended and shut the hatch.

Brambell looked around to see if anyone was paying attention. There was a knot of people at one end of the aft deck, talking or arguing, but they paid him no heed. His mind was unusually clear, and he remembered the directions perfectly. He maneuvered the joystick. The cables tightened, raising the sub from its cradle. When it was clear of the cradle, he pushed the crane stick sideways and the crane obediently swung away from the A-frame, carrying the DSV until it was dangling over the stern. Checking to make sure there was plenty of clearance, he lowered *John* to the water, where it settled in, still buoyant. He pressed the button that disengaged the hooks, and the DSV was free.

"Good luck, Antonella," he said to himself under his breath, as a rush of air bubbles around the DSV indicated Sax was filling ballast tanks. The mini sub sank beneath the surface. He watched for a few minutes as it went down and then disappeared.

Brambell felt a certain loneliness steal over him. He had to admit he was a bit in love with Sax. But he would see her again, and soon—he was certain of that.

Leaving the console, he wandered back into the hangar, feeling restless and anxious. He wondered what there was to do now. It did seem as if there should be more to do, and then it occurred to him what it was: stop this insane use of the nuke. He wasn't sure when that was supposed to be deployed, exactly, but it didn't matter: he could stop that right now.

At the far end of the hangar, set apart from everything else, was another draped submersible. It was not a manned DSV, but a smaller ROV. That, he knew, was the intended delivery vehicle for the bomb.

It would be a simple matter to make sure the ROV never delivered a bomb anywhere.

Antonella Sax worked the controls of *John* as it descended into the depths. She located the main panel, then punched in the code to deactivate the mini sub's AI and disable any surface override of her autopilot. She felt a sensation of warmth and security as the DSV was enveloped in darkness. She could almost feel the massive weight of water pressing in on it relentlessly, increasing with every meter she sank. There was a feeling of anticipation, of excitement, as she was about to perform perhaps the greatest mission ever conducted by a human being.

As she descended, humming a little tune to herself, she saw movement: a head poked out of a gap in the electronics, a small head with two beady eyes and a tiny puckered mouth. The mouth opened, exposing a single tooth.

"Who are you?" Sax asked playfully.

As if in response, the little creature crawled out of its hiding place and came over, curling up against her thigh for warmth.

She touched it. "There's a good boy," she said, stroking it as it relaxed in contentment. "There's a good boy."

60

GREG MASTERSON HAD gathered the mutineers in the rec room, adjacent to the staff quarters, to explain the plan of attack. They had arrived well equipped with weapons. Many had knives, but some of the ex-servicemen had their sidearms, as well. At the last minute, the group had been joined by two of the security guards who had been sweeping for worms, including the deputy security chief, a man named Vinter. Vinter was a godsend: he not only knew the layout of the ship by memory, but also knew its security protocols and codes.

As the men and women assembled in the room, Masterson thought about what was coming. He had no illusions. But what had to be done had to be done. That this crazy mission kept going forward, even in the face of obvious failure, suggested to him that the top officers weren't just affected by bad judgment, but may have actually been infected: perhaps all of mission control, or the entire bridge.

He looked around. Everyone appeared ready. "Okay, listen up."

Silence fell.

"We're very fortunate to be joined by Mr. Eyven Vinter. He was, or rather still is, deputy chief of security. I'm going to turn the floor over to him to describe the plan we've worked out."

Vinter, a massive man with a charismatic presence, stepped forward. "The primary goal is to take the ship's bridge. The key element will be surprise. The secondary goal is to take over, or at least incapacitate, mission control. With those two objectives complete, we will proceed directly to Ushuaia."

His tone was blunt and direct, and he spoke with a quiet, pleasing Scandinavian accent.

"The captain and officers will defend the bridge with a strong sense of duty. We may need to resort to violence. But no one on the bridge is likely to be armed. Only security is allowed to carry arms on the bridge—and there is no security there at the present time."

A steely look around the room. No one flinched.

"The bridge is designed to stop entry by anyone who might try to commandeer the ship. There are only two points of ingress, port and starboard doors. Quarter-inch steel. Under normal operations, those doors are left open. So we go in fast and hard, taking them by surprise, and seize control of the openings to prevent the doors from being shut and locked. Once we gain control of the bridge, then we turn the bridge's defenses to our own purpose by sealing the doors."

Masterson stepped forward. "Thank you, Mr. Vinter. Any questions?"

"What about the engine room?" someone asked. "Can't they shut down the engines from there?"

"Yes," said Vinter. "But once we're safely in control of the bridge, we can make our case, via the ship's intercom, which we will also control, to the rest of the crew. They can conceivably shut down the engines and power, but that will only render the *Batavia* dead in the water. Not much use in that—and not a good means of persuasion." He paused, and then said with quiet and unshakable conviction: "We will have the upper hand. We *will* prevail."

As Masterson looked out over the group, he saw that this man, with his rock-like presence and quiet voice, was having a galvanizing effect. "We can't wait," he said. "Word will leak out—it always does. So we're doing this now. Are you all with us?"

Everyone was.

"There are twenty of us. We're going to divide into five groups of four. We'll head toward the bridge, strolling easily through the corridors, chatting lightly, attracting no attention. We'll converge at the lower bridge deck below the companionway—but there will be no pause. Just keep up the momentum, rush the doors, and secure them. Those with firearms, cover the officer of the watch, the captain, and the other bridge officers. If they resist, shoot—but only as a last resort. Those with knives, take up a defensive position at the doors."

Masterson paused. He realized he was sweating. He felt afraid. But when he glanced over at Vinter, standing beside him, he grew reassured. *He* wasn't afraid. The man exuded confidence.

"What if the bridge doors are already locked?" someone asked.

"They won't be," said Vinter. "That's against all security protocols. But on the off chance they are—if there has been a recent worm attack, for example—then I will talk us in, as deputy chief of security."

Masterson divided the people into groups and sent them off on different paths, all of which would converge at the bridge. He led one group. They took a somewhat roundabout route forward, trying to look nonchalant. As they moved through the ship, Masterson was struck by the atmosphere on board; while some people were still going about their business, much of the crew seemed idle, standing about in agitated groups. Others were obviously inebriated, and one man lay in a corridor, empty bottle in hand, passed out. The withdrawal of security to sweep for worms, the lack of sleep, and the rampant suspicions among the crew about who might have been infected had caused a sharp deterioration in morale.

It only reinforced Masterson's belief that they needed to get this ship into port as soon as possible. They could deal with the worm infestation once people were off the ship—burn the vessel to the waterline, scuttle it if necessary, put everyone in quarantine until the infected could be identified. But decontaminating the ship wasn't his immediate problem. Right now, his problem was getting them the hell out of there.

As he walked, he felt the bulge of the .45 Vinter had given him. Masterson wasn't a gun enthusiast, but he'd hunted with his father and knew how to aim and fire a pistol. He hoped to God he wouldn't have to use it.

He led his group to the lower bridge deck, where the others were now converging. Without acknowledgment, they climbed the stairway to the bridge deck. The port bridge door was indeed open. Vinter was ahead of him, and he had his gun out. The man stepped easily through the door, Masterson following.

Everyone on the bridge was so focused on their individual tasks that no one even looked in their direction. Masterson watched as Vinter raised his gun, casually aimed, and fired at the officer of the watch, hitting him in the back. The sound of the gun going off was incredibly loud, and the man went down as if he'd been hit with a sledgehammer. The cold-bloodedness of it froze Masterson. This wasn't what Vinter had said was going to happen.

First Officer Lennart, who was standing next to the officer of the watch and was, to Masterson's surprise, armed with a sidearm, spun, drew and fired her own weapon with astonishing rapidity. Vinter was hit and thrown back against the wall. She fired again, the bullet whining just below Masterson's ear. She kept coming, kept firing; Masterson fell back through the door as a third round banged off the steel doorjamb; meanwhile, the rest of the bridge personnel were drawing weapons—they *all* had weapons—and were charging the mutineers, returning fire.

Vinter, up against the inside wall of the bridge, fired his weapon a second time and dropped Lennart with a bullet that, all too obviously, took out her heart and its attendant plumbing. He fired again, hitting another officer, even as he himself took a second round. He staggered back through the door, bullets ricocheting around him, sparks flying. He took cover behind the door, and a moment later it was slammed shut. Masterson threw himself against it to force it back open, but it was too late: it was sealed.

An alarm sounded on the ship's emergency system.

"Son of a bitch!" Vinter roared, blood pouring from an ugly wound in his shoulder and another in his forearm. There was confusion among the mutineers behind them.

A shot was fired in the companionway, then another. "We're under attack from behind!" someone yelled.

Vinter swung around and, still bleeding, charged down the stairs, gun still in hand. The others followed. Several security officers, converging on the scene, began shooting and took down a couple of mutineers, but were themselves quickly cut down by Vinter and some of the others.

"Retreat to staff quarters!" Vinter shouted. "To quarters!"

They raced along the maindeck, people scattering as they charged past. There was very little additional security to be seen. Vinter plunged down the companionway to the staff quarters; as they poured through, he slammed and dogged the door.

"Seal the doors in back!" he cried. "We can defend this space!"

The doors were sealed. Vinter leaned against the wall, his hand pressed on the gunshot wound in his shoulder.

"We've got to get you help," said Masterson.

The man gave an ugly laugh. "Get me some bandages and compresses and I'll be fine."

There was bewilderment and confusion among the mutineers who had managed to get back. "What the hell happened?" one asked.

"They were armed," Vinter said. "The presence of the worms must have changed the no-arms protocol. My fault." He sagged down into a chair as the rest gathered around. "We can hold out here—we've got food and water. And arms. It'll be hell for them to root us out—it would take cutting torches or explosives to get through those doors, and we'll be keeping a watch to nip any of that in the bud. Besides, they have other things on their minds."

"But…" Masterson felt overwhelmed with confusion. "What do we do now?"

"Stick to the plan. Take the bridge. There's some C4 in the security armory. We'll blow those doors. And I can hack our way into the shipwide intercom, rally others to the cause." He took a few breaths. "We've had a setback. But we can still do this. Discipline on the ship is falling apart. That's to our advantage."

Pounding began on the door to staff quarters, followed by shouting. Vinter rose, made a gesture to Masterson. "Talk to them. Tell them we want to take the ship to safety in Ushuaia. Get them to join us—if only to save their own lives."

61

GARZA GAZED AT the video image on his iPad, coming from the camera that had been lowered forty feet through the vertical engine air duct.

"Oh, Jesus, that's the mother of all breeders," he said, passing the iPad to Moncton.

Moncton gave a low whistle. "I'm not surprised. That's just where the flue makes a ninety-degree turn from vertical to horizontal. It's flat, protected, and particularly warm from the engine."

He passed the iPad back. "I suggest we go in from the side. Maybe we don't even need to cut a hole. But that means going back through the engine room and into the alcove holding the compressor and turbocharger."

Garza turned to the two remaining men on his team. "What do you say?"

"Let's do it."

Once again they descended into the bowels of the ship, Moncton leading the way. Garza was mightily impressed with Moncton. He was a rather odd fellow, with a curiously precise way of walking, almost like a dancing master: small and neat, but damn near unflappable. Garza could hardly believe how tough the guy was. Over the past hour, Garza had started to feel they might actually be able to overcome the worms, after all. While the things were still everywhere, they had killed three giant breeding masses and zapped countless loose worms, and that seemed to have put the fear of God into the things. They seemed less aggressive and more prone to run and hide than attack en masse.

He hadn't been able to raise the security chief, Bettances, on the radio since their last communication twenty minutes before. He hoped to God that didn't mean what he feared it meant.

A short trip brought them to the closed door of the engine room. While the ship was not under way, the engines were still throbbing gently, the main engine keeping the ship in position using dynamic positioning, and the synchronized generators supplying electric power.

Garza felt a twinge as they gathered at the steel hatch into the engine room. After their first encounter, Moncton had jerry-rigged a heavy-duty zapper on a long pole, which they had plunged into the jelly-like breeding mass. It had worked well. Electricity was deadly to the worms and it didn't take much of it to kill them.

"I'll go first," said Moncton.

Garza stood to one side, his two team members behind. They lowered their face shields and tugged on heavy gloves, poor protection though they were. Garza eased the hatch open. Moncton stepped inside, zapper at the ready, and he followed. It was hot and close. Bits and pieces of smashed worms lay about.

"The bodies are gone," said one of his men.

"Yeah. They sleep two hours, then wake up and act normal. They're probably walking around the ship as we speak."

"Right, right. Maybe we should've…" The man hesitated.

"Put them out of their misery?" said Garza. "Maybe."

The men fell silent. The engine room seemed normal, aside from the dead worms on the floor. The vent dangled open, and a dark liquid was dripping from it and streaking part of the main engine. The liquid, Garza realized, was draining from the breeding mass they had killed farther up the vent.

"The air supply, along with the turbo and compressor, is in the back," Moncton said.

Garza and the other two followed the ship's chief engineer down the main aisle of the engine room. The room was brightly lit and there was no additional sign of worms. Moncton reached the end of the giant main engine, ducked under a pipe, turned a tight corner, then stopped. There, in front of them, was a large galvanized flue, which came down through the ceiling and made a ninety-degree turn. It yawned open in a huge, mouth-like vent, six feet tall, looming over a mass of pipes and tubes—the compressor, turbo, and aftercooler. It lay behind a forest of pipes and valves.

Moncton whispered: "The mass is inside and below the elbow. I think we ought to try zapping it right through the galvanized flue."

"Won't there be a Faraday cage effect, the charge dissipated?"

"No, because the mass itself is a better conductor than the steel. The majority of the charge will go right into it."

"There's only enough room for one person to squeeze in there," Garza told him. "I'll go."

Moncton shook his head. "No. My turn."

Garza wasn't about to argue. He gestured for his two to stay back, their zappers ready. He followed Moncton into the tight space as far as he could.

"Get ready to run," Moncton whispered into his ear as he crouched, zapper pole in hand, working his way still farther into the jungle of colored pipes. Garza began to lose sight of the man in the knitted shadows. He waited. At any moment he would hear the crackle of the zapper as Moncton shot the side of the steel duct, along with the high-pitched screams of the worms inside as they were electrocuted.

Instead, he heard a rustling, whispering, scritching noise—*from behind*—followed by the sounds of things hitting the ground.

He turned. Both of his men were down—down without a sound—their heads covered with writhing worms, their arms waving feebly before flopping to the ground.

"Moncton!" he cried. "Get back—we've been ambushed!"

But there was no sound from ahead—except more rustlings and whisperings. And now he saw it: worms were gliding everywhere through the pipes, coming for him.

Garza jammed his zapper on a metal pipe and pulled the trigger; a sudden chorus of squealing arose as the worms jumped and jerked, falling off the pipe. He plunged backward, hitting several more pipes, zapping worm after worm, slapping and pulling them off him as they rained down from above. He was yelling at the top of his lungs, tearing off his shirt as the worms got inside; he leapt over the worm-infested bodies of the two men, and then—feeling the worms all over his body—he turned the zapper on himself, jabbing it into his chest and pulling the trigger in desperation.

It was like being hit by a truck: an immense jolt and flash of light, and he lost the use of his legs and fell to the ground. But even as he crashed to the floor, barely conscious, he realized the worms had dropped from his body. Crawling, trembling all over, he zapped himself again. Then he collapsed.

He wasn't unconscious; merely unable to use his muscles. He felt like an immense stone was on his chest, retarding his breathing. But the worms—the worms were crawling away. Fleeing him.

He lay there, trying to breathe, trying to clear his head of the millions of stars. After a moment, with an immense act of will, he managed to pull himself to his knees and crawl the length of the engine room, get to the door, climb over the metal lip, and seal it behind him.

Then he fell back on the cold steel decking and tried to get his jumping, tingling muscles back under control. It was in that moment he realized they had failed: they were never going to clear the ship of worms.

Because the worms were adapting.

62

THANK GOD, THOUGHT Gideon, that the nuke chamber was high-security and damn near impregnable. Glinn's QBA had proven correct: the ship had descended into chaos. They had just received word that a group of mutineers had tried to take over the bridge, killed Lennart and the officer of the watch, and were now holed up in the crew quarters. They had somehow taken over the ship's intercom and were broadcasting their message, steadily attracting converts to the cause. A group of people had tried to steal the ship's helicopter, and even managed to get it aloft, but the AStar had only gone a quarter of a mile before spinning out of control and crashing into the sea. There were also reports that the DSV *John* had been stolen and launched by persons unknown. The ship was overrun with worms. Garza had just reported the loss of his remaining team and the ship's chief engineer to a worm attack.

The people attacked by the worms, Gideon knew, were not dead, of course; they were going about their business as if normal, but all the while unconsciously doing the bidding of that thing down at the bottom of the ocean. And doing so while remaining resolutely certain their actions were justified and logical, even while they were carrying out sabotage and murder.

Inside the nuke chamber, Glinn and McFarlane, with the aid of two technicians, had used a ceiling-track winch to lift the nuke onto an electric dolly, specially built to transport it to the hangar deck for loading onto the ROV. All the electronics had checked out. Gideon had given the device a final once-over: the bomb was going to work perfectly. All that remained to do was set the timer.

Now the nuke was in a canvas sling dangling from the ceiling-track lift. Slowly, slowly, the two technicians lowered the device onto the cradle built to receive it, steadying it in gloved hands and rotating it into position.

Done.

The technicians unhooked the winch cables. Glinn went to the door and listened. Gideon could hear periodic muffled noises in the hall outside.

Glinn went into the back of the nuke chamber, unlocked a cabinet. Gideon was startled to see that it contained a small arsenal of firearms. Glinn sorted through them and removed five Colt .45 pistols in holsters, a stack of magazines, and boxes of bullets. He placed them on a worktable. "We may need to defend ourselves," he said. "Each one of you take a sidearm and load two magazines."

McFarlane quickly sorted through the weapons, Gideon following. The two technicians hesitated.

"Ever fire a weapon before?" Glinn asked them.

One shook his head and the other said, "I'm not sure now's the time to start."

Glinn leaned in. "This is no time for scruples." He pulled a pistol from the holster, ejected the magazine, demonstrated how to insert rounds into it, slapped it back into place, and showed them how the safety worked and how to rack the initial round into the chamber.

"Both hands on the grip when you fire. Understood?" He handed a gun to each technician. "It's a war zone out there. We need to do what it takes to get this device up to the hangar deck."

Gideon discarded the holster and stuck a gun into his belt.

Glinn turned to the nuke sitting in the cradle. "And now we'd better disguise that." He opened a life-preserver container—ubiquitous throughout the ship—pulled out a few preservers, and heaped them up on the nuke.

"Cover it with the tarp."

The technicians placed the tarp over and tied it down with straps, creating a vague, canvas-covered lump.

"What's it supposed to be?" asked Gideon.

"Chocks and dunnage," said Glinn.

"What's the hell's that?"

"No one's going to ask. Let's go. Two in front, two behind, guns drawn and visible. Sam, you watch our rear."

Glinn unlocked the door while one technician climbed into the seat of the motorized dolly. The nuke chamber was deep in the ship; they had to take it half the ship's length and up three decks in order to reach the hangar.

Glinn swung open the door. The corridor was empty. They reached the elevator without incident, not running into anyone and not seeing any worms.

The elevator doors shut and Glinn pressed the button for the hangar deck.

Even before the doors opened, Gideon could hear shouting. He drew his weapon, and so did the rest.

The elevator doors slid open to reveal a group of men waiting for the elevator. They, too, all had weapons—the main armory had apparently been looted—and they looked agitated.

"Hey—look who's here," one of them said, stepping forward. "If it isn't Eli Glinn himself."

There was a moment of tense silence. There were six of them, to Glinn's five. Gideon had the distinct impression the men were heading down to the crew deck to join the mutineers.

"You're coming with us," the apparent ringleader said, leveling his AR-15 at Glinn.

A shot rang out and the man's head jerked back. Then he crumpled to the floor, his assault rifle going off harmlessly. McFarlane stepped forward, smoking .45 now aimed at the man standing behind the leader. "You're next."

The sound of the shot seemed to shock the group into a momentary freeze. His own gun leveled, Glinn slowly stepped out of the elevator, with Gideon and McFarlane following. Glinn waved to the technicians to bring along the dolly.

The group of mutineers continued to point their weapons, but nobody fired. The ringleader lay on the floor, a pool of blood spreading from the ugly wound in his head. Even as they watched, a worm began to emerge from the wound. The other five backed up, frightened and uncertain.

Glinn spoke in a strangely calm, even warm tone. "Be careful where you put your trust, gentlemen. And now we will be on our way."

The group, sweating, moved aside and let them pass, McFarlane and Gideon keeping their weapons trained on them until they had turned a corner.

In a few minutes they came out onto the hangar deck. It was thankfully deserted, the hangar doors rolled open. The lights were already on and *John* was indeed missing. Glinn dismissed the two nuke technicians, telling them to return to mission control and join the teams sweeping for worms.

Standing at the far end, his bald pate shining in the sodium lights, was Patrick Brambell. He had pulled the canvas off the ROV and—inexplicably—was bashing at it with a sledgehammer.

"Stop!" Glinn yelled, raising his weapon.

Brambell looked up. "Dr. Glinn. Just the man I wanted to speak to." He took another swing at the ROV, the sledgehammer clanging off the titanium sphere.

Gideon could see immediately that the ROV had been given a pretty good working over. The propulsion system was in pieces, the mech arm torn away, the basket bashed off, and everything else accessible utterly destroyed.

"Step away from the ROV or I'll shoot!" Glinn said in an even tone.

"Do you realize just how absurd this whole scheme is?" Brambell cried. "We've been visited by an intelligent species—"

"I said, *step away from the ROV.*"

Brambell let the sledgehammer drop. "It's wrong to kill it. The creature's intelligent, probably more so than we—"

Glinn cut him off. "Who took *John?*"

"I'm glad you asked. Dr. Sax went down to open talks with the creature."

"Why?"

"Because it's her firm belief—and mine—that what is needed here is not violence, but communication—"

"*When* did she take it?"

"About half an hour ago."

At that moment a shirtless Manuel Garza appeared in the doorway of the hangar. At his heels was Rosemarie Wong, Prothero's lab assistant, along with a DSV handler.

Glinn continued to speak to Brambell. "Were you part of this?" he demanded, still pointing his gun at the doctor.

"I was indeed. Let me explain."

"Enough explanation. Get away from the ROV and lie face-down on the floor."

"Don't be ridiculous! You see, the ROV—"

"He's infected, of course," said McFarlane loudly.

"Me, infected? Absurd! Has the whole ship gone mad? At any rate, *I* know what I'm doing—even if you do not." Brambell picked up the sledgehammer and raised it again.

Glinn pulled the trigger, the report booming through the hangar space. A surprised look appeared on Brambell's face and he looked down at his chest. Glinn fired a second time and Brambell crumpled to the deck, as if in slow motion.

Glinn stepped back and turned to Garza. "You've come from the engine room?"

Garza was breathing heavily, and sweat covered his bare chest. "It's no good. We'll never be able to stop the worms—they're smart, and they're breeding too quickly." He jerked a thumb at Wong and the DSV handler. "These two wanted to help. They're clean."

"Indeed." Glinn turned to the man, but before he could speak Wong uttered a loud scream. A worm was sliding out of Brambell's nose with a long, sinuous motion. Gray, shining with body fluids, it seemed to keep coming forever.

With a grunt of disgust, McFarlane stepped over and ground it into paste with his boot.

Glinn gave this but a moment's attention. "Assess the damage to the ROV, please," he told the handler.

The man did a quick survey. "The hatch is still sealed." He opened the ROV's hatch, peered in with a flashlight. "The inside appears okay."

"How long will it take to repair?" Glinn asked.

The handler spent a moment checking the rear propulsion system, looking over the ROV's hull. He shuffled around and finally looked up, spreading his hands.

"Well?" Glinn asked.

"I'm afraid it's a total loss."

"What about the titanium sphere itself?"

"That's intact. Not much a sledgehammer could do to harm that. But the ROV itself is useless: no propulsion, no autopilot, no communications, and no internal power. It's just an inert titanium shell."

"But a shell still able to withstand pressure at depth?"

"Yes."

"How about buoyancy? With the nuke loaded?"

"Not neutrally buoyant, but it was designed to be only slightly heavy in order to help with ballasting."

"So the nuke *could* be put in the titanium sphere, and it *could* be towed to the detonation point—and it then *could* be detonated."

"Towed down?" McFarlane asked. "With what? I thought that stolen DSV was the last."

"We've got a spare," said Glinn. "Under wraps. The *Pete*."

"*Pete?*"

"Named after Pete Best," said Garza.

"So..." McFarlane turned to the handler. "Can it really be towed?"

"Perhaps," said the handler, sounding a little dubious.

"It has to be detonated six hundred feet above the *Rolvaag*," said McFarlane. "It's not likely to work higher or lower."

"That's correct," said Gideon. "The quick-and-dirty simulation I did showed that six hundred feet is the optimal detonation point for a liquid-liquid explosion. The numbers begin to fall off the closer you detonate it to the hulk."

"In other words, we're talking a suicide mission," said Glinn.

A silence.

Glinn continued, "Someone in *Pete* has to tow the nuke into position six hundred feet above the *Rolvaag* and hold it there until it goes off."

"Why not just lower it by cable?" asked McFarlane.

"If it goes off under the *Batavia*," Gideon said, "the shock wave will sink the ship. The ship has to be at least six nautical miles away."

"Isn't that a sacrifice worth making? So the ship sinks. We've got lifeboats."

"There are many reasons why that isn't going to work," said Glinn, "not the least of which is the chaos on board."

This was followed by another long silence.

McFarlane said: "I'll do it. I'll take it down with the *Pete*."

Glinn gazed steadily at McFarlane. "No. You've never driven a DSV. This will be a tricky operation, towing a dangling, inert load."

His eyes swiveled on Gideon. "Gideon," he said, "you're the obvious choice. You're now an expert in DSV handling. You're dying of an incurable disease. You'll be dead in nine months regardless. You can trade those nine months for saving the world— not to put too fine a point on it."

He spoke these frank truths in a steady, dull, matter-of-fact voice, not unlike an accountant reciting numbers to a client.

He continued. "A person who is staring death in the face is a special kind of person. A person who can do exceptional things. This will be one of those things."

Gideon couldn't immediately find his voice to reply.

The silence was broken by a sudden, sarcastic laugh from McFarlane. Everyone's eyes swiveled in his direction.

"Well, well," he said in a bitter tone. "It would appear that sometimes even the most obsessive behavior can bring positive results." He thumped Glinn on the back—none too gently. "Palmer Lloyd would be pleased." He turned to Gideon and extended his hand. "Congratulations, pardner."

63

Eyven Vinter leaned back in a chair in a small annex to the rec room. Standing beside him was the other security officer, Oakes, who had joined the mutiny at the same time he had. He felt exhausted by pain and was also suffering from a certain feeling of detachment that he knew must be shock from the gunshot wounds. Neither wound was fatal, at least not if eventually treated. But his injuries had rendered him useless. And their failure to take the bridge had temporarily demoralized the group.

But now the balance of power had shifted in their direction. "Get Masterson in here," he told Oakes.

"Yes, sir."

His job now was to put a little fire in the belly of Masterson. He saw that Masterson was key: he had a knack for recruiting people; he was at heart a good man; people trusted him. As second assistant engineer, he knew the intimate workings of the ship and could take the conn if necessary. Many had now flocked to their cause, and those who had not were paralyzed by the growing chaos and terror on board ship. Mission control had been neutralized. Even some of the security guards assigned to keep them bottled up on the crew deck had defected. The only remaining holdouts were the captain and the officers of the bridge, along with the cadre of top EES brass—Glinn and his group. They could literally walk to the bridge, maybe without firing a single shot. The catch was blowing the bridge doors, which had been designed to keep out terrorists and any others who might commandeer the ship.

Masterson came through the door. "How are you doing?" he asked.

Vinter could see that Masterson needed direction, encouragement. He grasped the man's hand. "I'll survive." He hesitated, adding a little theater: "That is, if we can get the ship to Ushuaia."

Masterson seemed to hesitate. "Those doors into the bridge—"

"Greg, I've got it all worked out. Oakes here managed to retrieve some C4 from the security armory. He knows how to blow those doors." This wasn't completely true, but Oakes had had some training in explosives in boot camp. "Blow the doors and then you all go in. You've got the numbers, you've got the momentum, and you've got the weapons."

"I understand. But the bridge is now armed to the teeth."

"If we don't get this ship the hell out of here, we're all dead. Fifty-eight hours to safety—keep that number in mind. Fifty-eight hours and this is over."

Masterson nodded.

"You're the leader. Everyone's looking up to you. You started this, and thank God you did. Now get everyone together and finish it. Let me tell you my plan." He leaned forward painfully.

"Blitzkrieg is the way to go. And—this is important—to make sure the bridge is not damaged."

He drew Masterson in still closer and began to explain how the mutiny was going to work.

Captain Tulley stood beside the helmsman. Like any good captain, he maintained a serene countenance, but inside he was seething. His ship was in chaos. Order had broken down. The worms were everywhere, at least in the lower spaces of the ship. The aborted mutiny had resulted in the death of both his chief officer and the officer of the watch, and the wounding of others; the blood was still on the floor of the bridge. The mutineers had managed to commandeer the ship's intercom and were continuously recruiting, while all other communications had been jammed or shut down by saboteurs. There were reports of widespread vandalism. Security officers had defected to the mutineers. And many people appeared to be infected by the worms, although it was almost impossible to tell just who had been infected and who hadn't.

Tulley was confident that the officers surrounding him were still clean; no worms had been spotted on the bridge. But, to be safe, he ordered all present to pair up and watch each other's backs.

He glanced down at the orders he had received from Glinn, brought to him in a handwritten note by Manuel Garza. The mission was going forward: they were going to explode the nuke. The ship was to remain in place until the order was received to proceed full speed ahead on a true north heading, in order to escape the shock wave of the blast. Garza had brought with him two security officers to lead the defense should the bridge be attacked again. The two, Garza had explained, were all he could find; the rest were unreliable and possibly infected, had joined the mutiny—or both.

Tulley knew a second attempt was imminent. And even as that thought crossed his mind, a massive explosion rocked the bridge, knocking him to the deck.

64

THE NUKE HAD been lowered into the ROV's titanium sphere and secured in the framework built to carry it. It took up most of the small interior space. Leaning in through the hatch, Gideon checked over the device one last time, examining the various critical components. It remained in perfect working order.

"Now to arm it and set the timer," he said. "How long?"

"Time to get in position?" Glinn asked Garza, who had just returned from his mission to the bridge.

"About thirty minutes, give or take," Garza replied.

"I might suggest a fifteen-minute contingency. More, and you risk being stopped by the Baobab. Less, and if you run into a glitch you might not be in position when the nuke goes off. You've shut off the bomb's remote-control mechanism?"

Gideon nodded.

"Very well. You won't be able to abort the countdown once you're underwater. Once that timer's set, there's no going back."

Gideon nodded again. Then he turned to the bomb, punched in the arming code. That activated the timer and LED screen. He verified that the nuke was armed, then carefully keyed in 45 MIN-UTES and pressed COMMIT.

Forty-five minutes left to live.

The handler shut and sealed the titanium hatch. Gideon turned and walked across the fantail deck to *Pete*, which had been rolled out and positioned under the crane. It gleamed in the morning light, yellow and white. Next, the ROV was attached to *Pete* using a heavy tow cable. The two would have to be lowered into the water in tandem—a tricky operation.

Gideon stared at *Pete*. The ladder was in place, the hatch open. It was all ready for him. But he did not move.

"I've manually disabled the *Pete*'s AI," said Glinn quietly, standing by the DSV's ladder. "I've done the same for the surface override—just in case somebody in mission control tries to stop you." He paused. "It's time…"

Gideon licked his lips, and then walked across the deck to the bottom of the ladder.

"Good luck," said Rosemarie Wong.

"Good luck," said McFarlane, with a wintry smile.

"Good luck," Glinn echoed. He held out his hand and Gideon shook it. In silence, McFarlane did the same. Gideon then turned and grasped the cold steel of the ladder rung, hesitated just a moment, and then climbed up. The handler was busy manning the crane controls. The small remaining group—McFarlane, Glinn, Garza, Rosemarie Wong—were on the deck, watching. Garza raised his hand in a farewell gesture.

Gideon gave one last look around: at the morning sun rising in the robin's-egg sky; the fantastically sculptured icebergs, licked by a slow and steady swell—and on the horizon, a distant ledge of dark cloud, heralding the approaching storm. He peered down the hatch into the dark interior of the DSV. Then he grasped the handhold at the top of the hatch, swung over, and lowered himself. As he took his place in the seat, he heard the hatch being sealed from above. Almost immediately he felt the crane lifting the DSV toward the ocean. By necessity, they were skipping the entire safety and operational checklist. *Pete* was a spare DSV; they hadn't expected to use it. It had been last checked out at Woods Hole, two months ago. It might just fail.

In that case, Gideon thought, he'd be dead a few minutes earlier. Not worth thinking about. What was worth thinking about was Lispenard's death. And her cruel life after death, her brain somehow preserved and still conscious, buried deep inside the Baobab. How strange and awful it would be, to be cut off from all sensory input, her mental processes co-opted by an alien lifeform for its own "thinking." It was a ghastly idea. But he could save her: with death.

He strapped himself in. This was going to be a lonely, one-way trip to oblivion.

Captain Tulley swam back into consciousness. He found himself lying on the deck, momentarily dazed, ears ringing, wreathed in acrid smoke. A moment later, as his head began to clear and memory returned, he fumbled for his sidearm. Two figures loomed out of the gray gloom. They grabbed him, disarmed him, threw him on his stomach, and he felt cold steel go around his wrists.

He tried to say something and was answered with a blow to the side of his head. The smoke was starting to clear and, from his position on his stomach, he saw the other officers of the bridge in handcuffs, being manhandled toward the rear bridge bulkhead. It had happened fast: a well-planned and -executed operation.

"So it's you, Masterson," he said, recognizing one of the men who had cuffed him.

"Yes. And I'm sorry, Captain, but we're taking over the ship. We're getting us out of here—and we're not taking any more chances."

Tulley was hauled to his feet, led to the back bulkhead, and chained there. The navigator and second officer soon joined him, and in a minute the rest were all shackled together. As the smoke cleared on the bridge, Tulley could see several bodies on the floor—the two security men Garza had brought and an able seaman, all apparently shot. The bridge windows close to the port door had been blown out and others were cracked. The main navigational station, with the radar and chartplotters, looked badly damaged.

But the mutineers were organized. In an emergency, resetting certain master controls allowed the ship to be conned completely from the bridge, bypassing the engine control room. Captain Tulley saw that this was exactly what Masterson was now doing. He knew that the man, as second assistant engineer, was capable of controlling the engine and propulsion systems.

But were the other mutineers going to be able to operate the vessel?

He looked around. They had an assistant navigator; they had a helmsman; they had lookouts; they had the ship's best electrotechnical engineer—and a few able seamen, as well. While the electronics in the navigation area had apparently been damaged in the explosion, they still had all the charts and navigation tools at their disposal. And a bloody cell phone these days would give you any necessary GPS coordinates. But as he assessed the damage, he realized it looked like it was going to slow them down. It would be a long trip to Ushuaia.

He watched the mutineers go about their business with focus and efficiency. Even as he was making these observations, he felt the telltale rumble of the engine, felt the ship begin to respond.

They were wasting no time getting out of there.

65

THE CRANE HOISTED the DSV *Pete* into the air, and Gideon felt the now familiar movement as it was swung overboard. Through the downward viewport he had a glimpse of the aft deck and the small group watching him, and then the DSV was lowered. He had a final glimpse of the surface of the ocean—and a mass of white water churning away from the ship's stern. What was this? Was the *Batavia* getting under way?

This speculation was cut short by a jarring landing in the water, made worse by the incipient movement of the ship. Bubbles swirled about the viewport and he heard the uncoupling of the hooks as *Pete* and its ROV companion were set loose from the crane.

As soon as the crane released the hooks, Gideon felt a sudden, sickening downward motion. Through the viewport he saw the heavy ROV swinging down underneath him, a dangling deadweight—and it sucked his DSV into the depths like a ball and chain, pulling him ever faster. The color of the water grew dark and then black almost immediately, as the DSV sank hundreds of feet per second in a headlong plunge into the depths.

Heart in his mouth, Gideon fumbled with *Pete's* controls. If he didn't arrest its descent, and fast, he would impact the seafloor—and it would all be over. He cleared the ballast tanks, one at a time, filling them with air to increase buoyancy. But even after this maneuver, the DSV continued to sink like a stone. Fighting down panic, he realized there was something else he could try—dropping the iron ballast weights. He was supposed to drop all four of them simultaneously when it was time to rise to the surface—except this time, he wouldn't be rising to the surface.

Pressing a button, he dropped one weight. The descent slowed, but the DSV went crooked, tilting a little. He dropped a second from the other side and the descent slowed significantly. But the DSV, unbalanced, was now listing by a good twenty degrees.

The headlong plunge to the bottom had ceased. Gideon leaned back with an exhalation of relief. *Great. Just great. Now I can die the way I planned to.* Through the downward port, in the headlamps, he could see the ROV dangling below by its cable, swinging slowly from side to side, causing his own mini sub to rock.

He glanced at the timer, running in a window in one corner of the main monitor. Forty minutes.

Where was he? He hadn't even had time to boot up many of the electronic and mechanical systems. He now switched on the most vital—propulsion, sonar, depth gauge, cameras, life support. Various screens flickered to life and the electronics began to boot.

It seemed to take forever for everything to warm up, but in reality it was only a couple of minutes. From the depth meter, he established he was three thousand feet deep and still sinking, albeit only a few feet per second. The whole DSV was tilted. It was damned uncomfortable being slanted to one side, but he reminded himself it was only for the next... thirty-seven minutes.

Now he had to figure out where the wreck of the *Rolvaag* was. Nothing but empty seafloor was showing on the sonar. He raised the gain, looking for the telltale smudge of the ship. It wasn't there. Nor could he find the sonar cloud generated by the Baobab. He fiddled with the controls, changing the gain, but it was indeed a blank seafloor below him. Somehow he had drifted away from the target area. How far had the *Batavia* gone before he was released into the ocean?

He felt real panic. Thirty-five minutes to go...and he had no idea where he was. He wasn't afraid to die—but he didn't want to die uselessly, for nothing.

...And then it occurred to him that the damn sonar horn was tilted. It was looking off to one side. Could he correct it, reorient it? Yes, he could. He worked with the dials until he had corrected for the twenty-degree offset—and there, to his relief, was the smudge of the *Rolvaag*, and the strange sonar cloud that indicated the presence of the Baobab. His position was offset about half a mile north of it.

This was perfect. It would be crazy to descend straight down onto the target: he would be a sitting duck for the Baobab, which would see him coming. But if he dropped down from his present position, half a mile away, he'd arrive on the ocean floor on the far side of the *Rolvaag* from the Baobab; he could then approach the Baobab unseen, using the ship's hulk as cover.

He would lurk behind the wreck, hidden from the Baobab; and then, two minutes before detonation, he would drive the DSV up to six hundred feet and hold it there until the end.

Time to get going. He filled one of the ballast tanks with seawater, and the DSV began to descend more quickly.

Thirty minutes to detonation.

In four minutes the seafloor came into view. He pumped out

the ballast tank and brought the *Pete* back to neutral buoyancy. Slowly, carefully, he let the sub drift down until the ROV was dangling only about twenty feet from the seafloor. Then he moved forward, toward the *Rolvaag*, half a mile away, careful to keep the wreck between him and the Baobab.

It was hell, controlling the DSV with the weight of the nuke dangling below. It never ceased swinging and pulling the *Pete* along with it, back and forth, requiring constant course adjustments. But he made decent progress and, within a few minutes, the hulk of the *Rolvaag* reared above him. He slowed, bringing *Pete* in behind the cover of the ship. He didn't dare turn off his lights during the forward movement; he hoped the glow wouldn't be picked up by the Baobab.

The two pieces of the wreck loomed up over him, its great rust-colored hull sweeping upward and out of sight. He came to a halt mere feet from it, well hidden from the Baobab. He shut off his lights and settled in for a short wait—his last. Funny, now that he was facing death—certain death—no thoughts came into his brain. Just the final steps he had to take in order to position the bomb, complete his mission. And—he smiled grimly—save the world.

Twenty-four minutes.

Suddenly, through the starboard viewport, he saw lights approaching. Bright lights. He was confounded: what the hell was this? He turned on his own lights and saw, with utter surprise, the DSV *John*—coming straight at him at flank speed.

66

ELI GLINN FELT the vibration of the ship's engines and knew immediately what had happened.

"What the hell?" Garza said. "The captain didn't have orders to move!"

"It's not the captain," Glinn told him. "The mutineers must have seized the bridge."

Garza shook his head. "Well, they're just a few minutes too late, aren't they?"

"So it would seem."

"Mother of God," said Garza, staring at the spot in the water where Gideon's DSV had disappeared. "That took guts. Even for a dying man."

"It's not over yet," said Sam McFarlane.

Glinn glanced at the man. His face was gaunt. He looked like a ghost. His eyes were sunken.

"Gideon might be a little crazy," said Garza, "but the guy's got luck. He hasn't failed yet."

There were shouts—and then Glinn saw a group of armed mutineers running toward them across the aft deck, weapons drawn.

The DSV handler took one look at them, then sprinted off in the direction of the hangar. A burst of gunfire rang out and he was cut down.

"Down!" the mutineers commanded, as they surrounded them. "Facedown on the deck! Keep your hands in sight."

Raising their hands, Glinn, McFarlane, Garza, and Wong were surrounded. They knelt, then lay facedown. The men searched them, removed their weapons, handcuffed them, and hauled them back to their feet. Glinn noted that one of the men had flecks of blood on his shirt—he had recently, it seemed, suffered a nosebleed.

"Where's the ROV?" the one with the nosebleed asked. "What just happened here?"

"What just happened here is that you bastards are too late," said Garza, spitting on the deck.

The men stared at him. They looked confused. "What do you mean, too late?"

"You'll see."

"We're going to lock you in the hold so you don't cause any more trouble," said the man with the nosebleed. "Come with us."

As they were being marched below, Glinn noted that much of the terror and chaos that had gripped the ship had subsided. The vessel had become more organized; the crew were going about their business with purpose. An unnatural calm had fallen. Was that because they were finally moving away from danger and heading for port...or because most of the crew had now become infected?

He glanced more closely at Prothero's lab assistant, Rosemarie Wong. Her lab coat was splattered with blood.

"Are you hurt?" Glinn asked.

"Not my blood," she said. "You know what's going on, don't you?"

"I'm afraid so."

She lowered her voice. "They're almost all infected."

Glinn nodded.

"And we're next. They're locking us up in a worm-infested hold so that we, too, can join the cause."

Glinn felt a sense of infinite exhaustion. But the Baobab would not prevail; Gideon would succeed in killing it. He wondered what would happen when the worm-infested ship and the parasitized crew docked in Ushuaia. But he realized such concern was pointless. If the Baobab was destroyed, there wasn't much the infected crew could do about it. On the other hand, if Gideon failed in his mission... then it would just be a matter of time.

He glanced at his watch: twenty-six minutes to detonation. As they'd been led below, he'd noted that something seemed wrong: given the sound of the engine, and the sense of forward movement, it was clear the ship wasn't reaching its normal cruising speed of twelve knots. Instead, it seemed to have plateaued at around four or five. Why, he didn't know. But at this rate, the ship wouldn't clear the six-mile radius of possible shock wave from the explosion. *Perhaps that will take care of the infection problem*, Glinn thought grimly as they descended into the darkness of the hold.

They were thrust through a bulkhead door into a dank, throbbing space in the very bowels of the ship. The door clanged shut, cleats were dogged from outside, and absolute darkness fell.

And then he began to hear, from all around, a rustling, scritching noise.

67

GIDEON COULD SEE that *John* was on a kamikaze mission, AI obviously turned off or overridden, the mini sub intending to ram him. He ramped up the propulsion and brought *Pete* around to face *John* while at the same time ascending as quickly as possible. But being tethered to the nuke made his DSV sluggish and difficult to maneuver. He realized that what he had to do, above all, was to protect the six propellers in the rear from damage.

Slowly, agonizingly, his propellers humming, the DSV rose, the tethered nuke dangling. *John* came on fast but erratically, and through either misjudgment or mishandling it missed ramming *Pete*, passing just to one side; as it swept past, Gideon glimpsed Antonella Sax working the controls, struggling to bring the DSV back around without the help of the autopilot. It was incredible: the senior exobiologist, in thrall to the alien life-form. What in hell was she thinking?

Now *Pete* was ascending faster, while below him he watched Sax's DSV make a loop, coming back around and heading for him once again. Gideon realized she was on a trajectory to hit his stern—aiming, rightly so, for the propulsion system.

There was nothing he could do, he realized, to avoid an impact. Quickly moving his joystick around, he rotated the DSV so as to put the propellers behind and watched, helplessly, as *John* came straight at him. Sax's calm, bland face could be seen illuminated through the forward viewport, staring at him as she closed in.

There was a terrific crash and Gideon was thrown forward, arrested by the safety straps, his DSV recoiling from the blow. A monitor cracked and a shower of sparks fell inside the personnel module. But the titanium sphere was built to withstand immense pressure, far higher than any ramming would accomplish. She couldn't sink him by ramming him—but she could make it impossible for him to deliver the weapon to the proper altitude.

Sixteen minutes.

As his ascending sub cleared the upper edge of the *Rolvaag*, the Baobab loomed into view. Gideon was shocked: it was now glowing from some sort of internal phosphorescence, a gigantic, pale, greenish-yellow thing that no longer looked like a tree but rather a vast polyp, swelling and subsiding as it drew in and expelled water.

He wondered if Sax could be reached on the UQC; if there was any chance of talking her out of this crazy defense of the Baobab. He switched it on.

"Antonella!" he cried. "Can you hear me?"

John was coming around for another swipe at him. To his surprise, her voice came back, calm and steady. "I hear you loud and clear."

"What the hell are you doing?"

"The question is, what are you doing?"

"I'm trying to kill that thing—which intends to destroy the earth. Don't you understand that you've been infected? You're being manipulated!"

At this, Sax gave a low laugh. "So you, too, Gideon, have drunk the Kool-Aid. This splendid and intelligent life-form comes to earth, and our response is to try to kill it? How sad."

"Yes: because it's a parasite, and it's going to kill us if we don't kill it first."

Another mild laugh of amusement. "You know nothing about it. I've been *communicating* with it, Gideon. What an extraordinary experience. I know what it wants, what it thinks, what it feels. It's come here in peace and goodwill—and it can't understand why you want to exterminate it."

This was nuts. And he saw that something else was coming in besides her voice transmission; some sort of data dump into the UQC. Was she trying to hack into his DSV? But even as he was getting ready to shut it down, her DSV was bearing down on him. He rotated *Pete*, once again trying to shield his propulsion. But this time he could see that Sax was coming in low.

She's going to ram the ROV containing the nuke.

He reversed the joystick and slowed his ascent so she wouldn't hit the ROV. But to Gideon's absolute horror, his maneuver only caused her to miss the ROV and come in just above it—the mech arm of the *John* slicing right through his tow cable. It snapped with a violent jerk, and, through the downward viewport, he saw the ROV plummet toward the wreck of the *Rolvaag* and disappear into the big gash in the hull.

Suddenly—untethered from the weight of the bomb—*Pete* shot up like an air bubble, rushing faster and faster, leaving *John* a rapidly dwindling cluster of lights in the blackness below. Out the side viewport, he had an extraordinary view of the gigantic glowing creature as he rushed upward past it, its vile orifice swelling and pumping; it writhed its branches threateningly toward him, but he was now moving so fast that he caromed right through their grasp, and a few minutes later the DSV popped up on the surface of the ocean, the mini sub tumbling about like a billiard ball before finally righting itself.

In pure astonishment, Gideon looked out the forward viewport. *Pete* was bobbing like a cork on the surface of the ocean. A few miles away, he could see the receding silhouette of the *Batavia*.

He glanced at the countdown. Twelve minutes to go.

What the hell, Gideon thought; his mission had failed but he might as well try to save his own ass. He jammed the joystick forward and headed the DSV for the ship.

Nine minutes to detonation.

He kept the joystick pushed to the maximum, but the DSV moved slowly at the surface, impeded by the heavy seas of the approaching storm. He was eking out a few knots at best. For whatever reason, the *Batavia* clearly wasn't going at top speed, either, but nevertheless it was still going faster than he was…and he was never going to catch up.

Eight minutes.

So the bomb had dropped into the *Rolvaag* itself. The quick-and-dirty simulation he'd managed to do in the short time available showed that the bomb, detonated on or inside the *Rolvaag*, would probably be insufficient: the steel of the hulk would absorb too much of the blast. He could only hope his calculations were off.

Six minutes.

He knew that the *Batavia* itself had to be at least six miles from the point of detonation, or the shock wave would rupture its hull. There was no way *Pete* was going to clear the danger zone, and as he saw the *Batavia* limping along, he realized it would not make it, either.

Four minutes.

At his current speed of two knots, he would be three surface miles from the *Rolvaag* when the bomb went off. Two squared plus three squared... what was the God-damned square root of thirteen? Three and a half miles—that would be his straight-line distance from the blast.

Two minutes.

He had to stop thinking about the blast. Instead, he thought of Alex. He pictured her face. He thought of her, freed from that monster. That was better.

One minute.

The light arrived first—a dull flash in the bottom viewport. And then, three seconds later, the shock wave hit and it was like being punched by a gigantic fist and all went black.

68

AFTER THEIR WOULD-BE jailer had sealed the hatch, Eli Glinn could make out the clang of his departing footsteps. They had been put in the lowest part of the hold, called the lazarette, which contained the ship's steering gear and enclosed the hull seals for the azimuthing propulsion pod. It was dark and hot. Below the steel-grate floor, he could hear water sloshing around and the sucking sound of a bilge pump.

He could also hear a gathering noise all around them, a chorus of rustling and scratching: the worms, emerging from their hiding places.

"The scientist in me," said Wong, "wonders how it works. I mean, you get this worm up your nose and into your brain, and then you're doing the creature's bidding. But you have no idea that's what you're doing. How do the infected people rationalize their actions?"

Glinn felt a certain comfort in the distraction this problem afforded. "Human beings," he said, "have a bottomless capacity for rationalization and self-deception. The worms simply jack into that capacity."

"True. But do you suffer amnesia? Do you remember a worm crawling up your nose?"

"I imagine we'll soon find out," said McFarlane.

In the darkness, Glinn was sorry he couldn't check his watch to tell the time. There were only minutes to go before the explosion. He wondered if the ship was inside or outside of the danger zone. He hoped inside, and that the ship's destruction would be quick.

McFarlane gave a shout. "Son of a *bitch*! Fucking worm!" Glinn heard him moving around, stomping and shuffling.

"Ugh!" Wong brushed off a worm and slapped at her clothing. "They're all over!"

He heard, around his feet, the sound of the gathering worms like the rustling of autumn leaves. He felt one begin to slide up inside one pant leg, then the other. He shook his limbs, slapping at the clothing even as he realized he was only delaying the inevitable. Maybe he should submit. But somehow he couldn't do that—the feeling of the worms crawling on his flesh was so revolting that he slapped and kicked at them, trying to shake them off. But there were too many, too many, and they clung to the skin in a sticky sort of way.

Garza was shouting, McFarlane was swearing, Wong was screaming. The hold filled with their cries. And still the worms came...

And then it happened. It was as if they were inside a bass drum and someone abruptly pounded it, viciously, with a mallet. It was a boom so deep and so violent that it shook Glinn to his very bones, shook the brain within his skull, shook him into oblivion...

But not for long. He came to lying on the grate, with a splitting headache, his ears buzzing. It was still dark. The scritching of the worms was gone—to be replaced by the sound of roaring water.

"Sam?" he croaked.

A groan.

"Rosemarie?" Glinn felt around and located her, giving her face a light pat, then another. "Rosemarie?"

She gasped. He helped her sit up. "My head," she murmured.

"You hear that?" came Garza's voice. "The explosion ruptured the hull. The ship is sinking."

"And we're locked in the hold," said Wong, her own voice strengthening. "From worms to water. Pick your fate."

Meanwhile, the throbbing sound of the engine had become a grinding noise. After a moment, it ceased altogether.

"Anybody have any ideas on how we might get out of here before we drown?" Glinn asked.

"No," said McFarlane in a low voice.

"I do," said Wong.

"Now's the time to tell us."

"We find out how the worms got in here. And we go out that way."

"That's right," said Garza. "And we *know* how the worms got in here: through the ventilation shafts. Even a hold as deep as this one—*especially* one this deep—has to have serious ventilation."

Glinn heard Garza rise and begin feeling along the slanted bulkhead of the lazarette, tapping the walls. There was a hollow bang.

"Here it is," he said. "And here's a gasket. Just follow the sound of my voice. We'll crawl out of here."

69

♦

GIDEON SWAM BACK from unconsciousness, racked with pain. It took a few minutes for him to think through what had happened and realize he wasn't dead.

The DSV was still floating on the surface of the ocean, but it was now upside down. His chair was on the ceiling, its straps loose and dangling. Something was wrong with his arm, and when he examined it he saw the ugly, shocking sight of a bone sticking out of his forearm, oozing blood. The interior of the sphere was wrecked, glass and wire everywhere, the acrid smell of smoke hovering in the dead air. The only light came in through the viewports.

But...the shell was intact and he was alive.

The sub had been battered severely by the shock wave, but the titanium hadn't been breached. He could see, outside the starboard viewport, the R/V *Batavia*, about two miles away. It was listing in the water, no longer moving. Even as he watched, the list grew more pronounced and he could see that the ship was launching orange lifeboats.

Dead air. He took a deep breath, felt a wave of dizziness. As he surveyed the interior wreckage of the sub, he saw that all life-support systems were dead. His only air was what was already inside the shell, and he'd been breathing it now for several minutes, perhaps even longer. It felt like the oxygen levels were dropping, as he was panting—or maybe that was due to the horrible pain of his broken arm.

He needed to get out. And that meant climbing down and exiting from below; since the DSV was floating upside down, its only hatch was on the bottom. He hoped to God the force of the explosion hadn't warped the hatch, trapping him inside...

Pushing aside all thoughts of anything but escape, he tried to move. His head was splitting, he was bruised and cut all over; glass was in his hair, blood was trickling into his eyes, and his arm was a fright. Every movement was excruciating.

He had to immobilize that arm if he hoped to be able to do anything. And he had to do it quickly, before he fainted from shock. Using his good arm, he managed to unbutton, then pull off his shirt. Gasping through the pain, he lashed the broken arm against his abdomen, keeping it in place. Clearing away debris with his good arm, he unsealed the hatch and—thank God—managed to open it. Water did not rush in—the air in the personnel sphere had nowhere to escape, and it formed a sort of bubble. The water was going to be cold, around fifty degrees.

So be it.

He eased himself down into the water until it was chest-deep. The shock of the cold took away some of the pain in his arm. The upper, flimsier personnel hatch was gone—lost in the shock wave. All he had to do was hold his breath, dive down and out, and then surface.

Which he did.

He came up next to the mangled, half-submerged DSV. He

grasped a projecting piece of metal and managed to crawl up out of the frigid water, where he stretched out atop the wrecked mini sub. There were plenty of handholds, which was good, because the seas were heavy and the sky scudding with dark clouds, the storm wind rising. God, he was cold.

But as he lay atop the bobbing *Pete*, shivering, he marveled that he was alive at all. It would be a shame if he died now. And just as he had that thought, he heard a sound, and a plane flew overhead, waggling its wings at the sinking *Batavia* and dropping flares and signal buoys.

He didn't know if the blast had destroyed the Baobab. Chances were, the force of the detonation—impeded as it was from inside the *Rolvaag*'s hull—hadn't been sufficient for the liquid-liquid explosion. But he did know one thing: they were all going to be rescued. And he had survived—at least, for the time being.

And then Gideon passed out.

Epilogue

GIDEON CREW, ONE arm in a cast fitted with a sling, strolled down Little West 12th Street in the now chic Meatpacking District of Lower Manhattan. Arriving at the nondescript main entrance to Effective Engineering Solutions, he waited under the eye of the security camera until he was buzzed through the outer door. He walked along a drab, painstakingly monochromatic exterior hallway, and was buzzed through the inner door and into the building proper.

Ahead of him lay the cavernous space he knew so well: a vast room, four stories high, with catwalks running around various levels of its periphery. Its main floor was taken up with a wide assortment of 3-D models, whiteboards, computers, bioelectric and biomechanical setups, and freestanding clean rooms draped with plastic. Technicians in lab coats walked here and there, making notes on tablet computers or speaking together in small groups.

Only one thing was missing, and Gideon knew what it was. The huge display of the Baobab and its surrounding ocean bed—which previously had taken up a good deal of the central section of the floor—was gone. In fact, everything related to the project seemed to have disappeared—completely.

"Dr. Crew?" A man in a business suit came up to him. "They're waiting for you upstairs. Please follow me."

Gideon followed the man to a nearby elevator, and they rode to the sixth floor. The man led the way through various white-painted corridors to an unmarked door, then opened it and ushered him through.

Gideon found himself in a large, tall space he had not been in before. It appeared to be a lecture hall, with a dozen curved rows of seats stretching up and back—in the form of a Greek amphitheater—from a low platform that stood at the front. Small skylights, set into the high ceiling, afforded views of the blue December sky. Behind the front platform lay a long wall of electronic and mechanical equipment, discreetly housed behind panels of smoked glass. A large model sat on a table atop the platform.

The man closed the door behind him and Gideon made his way down the aisle. Ranged around in the chairs of the two-hundred-seat hall were several familiar faces: Manuel Garza; Rosemarie Wong, the sonar and marine acoustics assistant—and Sam McFarlane. McFarlane was seated in the front row, stretched out, ankles crossed in front of him. Seeing Gideon approach, the meteorite hunter gestured at him, whether in greeting or dismissal Gideon couldn't be sure.

He had of course seen all of these people, one-on-one and in passing, during their recovery from injury and exposure, and at the various debriefings that had taken place. But this was the first time he had seen all of them together since the dramatic rescue, complicated by heavy seas, of the survivors of the *Batavia*.

Taking a seat in the second row beside Rosemarie, Gideon looked more closely at the model on the table. It appeared to be another re-creation of the seabed: the site of the *Rolvaag*'s sinking and the sprouting of the Baobab. However, this one was quite different from the initial model. Instead of the horrible, sprouting thing, there was a massive, ragged hole in the seafloor, as if it had suffered the impact of a giant's fist. It reminded Gideon of Aklavik, the unusual meteorite crater McFarlane had described witnessing in northern Canada: except on a far larger, indeed gigantic scale.

A door at one corner of the front of the lecture hall opened and Glinn appeared. He walked slowly along the wall of electronics, stepped up onto the platform, and turned to address the small gathering.

"Thank you all for coming," he said. "I thought it would be appropriate to formally conclude this mission with a brief discussion, held for those of you who were most responsible for its success."

He stepped forward and waved one hand toward the model. "Because, as far as we have been able to tell, the mission *was* a success. The liquid-liquid explosion, theorized by Sam and detonated by Gideon, seems to have worked. We've sent a research ship down to the area—on the sly, of course—and a sidescan sonar was towed across the entire area. The wreck of the *Rolvaag* is no more; there is a huge crater in the abyssal floor, as this model demonstrates; and it appears the explosion reached deep enough to kill all the parasitized brains. Dead and rotting remains of the creature were observed floating on the surface, but life has already begun to return to the dead zone."

"What about the radioactivity of the explosion?" Gideon asked.

"The ocean is a marvelous thing. Its incredible vastness—the thousands upon thousands of square miles of seawater surrounding the detonation—absorbed and dispersed it. While I wouldn't recommend taking any dives down to the bomb crater itself, as I said, the surrounding area seems to be flourishing once again. And—as we'd hoped—local and global seismic stations have chalked it up as a single, violent undersea volcanic eruption: nothing more."

He took a seat on the edge of the table. "All of you know some of the details. But I'm here to give you the complete picture. It would appear that the worms that had infected so many of the crew and scientific staff of the *Batavia*—and had, in effect, taken over the ship, at the behest of the Baobab—died along with it. At the moment of the detonation, they became somnolent. From what we can tell, they were in the process of drying up, dying— even as, of course, the ship sank, taking them to the bottom."

"And the infected crew?" asked Rosemarie Wong.

Glinn's face grew grim. "From what we witnessed, and from later reports, at the moment the Baobab was destroyed, the affected crewmembers became lethargic and confused. They refused to leave the ship. As the *Batavia* was sinking, many of them began suffering brain hemorrhages—presumably as the worms in their brains died." He paused. "The official report was that the undersea volcanic eruption sank the ship—which, after all, is not far from the truth."

"How many?" asked Sam McFarlane.

"I'm sorry?"

"How many lives were lost when the *Batavia* went down?"

This time, it was Garza who spoke up. "Fifty-seven."

Fifty-seven, Gideon thought. Add that to the hundred and eight who went down with the *Rolvaag*, and one hundred and sixty-five lives could be chalked up to the so-called meteorite. Not to mention Alex Lispenard; Barry Frayne; Prothero; Dr. Brambell—

others. It was tragic, truly tragic: but of course, it could have been much, much worse.

Apparently, McFarlane thought so, too, because—while at first his face hardened and he appeared about to say something—he relaxed and sat back in his seat.

Glinn seemed to notice this, because he turned toward the meteorite hunter. "Sam," he said, "the rest of us in this room are all employees or officers of EES. This was a job we had to take on. You did not. And it was your insights—into the depths of the root structure containing the brains, into the possibility of a liquid-liquid explosion—that helped destroy the Baobab."

McFarlane made a dismissive gesture. "Gideon here was the real hero. He assembled the nuke. He armed it, placed it. And he did so believing it to be a suicide mission. He was fully prepared to die so the rest of us could live."

"And Gideon has my eternal thanks, as well as the thanks of all of us here at EES. He will be around to enjoy that thanks, in the many forms it will take, over the coming months. But you— I know you're already planning to leave New York." Glinn patted his jacket pocket. "I have here a check for five hundred thousand dollars—a token of our appreciation for your contribution to the mission."

"Keep your check," McFarlane said.

Everyone turned to look at him. Even Glinn seemed surprised.

"Palmer Lloyd got in touch with me," McFarlane said. "Apparently, you'd already spoken with him."

Glinn inclined his head.

"In any case, he's sent me a check for many times that amount. And since getting the news, it appears he's improving by the day. In fact, he's back to eating his *mignonettes dijonnaise* with a fork instead of a straw."

"What are you going to do with all the money?" Garza asked him.

"I'm going to use half of it to establish a charitable trust in the name of my old partner, Nestor Masangkay. The other half I'm going to spend." And he stretched luxuriously in his seat. "There's this little island in the Maldives I've got my eye on. Only a hundred acres, but almost half of that is beach. On a good night, the bioluminescent phytoplankton is something you have to see to believe."

This was greeted by a brief silence.

"What about the worms?" Gideon asked. "Have you been able to determine how the Baobab was able to communicate with them—how it could direct the actions of the *Batavia* crew in such specific ways?"

"That's one of many mysteries that remain to be solved—if solve them we can. It appears—this is classified—that the creature emitted extremely low-frequency radio waves, similar to what we use to communicate with nuclear submarines. While we were at the Ice Limit, such waves were picked up by the US Navy, thousands of miles away. They think the Russians may have deployed a new submarine communications system—and it's driving them crazy.

"But there's an even deeper mystery that troubles us." Glinn stood again, paced before the model. "While the UQC was on—when you, Gideon, were speaking with Sax—a digital download came in. Perhaps you were aware of it. We rescued a dump of that transmission, in the *Batavia*'s black boxes, just before we abandoned ship. The download appears to have come from the creature—or rather, from the alien brain the creature was using for its intelligence and central motor control. We know that brain was very large, at least by human standards. We also know—thanks to Prothero and Dr. Wong, here—that it had come, against its will, across light-years of space and millions of years."

"That must have given it plenty of time to think," McFarlane said drily.

"We can only assume it came from a race more intelligent than ours. Its message was a mass of binary data—zeros and ones. Our engineers have been trying to decode it for three weeks now. It does not appear to have any relationship to numbers or mathematics or known algorithms. Nor does it appear to be language or some form of logical communication. And it does not consist of images." He paused again. "We believe the alien brain knew what was about to happen; it knew this would be its final communication with us. It must, therefore, have some importance. But the fact is, we're still working on it—and we have no real leads."

"Have you tried playing it?" Wong asked quietly.

Glinn looked at her, frowning. "Excuse me?"

"I said: have you tried playing it?"

"Playing it?" Glinn asked. "You mean, like music?"

"The underwater environment that the creature came from was, above all, an acoustic environment. Play it."

"How would we do that, exactly?" Garza asked.

"We know the alien heard, and understood, whale song. It listened, and communicated, digitally, via the Baobab. It stands to reason it would also have listened in to the numerous communications of ours that were transmitted undersea—ship to DSV, DSV to DSV—over the UQC."

Glinn thought for a moment. "But UQC is an acoustic, analog technology."

"Yes," Garza said. "And that would give the entity access to both analog and digital methods of communication. Not that this would help it any."

"The alien brain could only communicate digitally," Wong said. "But that doesn't mean it wasn't trying to send an analog signal. Prothero walked me through the technology once. It wouldn't know how to use an audio codec, of course—but there's no reason it couldn't have sent an uncompressed bitstream of audio data." She looked around. "What else would take up such a large volume, if not communication?"

"Sounds far-fetched," said Garza.

"It probably is," Wong said. "All you need to prove me wrong is to run it through a D-A converter."

Glinn had been listening silently to this most recent exchange. Now he walked over to a phone on the nearby wall, picked it up. "Hello? Get me the audio lab." A pause. "Who is this— Smythefield? It's Eli Glinn, in the auditorium. Bring me up a digital-to-analog converter and a set of powered speakers. Yes, right away."

Hanging up the phone, he opened one of the doors of smoked plate glass behind him, revealing a bank of rack-mounted computers. He pulled out a keyboard, turned on one of the computers, typed in a series of commands, then unspooled a TOSLINK optical cable, used for transmitting digital stereo, from the bank of equipment.

"I've transferred the alien download into this CPU's memory," he said.

Gideon noted that Garza shifted in his seat; scoffed. Clearly, he believed this was a waste of time. At least he refrained from saying so.

One of the doors in the rear of the auditorium opened and two men in lab coats walked down the aisle, carrying several pieces of equipment. Gideon, an audiophile himself, recognized them as an expensive Grace Design DAC stereo monitor controller, along with a high-end set of Dynaudio powered speakers. They placed the equipment on the table, plugged it into receptacles in the base of the platform, and then, at a nod from Glinn, left the room. Glinn inserted the TOSLINK cable into the back of the Grace, then used a pair of balanced XLR cables to connect the powered speakers to the controller. He turned the speakers on, raised the volume controls on their rear panels, adjusted the gain and the signal routing on the controller, then stepped over to the computer keyboard.

"Initiating playback," he said.

At first, nothing happened. And then a long, low, gentle sound came out, rapidly joined by others, and still others, in a mounting chorus. The strangest feeling Gideon had ever experienced in his life began to wash over him. It was as though he was in his chair, here in this auditorium in the EES building in New York City— and yet he was also everywhere and nowhere in the world, simultaneously. It sounded as if he were listening to, *experiencing*, the most beautiful music imaginable. And yet it was not music. It was something more than music: a form of communication so deep, so profound, so wondrous, as to be utterly beyond description. It was, he thought, as if he were hearing the singing of God. At the same time, he felt a vast psychological weight being lifted from his shoulders. The pain and sorrow that he bore, new and old, that had accumulated every day of his life like a second skin—the loss of his parents, the death of Alex, his own medical death sentence—all of it was gone, gone entirely, replaced by a kind of quiet, transcendent joy. As he sat there, transfixed, he felt the hinges of his mind begin to loosen. He became aware of the singularly unique sensation of being on the cusp of understanding the real meaning of life; as if incredible insights into the very purpose of the universe were about to be laid bare, something beyond language, beyond human understanding; but in order to receive this revelation he felt his own individuality, his own sense of self, evaporating into the cosmos...

And then, suddenly, the music stopped.

Gideon, gasping, came back to himself. On the platform, Glinn, staggering slightly as if from a physical blow, had shut down the audio system.

"I don't think..." Glinn began, and then stopped to take a few deep breaths and steady himself. "I don't think the world is ready for this."

But even though Glinn had stopped the playback, the indescribable joy, the release, that it offered to Gideon did not dissipate—at least, not entirely.

"It's a gift," he heard McFarlane say, his voice strange. "It's the alien consciousness giving us a gift as a way of saying thank you—for liberating it from its prison."

"A gift," Gideon repeated. And, looking over at McFarlane, he noticed that the bitter, brooding expression that seemed permanently stamped into the meteorite hunter's face—as deeply as an image embossed into a coin—had eased. It was as if he, too, had just shed the existential darkness that had followed him around, like a shadow, for much of his life.

Their eyes met. Slowly, McFarlane smiled.

Gideon returned the smile. Then, as he settled back in his seat, his eyes traveled upward toward the skylights—and the pure light that streamed through them, enveloping him in golden warmth, felt like a caress from creation itself.

A Note to Our Readers

More years ago than we'd care to admit, we wrote a thriller titled *The Ice Limit*. It was about an expedition to the desolate wastes at the frozen tip of South America, with the goal of recovering the world's largest meteorite.

The expedition did not go quite as planned. It was a dark story and the ending was rather grim and enigmatic. We believed at the time that no further explanation was required. As with the famous *Twilight Zone* episode, "To Serve Man," there appeared to be only one possible outcome after the final page was turned.

However, we began to get letters and emails asking exactly what *did* happen after that final page. And demanding a sequel to the novel.

We thought such requests would die down over time. They did not. We continued to receive them until they totaled in the many thousands. Even today, at virtually every book signing we do, somebody asks us when we are finally going to write a sequel to *The Ice Limit*.

Eli Glinn was a character we first introduced in *The Ice Limit*, and he continued to appear in several of the books that followed.

In the mysterious way that fictional characters sometimes take on lives of their own, Glinn too began to insist that we tell the rest of the story—he even worked behind the scenes, as it were, to make it happen. Glinn roped in Gideon Crew, our newer series character, in his obsession with the "meteorite." That was when we realized our readers were right: the story and characters *demanded* a sequel. Once we understood that, we knew the time had come to set sail once again.

We did, however, take pains to ensure that this new book was not just a story for fans of *The Ice Limit* or Gideon Crew, but rather a stand-alone novel that anyone could enjoy, whether or not they had read any of our earlier fiction. We hope that, in retrospect now, you agree, and that you have enjoyed your fictional journey—whether for the first or the second time—to the Screaming Sixties of the South Atlantic...and beyond the Ice Limit.

ABOUT THE AUTHORS

The thrillers of **DOUGLAS PRESTON** and **LINCOLN CHILD** "stand head and shoulders above their rivals" (*Publishers Weekly*). Preston and Child's *Relic* and *The Cabinet of Curiosities* were chosen by readers in a National Public Radio poll as being among the one hundred greatest thrillers ever written, and *Relic* was made into a number one box office hit movie. They are coauthors of the famed Pendergast series, and their recent novels include *White Fire*, *Blue Labyrinth*, *Crimson Shore*, and *The Lost Island*. In addition to his novels, Preston writes about archaeology for the *New Yorker* and *National Geographic* magazines. Lincoln Child is a former book editor who has published six novels of his own, including the huge bestseller *Deep Storm*.

Readers can sign up for The Pendergast File, a monthly "strangely entertaining note" from the authors, at their website, www.PrestonChild.com. The authors welcome visitors to their alarmingly active Facebook page, where they post regularly.